More praise for
JACK FAUST

"Powerful...One of the classic fantasy legends...
brilliantly retold."
—*Denver Post*

"Vivid...glorious...a bleakly comic, richly imagined novel...
deepened by those moral nuances which are the hallmark
of [Swanwick's] work...JACK FAUST rampages to its close at light speed,
with all sorts of contemporary icons and horrors
winking in and out of view: snippets of *Metropolis* and *On the Road*,
Freud and *kristalnacht*, Rupert Murdoch and deranged snipers in towers.
I shut the book feeling as though I'd just ridden
a particularly vicious roller coaster through our century:
breathless, overwhelmed, and none too certain
of the solid ground underfoot."
—Elizabeth Hand, *Fantasy & Science Fiction*

"Highly recommended...This is a wonderful
and wondrous retelling of Goethe's masterpiece
and puts a whole new spin on the original story...
Swanwick's considerable reputation is about to receive another boost."
—*Booklist*

"[It] slowly and quietly impresses you with its brilliance."
—*Tampa Times & Tribune*

"Every line counts. The target of [Swanwick's] pen is us: here and now."
—*Washington Post Book World*

"Immensely creative and surprising...
Swanwick's writing is effortlessly lyrical
and his extrapolation of a world given technology
before its time has the chill ring of truth.
This one will leave you thinking long after you've finished reading."
—*Middlesex News*

Other Avon Books by
Michael Swanwick

THE IRON DRAGON'S DAUGHTER
STATIONS OF THE TIDE

jack FAUST

MICHAEL SWANWICK

AVON BOOKS ◆ NEW YORK

AVON BOOKS, INC.
1350 Avenue of the Americas
New York, New York 10019

Copyright © 1997 by Michael Swanwick
Front cover illustration by Greg Spalenka
Inside back cover author photograph by Standard Photo Group
Visit our website at http://www.AvonBooks.com
ISBN: 0-380-79070-X

Library of Congress Cataloging in Publication Data:

Swanwick, Michael.
  Jack Faust / by Michael Swanwick.
    p.   cm.
  1. Faust, d. ca. 1540—Fiction.   2. Magicians—Germany—Fiction.   I. Title.
PS3569.W28J33   1997   96-53679
813'.54—dc21   CIP

First Avon Books Trade Paperback Printing: September 1998
First Avon Books Hardcover Printing: September 1997

AVON TRADEMARK REG. U.S. PAT. OFF. AND IN OTHER COUNTRIES, MARCA REGISTRADA, HECHO EN U.S.A.

Printed in the U.S.A.

OPM 10 9 8 7 6 5 4 3 2 1

FOR MARIANNE
I lay this book at your feet,
alongside my heart

ACKNOWLEDGMENTS

I am grateful to Gregory Frost for his generous encouragement and wise advice; Dr. John Cramer for demonic algebra; Elizabeth Willey for *Simplicissimus*; Patricia Ma for nursing procedures; Stanley Reynolds and the crew at the Bureau for insights into *Vibrio cholerae*; Jennifer Stevenson and Greer Gilman for medieval birth control methodology; Albert Hodkinson for London; Pamela Willey, Leslie Goldberg, and Barbara Frost for outlining Margarete's executive responsibilities; Bob Walters for paleontology; Janet Kagan for French translations and landscaping; Bronwynn Elko for astrological terminology; Steve Fisher for lyrics and musicological advice; Maria Delgado for Spanish birds; and the staff of the Roxborough branch of the Philadelphia Free Library for general research. Microbiology, epidemiology, and emotional support were provided by the M. C. Porter Endowment for the Arts.

The new Philosophy calls all in doubt,
The Element of fire is quite put out;
The Sun is lost, and th'earth and no mans wit
Can well direct him where to looke for it.
—JOHN DONNE

A sudden burst of sunshine seemed to illumine the Statue of Liberty, so that he saw it in a new light, although he had sighted it long before. The arm with the sword rose up as if newly stretched aloft, and round the figure blew the free winds of heaven.
—FRANZ KAFKA

From Hell, Mr. Lusk
—JACK THE RIPPER

jack FAUST

𝔗RINITY

Wittenberg at the birth of the century was a microcosm of the human world, a walled and fortified city of six thousand souls, twice that when the university was in session, an island by virtue of moats and the Elbe, smugly ignorant of all that lay beyond the town walls, as wicked, crowded, and devout a place as any on Earth, and as ripe with life as an old pear that sloshes when shaken. It ran by magic. All crafts and professions were simple compilations of formulae and rituals, not because these methods had been investigated and proved effective, but because they had been so taught by elders who had in turn learned from their elders in an unbroken line of authority reaching back to Antiquity. Exhausted mines were sealed to give gold and diamonds the time to grow back. Mares could be impregnated without stallions—so said conventional wisdom—by presenting their haunches to a steady west wind. Nothing new had been discovered in living memory. Nothing was truly understood.

There was a castle to one end of the town, two monasteries to the other, and a cathedral in its center. Church bells tolled the canonical hours—matins, prime, tierce, sext, nones, and vespers—six times a day. These hours varied in length with the waxing and waning of the seasons, but nobody kept strict schedules anyway. More precise measurements were not needed. The Elector's soldiers protected the city from the armies of foreign states, duchies and principalities, ecclesiastical holdings, free imperial cities, margraviates and landgraviates, baronies, and other independent powers—of which the weak and hopelessly divided Empire had somewhere between two hundred and two thousand, depending on who was doing the counting. The Augustinians provided the core faculty for the university, and the Dominicans saw to the propagation of the faith and the salvation of its congregants.

Land within the walls was unspeakably valuable and therefore overbuilt. Houses shouldered each other across narrow streets. Balconies and extensions were built from the upper floors, competing for air and sunshine like trees in the Black Forest. Attic windows almost touched, making it possible for many an adulterer to crawl out one and into his lady love's opposite. There were alleys so overhung with additions they were almost tunnels and light touched the cobblestones only at noon when the sun shone straight down between rival eaves.

The city stank at the best of times and festered in the summer heat. Every occupation—tanner, baker, dyer, knacker—had its own distinctive smell. A student for a bet had once made his way blindfolded through the labyrinthine passages from Rostockgate to Coswiggate guided by his nose alone.

Slops were thrown from the windows, and the sewers ran down the middle of the streets. Rain and the river took care of all garbage.

Most houses were wooden, and even stone buildings had oak frames and walnut floors, thick planks dead for centuries and drier than dust at the heart. The grander houses had wooden shingles and the poorer thatch. Stables were crammed with straw and hay. Warehouses were stuffed with English wool, Russian furs, and silks from the Orient; with cooking oil, varnish, turpentine, and pitch; with bushels of saffron and corn and salt fish; with candles by the gross; and above all (for Wittenberg was famed for its booksellers) with reams beyond counting of paper waiting to be made into broadsides, Bibles, almanacs, brochures, treatises, manifestoes, breviaries, account books, and Latin grammars.

Within this steep-roofed mountain of dried and seasoned wood, the citizenry was as snug and content as a colony of mice in a pile of brushwood, neither knowing nor caring that it had been heaped up to serve as the midsummer bonfire. The granaries were full, the craftsmen, innkeepers, and three-penny merchants prosperous, every burgher fat and surrounded by children, every wife pregnant yet again. They were not aware of the madness that lurked within their own minds.

For at the height of this endless August an irrational discontent possessed the city, as darkly inexpressible as the revulsion that touches a drunken soldier just before he torches the house and barn of a peasant suspected of holding back food for his own use. All of Wittenberg was in a doze, caught in a pleasant suicidal fantasy of the spark that would come to liberate its timbers into explosive fire. The citizens twisted, moaned, and writhed in their sleep, yearning for the broom of flame that would sweep clean the fetid streets of the garbage and accumulated obligations of the past. The very buildings themselves dreamed of holocaust.

From one lone chimney in the heart of the city, a wisp of smoke curled up into the heartbreakingly blue sky.

Faust was burning his books.

With a shower of sparks, Thomas Aquinas was consigned to the flames. Pages fluttering, a slim manuscript book of extracts from Pythagoras—which Faust had held for half his lifetime against that happy day he finally encountered a complete *Works*—flew into the fire. Bouncing from the blackened back of the hearth, Andreas Libavius's *Alchymia* entered that mystical alembic which would transform its gross substance into the rarefied purity of its component elements.

Faust worked systematically, condemning no book without a hearing, riffling through each text until he found a demonstrable lie, and then tossing it atop its dying brothers. Half his library was in the fireplace already, so many volumes that they threatened to choke the flames. A touch of wind coming down the chimney filled the room with the stench of burning paper and leather. The smoke made his eyes sting. Calmly, he gathered together another armful.

All his life he had devoted to these detestable objects, and in return they had done nothing but suck all the juice and certainty from him. They were leeches of the intellect. If there was a true word to be found in any of them, then it was surrounded by a hundred indistinguishable lies. To possess one simple truth, he must accept an Alexandria of nonsense into his brain. These piously regarded falsehoods had for long years crushed his head in the book-press of scholarship, squeezing all hopes and ambitions from him, leaving nothing but a dry, empty husk.

No more.

From boyhood, all his passion had been for knowledge. He had ached to hold within him the compass of all lore and learning, to read the book of Nature and so comprehend the mind of its Creator, to be that more-than-mortal man, that *Magister Mirabilis* who would synthesize and reveal all, and so raise Mankind from the muck of superstition, disease, and ignorance, easing human misery and undoing the curse of toil, filling the nations with clean white cities and joining all in a single commonwealth under one king and that king Reason itself.

Too late, he saw his ambitions for the folly they were. His youth and money were gone and he had nothing to show for them. Nothing but books, books, books . . .

"God damn you," he whispered.

The room swam in the heat and for an instant he saw the slim white tapers of his father's funeral wavering like beeches through the drowning waters of the Mediterranean. He saw swans rising from the serene lake of his childhood, and it seemed to him that the past was a garden from which he had been expelled and which he could never regain.

At that moment Wagner appeared in the doorway, yawning and pasty-faced in his cotton nightgown, though it was late afternoon. He rubbed his eyes against sleep and the fumes, and then gawped like a fish as he came suddenly awake.

"Magister!" Waving horrified arms, he advanced into the smoke. "What are you doing?"

Faust extracted a volume of Galen from his armful, letting the rest spill to the floor. He waved the Greek physician under the young man's nose. "Have you ever cut open a human body, Wagner?"

"Before Jesu, never!"

"If you had—if you had . . . I served for a time as a physician in the Polish army. So much sickness, and so rarely did my medicines work! During the campaigns against the Turk, I stitched up wounds and sawed off legs by the hundreds. So this elaborate horror you show for the sanctity of the dead is quite incomprehensible to me. How can it be moral to gaze upon the shattered organs of living men, knowing you can do nothing for them, but sinful to look at the undamaged organs of those who no longer suffer pain? I assure you there is more horror in cutting open a body when it can still scream.

"Thus I began a series of investigations into the origins of disease. I quickly found that there were organs described by our good friend Claudius Galen that are not to be found in human beings at all. Why? Because in his priggish regard for the sanctity of man, the old fraud examined instead the insides of butchered pigs, from which he extrapolated a similar anatomy for the human body. Pigs! For thirteen hundred years we have doctored the sick as if they were swine, and all on the word of one who could be disproved by any idiot with a knife and a corpse."

"Speak not so of Galen, sir! Not of that greatest of anatomists, that divinely inspired father of physicians, that—"

"Father of lies, you mean." Faust clutched the Galen so tightly his knuckles turned white. "Here is another perjurer who will not mislead one more honest man!"

He skimmed the book into the flames.

With a cry, Wagner ran toward the fireplace. He was buffeted back by the scholar, who then seized his arms and grinned wildly into his face. "The world is better off without such quacks, bleeders, apothecaries, and barbers—let us go to witch-women and root-gatherers instead. Or, better, let us not go at all." Thrusting Wagner back disdainfully, he seized another book. "Ahh, now here is a treasure, Averroës's *Commentaries* on Aristotle in a tolerable translation from the Arabic by Gerard of Cremona." He lasciviously stroked the red leather boards, knowing well how his pupil ached for the chance to pore through it. "A liar's gloss on a liar's lies. Surely this is a rare criminal."

He cocked his arm.

Desperately, Wagner said, "Sir, please consider! These books are of value, Magister, of monetary value if nothing else."

Faust stopped, looked down at the younger man. "How old are you, Herr Wagner?"

"Seventeen years, Magister."

"Four years, then, you have studied the trivium—grammar and rhetoric and logic—things which are of no value in themselves save that they order and organize human thought in order to facilitate further learning. And what have you learned?"

"Great things, Magister."

"*Nothing!* Why can a bird fly and a man not? What star or curse or vapor causes plagues? What monsters live within the ocean's lightless depths? What makes the sky blue? These are questions a child might ask, and yet you cannot answer me."

"No man can."

"Exactly." He chucked the book into the flames, ignoring the sound that burst from Wagner's throat like the cry of a small bird. "All these books and a thousand more I have read, traveling great distances at times to win the privilege, and they, the accumulated wisdom of the ages, can help me answer none of them." He reached for a folio book bound in tooled kid with gilt tracery, Ptolemy's masterwork, the *Alma-*

gest. But before he could firmly grasp the volume, Wagner had wildly flung himself forward and wrestled it away. "Give me that!"

Hugging the *Almagest* to his chest, Wagner cried, "Hear me out! For three years, master, I have gone every night to make your measurements, out to the Roman tower in Spisser's Wood. Have I not? I have been your poodle, your loyal ferret, your most obedient servant. In rain and snow I have gone, against the chance the weather would break. And when the weather was clear, I climbed to the broken top of the tower and there with instruments of your own devising, with torquetum and cross-staff and sighting tubes with spider-silk grids, made measures more perfect than any man had before—"

"The measurements." Faust laughed bitterly. "For two sleepless days and nights I have struggled to make sense of them. All orbits must be circles, so says Ptolemy, for just as all things *sub lunae* are imperfect so must all realms beyond be perfect, and the circle, being infinite, is perfection itself. Cycles and epicycles, deferents, equants, and eccentric spheres of ethereal crystal have I plotted, and all in vain. The discrepancies between what is and what ought to be still remain. Where measurement is perfected, the variance revealed is greater than before. Every correction requires yet more subtle corrections. It is as if the planets did not revolve about the Earth at all. But if not, then . . . what? Their paths are regular enough that there *must* be meaning in them. Yet the more I try to impose reason upon the unruly universe, the further it moves from comprehension. It is this nut I have been trying to crack with my forehead until my poor skull is bruised and shattered and black." He clutched his head, swaying.

"The notes!" Wagner cried in sudden dread. "Where are they?"

For a long moment Faust glowered at his junior with glittering and sardonic eye, like a magician staring down his fascinated audience prior to pulling some fantastic illusion from his sleeve. With slow deliberation, he said, "Fool! How do you think I *started* the fire?"

"Oh," Wagner said. It was the softest of sounds, almost a sigh. He sank to his knees, still hugging the Ptolemy, and began to rock gently on the floor.

"Stand up!" Seizing the youth by the roots of his hair, Faust hauled him to his feet. "If you wish to save these books, these oh-so-precious books, why then, I will let you try."

Wagner looked up with tear-stained face. "Sir?"

"We will debate, you and I, whether these books deserve to exist. Surely this is fair, for if the truth is on your side, no amount of oratorical trickery can prevail. Should I win, let the flames of damnation take them! Should you win . . ." He hesitated, as if thinking. "Should you win . . . Why, then my library is yours."

Wagner's eyes grew wide with astonishment, all horror, all fear wiped clean in this instant of greed and wonder. "Agreed!" he gasped.

"Before we begin, though, let us limit the terms of our argument. All the breath in your body could not begin to defend every book page by page. So we must choose an epitomal selection to debate. Now, what are the three legs of learning— eh? The three legs upon which all else depends?"

"The—the trivium, Magister, rhetoric and logic and . . ."

"No, no, no! All the material world consists of that which is beyond our touch, that which can be examined, and ultimately upon that which can be determined by the study of these things of the reasoning of their Creator—which is to say the realms of astronomy, physics, and teleology. Would you agree?"

"Who could deny it, master?"

"And the three books from which we derive all our lore and learning on these matters—surely you can name them? No? There in your arms lies the *Almagest*. All other works on astronomy are mere gloss and corruption. So much for the cataloguing of existence. Here"—he slammed a second volume, as great as the first, though less expensively bound, on top of the Ptolemy—"is Aristotle's *Physics*, and that accounts for your mechanics. Which leaves the design of physical existence. For which we proffer . . . ?"

With a sudden wrenching motion, he turned and seized two black folios from the wall; gripping each by their bottoms, he stood spraddle-legged, in the posture of Moses with the tablets. "My grandfather published this Bible in old and new testaments in Mainz, long before I was born. What finer prize could I offer?"

Wagner staggered as they were slammed into his arms.

"Now! Three works in four volumes, the round world contained in a squared triangle. Let us contend."

"I stand ready."

"Bravely said. There are, as William of Ockham has asserted, three sure sources of knowledge: the self-evident, experience, and Scriptural revelation. Would you agree?"

"That is beyond denial."

"We shall then begin with the *Almagest*. Ptolemy himself has said that astronomy is a form of mathematics. Hence it is a perfect exemplar of the self-evident. If there is a single flaw in an equation, the whole is necessarily wrong. Which being so, your measurements by themselves discredit him."

Eyes shining, Wagner said, "Not so! For Ptolemy's observations have stood the test of time. Whereas my own could easily be flawed by reason of weariness or some lenticular effect of the atmosphere or some other cause beyond the capacity of my imagination to comprehend."

"Surely, however, reason can correct any lack in your perceptions even as ground lenses can correct a weakness in optical vision."

Wagner licked his lips. "But if the organ of rational thought be imperfect—as what man's is not?—then it can no more apply the logic of its own correction than a man may touch his elbow with the hand of that same arm."

"If you cannot trust your senses, nor reason them back into coherence with the known facts of existence, it necessarily follows that truth is *ipso facto* unknowable to you. We must reject then the self-evident, commonsense interpretation of existence, for you lack the mental equipment to verify it."

"Ah, but Ptolemy's judgment was infinitely superior to my own."

"Was it?"

"Yes."

"How do you know?"

"By the verification of a hundred witnesses and scholars."

"There is a children's game—you have surely played it—where one youth whispers a sentence in a second youth's ear, and that friend whispers it to a third, and so on until it has passed through twenty ears and as many mouths. The last speaks his treasure aloud, and it has no relation whatsoever to the original. A true word enters through the river gate and by the time it departs down the road to Coswig, it has become a lie. The hearsay of hearsay is not admissible as scholarship." Faust sighed. "You are fallible because you are human. All men are fallible. Ptolemy was a man. Ptolemy was fallible. *Quod erat demonstratum.*"

He took the *Almagest* from Wagner's arms and slammed it down on the worktable. "We arrive now at the second leg of our triangle. Aristotle must stand in for those truths derived from experience. His *Physics* asserts that physical laws are determined by distinctions of qualities." He took that volume from Wagner's arms and leaned it up against the Ptolemy, so that together they made an inclined plane whose lower end overlapped the table's edge. Opening a chest, he rummaged within, and removed two fist-sized spheres.

"Here are two balls of equal size but different composition, for the one is made of pine and the other of granite. The stone sphere, you will note, is significantly heavier. Their intrinsic qualities could not be more different. We will place each at the top of this ramp and simultaneously let them go. Which will hit the floor first?"

"The granite one, necessarily."

"So Aristotle would have you believe. And for most scholars that citation would suffice. We, however, will prove or disprove it from our own experience."

He let go the balls.

They rolled down the book, fell through the air, hit the floor as one. Faust raised his eyebrows.

"So much for experience. So much for Aristotle. I have removed two legs of your triangle, Herr Wagner, and you are left standing uneasily on but one."

"Truth," Wagner said boldly, though his voice wavered slightly, "springs from direct and divine revelation. Scientific inquiry, for which we have only the evidence of our own fallible senses, can be merely the calculated deception of Satan."

"So." Faust laid Ptolemy and Aristotle to bed in the flames, then lowered his hands upon the twin folio volumes of the Bible. "We must put all our trust and faith in this one book, eh? This one divided book, which all devout men take to be the divine revelation itself, perfect and immutable, the sole and single source that cannot be contradicted nor contradict itself. Where all man's ways prove unreliable, revelation cannot fail us."

"Yes!" Wagner cried. "Yes."

"You will stake your all, your soul itself upon this book?"

"I will."

"Tell me, then. How many days did Noah abide in his ark?"

"What?"

"It says in Genesis, '*And the flood was forty days upon the earth.*' That seems straightforward enough, eh? Then, but a few lines further down, '*And the waters prevailed upon the earth a hundred and fifty days.*' Which one is correct? They cannot both be correct. And if one is a lie, what does that say about the purported author of the book?"

"We—we do not know the *length* of days in those ancient times, and it is possible that the one citation gives that duration in the measure of our day and the other—"

"Bah! Sophistry!" Faust flung the books atop the fire.

With a wild cry, Wagner fled the room.

"So much for the old white-bearded man," Faust muttered. "So much for the Creator and Preserver. Who was it hid the knowledge from human eyes in the first place?"

Alone in the smoky room, Faust found himself staring at the front wall where the chimney formed a stone nose between the glowing rectangular eyes of two windows, so that he seemed to be standing within a human head. It was no common head, but that of a hero, large of eye and spacious within. The conceit came upon him that this study was a perfect simulacrum of his own brain. Here was his worktable, overflowing with scribbled charts and figures and glass retorts, there the lodestone wound thick with wire to multiply its potency, and overhead a stuffed alligator from the Orinoco quartering the room with excruciating slowness, a bit of mummery hung from the ceiling not so much to repel demons and negate their baleful influence on his experiments as to intimidate gullible clients. The skull of a whale (a small one) was propped up in one corner alongside a teaching device wherein a wooden roller in the form of two cones joined at the base could be made to seemingly roll up an inclined but diverging pair of boards. Nearby were the petrified thighbone of a pre-Adamic giant and an iron stone which he had with his own eyes seen fall from the starry sky. Each curio and device could be read as the visible symbol for some acquired skill or science Faust had crammed disorganizedly within his noggin. Each would greatly impress the ignorant. Yet they were but clumsy models for the real world outside, and however ably he might arrange and rearrange them, he could never bring that outside world within.

Faint noises of commerce and flirtation arose from the street. Somebody was shouting. Children laughed. He ignored these sounds as irrelevant, distractions from the Gordian knot of logic he must focus his intellect upon. For, paradoxically, in his excited and despairing state he felt himself closer to a true insight into the universal essence than ever his studies had brought him, so close that all the world suddenly seemed insubstantial to him, no more than shadows cast on the back of his skull or the filmy membrane of a bubble so infinitely immense its center was everywhere, its interior unknowable, and its surface the phenomenal world.

Without bravado, Faust held himself to be as learned as any man alive. Yet all he knew with any assurance was that he knew nothing. Therefore it was pointless to look for help from native minds; he must seek elsewhere, in realms greater or lesser than human. He must assume, too, that the knowledge he sought existed somewhere, else all his strivings were for naught. So, then. Where?

Faust had no delusions of Heavenly aid. An involved and benevolent deity would have helped him long years ago when, young, he had yearned for knowledge as achingly as now and with far fewer stains on his soul. So. He must deal with realms or domains or powers that might be devils or spirits or creatures that were neither but something beyond his merely mortal comprehension.

Assuming such beings, they must necessarily be far beyond him, existing in realms unreachable by human effort. In his alchemical studies he had worked with athenors, alembics, and solutory furnaces, manipulating such mordants, caustics, and solvents as were employed in mining and in the dying of cloth. But he had also engaged in researches involving the exhausted bodies of prostitutes, both female and male, the sacrifice of animals, and the obscene deployment of stolen Communion wafers in black Masses and other unwholesome rituals. There were two traditions of alchemy, and he had sought out—and paid—exponents of each, not only metallurgists and assayers but wizards as well, mountebanks and teachers of the esoteric traditions, followers of Hermes Trismegistus and worshippers of Saint Wolf alike. And it was all flummery. He knew for a certainty that none of them were in contact with such allies as he sought.

These allies, therefore, must locate Faust, for he could not contact them. Which meant that—denying the possibility of failure, for that was folly and despair—they must be already searching for him, for otherwise the contact could not be made. Therefore he possessed some thing or quality these beings or forces desired, be it worship or service or his very soul itself. There must be ten millions of people in Europe alone. Beyond that? In Hind and Cathay and Araby, in Africa and the new Indies? Unimaginable numbers. What had he to offer that no one else in all these swarming legions had?

One thing only: that he was seeking them.

It took a rare man, a great man, to break free of the encrusted prejudices of his age, to cast his thoughts into the dark and silent regions where the minds of such allies awaited him. And awaited him anxiously. For surely a man such as himself was no unworthy prize.

If they were seeking one such as he, and their thoughts touched his in the dark, then he and they could strike a bargain. He did not need the magical idiocy of diagrams or devices, of nonsense syllables or implements with evil histories. There was no need even to leave the room. He could win all, achieve all, here and now. It required only an act of will.

He had but to offer himself up.

A shiver—of anticipation or fear, he could not tell which—passed through Faust. The room felt unaccountably cold. Slowly, he spread his arms.

A book fell off the burning pile onto the hearthstone and, falling open, burst more furiously into flame. It threw up smoke like a black flare, but Faust did not stoop to retrieve it.

He stood unmoving, wondering at his own abrupt and incomprehensible inability to act. He did not fear damnation. Nor did he give a fig for the common opinion of Mankind. There was nothing to stop him but fear alone—fear that his reasoning was wrong. Fear that the offering would prove him a failure.

For the briefest instant he stood irresolute.

"Here I am," Faust said convulsively. "I open myself to you." For his part, Faust knew, he would gladly worship demons, willingly give service to monsters unspeakable, if that were what they wanted. Eat filth, murder children—whatever they required, that would he do. Whatever the price, he would pay it.

The smoke swirled about him chokingly, dizzyingly. He could see nothing now, feel nothing. Afloat and lost in the grey smoke and ruin, Faust emptied his brain of all thought, all reasoning, all words, surrendering everything but ambition itself. He made himself first passive and then silent, ignoring the blacksmith-bellows pumping of his lungs, the tidal surge of blood in his veins, and finally the faint crackling that underlay thought itself, accelerating toward zero, until all that was left was unmediated will, and that will a hunger, an open mouth.

He stood reduced to his essence, an uncarved block of marble awaiting the carver's hand, a palimpsest scraped clean of old ink and ready for the quill, as eager for knowledge as tinder for the flame. The noise of the fire rose up in his ears in a babbling roar like a million voices all joined together into a white surf of sound, flooding his brain, drowning the last semblance of reason. He fell into a perfect stillness.

Cycling ever quieter in perfect silence without expectations
falling into a timeless state outside his control
where human thought ceased and
nothing existed nothing
but the void
and

From the heart of nothingness, a voice spoke:
Faust.

ℜEVELATIONS

A puppeteer had drawn a crowd to the college street side of the market-square. Disembodied, locationless, Faust saw it all, the traveling horn-merchant's booth where gallants pored over tortoiseshell combs and boxes cunningly crafted to win the coldest female heart, the lean scrivener hurrying by with a bribe for the mayor, the bulldog woman with a stack of men's hats in either hand and another upon her head who could not speak but only bark yet was a shrewd dealer nonetheless, and the legless veteran of a Venetian warship with his begging bowl as well. A lesser mob clustered by the Jew street end, where a barber had set up chair and basin and was preparing to yank a festered tooth "within three pulls." He knelt heavily upon his apprehensive victim's thighs and nodded to his burly volunteers. Two of them seized the man's forearms while a third dug his fists into the hair and pulled back.

The crowd surged forward.

"Portugals! Portugals!" sang the orange-monger. Faust's vision was fragmented, as if he had a thousand eyes turned every which way, at now a scrannel dog slinking hopefully beneath the sausage-maker's glare and now a buxom towns-woman buying a choicer cut of meat with a furtive kiss behind the butcher's booth. Tied to the whipping post at the center of the square was a Rostocker who, for selling bad wine, had been forced to drink a quantity of his own merchandise and endure having the rest poured over him. The man had puked before losing consciousness and pissed and beshit himself af-terwards. Those who came close in order to benefit from the lesson of his example (and there were many such) either pur-chased oranges first, to hold before their noses, or else soon after regretted not doing so.

The puppeteer was presenting the rascal tale of Old Vice, an edifying and uplifting play with enough shrieks and drub-bings to satisfy the most demanding audience. The playboard was held over his head and a kind of curtain fell from it, was cinched at his waist, and then fell again to brush his boots. Children had pushed their way to the fore, but adults watched as well: housewives in their market-day finery, rough-faced farmers leaning protectively over their baskets of produce, an officer from the castle who sat back in his saddle with a smile and stroked his mustache, remembering a disreputable inci-dent from his youth. A frog-skinner laughed, even as her nim-ble hands emptied one bushel and filled another. On the stage Old Vice howled as his little boat tossed on imagined waves, the puppeteer bending at the waist and swaying at the knees to simulate an ocean squall.

A roar rose up from the far side of the market. "*One!*"

The audience turned, craned necks, saw nothing. The puppeteer froze, his hero's crescent-moon boat canted over almost sideways. "One?!" Old Vice waved his stiff little arms hysterically. "One what? Oh! It must be a sea serpent come for me!"

An aged fishwife leaped back as a passing cart-horse voided itself close enough to spatter her skirts, and began to vigorously scold the wagoner, who folded enormous arms and cocked his head in a bored manner. Neither noticed the young woman gliding by with a faraway smile on her lips and a tightly folded letter in her hands. Two angel-faced shoemaker's apprentices skipped past her, singing a glee in catches. One missed a note and his comrade playfully shoved him sideways against a confectioner's display, upsetting a tray of honeyed hemp seeds sold as a specific against women's cramps.

"*Two!*"

"Two sea serpents! Oh, woe!—what is to become of me?"

A student burst through the crowd, running across the plaza barefoot and in his nightgown, flapping his arms like some extravagant great bird.

"Help! Help!"

Old Vice disappeared from the tiny stage and was replaced by the gawking face of his manipulator. The children were pointing and laughing at the hairy-legged student. "Please!" he cried, running from citizen to citizen without pausing long enough for any one of them to react. "Somebody must help the Magister! He's setting fire to everything!"

"Fire?"

At that dread word all laughter ceased. Brother Josaphat, a great bruiser of a monk, as wide as he was tall, and not at all a short man, stepped out of the crowd. He placed himself in the student's path and so stopped Wagner in his headlong flight. "Who is setting fires?" the monk demanded. "Where?"

"It's Magister Faust, he—"

"The astrologer Faust?"

"Oh, no, no, no! The scholar Faust, good brother. He is a most learned doctor of natural philosophy who teaches at the . . ."

"Yes, yes, I know who you mean. Where is he?"

"He's—he's—he's—"

Brother Josaphat picked up Wagner by the shoulders and shook him roughly enough to restore sense to his head. Then he turned the student around and set him down again. "No more babbling. Lead us there and we will follow."

The rescuers thundered up the stairs, some bearing buckets of water that sloshed as they ran, others with bags of sand kept convenient for such emergencies, and still others with axes and hooked poles for pulling down draperies and chopping out walls. First came Wagner, followed by the mountainous Brother Josaphat and several merchants, some farmers who had already sold their wares and found the free nature of this diversion much to their liking, along with neighbors, laborers, idlers, even a pair of white-bearded, black-clad Jews. And of course the children, impossible even with kicks and curses to keep them away, shrieking with excitement. The puppeteer, hung all over with his moppets like so many bunches of onions, brought up the rear, a gaping scarecrow of a man, all bright eyes and beak nose.

They found no fire save that overspilling the hearth, but only Faust himself, vacant-eyed, mumbling, and incoherent. Somebody threw a bucket of water into the fireplace and the resultant explosion of noise and steam and smoke so unnerved the shakier elements of the throng that they began pulling down shelves and smashing in walls with frantic earnestness.

But then a clear-thinking Jew threw open the windows and fresh air entered the room. The smoke blew away and everyone paused in what they were doing, confused and blinking, stamping their feet uncertainly. The monk, fists on hips, scowled at the mess and confusion. "Disgraceful!"

"Oh, master, dear master." Wagner took one of the scholar's cold white hands into his. "Tell me you can hear me."

But Faust's eyes showed no response. His lips continued their idiot mumbling, and his face was beaded with sweat. Brother Josaphat peeled back an eyelid, laid his hand over the brow. "Fever," he declared. (Several of those closest shrank away, were frowned back.) "Put him to bed."

They put him to bed.

On the way out, the puppeteer seized the opportunity to steal a breviary of some small value, but as it chanced to belong to Wagner, no harm was done.

"Why do you show me this?"

All these events Faust witnessed at a remove, dispassionately viewing the players, himself among them, from all aspects at once, as if through the shards of a shattered but still enchanted mirror. They were all one in their insignificance, the hat-woman and the Jew, the monk, the farmers and the thief, flies upon the common dungheap, negligible. The petty comings and goings of Wittenberg coursed through his senses in a headlong stream of pictures/smells/textures/sounds whose significance he had not the time or concentration to sort out. But always a fragment—the most important one—of his attention was focused inward, into that dark and airless space where the voice had first spoken:

Faust. It was the smallest of whispers, a voice calling from a distance more than a universe away and yet simultaneously more intimate than his own thought. It was a voice powerful with hate. The malice of it seared him like a murderer's iron-hot grin in the night. *Vile and ignorant insect, we show you this so that you might understand. There can be no physical commerce between our world and yours—the gulf that separates us is too great. Only information can wing that chasm. Only words and thoughts. We can speak solely in the silence of your mind. Tell no one of us. You will be thought mad or worse.*

"Who are you?"

Those you summoned.

"Make yourself manifest."

His study re-formed about Faust with such hallucinatory clarity that the very air sparkled. The room was uniformly lit and without shadows, as if every object shone in the perfect light of its own nature. Here was his table, half-hidden under a futility of papers and blown-glass vessels, here the lodestone and there the alligator, here the charts of Irlandah al-Kabirah ("Ireland the Great" or "Greater Ireland" by his tentative translation) across the western Atlantic, with each stone city drawn and named in the fine and flowing script of the Arab geographer Idrisi, which he had, despite misgivings, bought from a Portuguese traveler who had sworn them stolen from the library of Henry the Navigator himself. So detailed a simulacrum was it that, had he not witnessed himself being put to bed, pale and muttering, he would never have doubted its reality.

A gleeful sensation seized him then, an involuntary roar

of triumph that rattled and shook him down to his foundations. "Who are you?" he repeated.

From nothingness, a figure composed itself. It was protean, monstrously so, shifting restlessly from form to form but fixing on none. The glistening skin and black stone eyes of a manatee gave way to a living construct of trumpet vines growing over a crude armature of oak planks. A flower closed in a wink to become a wet orifice that swallowed itself and sprouted tin crystals. It hurt Faust's eyes and wrenched his guts to look upon the creature, for its surfaces came together disturbingly, as if comprised of too many dimensions and those dimensions failing to come together in any sane fashion. To look upon it was to intuit (dimly, as in an uneasy dream) a universe in which four right angles might combine to form a triangle or six cubes stack into a sphere. "We are legion. A hundred libraries such as you have burnt could not contain our name."

"Begin, and I will tell you when to stop. Tell me who or what you are."

Dipping what might be a finger into the hearth, as if to pick up ashes, the creature wrote in bold black letters upon the white-plastered wall:

$$m_e \rho h = i \delta t_0 \Phi H \mathcal{E}_L \sum_{k=1}^{n} S$$

"Mephistopheles," the scholar repeated, charmed by the complexity of the equation, the implication of secret algebras lying within. "And the meaning?"

"The first symbol, m-subscript-e, represents the rest mass of an electron. This is multiplied by the mass-density of the universe times a constant measuring the size of quantum effects within any given system. In your universe this expresses itself as 6.6261×10^{-34} joule-seconds, a laughably small quantity, by the way. Which is done in order to establish a benchmark for a comparison of our relative energies. The derived whole is not, you understand, so much a name as it is an address, an expression of our relationship to your world.

"Returning to the equation—forgive me if I oversimplify—we determine this value by multiplying the square root of negative one by the variance of t-subscript-zero, the age of the universe, times the wave function of the universe times H, a constant for the rate of expansion of the universe. You see how neatly it all fits together? *Epsilon*-subscript-L is of course the permeability of the universe to information, and the *sigma* is a sum over standard values for S, where S represents—"

"I can make no sense of any of this!" Faust cried in dismay.

A crystalline human form, perfectly proportioned in all organs but one and that one grossly swollen, dissolved into a being with the stench and murky coloration of brackish water. "Calm yourself, little monkey. You will. For now, let it suffice that our universe exists at higher ambient levels of heat than you can comprehend. A window between our worlds the size of your head would let such energies pour from us to you as would melt the Earth like a candle.

"Under such conditions, both chemical and physical interactions transpire almost instantaneously, and thus signal occurs and information is processed with a rapidity inconceivable to you. Time also flows at a correspondingly greater pace. Even as we speak, a hundred generations of our kind are born, grow old, and die. This entity you see is an artificial construct, a homunculus or marionette by analogy, operated by vast numbers of our kind. You do not speak to an individual, but to the collective race. It is the only way we can communicate."

"Where are you?"

"That is no easy question." The Earth blossomed in Faust's vision. He saw it, serene and noble, and beauteous enough to fill his eyes with tears: blue with oceans, white with clouds, and so seemingly small that no least trace of humanity showed. He was given to know that the Earth revolved about the sun (and here was the solution to his muddled calculations!) for only an instant before his vision was yanked back and he saw that the glorious sun, great father Apollo himself, was but one star of many, and then was yanked back again to see that those many stars were an insignificant fraction of a whirlpool galaxy so vast that the light from a star at one edge would take a hundred thousand years to reach the other.

Again he was yanked back! Now he saw that the bright wheel of suns was only one of countless such, spinning, turning, and tumbling masses of many-colored stars. Next, that these galaxies were but an island in an archipelago of such. Then, that the archipelagoes themselves were arrayed within greater structures and those greater structures revealed as minor parts of still greater. Until finally he saw the cosmos whole and entire, a strangely twisted marble such as he might hold in his hand.

Drunk with wonder, Faust could only marvel. This was not the stately clockwork elegance of classical astronomy, but instead a wild and savage kind of glory that poured wonder upon wonder, surprise upon surprise, and each one nestled within embracing equations of such compelling logic that once known they could not be denied.

"Imagine this, your cosmos," Mephistopheles said, "as a bubble. Within it, a single set of conditions and laws uniformly applies. Without it, time is not spatialized nor space unpacked; they cannot even exist. Imagine that there are many such bubbles, each with its own unique set of laws. Our cosmos is one such."

"This is enlightenment beyond avarice!"

"It is nothing. You are like a beggar who stands in the doorway of the Emperor's kitchen, smelling the odors, and thinks himself within reach of all his desires. But we stand prepared to give you not just the food, the kitchen, and the castle, but the Empire as well, and the armies that will conquer those lands beyond if you wish.

"Though we can give you nothing more than knowledge"—the voice came from within a crawling mass of bright-eyed bats who clutched at each other with sharp claws and showed needle teeth to the scholar—"our knowledge is absolute. We have mastered all sciences, perfected all technologies. We can show you events from the distant past, the solemn rituals of Nippon and pagan ecstasies of undiscovered Western lands, the priviest moments of pontiffs, the rutting of kings and queens. With our aid you can remake the world, bend the strongest men, the most beautiful women to your will. You can obliterate enemies, reward friends, rule nations in secret or open as you wish. Whatever you ask to see, we can show it. No knowledge shall be hidden from you. Surely this is worth the pittance we ask in return."

"In return—" Faust said with sudden apprehension. "Yes. Yes, what do you want of me in return?"

"Only that you listen."

"Listen? Why?"

The room vanished. Faust stood beneath a grey sky. Identical clapboard houses were arrayed in a grid to all sides of him like barracks, enough to house a city. A walkway stretched from his feet to a windowless, many-chimneyed structure. Its bricks were blackened with soot. Heavy smoke gushed from its stacks. A cold autumn wind pressed down on the smoke like the rejecting hand of Heaven, forcing it to the ground.

The stench was beyond belief. It imparted a foul taste to Faust's mouth. He smacked his lips uneasily. Where the smoke touched his flesh, it left a grey, faintly greasy deposit.

"Why am I here?"

There was no answer.

He walked forward. Gravel crunched underfoot. It was eerily quiet. Despite the many buildings, there were no voices, no sounds of human commerce. Not a bird sang. In all this desolate tract, only the smoke moved.

He passed blind windows and vacant walls. Something creaked, regular-irregular, not loud but impossible to ignore. A door swinging, all but imperceptibly, in the breeze. As he passed it, Faust glanced within.

A glimpse—no more—of an empty classroom. Desks were arrayed in neat lines; their surfaces were scratched and scarred with use. Upon the walls hung violins by the hundreds, all sized to the hands of children, all silent.

He strode on, unaccountably disturbed.

The walk took Faust to the blackened building. The cold breeze died. The crunch of gravel ceased. He laid a hand upon the structure's metal doors and found them warm to the touch. A sudden dread seized him then and he could not open the doors. He could not. There was no power or reward great enough to make him look within.

But when he started to turn away, Mephistopheles stood at his side. The creature had taken on a nearly human form. He was red-skinned, sharp-chinned, and hook-nosed, with long and slender waxed mustaches. A long prehensile tail rose from clownishly striped pantaloons to sway its spearpoint tip over one shoulder. A plume bobbed from a ridiculous cap. He was the very picture of a comic devil from a low farce. There was no mistaking him, however, for an aura of ravening madness radiated from beneath the rouged cheeks, the sly and painted leer, as if a werewolf crouched just beneath the skin. He touched Faust's forearm and at this genteel gesture the scholar shuddered.

"You must look. There can be no misunderstanding between us."

"No. Please . . ."

But Mephistopheles was already pushing at the doors, already swinging them open.

"Do not look away! If you flinch, if you cringe, if you deny what you see, there will be no compact between us. None of this exists yet, but if you enter into our service, then it will. This is the price you must pay for knowledge: You must understand and acknowledge its consequences."

The doors slammed open.

Faust saw.

It was impossible. Unbearable. All chance of accord with this fiend vanished forever. He could not. Could not. Not with *this* before him. Abruptly, Faust found himself crying, not only out of disgust and pity for the reeking horror he was forced to witness, but for losing the infinite wealth of knowledge offered him along with it. He had come so close! It was maddening to think upon.

He did not, could not look away.

"How . . . how can"—savagely, he slashed an arm down before him in absolute negation of all he saw—"such be? How could God allow it?"

"God? You fool—*there is no God!*"

The words struck Faust like a great bronze clapper, shattering the crusted certainties of a lifetime, reverberating, setting up echoes that washed back and forth through his being in slowly lessening waves, leaving no atom unshaken, no belief untouched. There was no God. He knew this for the truth, recognized it as such on an almost physical level, for it summed up everything he had ever thought or reasoned. It resolved a thousand doubts. It left no question unanswered. There was no God! Everything was possible now. Nothing was forbidden.

This moment of bleak liberation from belief would have been exhilarating at any other time. Standing before the charred building's open doors, he could feel nothing but despair. "What purpose," he asked, "is served by showing me such a thing?"

"I am delighted that you should ask." Mephistopheles jauntily twirled a mustachio. "It is, quite simply, our will that your race should die. You live so much longer than we, you see. Ours are mayfly lives alongside yours. In time, a long time even by your standards admittedly, our race will grow old and die—there are reasons why this is inevitable and should you wish, we will happily explain entropy and the tyranny of thermodynamics to you. Yet here, where time runs slowly, your feeble and noisesome kind will survive our extinction. This is intolerable. It offends us.

"So we will give you all the knowledge you desire. So much, indeed, that your race will choke upon it. We will give them the tools to commit every crime and outrage their fecund imaginations can devise. Through you, we will give them power without limit and they will inevitably use it to destroy themselves in a symphony of horrors." He gestured lightly at what lay beyond the doors. "Horrors so great that when they have run out of victims, the last survivors must inevitably surrender themselves to their own atrocity machines.

"Then, with existence scoured of your verminous breed, we can die."

"This cannot be!"

"It must be."

"You said—you showed me the cosmos, stars beyond number, and named it but one of an effervescence of bubbles in the matrix of being. We inhabit an insignificant world in an obscure corner of a forgotten galaxy of a cosmos that can never influence yours. It can hardly matter to you whether we prosper or fall."

"If you were dying, Magister Faustus, and a cockroach chanced to scuttle upon the bedside table, an inch from your clenched fist, and you knew it would live to see the dawn denied you—what would you do?"

Faust's eyes felt dry and gritty. It was painful just to keep them open. A ferocious anger rose within his breast at all the human race for having within it the potential to create the grotesquerie before him. Bastards! Weaklings! Were it not for their failings, their undisciplined appetite for cruelty and destruction, he could achieve in an instant such insight and enlightenment as all the philosophers of the ages had sought and been denied. Knowledge without limit was his for a word.

"Surely," he cried, "this is not inevitable. Surely humanity could take the knowledge you offer and use it to ennoble itself. Surely they could apply it wisely and without folly."

"They could," Mephistopheles said dryly. "But will they?"

"This is hard, very hard," Faust said. Then, convulsively, "Must I obey you?"

"Do what you will. Only listen."

"I have never turned away from the truth . . ."

"Then do not turn away now."

For a long time Faust was silent. Ashes drifted across his shoes, but he did not move away. Seeing was the hardest part; once he had looked, enduring was, by contrast, easy.

"On them," he said at last, "be it. I believe that Mankind can endure any truth and, more, that with the perfection of knowledge we will and must ascend toward the perfection of spirit. We are not animals! But if I am wrong . . . If the common run of people cannot rise to the challenge of knowledge, if the only check on their passions is ignorance, then they deserve whatever they bring down upon themselves. I wash my hands of them."

He turned from the open doors.

And found himself home again.

Mephistopheles reclined lazily upon the study table, raised slightly upon one arm, head turned coquettishly. He retained the comic devil's visage and plumed hat, atop the nude body of a certain plump whore whose favors Faust had from time to time employed. He scratched up a louse from her cunt hair and ate it. His eye glinted mockingly.

"Sweet Faust," he purred. "Ask me whatever you wish. I will deny you nothing."

THE NEW PROMETHEUS

For seven days Wagner nursed Faust through his fever. He knelt by the great scholar's bed to spoon broth and watered milk into his mouth. He changed the bedclothes when they were soiled. To bring down the temperature, he soaked folded cloths in tepid water and placed them on Faust's groin and in his armpits. He knew to rub alcohol over the pale limbs and Christ-long torso, and to shift the body periodically so that it did not develop bedsores, because he had lost all three of his sisters to fevers and had helped his mother nurse each one through her final illness. Brushing Faust's hair every morning, he would remember each of their dear faces, white as marble, still and angelic on their death-sheets, and hot tears would flow down his face and the back of his throat.

Nights he slept, as always, in the trundle bed at the doctor's feet. But he did not sleep easily; he would awaken at a change in the tone or tempo of Faust's constant murmuring, and was often jolted upright by a sudden cry of wonder or alarm.

Visitors came—the landlady, neighboring scholars, even the heavy-footed Brother Josaphat—to offer condolences, soup, and nostrums which invariably had a history of miraculous cures when the doctors themselves had despaired and inevitably had no effect whatsoever save upon the difficulty of Wagner's daily laundering of the sheets.

Still, for most of the day and all of the night, Wagner was alone. In his weakness, he could not help remembering the long voyage by foot he had made to Wittenberg, so many years ago, how he had slept in barns when allowed and haystacks when not and his cloak when neither were available, eating stale bread from his wallet and whatever fruits and plants the wilderness had to offer along the way (but he was a village boy and had enough woods-lore that this was not the hardship it might have been) and drinking only water from streams, for his mother had often warned him that still water caused seizures.

A fearful and exhilarating time it had been for a young man. He could scarce believe now he'd had the courage then. For he had never before left his native Kreuzendorf. But he'd conceived a great enthusiasm for learning at the Latin school, and studied so diligently that with good master Paumgartner's help he had managed to extract a promise from his father that—somehow—when the time came, money would be found to send him to a university.

So that after his father had died and his mother been taken into his Aunt Scheurl's household, what other opportunity was open to him other than to turn his cap toward the nearest university town? He had neither home nor patrimony, lacked the money to be apprenticed to a trade, and was too young to have any skills worth the hire. All he had was a love of learning and the fiery desire to read the odes of Pindar, of which he had heard much and seen nothing.

Empty-stomached, Wagner had walked the streets of Wittenberg in a marveling daze, staggered by the height of its buildings—five stories, some of them!—and the plenitude of stone-paved streets. He had determined to kneel before the first teacher he met and beg to be accepted as a student, in exchange for his unquestioning service as a servant. But so weakened was he by his privations that in the actual event he collapsed facedown in the dust.

To his eternal joy, the scholar at whose feet he had flung himself had been Faust.

Faust, amazed and amused, had taken the starveling to a tavern, bought him a plate of sausages and a mug of beer, and grilled him on his Latin verbs and then probed his far more elementary grasp of Greek. "Good enough for a provincial," he had concluded at last, and so the deal had been sealed.

Wagner could not help remembering all this and then, blushing with guilt, wondering what was to become of him should his benefactor die.

"Call in a doctor," Brother Josaphat commanded on his second visit.

Wagner's heart leaped. "You recognize the disease? It's curable? You have no idea how relieved I am to hear it. I had almost given up hope he would ever recover his wits."

"For photons of uniform energy," Faust mumbled, "the energy flux of the photons at the point of interest is related to the absorbed dose rate . . ."

"Listen to the man! He's dying. Doctors can't help that. But they have drugs and methods to revive him long enough to confess his sins and receive the sacrament." The monk's angry gaze took in the plenitude of scientific and pedagogic devices upon the walls with here a lute and there a steelpoint engraving of a rhinoceros but never a crucifix to be seen. "Can't you feel the demons thronged about your master, eager to drag him down to the shit-pits and cesspools of Hell? Faust has frittered away his life with grammar and pagan scribblings. But the Lord is all-forgiving. An instant of repentance, an act of true contrition, and his soul can evade their clutching talons and wing its way free to Heaven."

Brother Josaphat was so exercised by his speech that when he paused, he was panting like a dog. His hands and jaw clenched hard enough to bulge the veins on his forehead. Delivered thus, his simple message of Christian redemption sounded like a threat.

"The spectral emissivity of a thermal radiator is the ratio of the radiance of the radiator in a given direction to that of a black body at the same temperature."

"He despises doctors!" Wagner cried, horrified. "Many a time I've heard him say—"

"You can help him die into the eternal life of the Father," Brother Josaphat growled, "or else consign him to burn in the endless night of damnation. Think hard—and think of the welfare of your own soul as well!"

"Sir, you judge my master too harshly. I assure you there is nothing impious in the examination of Creation."

"In isometric transition a metastable nuclide is converted into another nuclide of the same element with emission of gamma rays."

"It's the devil's own syllabary!" The monk stamped his foot in outrage. "I'll listen to no more."

He left.

So it was that Wagner, with guilt and trepidation, searched through Faust's chests and belongings until he found the small store of coins set aside to last through the new semester's fees, and from it extracted enough to pay for a physician. Then, on the advice of Frau Wirten, the landlady, he sent for Doctor Schnabel.

Doctor Schnabel was famed for having an educated nose, an enormous and complexly sensitive olfactory instrument with which he could almost instantaneously diagnose diseases, identify subtle changes in the progress of an ailment, and infallibly predict the onset of a patient's death. He entered the room with a rush and a swoop, flinging the door aside as if the fate of his patient were too precarious to wait upon such niceties as knocking. He was seated at the sick man's bedside almost before Wagner could bring up a stool to slide beneath him.

Frau Wirten, who was a simple creature and a dwarf as well, was a great admirer of the grotesque and loved tales of demons and murderers, and things medical above all. She appeared in the doorway, like a scrap of paper drawn up the stairs in the wake of the doctor's passage. Lips tight with excitement, she tiptoed into the sickroom.

The doctor leaned low over Faust, passing his great nose over every inch of the scholar's body. He stroked the forehead with a slender white finger and then closed his bright, pink-lined eyes as he held that finger under his nostrils and inhaled noisily. With a flourish, he produced a spotless white handkerchief to wipe the finger, and then daintily drew up a corner of the imperfectly laundered nightshirt for nasal inspection.

All the while he addressed them both in a sonorous, confidential manner:

"My dear late mentor, Doctor Geier, rest his soul, would not only smell the excrement of his patient but—you'll scarce credit this—*taste* it as well, and do you know why? To impress the client, you see. The sick prince (or merchant, or whatever) would think to himself: 'To what extremes he goes for my sake!' And would resolve to pay particularly well upon his recovery. For in those days, the fee was contingent on recovery.

"Well, those were primitive times in some ways. These days we handle such matters in a more civilized manner, and require a set fee which is due us for our labors whether one recovers or not." He paused and peered significantly over his spectacles at Wagner. "That's in the way of being a jest, my solemn young friend."

Wagner colored. But Frau Wirten's laughter spiraled into the air, bright-feathered and approving. She pushed her way forward and poked the unconscious scholar with a bony finger. "Is he going to die?"

A tolerant smile that shaded into sadness and then resignation before reaching full growth as a heavy sigh. "I'll not lie to you," Doctor Schnabel said. "There's no sepsis, and that's hopeful. No pustules, cankers, or emission of fluids. Were Magister Faust a tradesman or a monk or even a courtier, I would say: Leave be! Let sleep and nature run their course. But your tenant, alas, is a learned man, and the ensuant overexercise of his imaginative faculties leaves him prey to mental vapors, horrid imaginings, and nonconforming behavior. In short, madness. I am, in fact, working on a taxonomy of such *bizaria* in the form of an instructive booklet (I shall have to commission woodcuts; terribly annoying expense, but necessary if one wants to reach the masses) listing the follies of the famed and the obscure alike, to be called *The*

Madness of Scholars." His eyes grew dreamy. "What name shall I give Faust's affliction? Magic-mad, perhaps, or alchemy-mad?"

Scandalized, Wagner seized the doctor's arm—Frau Wirten gasped to see it—and kneeling, imploringly cried, "Sir! Surely this judgment is premature. I refuse to believe the Magister is mad, particularly since he remains unconscious; a man may say things in a fever he would never say otherwise. Think of your patient's reputation! I beg you, apply yourself to his cure."

Doctor Schnabel came to himself with a start. He sighed again in a professional manner.

"This will be a close thing, a very close thing indeed."

He rolled up his sleeves, as if preparing to literally wrestle with the forces of life and death over the fate of his patient. Then he opened his handbag and removed two cloth bags with wooden-nozzled hoses, several paper-wrapped packets of pilled and powdered drugs, and a jar of leeches. From the leather pouch upon his belt, he selected the sharpest of many blades. "I'll need a basin, two if you have them. Three would be best."

"In vertebrates the hormone-producing organs are the adrenal cortex, the ovaries, the testes, and the placenta."

Returning to the room with a basin in either hand (Frau Wirten carried the third high over her head), Wagner said, "I must ask, sir, that you tell of any procedures you may intend before they are put into effect. This is no reflection upon your abilities!" he hastened to interject. "But the Magister has very definite views on certain aspects of the healing arts."

Frau Wirten bristled, but said nothing.

"Stereoisomerism is of importance in nature not only for

carbohydrates but for all compounds where stereoisomers are possible."

Doctor Schnabel leaned forward to sniff Faust's eyelids and the crinkles at the edges of his eyes. "This man is twenty-nine years old—am I correct?"

"Thirty or thereabouts, yes."

"Twenty-nine," Schnabel said firmly. "His Saturn is in the third decan of Aquarius." Squinting, he moved his lips in silent calculation. "Not *quite* thirty, then." Then, turning to address Wagner directly, "My approach is orthodoxy itself. The body is a microcosm, subject to the laws of growth and decay. In much the same way that the macrocosmos is a single organism, so too every being is his own small world, self-contained and self-regulating. It is for this reason that each individual's disease is unique."

Frau Wirten smiled and nodded as Schnabel spoke, holding one hand down with another, to keep them from launching upward into applause. Wagner, however, remained uncertain.

"But what specifically," he asked, "do you propose?"

"Your master's brain is overheated, due to an imbalance of humors in the bodily fluids. He must be purged. We will begin simply by toning his body with an enema, an emetic, and an expectorant. Any competent farmwife could do thus. But then he must be bled, in order to cool the fever and relieve him of impurities, and *that* will require all of my curative powers, for with too diffident a purging we cannot stop the course of his deterioration, and yet with too great an excision he may well die. It is all a matter of balance, the restoration of which requires both skill and experience."

"Why are there two enema bags?" Frau Wirten asked eagerly.

"The second, dear lady, is for the clyster, which is the complementary other half of an enema. When we are done, it is possible that the good scholar may not be able to take in food by mouth. In which case we will prepare a soothing mixture of broth and wine and insert it—thus." He gestured. "You see?"

"Ah," she said, appalled and fascinated. "I never realized that nourishment could be taken in by that particular orifice."

"Indeed. Such specialized knowledge is the province of a professional such as myself."

Wagner straightened his shoulders and took a deep breath. A little fearfully he said, "Sir, I have listened to your intended course of action, and I can authorize none of it. Doctor Faust has often spoken on such methods, and once made a careful comparison of the health of people who are bled against that of those who could not afford it. The conclusions he held inescapable, that purging is deleterious to the health."

"And where has it gotten him?" cried Frau Wirten, unable to contain herself. "I myself am bled every month at the full of the moon, and look at me. I have not been sick since that time two years ago when my head swelled to three times its—"

"Yes, yes, yes." Schnabel opened the jar and drew off a small cupful of leech-water. The actions roused the bright denizens of the jar and they struck at its inside surface again and again. He was careful to keep his fingers away from them. "I am aware that Faust was at one time employed as a—surgeon"—his voice dipped ever so slightly, passing lightly over his opinion of the occupation—"in the service of Poland, and that he was no believer in prophylactic bleeding. But we shall change his opinions, I assure you." He opened a twist of paper and deftly tapped in a dram of white powder. "A year from today he will be the most fervent of believers. He will sing on his way to the knife, and skip merrily on his way back from it."

"I must insist." Wagner shook off Frau Wirten's reproving hand from his arm.

Doctor Schnabel withdrew a small rod from his pouch and stirred the mixture briskly. "We'll begin with the emetic. If you would be so kind as to hold the basin, I'll guide his head."

"You must leave, sir," Wagner said sternly. He went to fling open the door and found it had never been closed. So he contented himself with throwing out an arm and gesturing dramatically down the hallway. "You are not welcome here, nor will you be paid for your efforts, nor do you have the authority to do anything to this good man."

Doctor Schnabel looked up, annoyed. "If you cannot refrain from this confounded bleating and squeaking, young fellow, I shall have to put you out of the room."

Wagner gestured again, this time with an accompanying stamp of his foot. "Out!"

It had no effect. Schnabel remained bent over his medications, with Frau Wirten hovering anxiously behind him.

Sheepishly, Wagner returned to the sickroom.

"Friedrich Wilhelm von Wondheim," Faust said, "was bled to death over the course of six weeks."

A puzzled frown crossed the doctor's face. "What is he saying?"

Faust opened his eyes.

"Karl Melber died from loss of blood as well, as did Frau Tucher, Heironymus Nützel, Bettina Hotzschuher, and Charlotte Koestler. Berndt Plitz was felled by an overdose of mercury administered as a supposed cure for *morbus gallicus*. Lafcadio Romano was similarly poisoned, but has recovered

with only moderately severe nerve damage; it is a neighborhood joke to offer him a bowl of soup. Frau Wieruszowski
and her unborn twins would be alive today, had her husband
had the sense to summon a midwife." Faust sat up, eyes blaz-
ing. "All of them are dead within the past year, and who do
they have to thank for it but you?"

Doctor Schnabel started to his feet, scattering instruments.
"How can you know all this? The mercury cure is a proprie-
tary—I perfected the methodology myself. How dare you—"
He broke off, suddenly suspicious. "Have you been following
me about? What unholy power do you have?"

Behind him, tiny Frau Wirten hurriedly made the sign of
the cross.

"Say that the devil whispers in my ear, if you wish. Say
whatever nonsense you like. What failings of mine could com-
pare with your hideous complacency? Accused of murder,
you rush to defend the secrecy of your quack inventions. You
refuse to even look at the truth—which is that you have no
idea what you are doing. The blood serves three purposes: It
carries nutrients to all parts of the body. It takes away the
dead cells. And it contains infinitesimal platelets that fight and
destroy the animalcules that cause disease. In bleeding your
patients, you depress their natural defenses and by thus weak-
ening them, encourage infection and promote the very diseases you are sworn to combat."

He stood, the embodiment of wrath. The two doctors faced
each other across the dim room, the one visibly shrinking from
the violent anger of the other. With a squeak, Frau Wirten
retreated to the shadows.

Schnabel smiled weakly, placatingly. "It is your madness
speaking now. You must lie down and rest."

"Oh, you are a blockhead indeed. You are as ignorant as

snot! Shall I delve deeper into your incompetence? Very well. The woman you petitioned to have burnt as a witch, and who subsequently fled Saxony altogether, was no more than a simple herbalist, whose plain cures were vastly more effective than your own poisons and nostrums. There are five citizens in the graveyard because her absence drove them into your arms."

"Sir, you must control yourself. Your humors—"

"No shame yet? I will hold up a mirror to your ugly mug that will make even you blush: Your own brother died when you cut him for the stone." Faust picked up a fireplace poker and lashed it angrily in the air. "Do you remember how he smiled and squeezed your hand before the operation? How lovingly he kissed it? How, gazing into your eyes, he told you to ignore his screams, for he knew your hands, your brotherly hands, would heal him? Your hands. He would have lived, had you thought to wash those hands first! Oh, I should smash your thick skull in for you—it would be a mercy!"

With a choked cry, Doctor Schnabel flung an arm before his eyes and stumbled from the room. Frau Wirten went bouncing after him, arms flapping like a child's.

Faust laughed and threw down the poker.

"Fill one of those basins with water," he said. "I must wash and dress. Make certain the inkwells are filled. Sharpen a dozen quills."

"Magister!" Wagner cried joyously. "You're—"

"Quickly, quickly now. We must take up the pen. The world awaits my reshaping words." Faust paused and swept a scornful glance toward Schnabel's scattered instruments, his knives and clyster, his potions and leeches. "First, however, clear away this trash."

Wagner leaped to obey. For one bright instant, all was well.

Far into the night and for many nights thereafter, Faust dictated letters to all the great men of Europe and a myriad of the lesser as well, outlining his discoveries and insights. To Johann Tritheim, the Benedictine abbot of Spanheim, who published under the humanist name of Trithemius, he confided the information that colors are but fractions of white light and that white light is compounded of mingled colors. To Konrad Mudt, known to the learned as Mutianus Rufus, he described a force to be found in lightning bolts and easily demonstrated with strips of metal and fresh frogs' legs, and proposed devices by which it might be harnessed. To Johann Weiher, body physician to the Duke of Cleves, sometimes known as Wierus and other times as Piscinarius, he offered a close description of the circulation of the blood, along with observations on the purposes of the minor organs. Pamphlets he dictated as well on painless surgery, the origins of disease, the outlines of a calculus for problems dealing with rates of change, and more besides, enough to sate the appetites of an army of booksellers.

All these documents he signed NEOPROMETHEUS, explaining to Wagner that his own name was but little known and in the cause of spreading enlightenment there was no point in modesty. "Not," he said, "when my revelations are so great as to dwarf those of all the scholars and savants of Antiquity and modern times combined. Either I am the New Prometheus or I am completely deluded. There can be no middle ground."

Wagner wondered greatly, but wrote as he was directed.

While he scribbled, Faust drew: diagrams of the molecular structure of crystals, the orbital mechanics of planets, detailed maps of an Antarctic continent, a mathematical proof for the convergence of infinite series, plans for what he called "leaf-springs" to make carriages ride more smoothly, calculating machines, difference engines, steam-driven mining pumps. These were included with letters explaining their import.

"These are strange observations," Wagner commented after a letter to Düsseldorf on the economics of supply and demand. The ideas passing beneath his pen were dizzying; he needed a month or three for each, to judge its validity and absorb its implications. Instead, he had but the minutes of their dictation before more ideas were piled upon him, each as challenging as the earlier. Strange and aching things they were to wrap his thoughts about; it would be easier and less painful by far to dismiss them all without thinking. From any other source he would have. "When did you find the time to gather such detailed information on the quantities of grain and price of bread in so many cities over such a period?"

"Inspiration, Wagner! Inspiration! The facts follow logically upon the insight."

"But—"

"A fresh sheet of paper! Has the cramping in your hand subsided yet? There is much to do. We owe it to posterity not to rest."

The weeks passed like a fever dream: Wagner wrote and wondered. Faust drew up plans for impossible machines. He designed buildings like no man had ever seen or wished to. He talked of prodigies to be found in a drop of water, and drew up plans for an instrument of tubes and lenses that would display them to others. Briefly melancholic, he spoke of soldiers dying of sepsis after successful amputations. But his sadness did not last. "In the morning," he said, "you must go to the lens-grinder. I require several pieces from his stock and many more that must be ground to my exact specifications. I will provide you with a list." He started to scribble, then looked up wildly. "And linen! I must have linen!"

"Linen?"

"To fly with. We shall build me wings such as have never been seen before—wings as round and spherical as the world."

Faust laughed.

Wagner's days were thronged with errands. He was sent running from carpenter to brass-worker, from tinsmith to apothecary, fetching herbs from the fields outside Wittenberg and commissioning lengths of copper wire that were thrice rejected as being too thick. For two leather-tubed optical devices in particular, Faust was especially anxious; he promised double payment for their rapid completion. And yet Wagner, who had gone through every chest and bag in the scholar's rooms before calling upon Doctor Schnabel, knew exactly how little money his master had, and worried for his finances.

Faust's excitement reached climax on that day when the instrument-maker's apprentice finally appeared at the door with two tight-wrapped packages. Chortling, Faust unwrapped the smaller and placed the commissioned device on the table.

The leathered tube was angled upon a stand, with knobs to adjust the distance between lenses, clips to hold thin rectangles of clear glass, and a mirror to reflect sunlight up through the glass and into the tube. Faust set it up anxiously, drew a drop of water from a glass of stagnant pond-water Wagner had fetched from beyond the city walls the day before, and, placing the drop on the glass rectangle, put his eye to the tube and adjusted it. For a long instant he was still.

Then he *crowed*.

"It's true!" Explosively, he seized Wagner by the shirt and swung him before the device. "Look!" Faust commanded, forcing his head down with one strong hand. "Tell me what you see."

"I—my reflection, Magister. The reflection of my eye."

"Idiot! Keep both eyes open. Look through the tube. Turn this knob slowly until a clear image comes in view."

Hesitantly, Wagner obeyed. The lens was a bright formless circle at first. Then vague shapes appeared, condensed, and abruptly sharpened. With a cry, he drew back from the device. "It's filled with monsters!"

Faust chuckled. "Not monsters, my dear Wagner. Not monsters—the future."

"I . . . I don't understand."

"No, of course you don't." Faust unwrapped the larger packet and quickly assembled the second device. "You have eyes and yet you cannot see." He ran loving hands up and down its delicately tooled barrel. "Ah, but *here* is the invention that will make my name echo down the ages! No learned fool or scholarly tortoise, however encrusted he might be with degrees and years of tenure, barnacles and moss, can fail to be convinced by what it will show."

"What is it?" Wagner asked unhappily.

"Who cares for names? Call them what you will. Assemble words from the classical languages. Name the one 'microscope' and the other 'telescope.' From the Greek for 'small-seeing' and 'far-seeing.' I have no interest in the matter. It will be clear tonight. I can make my first observations. And to-morrow—the baths. Oh, how the Leucopolitans will praise me! How delighted they will be."

Abruptly, he set his telescope aside and went to the window. Placing both hands on the sill, he leaned out straight-armed and stared up at the moon. Pale and full, it hung in the dark blue sky of late afternoon. For a long moment he simply stood unmoving. Then quietly he said, "Do you think we shall live to see men walk upon the moon? Is it possible so much can be accomplished in a single lifetime?"

"Walk upon the moon?" It was a comic notion, the sort of flying-horse-and-ten-leagues-boots lie one used to set a small child to laughing and clapping. But Wagner was no child, and Faust was a man nine years into his third decade, far too old and, one would have thought, dignified for such frauds and whimsies. Wagner was baffled. Was Faust speaking meta-phorically? Could this be some manner of allegory?

His master returned to the instrument. After several more minutes peering through it over the rooftops and at the moon, he straightened, sighed, and said, "I need to see the planets! Will night never come?"

"Soon, Magister. The sun is going down."

Turning his back on the window and the city, sky, and moon it framed, Faust said irritably, "The Earth is tilting *up!*"

It was in that instant that all the bits and pieces of the last few weeks came together in such a way that Wagner could no longer deny to himself what all of Wittenberg was soon to learn: that the famed and learned scholar Johannes Wilhelm Faust was mad.

4

FLIGHT

Like storks to the Low Countries or plague rats to the seaports, the students had returned to Wittenberg. The young vaga-bonds were everywhere, exasperating and enriching the townsfolk, boasting and swaggering and fighting mock duels, energetic, boundlessly curious, eagerly poking their noses into everything, like so many thousand human puppies.

They scattered before Faust as he swooped down the castle road with a stride so long he almost flew. Two black-and-white Dominican monks coming out of the Schlosskirche scowled upon seeing him. (Smile and nod) Mephistopheles suggested. (That will infuriate them.) And so lighthearted did he feel that Faust complied, throwing in a merry wink for good measure. He was rewarded by the sharp hiss of indrawn breath as he hurried by.

Wagner trotted after Faust, rendered tortoiselike by the

enormous basket he carried upon his back, on its way to the harness-maker's to be fitted with leather straps for the flying-device's suspension ropes. "As soon as that's done," Faust called over his shoulder, "you are to bring my telescope to the bathhouse."

"Yes, Magister," Wagner muttered sullenly.

(Tell him not to dawdle with the harness-maker's daughter) Mephistopheles said. (The one with the tits as big as Westphalian hams. She's in heat, and if she catches his eye you won't see him again until morning.)

"And no talking to any girls!" Faust said. "I know your ways."

"Magister!"

"I must demonstrate my invention to the Leucopolitans. This is important! No—imperative! If you do not have it there and set up within the hour, I promise you I will thrash you to within three breaths of your life."

The *Sodalitas Leucopolitan* (the "white city," as its resident poet, Ricardus Sbrulius, was unfailingly careful to point out, came from the color of the Elbe's sands and not from a bad etymological back-construction of "Witten" as meaning "white," which it most decidedly did *not*) was the least Germanic of learned societies in all Germania. No minutes were kept, dues collected, or meeting announcements sent out. It convened in taverns or in the rooms of its various members as the whim to discuss matters philosophical hit them. But once a month they met more formally to bathe, talk, and debate, at which time Sbrulius inevitably referred to them as the Knights of the Bath.

(Oh, what a wonder for marveling eyes to see!) Mephistopheles exclaimed. (All the finest minds and wits in Saxony with their butts and balls flapping in the breeze.)

"Be silent," Faust directed him. "This is no time for your cynical remarks. Those you mock are philosophers, poets, and lovers of the truth. There are no more honorable men anywhere, nor any whose good opinion I value more."

(Indeed? Would you care for me to show you how today's meeting will go?)

"No! I forbid it. You have contracted to tell me of things *as they are*. Let the future tend to itself. Once shown, what freedom would I have to act contrary to your visions? I shall discourse with the society as a learned man among equals. More I do not need."

(Put a thief among a hundred honest men, and within the hour they'll have relieved him of his purse and trousers. Set a whore among schoolgirls and see how long her virtue lasts! Sell a Moorish slave to the College of Cardinals and he'll be worshipping demons by nightfall. You go to put your head in a den of intellectuals and thinkers. I fear that they will drive you mad.)

"Pish."

Here Faust's way parted from Wagner's. The younger man, grown accustomed to his master's new habit of mumbling to himself, cast a fretful glance back at him, but made no comment.

Wagner placed his master's leather-bound calculations on a small table in the grassy yard at the rear of the bathhouse, and then erected the telescope alongside it. The summer baths were separated from the yard by a waist-high fence and sheltered from rain and sun by a high wooden roof. This pleasant arrangement allowed gentle breezes to flow freely over the bathers. Beer was available, and soap, and attendants rapid to scratch a back or fetch a thick, clean towel. Gentlemen were encouraged to bring musical instruments for their amusement. Out of a common regard for decency, women were allowed nowhere near. A man could pull himself out of the shallow common bath and amble over to the fence to pee on its pilings without interrupting the erudite disputation.

It was a paradise for scholars.

A socketed brass band was looped about the barrel of the telescope, so that it could be set up on a wooden tripod of the sort surveyors or architects used. Wagner struggled with the balky device, equally anxious to keep it away from the piss-marshy regions of the lawn and at the same time remain close enough to eavesdrop upon the learned discussion.

Sbrulius sang:

> Come to the bathhouse, rich and poor,
> The water is soothing, to be sure,
> There's fragrant soap to wash your skin,
> A sweat box that we'll put you in;
> And when you've had a healthful sweat,
> We'll cut your hair, your blood we'll let,
> After which, a good brisk rub,
> And a pleasant soak in a nice hot tub.

The Leucopolitans applauded and he put aside his lute with an ironic bow.

Beckmann, lounging against a spigot post, turned to Faust. Beside him, a dribble of water spattered from a brass mackerel's ugly mouth. "There's talk the Dominicans are planning to bribe a tame priest to preach a sermon against you. What in Heaven's name have you done to rile them so?"

Faust made a dismissive gesture. "I told Brother Josaphat that the original of his name was no Christian saint at all but a heathen god known as Bodhisat, revered in India for sitting many years beneath a tree. In the eighth century, John of Damascus popularized his tale with a fanciful translation from a corrupt Arabic text."

If Beckmann had a single fault, it was his distaste for conflict in any form. A deep and abiding sadness came into his eyes that only emphasized his long-faced resemblance to an old and peaceable hound. "Now why on Earth would you tell him a thing like that?"

"Because it's true."

Sbrulius laughed. "That, dear Faust, is the single worst argument you could have raised. Many things are true. Few are proper. Fewer still are desirable." He was not the most powerful of intellects at the university—his gifts being poetic rather than analytic—and thus in conversation relied heavily on paradox, metonymy, litotes, hysteron proteron, and other such light rhetorical devices. He had no enemies but those earned by his compulsively indiscriminate womanizing.

"I had thought," Mette said darkly, "it was for your heterodox and potentially heretical new cosmology." He was a lean man, a theologian, and avidly ambitious for a more honored place within the society and in the university as well. Fat and lazy old Balthasar Phaccus shrugged and stretched out a hand for his stein.

"That too, perhaps. The fact—I know you are tired of hearing this, but a fact it is—that the Earth and other planets all revolve around the sun must necessarily be controversial. I admit it. So radical a revision of common prejudice is bound to make enemies.

"Still—I have heard of Brother Josaphat's displeasure from sources of my own. His face didn't break out in pimples because he thought the sun had been insulted. It was the slight upon his name that raised his ire."

(Well put) Mephistopheles said. (Tell them about his masturbatory practices.)

"Good friends!" Beckmann cried, horrified. "Let us discourse as scholars, without *ad hominum* attacks. Faust—there is no need to slander Brother Josaphat, however much he may invite such treatment. And Mette—it is scandalous of you to call Faust's theory heretical. Nicholas of Cusa proposed much the same thing when he wrote that to a man standing upon the sun the Earth would seem to revolve about him. This is no more than a restatement of his idea."

"No!" Faust cried. "Save me from such defenders as you, good Beckmann! You will defend my thesis to oblivion. I assure you that what I intend is nothing less than a total revision of our understanding of the universe. Look upon my figures. Wagner! Bring the book! You will see the beauty, the elegance, the compelling logic of my system. Look! Look! See for yourselves."

To Faust's dismay, it was of all people Phaccus who grunted and heaved himself up from the bath. Like a walrus, he waddled to the fence, slapping his hands against his buttocks to rid them of excess water and then holding them out to an attendant to dry. With Wagner respectfully serving as a book-stand, he casually flipped through the manuscript, perusing one page in five. Then, meditatively scratching the underside of his ample belly, he returned to his place at the lip of the bath.

Finally, he spoke. "It's a very pretty conceit, but what's the point? To justify a rank of numbers? *De minimus*, my dear. If you are to turn the universe upside down, you must have some compelling reason to do so."

"At any rate," Mette said, "it all falls apart at a touch. If the Earth revolves about the sun, then what does the moon revolve about?"

"Why, the Earth, of course!"

The Leucopolitans all laughed.

"You see? You retreat from your heliocentrism at a word," Mette said.

(A touch!) Mephistopheles cried. (Sound the trumpets so the citizenry may be assembled to witness what brilliance among us dwells!)

"All bodies have a mutual attraction for one another," Faust said testily, "in direct proportion to the product of their combined masses and inversely with the square of distance between them. The moon, being proportionately closer to the Earth, is caught in its gravitation field and the two together revolve about a common point within the Earth, and thus orbit the sun as a dual planetary system. If you would examine the mathematics, you would see this for yourselves."

"This is complication piled upon complication!"

"Not in the least. If you but imagine the structure of space as being—"

"Faust," Beckmann said firmly. "Your colleagues have, gently and with good humor, demonstrated your error. Do not cling to folly."

"It is not folly, which can be proven in three words: Jupiter has moons! I have seen them through my lenses."

"Oh, this is too much."

"Not the lenses again!"

"Come out tonight, all of you, and I will show you."

"Out of doors on a moonless night?" Mette sneered. "Only fools, footpads, and astrologers stray where there is no light. I have no desire whatsoever to have my head bashed in by some nameless thug, thank you. Let somebody else martyr himself upon the altar of your faulty scholarship."

Exasperated, Faust surveyed his naked compeers, one by one. Except for Mette, who glared at him like a basilisk, not one would meet his eye. Even Beckmann looked away. "Then—Wagner! Bring my lenses here. I shall demonstrate the efficacy of this new tool." He went to the fence and after some clumsiness had his telescope set up and adjusted. "Look there, through the gap between buildings a small fraction of the city walls is visible, and beyond it a stand of trees. If you look through my lenses, it will seem that the trees leap toward you. You will be able to count the leaves. If there is a bird on one of the branches, you will be astonished to see its beak move in song and yet be so distant you cannot hear the song itself. Now look down below, where the stream that meanders by the bottom of our lawn is crossed by a stone bridge . . . Do you see how two housewives have paused on their way to market to gossip? Through my tube you can see a wonder: their tongues wagging in silence. Come, Mette, my doubting Thomas, you shall be the first."

Mette looked away, saying nothing.

"No? Then—Sbrulius, Phaccus? Come, gentlemen, who will be first?"

Sbrulius sauntered casually to the tube and bent to peer through it. Under Faust's direction, he aimed the tube at the distant bridge and adjusted the focus. For a moment he was silent. He raised his head from the tube to look at the bridge, and then returned his eye to it again. "Remarkable," he murmured. "Does it see through walls as well? Which way is the women's bathhouse from here?"

(Marvelous! The invention is but a day old and already

Magister Sbrulius contrives to find a way to make it serve his lust!)

"Beckmann!" Faust cried. "Surely *you* will not refuse the entreaty of a friend and fellow scholar. Please."

When Beckmann looked up from the telescope, a thoughtful expression came into his eyes. "An . . . interesting tool. But is it necessary? As Mette reminded me just yesterday, Aristotle described this exact same phenomenon long ago."

"He did not!"

"Indeed he did," Mette smugly interjected, "in his *Physics*. He described how stars can be seen in the daytime from the bottom of a dry well. The well itself obviously serves as does this tube, denying excess light entry into the passage. The place of the lenses would be taken by coagulating layers of air. So your device is nothing truly new."

"You will note, too," Sbrulius threw in, "that Aristotle's observations were clearly all made by the unassisted eye. From which we may assume he found this device of no merit in the advancement of science. And what is good enough for Aristotle is surely sufficient for us."

"Mette!" Faust cried. "You are an honest man. Your arguments, though wrong, are based upon reason. Let you, my harshest critic, become my first convert. Here is the telescope. Come, look, understand!"

Mette shook his head bullishly.

"You will not even look?" Faust cried, astonished. He gestured toward the device. "Either I am right or I am wrong. How can you refuse to bend the inch or two it would take to put your eye before my telescope and *see*?"

"I have no need to expose myself to your flummery," Mette said with dignity. "I believe in order that I may know. I do not know in order to believe."

"I marvel at your spite. Of what possible benefit can this willful ignorance be to you?"

"Spite?" Mette rose to his feet, fists clenched, face pale. "Ignorance? You have decided to set yourself above your fellows; we are to provide the altitude by letting you clamber up the mountain of our praise; which praise is to be heaped before you in exchange for the wildest and most fanciful of whimsical nonsense; and you dare speak to us of ignorance and spite?" He shrugged off Beckmann's restraining hand, but nevertheless subsided again into the bath. "Your immodesty ill becomes you."

"This is astonishing!" In his anger, blood rushed to Faust's head. His face felt stuffy and hot. "You debate my points before I am finished making them. Your minds are set against me even before I can voice my reasoning. Your words have the stale sound of well-rehearsed arguments. It is almost as if—" He paused. "It is almost as if you had all formed a cabal to conspire against me."

(Oho! The light dawns.)

Uncomfortably, Beckmann said, "We had a discussion together the other day, yes. But you must not think we were *plotting* against you! It merely seemed wisest to form a consensus of opinion before hearing you expound upon your new . . . notions."

For a long moment Faust could not speak. Then, when he could, the words came pouring out of him in a torrent, unstoppable, driven by anger and betrayal:

"I am appalled. I came here before what I thought were the noblest minds in Christendom, to dispute and prove new insights into the nature of the universe. For you I reserved the honor of being the first to learn of these wonders in detail.

But the truth means nothing to you! You contaminate everything about you with putrefaction and ignorance. You beslobber and besmirch all that is beautiful and good and then try to convince the world that it is better off for your tasteful leavening of excrement. You quibble and quack and chop logic while revelation is yours to be had for the asking. This is unbearable! You are—"

(Yes!)

"You are driving me—"

(Come, say it!)

"—mad!"

(Thank you, Faust. My thesis is proved. Let us depart.)

That evening, not long after sunset, Faust went shouting through the marketplace. With Wagner reluctantly trailing behind clutching the telescope, he summoned the citizens to rise from their sleep and come out to behold the stars. "See the rings of Saturn!" he yelled. "Planets new to mortal ken and moons in profusion! Galaxies and nebulae! Wonders beyond cataloguing!"

When nobody emerged from their houses, he bellowed and roared and slammed on doors with his fists. Reaction varied by the temperament of those within. Some laughed; some scolded; some dragged furniture against the doors and shouted loudly for the watch.

Tears of rage and disappointment filled his eyes. "I offer you *enlightenment!*" he screamed. "I offer you truth!"

Nobody came out.

Finally, dejected, Faust returned to his rooms. He sent the humiliated and dispirited Wagner to bed. Then he sat up late into the night with Mephistopheles and a bottle of wine. The devil manifested himself as a small black-furred monkey with malevolent red eyes.

"I have written," Faust said dejectedly, "literally hundreds of letters, and received not one reply."

Mephistopheles hopped up on the writing desk and began to search himself for lice. Offhandedly he said, "The posts are unreliable and even at the best of times a letter can take weeks to move a few score miles. Mud slides, robbers, the rumor of dragons in a mountain pass—any of these things can isolate a city from the outside world for months."

"Still, my messages go out by every post, and some of them do not have far to travel. Yet from Erfurt, from Heidelberg, from Kraków, there come no replies." His goblet was low; he tipped the bottle over it and poured. "Why do you appear in such a grotesque form?"

"I do this in honor of your race. If you compared the human genome with that of chimpanzees, you would find that ninety-eight percent of the DNA was identical. You are only two percent distinguished from an ape. Two percent!" Mephistopheles placed his fingers to his anus and then to his nose, repeating the action several times before he was satisfied. "Yet, strange to relate, I swear that from my perspective the differences seem even less."

Faust shook his head dismissively, wrapped both hands about his goblet. "I publish pamphlets that nobody buys. I bring scholars into my study to look through my microscope and they go away shaking their heads in bafflement."

"Patience. Rome was not corrupted in a day." The monkey began playing in a bored way with his genitalia. "I fail to see, however, why you should wait upon the post when you can have the same information by merely asking."

"You can do this?"

Mephistopheles yawned, baring tiny razor-sharp teeth.

"Tell me, then. How were my letters received?"

"Trithemius has written to the mathematician-astrologer Johann Windling, calling you a fool, a mountebank, and a vain babbler who ought to be whipped. Mutianus Rufus considers you a charlatan. And our beloved Piscinarius is telling all who will listen that you are a drunken vagabond. The carriage-maker in Nuremberg, however, is enjoying great success with your design for the leaf-spring. The Emperor himself has heard of your innovation and ordered all his carriages replaced."

Faust made a disgusted noise.

" 'Tis but proof that it's easier to make the ass smart than the head." Mephistopheles dipped a long-nailed finger into the ink pot and meditatively stirred. "You'd do better to take my advice and stop wasting your time on humanists, thinkers, and philosophers—they are misers who dearly love their hard-earned and long-hoarded knowledge. Your revelations would bankrupt them—can you wonder they will not listen? Let me give you instead a list of merchants and mechanics, tool-makers, and other tradesmen, with practical suggestions for the improvement of their businesses."

"I have diamonds to pour at the feet of the wise and you wish me to muck out the stables of fools."

"Exactly so."

Dejectedly, Faust put his chin in his hand. "What wonder can I present these lard-headed idiots that will convince them? What marvel is there that they cannot refuse to see?"

Mephistopheles shrugged.

"My balloon . . . how goes it?"

"The linen merchants are beginning to grumble that you intend never to pay them for their cloth. The varnish-dealer too has expressed his doubts. In consequence, your seamstresses have made your commission a lesser priority and set it aside whenever cash work comes to them."

"Money again! When the balloon ascends, there will be money in plenty. It will fall from the hands of the great and powerful like rain. I shall be showered with riches and honors."

Mephistopheles made a disbelieving face. "Patronage is a notoriously unreliable source of funds."

"What would you have me do?"

"A simple word in the ear of a councilman you know well: 'Timonias,' say you. 'Saint Martin's day. For the sake of a certain lady.' Say also that you are in serious need of silver. He will help you to the uttermost of his ability."

"Oh, vile! You urge extortion on me."

"How swiftly you see to the heart of things!"

"I will not heed such advice."

"Pity." Mephistopheles drew out his finger and with obvious pleasure lapped up the ink with a long black tongue. "Then honesty requires that your balloon rely on the more traditional method of ordering goods and not paying for them."

"They will be paid for. I swear it." The scholar sighed again and drained his cup. "But, oh, sweet misery. How long can this go on?"

"Through the winter, at a minimum. I promise you, Faust, that if you hold true to your course you will achieve all you desire. But you will have to pay the freight in advance. You must endure cold and hunger and the taunts of fools."

"Must it be?" Faust groaned.

"It must. To triumph, you must first suffer as much as ever a scholar did."

It was as painful a winter as the devil predicted. Faust lived frugally, feeding upon barley and oats, drinking water rather than beer, going for months on end without so much as a scrap of meat. He sold the better of his two gowns and patched the lesser. He heated his rooms with driftwood and deadfall.

It hardly mattered that few attended Faust's regular lectures, for he was the *mathematicum superiorum*, the professor of astronomy for the university, his chair endowed by the Elector himself. It provoked criticism, but his position was secure. So he told himself. Still, it stung.

The worst of Faust's many humiliations was how the students flocked to his afternoon lectures, which he offered free for all who cared to attend. They came to laugh at his outlandish pronouncements, to jeer at what they should be receiving with prostrate gratitude. He glowered at them and shifted his shoulders like a great bear (there were white bears in the Arctic regions, and primitive but fearless peoples who hunted them with bone-tipped spears; he had seen them) and stubbornly continued his lecture, for he wished to reach that one student in a hundred, a thousand, whose eyes and ears and mind were not closed but open. Who might actually learn from him.

He lectured himself hoarse. He spoke to all who would listen. Not many would listen.

As winter turned to spring, the number of students at Faust's lectures dwindled. The mockers and braying asses fell away as their studies became more demanding and the sport grew old. Finally there was only a handful of the most promising young men. And Wagner, of course. Outwardly they were an unlikely lot, and in ways inwardly as well. For the sake of the two who had not the Latin—and were consequently flunking their other courses—he lectured in good honest German. This only increased the public scorn.

During the lectures, Wagner took notes his master intended to rework as textbooks. Because there was not the money to have them bound, Wagner tied them up with bits of string begged from an indulgent butcher.

Faust's debts grew.

So much of a scholar's income came from examination fees that it was common to spend most of each year in debt. The merchant who did not extend credit would have quickly gone out of business. The trick lay in knowing the seasonal rhythms of poverty and coin-lack for all professions, so that credit could be offered in times preceding affluence and denied where that affluence would never come. This seasonal indebtedness masked Faust's greater liability. No one creditor had advanced him too much money. Yet many had advanced him all they dared.

His scant wealth he trickled out a coin at a time, in order to keep work on his balloon from ceasing altogether.

Finally, on a warm spring day not long before the examinations were to begin, news came that the great balloon was ready.

Wagner was given a brush, a bucket of paste, and a handful of quickly printed handbills and sent about town to plaster the walls with notices:

Come Witness

THE ASCENT OF *DAEDALUS*!

! !

Humanity Freed from the Tyranny of Earth

The Dream of the Ancients Become Cold Hard Fact

THE FLIGHT OF EAGLES ACHIEVED BY MORTAL MAN

o o o o o o o o o o o o o o o o

This Miracle to be Demonstrated on

The Feast of the Ascension

—Market-Square—

| |

Noon

"What new impiety is this?" Brother Josaphat demanded. He had stopped Faust on the street and thrust a poster into his face, too close to be read but not so close he could not see the size and force of the monk's enormous fist. Faust smiled.

"You must wait and see."

"Only birds, angels, and saints can fly. And you are none of the three."

"Neither angel nor saint, I readily agree. But a bird is no difficult thing to be, I think. You yourself are as odd a bird as I've ever seen."

With a roar of incoherent rage, Brother Josaphat crumpled the handbill and threw it in Faust's face. Then he turned and stormed away.

The balloon slowly filled, swelling and rising up above the market-square like some hallucinatory great skull. Faust oversaw the hose and leather funnel arrangement that fed it hot air, while Wagner kept the fire fueled. By slow degrees the balloon lifted from the ground, tugging at the ropes that held it captive. Its yearning to lift grew stronger.

The crowd was enormous. It had to be held back by a line of burly students, all of them volunteers eager to have a place in this diverting enterprise, whatever their opinions of Faust's sanity, and all of them certified reliable for the task by Mephistopheles himself.

The balloon continued to grow. The linen was sewn in three concentric circles, black at the top, then blue, and after that an unbleached white, and heavily varnished with a solution of elastic gum, so it would hold the hot air. "Silk would have been better," Faust murmured, staring up at it, "and hydrogen better still."

"Hydrogen?" one of the students asked.

"It's abundant in water. Helium would be best of all."

Faust stood by the wicker basket.

Two ruffianly students—Fritz and Karl, both favorites of his—held their hatchets ready to cut the anchor ropes. Nearby sulked a third, Hans Metternich, who had been told by Faust that if he were to attempt this simple feat he would slice open his own leg and—worse—unbalance the basket, spilling its passenger upon the ground. "Wait for my word." Faust jovially wagged a finger at them. "Don't let my air-carriage leave without me."

The balloon was filled at last, and the hose thrown aside. Now, horrified, members of the crowd were seeing what had evaded them before, that the circles of cloth, inflated, formed the perfect semblance of a great eyeball, staring upward. Faust, climbing into the basket, made the monstrous eye bob slightly, down and then up again.

Somebody in the crowd seized a stone and made to throw it at the balloon. Hans, vastly more alert than he ever appeared to be in class, wrestled the would-be assailant to the ground. All in an instant the mood of the crowd shifted. Brother Josaphat pushed through it, toward where Hans and his adversary wrestled on the ground. Fights broke out here and there. Wagner had been adjusting the balloon's ballast bags; now he turned to reinforce the line of students.

But Faust seized Wagner by the rear of his belt and hauled him back. "No, no, my young friend," he said jovially. "You have served me well and faithfully—you must have your reward." He was in great humor; everything seemed amusing to him, as if he were on the inside of an enormous joke that the entire rest of the world lacked the perspective to see.

When he had hauled the horrified Wagner in with him, Faust waved a hand to his young hatcheteers. "Now!" he cried. Blades flashed, and with a double jerk the anchor ropes parted.

The balloon lifted.

It ascended slowly, perpendicularly, with no sensation of movement at all. To Faust it was as if the world had, with infinite gentleness, drawn back a pace from him. What an instant ago had threatened to become a mob was now silent with reverent astonishment. Hans and his opponent rolled apart, stood, gawked upward.

Falling to his knees, Brother Josaphat lifted his hands to the heavens and began loudly to pray against this violent rupture of the natural order. "Lord, send down your lightnings!" he cried. "Let avenging angels strike this blasphemy from the sky!" Among the still faces, one bobbed wildly up and down, the artist Cranach, sketching madly, head going from sky to paper and back as his hands flew across the paper. A stone flew, but fell short. The thrower was dragged to the ground by Fritz, Karl, and Hans. Fists rose and fell.

Faust impulsively seized a ballast bag and emptied the sand over the upturned faces. He laughed as they squinted and scowled, waving hands like so many picnickers warding off wasps. "Stay upon your knees, Brother Josaphat!" he cried. "I will stay in my balloon. We'll see which of us reaches Heaven first!"

A perfect stillness surrounded him, and he was filled with a fantastic elation. Looking down upon the dwindling people, he felt a mingled scorn and love for them all. The dear little people—they were like ants. He could throw down his shoe and crush them all! If he were to spit upon them, they would drown in his saliva.

Wagner stood frozen at his side, clutching the edge of the basket. His eyes were wide as saucers. His face was pale with wonder.

The balloon rose above the church steeple. The town and its streets were laid out below, clearer than any map. Then the wind caught them (but they felt no wind) and they were pushed over the castle. In the courtyard soldiers gaped up at them. It came to Faust that it would be the easiest thing in the world to drop rocks and even gunpowder bombs upon them, that fortresses and city walls meant nothing in the bold new world that was a-borning.

"Well, Wagner," Faust said jubilantly, "do you still think me mad?"

Wagner turned, all in one motion, and threw his arms about the scholar, burying his head in Faust's side. "Master!" he cried. "Forgive me for doubting you!"

Not half an hour later, coming down in the fields five miles from town, the basket would tip over and send Wagner tumbling. The leg he would break was to be a small price to pay for having flown, but it would complicate the return to the city greatly. For now, though, all was perfect.

"We have been through a long, dark winter," Faust said. "But now it is spring, and all Nature favors us and our work. All of Europe will lie at my feet. I see nothing but fame and riches before me."

The next day Faust's creditors gathered at the town hall and collectively swore out a complaint against him.

FALSE DAWN

In the hour before dawn, a chill and indirect luminance infused the cloudless sky over Wittenberg. A swallow, hunting mayflies, mosquitoes, and other riparian delights, swooped out of the light and into the shadowy town. Five great looping dives carried it over the dark and empty streets, past the warehouses and the church tower, over the university and the castle and into the light again. For an instant it saw two men in a cart down below it, and then it was out among the western fields and all the town, with its wealth and people and problems, dissolved to nonexistence in the all-abiding and universal solvent of the eternal now.

In a garret room under the city wall, a student who had spent all the night and most of two candles struggling to translate ten pages of Cicero's immortal rhetoric heard the *clop-clop* of hooves and creaking of wooden wheels. His head jerked up and he stared numbly at the plastered wall, thoughts a jumble of Roman glory and memories of a long-ago journey to Paris. "Somebody's out early," he said aloud.

The cobblestones were cold and damp. A rat fled from the cart-horse's hooves. It scuttled over a landscape of puddles and wagon-ruts, hoofprints, and scraps of brick, to a sheltered spot where a broken wheelbarrow and a rotting plank conspired to hide an opening to its lair. Pausing at the mouth of the hole, it looked back at the men, eyes glittering like marcasite beads. In the distance a dog barked. With a disdainful flip of its tail, the rat turned and was gone.

White-bearded old Methuselah, who lived rather like a rat himself, in an oaken barrel half-buried in the work yard of a kindhearted carpenter whose name he did not know, was next to see the wagon pass. Snug in his abode, crouching naked and on all fours, he turned his head as it went by, dragging his beard against the ground. His voice rose up in a howl: "Oh Lakedaimonians, breakers of splendid horses, violators of Hesychia!" he cried. "Your limbs are shackled to shameless hope; your brows wreathed in victory beside Alpheos' water. Ixion, fixed on his winged wheel, spun in a circle, cries aloud this message to mortals: Wide is the strength of Wealth; an end in all bitterness awaits the sweetness that was wrong— best of all things is water." He had been a scholar long years ago, before losing his wits through the memorization of ancient texts, and his mad recitations were still a popular diversion at student feasts.

Hearing him, the young man grinned and dug into his purse for a scrap of bread to throw. His bandaged and splinted leg ached and throbbed with every jolt, and he shivered with the cold. But he felt oddly sure of himself, serenely quiet, willing to accept whatever might come. Each thing he saw, he looked at for the last time, and the twinge of fear this brought only made them all the more precious to him. "It's going to be a beautiful day."

His dark-bearded companion grunted. He was, despite the season, winter-gaunt, and his heart was as disturbed as the younger man's was tranquil.

Ahead of the cart, pacing it, unseen and unfelt by any but the older man, a dancing sprite of malice skipped nimbly over the town. His feet were two dark flames touching here the mossy lip of a well, there a thatched roof, now a door stoop, and again a window frame. His laughter sounded only for one set of ears.

The wagon came to a stop in the plaza between the castle and its church. The western gate was still locked. To the east of town, outside the Rostock gate, where they could wait in sunshine instead of shadow, several garrulous old Slavic farmers would be sitting in their wagons, sharp-eyed to pick up the least scrap of gossip and loose-tongued to set it down again. Here, they had only the guard to get by, and the driver of the cart had been assured the guard this morning would be hungover and incurious.

The bearded man was in the darkest of moods. It was a hard thing to be skipping out on his debts. But if it were to be done, it were best done now: The examinations began in less than a week, and who would expect a teacher to disappear before collecting all those fat fees? By the time anyone was convinced he had fled, he would be long gone. And he would have good advice on which roads to take. He did not fear pursuit. Only the bitterness of shame.

The morning breeze carried the sulfury tang of swamp air over the walls, and the putrefying essence of stagnant moat-water as well. These smells mingled and merged in an alchemical marriage with the ordinary street stench of humans, dogs, and scavenger pigs to form a bouquet as rich and pervasive as an outhouse fart.

Deaf and distracted old Brother Jerome hurried across the square. The younger of the men hailed him cheerily, but he paid no mind. Without a glance at either, he scurried up the Schlosskirche steps, took a key from his cassock, and unlocked the church doors. The week's notices fluttered briefly. Then the doors slammed behind him.

The horse snorted.

The younger man slapped his jacket with both arms. "You'll be happier once we're on the road," he said.

"Nothing will make me happier. Nothing but—" The elder stopped abruptly, and cocked his head as if listening to a suggestion. "Yes," he said with sudden energy. "Yes, that's exactly what I'll do."

Brusquely, he seized a rope and began to undo its knot. Throwing a tarpaulin aside, he dug into the bags and trunks like a terrier, emerging after a few minutes with a blunt German hammer, several nails, and a parchment sheet. "Wait here," he said.

He walked up the castle-church steps with the sheet of paper in his hand, disappearing into shadow, then reappearing again. Posters covered the doors—examination notices, satirical broadsides, theses presented for debate—tacked one on top of another in places an inch thick. He tore them down in great handfuls and flung them away. Then, with fifteen solid hammer blows, he nailed up the chart. The boom of those blows echoed over the city, louder than a drum.

At the sound, pigeons scattered and the younger man glanced nervously over his shoulder. In his garret, the student looked up stupidly, shook his head, sighed, and set aside Cicero for a bowl of wash-water. Brother Jerome frowned faintly, half-turned, and then decided it had been his imagination. Nobody else heard.

The gaunt dark-bearded man threw the hammer into the back of the wagon and climbed up in the front.

"There!" he said. "That will rattle their provincial little world. That will shake them more thoroughly than they have shaken me. I have lit the fuse to a bomb, Wagner. All the gunpowder in the world crammed within that church would not set off an explosion half so grand as mine." He waited for the questions he knew were coming.

But Wagner did not need to ask or even know what the poster said or meant. There was no least trace of fear or mistrust in his mind any more; the flight of the *Daedalus* had restored all his lost faith in Faust. He had walked through the dark night of disloyalty and emerged with his faith stronger than ever. He had now a sure and abiding confidence that he would never doubt his master again.

Inside the church, Brother Jerome stared steadily up at a particular corner of the stained-glass window of Saint Ceraunos, waiting for the light to hit it *just so*. This was his special gift, to pinpoint the moment of dawn through the shifting seasons, even on the most overcast of days, and though he could not have told exactly how he did it—Brother Jerome was not a verbal man—yet he enjoyed some small fame for this knack. When he judged the moment right, he seized the bell-rope and hauled down on it. The bell resisted, swung, reverberated. He let the rope run silkily up through his callused old hands, and then stretched, grabbed, pulled again. Brother Jerome could hear the bell only faintly, as if it were being sounded underwater by mermen in a distant Atlantean city. But he could feel its vibrations. Those he could sense as well as any man.

Wagner looked up as the bell rang. Faust did not.

From the Coswig gate came the groan of wood and metal. The guard was opening the city for the day's traffic. Outside, the world would be bright with promise. The sun had risen.

It was morning.

Faust climbed up on the cart. He made a clucking noise and shook the reins. The horse pricked up his ears and lifted his heavy legs.

The cart pulled away from the church, through the gate, and down the road. Left behind, the chart was a luminous white rectangle on the church doors. On it, a hundred-some neatly penned but eccentrically placed squares were arranged in nine rows, not all of them continuous. Numbers and symbols abided in each square. Notations dwelt here and there in the margins, defining the significance of atomic weights, valences, electron shells, and such esoterica, to enable the clever to decipher its use and meaning. Atop all, in Faust's finest Gothic script, ran the heading: PERIODIC TABLE OF THE ELEMENTS.

Practical designs

His second night in Nuremberg, Faust went for a stroll with
the devil. They walked east, past the convent of Saint Catherine, where the *Meistersingers* held their singing schools, toward where the Pegnitz passed through fortified breaches of
the wall in two branches, forming a slim green island in the
heart of the city. Six stout bridges enabled it to be used as a
park and commons; they crossed one. It was that pleasant time
just before sunset, when the air is clear and colors soft, and
the towers of the city wall—by a myth proudly attested to by
its citizens, there were three hundred sixty-five in all, one for
each day of the year—present themselves at their finest. It was
a Saturday and all the best people had come out to walk and
be seen, in clothes not quite opulent enough to run them afoul
of the sumptuary laws.

(You listen to me) Mephistopheles grumbled (but you never take my advice.)

"That was never our understanding," Faust said sharply. He bowed to a passing burgher, who returned the honor with a complacent bow of his own.

(You are like the boy who is so anxious to build a tree-house that he slams the lumber down in the garden before the oak is out of the acorn. It is impractical to think you can revolutionize the science of your world without first improving its technology. If you attempt to build your tree-house now, you will only trample down the seedling.)

"I am a scholar, not a mechanic."

(To remake the world requires hammers as well as books, sweat as well as words. A revolution is not a picnic. You can name as many quarks as you like, as whimsically as you will, but all your elegant reasonings will convince nobody. Belief requires proof, and for proof you'll need a cyclotron.)

"Put aside these futile arguments. Divert me."

(Oh, very well.) Mephistopheles had incarnated himself to-night as a tattooed American savage, clad only in a loincloth, with wooden plugs in his earlobes, a long spear, and a small leather pouch hanging from a thong about his neck. His hair was shaven halfway up his head and macaw feathers sprouted from his topknot; his teeth had been filed to points. Yet his poise, posture, and proud stare were simple and unforced, so that he presented an odd mixture of the noble and the brutish. (What variety of learning would best suit your current mood: physics, chemistry, biology?)

"Show me a new creature," Faust said, thinking of the order *Dinosauria*, those monstrous Titans which had ruled the world for so many millions of years and whose existence he had first learned of in a tavern on the road from Wittenberg to Nuremberg. "Something so unfamiliar to me as to rouse my sense of wonder. Something stranger than giraffes and more dangerous than electric eels. Something pleasant to the eye and yet baffling to the mind."

Mephistopheles slung his spear across his shoulders and hung both arms over it, semicrucified. (Strangely dangerous and pleasantly baffling.) His mouth twisted in a cruel smile. (I have just the thing. And look—here comes one now!)

A young and modestly dressed woman passed them, with a fleeting smile and a nod of recognition. When Faust looked after her, the devil took his arm.

(She's a pretty thing, isn't she? Our landlord's lovely daughter. She'd lift her skirts for you in an instant if her mother were not present. Ah, but the mother is hardly better herself; a soft word and a grope in a dark place would win her, too. She has no face worth looking at, I'll grant you, but all cats are black at night.) He pointed his spear across the water, to where a dark-haired maiden gazed moodily from a window over the river. (That quiet woman with the deceptively modest eyes as well. But she's poxy and you'd regret it soon enough.)

"What! You'd serve as my pimp?" The scholar could not help but laugh. "Is there no end to your talents?"

(Information is information, Faust. Knowledge is knowledge. I make no distinction between the high and the low.) Several paths wound their way through the island. By common consent, they followed one that ran along the river for a time, then looped inward, through a scythed meadow and under the trees. (Returning to the subject of our landlord's wife and daughter, though. Were you willing to put in a solid month's intrigue, with lies and flowers, forged letters, small kisses, and cunning promises, you could have the both of them in the same bed at the same time: daughter competing with mother, experience vying with youth. Each one mad to prove herself the better fuck. I see that the thought interests you!)

"I find this hard to believe—that women, whom I have always revered as purer and more spiritual than men, should behave so sordidly."

(More sordidly than the men who would use them so? Didn't you yourself, during your student days in Kraków, once pay two women to—)

"Those were whores! Degraded creatures, scarce worthy of the sacred name of Woman. It is foul of you even to mention the two in a single breath."

(Women are as lascivious, unfaithful, and coy as men, Faust. But men have created the lie otherwise, in order to keep them in control. Control is born out of scarcity, and to render scarce something everybody can and most wish to do requires a sound foundation of denial and deceit.)

Their way passed through a grove of lime trees, planted by the city fathers expressly to refresh strollers with their scent. When Faust paused to savor the blossoming fruit, Mephistopheles shook his spear at a tall and striking woman on the path ahead. A rich-dressed Netherlandish merchant walked with her, smiling indulgently. (Here comes a famous courtesan, one who has slept with so many princes that now she is as respectable as any ten married women. A night with her would cost you a month's wooing and more silver than you possess. A sizable investment to make purely on speculation and faith! And yet many a man who would not buy a turnip on such terms is at her beck and call. Would you like to see what her friend, Herr van t'Hoort, has not—the quality of merchandise that lies beneath those fine and regrettably concealing clothes?)

"You can do that?"

(I am in your mind. I need but your command.)

"Show me, then."

Mephistopheles unlooped the pouch from about his neck, and emptied into his palm what looked at first to be pebbles but were in fact the bleached skulls of small birds. He clapped his hands together, pulverizing the skulls, and then blew the resultant powder into the air. A fine mist or haze imposed itself upon the world, making its colors swirl and swim.

When Faust's swooning vision cleared, he found himself looking at the courtesan's nude body. She was approaching middle-age, and one could see that all her features had softened; that her chin was not so straight as it had once been; that her belly was less firm than of yore; that her large-nippled breasts were now distinctly pendant. Yet still her strong legs and heroically long torso made of her a perfect Amazon among women save only for the fact—hardly a flaw—that she had sacrificed neither breast to the perfection of her archery. Even in decline, she was a sight well worth the seeing.

As the harlot approached, Faust bowed deeply. The admiration he felt for her must have shown in his smile and eyes, for she stopped briefly to flirt. "You are dressed," she said, "as a scholar. Yet you bow like a courtier."

Faust met her eye steadily, resisting the urge to look lower and more lecherously. Her lips were wide and moist. Her eyes were blue and fearless, those of a woman who would do as she liked and apologize to none for it afterwards.

"It is your beauty makes me one, madame—briefly. Standing in your gaze I feel ensplendored, and the equal of any man." The merchant van t'Hoort frowned slightly, but was waved back by a flutter of her milk-white hand. "In a moment you will withdraw your radiance and then I shall fade back into the threadbare and humble scholar that I am without the enchantment of your presence."

"You have missed your calling, sir." Her eyes glittered with good humor. In the fading light, her complexion was exquisite and continued so into regions where she could never have suspected his eyes could follow. Her navel was as deep as a thumbprint pushed into fresh dough. The hair upon her cunt was downy and golden. "There's many a woman in court would sigh to know such a man has willfully denied her such honeyed lies."

She offered her arm to her escort, and with a swirl of invisible silks proceeded on her way. Faust stared after, watching her buttocks dimple merrily with every step.

(Bravely done! Had it not been for her companion, her good sense, her professional ethics, and the phase of the moon, I do affirm that come morning, we'd find her feeding you breakfast in bed.)

With mingled wonder and dismay, Faust said, "Are all women so easy, then? Can they all be won with a word, a smile, a bright scarf, or a handful of coins?"

(All human beings have their price, and quite often it is surprisingly small. The trick consists of knowing exactly *what* that price is, when they themselves do not.) They stopped now to admire a troop of boys improving their archery by shooting at a straw Saracen. Hard proud cries rose up every time an arrow struck its mark. (But let us extend our experiment. I shall continue to strip bare the good women of Nuremberg to your eye. You shall pick and choose among them; and I shall describe for you the consequences; in this way I guarantee you a companion tonight who is available, pliant, lusty, and pleasing to your every sense.)

"Do so!"

For the span of that enchanted evening, every woman Faust saw was revealed to his marveling vision, retaining jewelry, shoes, hats, and other ornamentation, but not a wisp of concealing cloth. The range of feminine possibility was spread before him. Mephistopheles played the part of solicitous merchant, pointing out the merits or hidden flaws of each, and exclaiming over their reasonable prices. Every woman, it seemed, was available to him. All of Nuremberg was his harem.

He strolled the island in an ecstasy.

Everywhere was beauty. Here a herd of tame deer scattered before the approach of a short and compact woman, all thighs, bust, and belly, who blushed happily at his glance and quickly looked away. (There's peasant blood in her) said Mephistopheles. (That sort can swing a hoe all day or plow a man all night, yet her husband gives her precious little opportunity to demonstrate her endurance. She's yours for a lie or three.)

Bowing, smiling, Faust progressed down the pathway. A handful-and-a-half of slim nymphs approached, chattering, hands swooping like birds, flesh luminous. A few were plain and several were not; yet their bodies each expressed beauty in its own way, some lush and some elegant, some spare and others extravagant. Two things they had in common: that their hair was cropped short, and that they wore no ornamentation but crucifixes that hung between their slight, plump, emphatic, subtle, and exuberant breasts. With a start, Faust realized that they were nuns. (Access is the problem here, yet I could point you out two or three who might be convinced to leave a ladder leaning against the back of the convent wall.)

"They are brides of Christ!" Faust said, shocked.

(Oh, that won't bother them.)

The nuns passed with cheerful greetings and as they did Faust saw that one—slim-hipped and almost boyish of figure—had vivid red semicircles upon her breasts and belly and clustered upon the insides of her thighs. Briefly he was baffled. Then, all in an instant, the crescents resolved themselves into human bite-marks, such as only passion could have produced.

Faust blinked; Mephistopheles smiled and said nothing.

A pregnant woman walked by, made radiant as the moon by the grace of her belly; her flesh glowed with health. (Threaten to bankrupt her husband.) A slim girl, barely of age, with coltish legs and new-budded breasts. (Seduce her sister and she'll do the rest.) A councilor's red-haired wife, proud of bearing, with fat breasts and pubic hair like a dark flame. (Use force.)

"I am in a daze," Faust said. "How will I ever choose?" Already, darkness was seeping up from the ground. The Kaiserburg atop its rocky outcrop shone bright with reflected sunset; the stone buildings clustered below caught a dimmer light, which their orange-tiled roofs warmed and made into a single smearing brush-stroke of color; below them the trees were cool and shadowy green; an inn twinkled within their branches, one of several on the island. Lanterns had been hung from long poles in the tavern's forecourt, where wooden tables were scattered upon the grass. A boy went among them with a long candle-and-stick device, deftly lighting each.

Waiters with trays of food hurried in and out of the tavern. The festive crowd on the lawn moved in bright and languid swirls, laughing, raising up toasts, flitting from table to table. The women, nude, bright-eyed, were like woods-sylphs; the

men, in slash-sleeved doublets and pants cut so as to display
their best attributes, courteously danced attendance upon their
ladies' grace. Several of the younger women had plaited flowers in their hair, and one of their swains, in response had, with
two sticks and a kerchief, made for himself a pair of antlers.
They danced, hand in hand in a ring, to music that drifted
softly from a trio of lutists and horn-player seated on a bench
by the tavern door. No fairy gathering could have been more
delightful to the senses.

(Here comes the mayor's wife.)

A woman of enormous bulk and even greater dignity wallowed slowly up the path, escorted by her equally dignified
but otherwise unnoteworthy husband. Her legs were thick as
tree trunks but suety-soft, bulging out into such buttocks as
would have disgraced a hippopotamus. Her ample breasts
draped themselves limply across a belly soft as a pudding,
and so large that had it *been* a pudding, it would have fed
multitudes. The nipples were brown as leather, and the mys-
tery between her legs was hidden by bulging, sagging flesh.
Everything was in motion, loose and jiggling. She favored
Faust's appalled bow with the faintest of condescending nods,
and passed grandly by. Glancing after her, he saw that she
was heading straight for the mounded arrays of hams and
fowls, sausages, roast boar, jugged hare, and peppered beef
that were testing the tensile strength of the wooden tables.

(A lady who greatly favors meat) Mephistopheles said
dryly. (I trust her husband has similar appetites.)

"You are unfair to that poor woman. Clothed, she would
seem perfectly normal. I would pass her by without a second
glance."

(Exactly my point) Mephistopheles said. (Human beings

are far more grotesque than your dulled aesthetics give them credit for being.)

The light was draining from the sky as they crossed the Pegnitz once again, away from the pagan isle and back into the clean, narrow streets of the city. Reluctantly, the naiads and their retainers were leaving Faerie. Everywhere to be seen were promenaders making their slow ways home; Faust felt and shared their reluctance for the evening to end. Staring hungrily after the nymphs sifting slowly into obscurity, he said, "They are all so desirable that I cannot choose among them. I could be happy with any."

(Then follow me.) Mephistopheles turned down a wide dirt lane between the city armory and a small church. (I know of a woman who, I swear, fits your mood perfectly.)

Skeptically, happily, Faust followed.

He was halfway down the lane when a small door opened in the side of the church and someone emerged.

Faust stopped in his tracks. The woman—if woman she was—stood briefly before him in the holy grace of her una-dorned flesh, for Mephistopheles had not yet lifted his spell. Her breasts were small and perfect: no larger than two clenched fists, and tipped by the pinkest of nipples set off from her milky skin by the merest hint of apricot. The complex and inevitable swell of her belly drew his eye gently downward to where a soft and youthful down covered her most private of organs, like fine moss upon finer porcelain, before a chance movement of her hands hid it behind her prayer-book. Her knees and toes blushed a faintest rose.

She looked as innocent as Eve before the Fall.

All this in an instant. Then the young woman had passed him by. She gave him the briefest of glances as she passed, and there was in them not so much as a spark of lascivious interest. He would have known if there had been.

"Who is she?"

(Oh, Faust, you don't want *her*.)

"I want her. Tell me her name." The woman disappeared around the corner. Her hair was pale brown with gold highlights, parted in the middle and chastely combed back, to be captured and bound by a small black ribbon, and then cascade free again in loose curls that did not quite reach her delicate waist.

(Direct your lust elsewhere. She is a pious and virginal girl, totally lacking in carnal experience. You cannot have her. It is an impossibility.)

(You said—)

(I said that everyone has her price. Sometimes, however, that price is too high. If you had the money and position, you could petition her father to marry her to you, and I guarantee you she would work as passionately to please her husband as would any other woman. But here you are a stranger, all but a pauper, and a man without friends or influence. She is young and inexperienced. Your slightest approach to her would send her scampering away like a deer affrighted in the wood. You could assault her in an alley, perhaps. But what you want, Faust—her, willingly, tonight—cannot be had. Yes, she could be seduced. But believe me, you lack the patience it would take.)

"I could be patience itself if—her name! You haven't told me her name."

(Margarete Reinhardt.)

"Margarete! How that name transports me! I must win her."

(Faust, listen to me: There is a door not many streets from here, behind which a woman waits for her lover in perfect darkness. She does not know he's been delayed. Go there, knock once, and step boldly within. In an instant she'll slam the door shut, throw you down upon the floor, and rip open your trousers with her teeth. Then she'll crouch down over your body—for she has already shed all her clothing in antic-ipation of this moment—and impale herself upon you. She's a gorgeous creature and as pleasant a tumble as any you've had. When she realizes from the flavor of your mouth and the rough unfamiliarity of your caresses that you are a stranger, she will experience an instant of terror and confusion. But then her lust will be magnified by the very wantonness of the act, and she will redouble her lewd efforts. She will do things with you that she has never done before, even with her lover. And when you leave, she will whisper in your ear a time when next her husband will be away and the lamps all dark.)

"Are you done?"

(As ever, I am your slave. But to win this girl, who is hardly more lovely than a dozen others in Nuremberg, and totally lacking in the erotic experience a man of your age re-quires, would take you over a year. A year, Faust!—and not a year of flirtations, small favors, and stolen kisses, but a year wherein you must harshly discipline yourself to show her no favor, no special looks, no least sign of your ardor. A year, moreover, spent in such enterprises as you have stoutly re-fused to enter into. It's hopeless, my friend.)

Faust stared down the lane, marveling at how ordinary it seemed to the eye, how special to the heart. A trickle of water in the ditch alongside it caught the light and turned a palest silver. "Oh, intersecting lines of destiny!" he said aloud. "Oh, holiest of streets!" Then: "What was it you said? About how I can win her?"

Mephistopheles sighed. (Not with money.)

"No, of course not!"

(Yet it will take money to win her. The Reinhardts are not the wealthiest merchant-clan in the city. But they stand high in the second rank. To approach her in your penniless state would raise the suspicions of everyone involved. Including her.)

"I am certain such crass considerations wouldn't matter to Margarete. You said yourself that she was innocent."

(If a clumsy unfamiliarity with the arts of love is innocence rather than mere ignorance, why—)

"Shut up! I will not tolerate you speaking thus of an angel!"

(She is human. I can show you the contents of her chamber pot if you need proof.)

"Scoff as you will. Your denials and evasions only make me desire her the more."

(Do they?) Mephistopheles said casually.

Faust chewed his lip, thinking. Then, impatiently, he said, "You know what I want. Scan the future and advise me on how best to achieve my goal. But no more! You are to tell me of nothing that does not directly relate to my Margarete."

(Well, if you're determined, then the road to her bed begins at the tollhouse of her parents. If we hurry, you can catch them before they reach their door.)

Faust doffed his hat to the Reinhardts. They were a conventionally respectable couple, the man clad in modest velvet and his wife in, of course, nothing at all. She was a matronly woman, inclining toward the stout, with a hard jaw and a shrewd eye that yet had a glint of humor in it. Hers was a body pampered and well fed, so that it had grown lush, rounder here and pinker there, but everywhere smooth and firm. Faust felt an irrational urge to run his hands up and over every curve and rump of her, and thought, yes, here indeed was the mother of his Margarete. Hers was a beauty past its prime, but the remains of that beauty were there to be seen. An irritated thought directed at Mephistopheles restored her clothing; up and down the street, nymphs disappeared back into human guise; the enchantment dissolved from the evening; and Nuremberg was Nuremberg again.

"Good evening, Herr Reinhardt. Frau Reinhardt."

They returned him cautious nods, of the sort one offers to those whose station is unknown, and Reinhardt said, "Do I know you, sir?" with a coolness that suggested he did not. He was a sandy-haired man with a round and gullible face, which misleading appearance must surely have served him well in many negotiations.

"Sir, I am a stranger to you. Yet I have business to conduct in this city, and you are well known not just for your acumen in matters of commerce but for your probity as well."

"Not at all, not at all," the merchant said in a pleased, dismissive way. His wife actually smiled. "And you, sir? Your name?"

"I am, sir, your humble petitioner, Johannes Faust."

"The aerialist?"

"You have heard of me, then. That makes matters easier. My air-carriage is, indirectly, why I am here. My ascent, you see, so excited the mob that upon my return they destroyed the balloon and then, their savage lust unassuaged, attacked my house and burnt it to the ground. I was fortunate to escape with my life. All I had was lost." The lies came surprisingly easily; Faust was unhappily amazed to discover such a talent lying dormant within himself. "To my lasting shame, I had to leave debts behind me. I had greatly hoped for patronage, but . . ."

As they talked, all three continued to stroll, at a politely unhurried pace, toward the Reinhardts' house. For, though the moon was full and children were out playing in the streets, it was getting on time for all decent, moneyed folk to be safely abed. Had they not had the good fortune to live in a large city, their doors would have been bolted long ago.

"If I may say this without giving offense," Reinhardt said in a friendly but carefully formal manner, "you suffer from a common affliction of the imaginative. Your creation—brilliant! If you can yet find a sponsor for it, I would travel a far distance for the privilege of seeing such a thing. But of what *practical* use is it? Genius is not an easy ware to peddle. Had you turned your prodigious intellect to something lesser and yet more easily commodified . . ." He shrugged. "I am sorry to be so blunt with you, sir, but these words are kindly intended. I could not possibly bring myself to invest in your flying-device."

"Pray, don't misunderstand me! That was never my intention." Faust hesitated, then said, "I also invented something of more practical utility: the carriage leaf-spring."

"That was yours?" Reinhardt asked, while simultaneously, his wife exclaimed, "So *you* are Pfinzing's mysterious Wittenberg savant!" Her hand closed quietly about her husband's forearm and squeezed, a private signal which, a whispered word informed Faust, meant that he was to be alert for opportunities for profit.

"Herr Pfinzing has done extraordinarily well by that device," Reinhardt said. "Yet if you have come here to litigate for a share in his profits, I must hope that you obligated him to a sound contract. Pfinzing is an honest man, but hard."

They had reached the Reinhardts' home now, and stood by its stoop.

"He is welcome to his profits," Faust said. "I have"—and only the devil could've detected the hesitation in his voice, or guessed what a distasteful chore to which he had just committed himself—"many more ideas of similarly practical utility."

A look passed quickly between the Reinhardts, and then the husband seized Faust's hands heartily. "Then come inside, good friend. If we are to talk business, let us talk seriously and in comfort. I'll put you up in our guest room."

They stepped within the house. Frau Reinhardt disappeared in search of candles. Standing in the moonlight with one hand on the door, ready to close it as soon as his wife returned, Reinhardt said, "Now—forgive my eagerness—but what exactly did you have in mind?"

"For one, an optical device which so manipulates light that distant objects can be seen clearly. I have used it myself to—"

"Yes, yes, but remember I asked you for *practical* devices. None of this dew and moonshine!"

Before Margarete, this dismissal of his greatest discoveries would have enraged Faust. Now he schooled himself to say, "Nothing could be more practical. The military potential, particularly for ships and port cities, should be self-evident. With its use, pirates can be evaded, cities and fortifications given hours more preparation against attack, and the deployment of enemy armies discerned from a distance." Nuremberg was a major foundry site; foundries meant armaments; Nuremberg was famous for its cannons throughout the civilized world.

Faust knew that the trivialization of his great invention could not fail to interest his host profoundly. "I call it"—he hesitated for an instant, considering his audience—"the spy-glass."

Frau Reinhardt appeared with candles. She gave one to her husband. "I'll see if there's any meat left over from supper, and bring it to your office," she said, hurrying away again. "Perhaps there's still bread." Her voice echoed through the house. "Margarete!" she cried. Then, fretfully, "Where is that girl?"

The office was snug, wood-paneled, efficient. They took chairs, and Reinhardt cleared the clutter from a table and drew out several sheets of foolscap from a drawer.

"I have also invented means of drawing a finer and stronger gauge of wire than has hitherto been commercially practical, and can also cast various metals in larger sections than has been previously considered possible. But these things require a substantial investment of gold. The spy-glass can be created quickly by only a few craftsmen, at minimum outlay, and then sold for a quick and sure profit."

"A commendable approach. I encourage you to continue your thoughts along such lines. In fact, I think—ah, daughter!"

Margarete appeared in the doorway, dressed in a long white sleeping-gown and holding a candle that set her face aglow. In her hand was a platter with two glasses, a bottle of wine, and several slices of cold roast beef hastily placed between cut slabs of bread. She looked at Faust without recognition, and smiled politely.

In an uncharacteristic display of whimsy, Mephistopheles filled the dim house with fireflies, parrots, winged sprites, dancing lights, and elfin laughter, all rising in chaotic spirals.

Monkeys howled and elephants raised their trunks and trumpeted. Heavy ophidian things crawled and slithered in the dark corners.

So bewitched was Faust that he hardly noticed.

THE INQUISITION

They came, masked, for Faust at twilight. He was returning to his workshop from an inspection of the new card-guided weaving machines when they stepped from the shadows, knives drawn. It happened so fast he couldn't tell how many ruffians there were. Four at least: one who stood menacingly before him while a second wrestled his arms behind his back, a third who thrust a sack over his head, and a last who bound his wrists. There might have been more.

"Cry out and you're a dead man," one growled.

"It's all right," another whispered, "we're friends."

For a brief reflexive instant Faust struggled, silently crying out to Mephistopheles for the names of his attackers, their intentions, and a way to outwit and escape them. But Mephistopheles did not answer.

So he went quietly.

Blinded and dizzied, Faust was led up stairs and down streets, through buildings, and out into the open again. He was almost immediately lost, but this did not stop his captors from threading him through a long and wearying maze of sudden turns, reversals, and similarly unnecessary complications. When he lagged, he was cuffed back up to speed. It was terrifying.

But even so, he could not stop thinking of Margarete.

He saw her every day. Clad in rough clothes and leather apron, with an artisan's large beret atop his head, Faust spent all his waking hours in the workshop, trying to achieve through labor if not peace then a kind of numbed tranquillity. He gave lectures, demonstrated techniques, taught classes. With the aid of a changing crew of craftsmen and skilled artisans, he built working models of myriad new devices. As occasion demanded, he had guild-masters working the bellows for the forge, and men who owned their own foundries puffing as they turned the great wheel of the grindstone.

Always Wagner stood at a writing desk in the corner to make fair copies of his notes and plans. Messengers sat three to a bench waiting to fly these copies to the presses or to anxiously waiting workshops, as need required. Yet all this activity was haunted by Margarete, the thrill of her footstep in the doorway, the jolt of her glance, the tension of her absent voice like a rising musical note endlessly prolonged.

Frau Reinhardt, concerned that their guest was overworking himself, often sent Margarete over with a bowl of soup or a bouquet of white roses. At such times the young woman usually lingered a bit to brighten his day with laughter and small gossips about the comings and goings of the household. Other times she came of her own will, for she was

infinitely curious about his work, and listened to his explanations with a clear and avid intelligence, asking questions
that cut to the heart of whatever he was trying to convey.

"If only *everyone* were so quick of understanding!" he
growled once, staring hard at a blushing founder's apprentice
who had miswired a rotor and was now pouring salt on the
smoldering remains of the resultant fire. Margarete laughed
and casually, meaninglessly, squeezed his forearm. The
warmth of her flesh shot through him like voltage through a
hot-wired frog's leg. One moment's pressure of her pale white
hand against his skin, almost Aethiopian from exposure to sun
and forge, and then no more. There was a flip of skirts, and
he did not have to turn to know she was gone.

Leaving him to begin waiting again for her return.

"Through here," one of the thugs said with a shove. Faust
went stumbling down a short flight of stairs. An unanticipated
floor sent him crashing to his knees.

Again he cried out silently for Mephistopheles.

Again there was no reply.

He tried to stand, but was shoved back down so hard he
cried out in pain and fear that his kneecaps would crack. The
bag was whisked from his head.

He was in a dark windowless space, impossible to guess
its dimensions. It smelled of pitch, hemp, raw wool—a warehouse. Two of the dagger-men stood at a distance with lanterns held so that they shone into his eyes. Between him and
them, a black silhouette, was a table made of a plank laid
across stacked crates. Five men sat behind it, their faces hidden by the darkness. Shadows streamed from them to him.

To one side a scribe stood, a barrel for his writing desk.

He had a long, pointed nose twice the length of his quill. Another mask.

One of the faceless men leaned forward. "Remain kneeling. Speak only to answer questions. Disobey and die."

The Reinhardts had set Faust up in one of three rental properties which, together with their own house, framed a common garden courtyard. It had formerly been the shop and habitation of a pike-and-swordmaker who had lost most of his trade as the demand for such weapons trended increasingly toward the ornate and ceremonial, qualities which his heavy and functional weaponry lacked. On his death both sons had gone into the wool trade with an uncle, leaving behind the tools Faust now found a useful start for projects of his own.

For a season this workshop became the intellectual center of Nuremberg. Instrument-makers, gunsmiths, lawyers and clerks, ambassadors, famed creators of clock androids, artists, architects, merchant lords, able men from every walk of life converged upon it to witness the assembly of fantastic new creations, and the best of them were afterwards invited up to Faust's modest rooms above the workshop for conversations and arguments that lasted deep into the night.

Almost as fabulous as the inventions themselves was the method by which Faust introduced them. Men and machines would be assembled and the workshop rebuilt for the creation of the one particular device. The workshop was, however, unbuilt as soon as the prototype was made—to be reconstructed elsewhere by these same workers under the careful eye of the new-made master of a novel and lucrative trade.

Nuremberg was quick to see the potential of the spy-glass. The commandant of the city forces, in an incident widely reported, stood upon the city walls looking out over the surrounding lands and the troops arrayed at varying distances for purposes of the demonstration, then raised the glass higher, to the horizon, and coolly joked, "I can see Augsburg burning."

The electric generator and motor were a less celebrated but more pervasive success. Their presence spread daily. Several smaller mills along the Pegnitz were converted to the generation of electricity and wires strung crazily up into the city to a constellation of makeshift laboratories where a new class of electrical artificers was busily inventing, studying, and building production models to Faust's sketches. A young entrepreneur had set up a static charge generator in the narthex of Saint Lorenz and was charging a penny apiece to those who wished to feel their hair stand on end and shoot blue sparks from their fingertips. Another, at the convent of Saint Catherine, was electrocuting dogs. Many important discoveries had been made, and one apprentice killed through his own carelessness. Those lucky enough to be involved couldn't have been happier.

"State your reasons," the faceless man said, "for appearing before us."

Faust shook his head in confusion and disbelief. It was as if the man were speaking a language identical in sound but not meaning to German; the words were all familiar, yet they conveyed no sense to him. He opened his mouth to say so.

"You know them already," said a voice to his side.

Turning, Faust saw Reinhardt, similarly bound, kneeling on the floor beside him. The merchant's round and freckled face was strained and white with anxiety but determined; it did not seem at all foolish now. He did not look at Faust. His gaze was fixed upon his interrogators.

"Reinhardt," Faust said. "What madness is this?"

"*Silence!*" the faceless man roared. Rough hands seized Faust's arms. "Another outburst like that, and you will be punished."

Reinhardt cast Faust a terrible look, but no words of comfort. To the faceless men he said, "I intend to buy a row of houses and have them razed for a factory, in which I will build in quantity a new variety of gun. You have my figures already, I believe."

"We have seen your figures, and we doubt them. Why should it cost so much? A gun shop could be established for a fraction of what you ask."

"You are usurers!" Faust cried, suddenly enlightened.

Reinhardt stiffened in horror.

Two of the men behind the table rose halfway to their feet; one slammed both hands down upon its wooden surface; another chuckled softly to himself. The scribe shook his head, perhaps sadly.

Out of nowhere a fist struck Faust in the face. He cried out as heavy boots kicked him in the ribs, the stomach, the side. Then fingers knotted in his hair and pulled back, painfully forcing his chin upward. He found himself staring through tears of agony into the bone-white and moon-blank face of a carnival mask. It had no mouth, but a quick twist of the head gave him to know that its occupant was smiling down on him in no friendly way. Something cold and razor-sharp, surely a knife, tickled his throat.

Horrified, Faust realized he was about to die, and he didn't even know why. Where was Mephistopheles? How could that unclean and maleficent spirit have brought him this far and then abandoned him? It made no sense. It was enough, in this moment of terror, to make Faust doubt his own sanity.

"That should do."

Faust was abruptly released. He crashed to his knees again. Where the knife had been, his throat itched terribly. He would carry the memory of that blade for a long time to come.

"When the Bishop of Würzburg burned his Jews," a faceless man said with imperfectly repressed anger, "the citizens of Nuremberg did the same. An entire generation has grown up free of their pernicious influence."

"Amen to that," said another. The lantern-bearers behind him shifted slightly, sending shadows bouncing about the immense room. No least fraction of light, however, reached his face.

"Yet this blessing, as all agree it is, comes at a price. Even vermin have their uses. Christians cannot charge interest. Believers condemned of usury are put to death. Few men are charitable enough to risk lending money without hope of gain. A vigorously expanding economy requires credit. This is the conundrum which—"

"Enough!" a third man said. "We are not here to justify ourselves. Reinhardt, if you satisfy our inquiries, funds will be made available to you at such terms as are necessary. If, however, your answers are evasive or incomplete"—a droplet of what could only be blood trickled under Faust's shirtfront and down into his chest hairs—"well, money-lending is a serious business. Faust, you are here as a witness. I remind you that not all witnesses are innocent. Any further attempt to undermine the dignity of this council will be dealt with appropriately." Strong hands touched Faust's shoulders lightly, were gone.

Faust shuddered.

Reinhardt's face was a mask in stone.

One who had been silent until now, a heavyset man with a slow and judicious manner of speaking, now addressed Faust. "This new firearm of yours, this 'repeating rifle' . . . Exactly what do those words mean?"

Speaking in as forthright a manner as he could counterfeit, Faust said, "They mean that a marksman will be able to fire ten shots from a single weapon without reloading. The gun's rifled barrel will impart a spin to the bullet, resulting in a flatter trajectory, increased range, and improved accuracy. A uniform bore will make it possible to manufacture cartridges— combining shot and a measured charge—that can be used in any and all of these guns, making the reloading time negligible. In combat one soldier thus armed will be the equal of a score with flintlocks."

"Who will manufacture these cartridges?"

"I'll want to build a powder mill for that purpose," Reinhardt said. "Eventually. For now the cartridges can be contracted out to the city armory."

"All this our spies have told us already," the first man said. "It helps, however, to hear these things said clearly and in order by their originators. Some of it, I admit we found— still find—difficult to accept. The tolerances you project for the bore of your barrels, for instance, seem to this grizzled old head an arrogant and unrealistic fraud. But let that pass. For argument's sake, we will not challenge it." He drew himself up sternly. "But answer this question, and answer it well. Everything hinges upon what you now say."

Faust took a deep breath to calm himself. "I stand ready."

"Explain to us this process you call—mass production?"

*   *   *

As time passed, Faust had found himself regretting the scholar's life less and less. One day Konrad Heinvogel, who had studied under Bernhard Walther, the onetime assistant to the great Regiomontanus and a noted astronomer in his own right, came to the workshop clutching a copy of Faust's *Starry Messenger* (obtained with tediously recounted circumstantiality from an itinerant bookseller who had months before passed through Wittenberg) and knelt on the dirty floor, tears in eyes, to kiss his hand. He was sent away with a telescope of his own—an example *gratis* of the optics workshop's finest work—a hastily scrawled almanac of productive times and coordinates in which to search for new planets, and a few trenchant observations on the nature and orbital mathematics of comets, which Faust dared hope might find fertile ground within Heinvogel's head.

But it was only a passing incident. Faust found himself increasingly involved in the greasy-handed business of engineering, and valuing the application of knowledge to practical problems above its mere acquisition. "Knowledge without utility is sterile," he told Wagner. "I would praise the creator of an improved water pump far above he who had spent his life assembling a catalogue of the names and spectra of all the visible stars in the heavens."

He smiled to see that Wagner carefully wrote down his words.

"Mass production," Faust said, "entails two chief elements: interchangeable parts and the assembly line." He gained confidence as he spoke, for in explication lay his chief talent. As he developed his argument, however, he found his hands straining against their bonds. He was a gesturer; as he lectured his students, his hands would rise and fall like swifts or leaping salmon, urging the words out of his brain, ushering them from his mouth, guiding them out into the world, and thrusting them upon his audience. His bonds hobbled not just his hands, but his speech as well.

Something moved from the shadows beneath the table—a cat. It padded out into the dim light, then collapsed all at once upon the floor. While not daring cease or slow his speech, Faust found himself staring at the creature.

It was not a handsome cat. Scrawny, crook-tailed, and covered with a coarse and matted black pelt, the beast was clearly one of the city's lowlier mercenaries, one who defended its merchandise from a diffuse army of rats and mice in exchange for the occasional saucer of milk and first claim upon the bodies of the fallen.

It began to groom itself.

Faust knew his rhetoric. He marshalled his arguments, shaping his speech to his auditors' reactions, enlarging on points they seemed puzzled by and skimming quickly past what they appeared readily to accept. And all the while he watched the cat.

It was such a homely and quotidian thing that he found himself reassured by its presence. It was a living reminder that this was, after all, no Star Chamber or subterranean crypt but somebody's warehouse. The inquisitors were men of business, the ruffians their sons. Only circumstance made all this seem sinister. Come morning, doors and windows would be opened and the oppressive miasma of night would be blown away by sunlight and the early-morning breeze. He thought how dark his own nights were, when he would beg Mephistopheles to show him Margarete's sleeping body. She slept modestly, wrapped in sheets and blankets, shrouded in a nightgown that revealed nothing.

But it was the work of an instant for his imagination to strip these virginal coverings from her.

"I can serve you better than that, if you like," Mephistopheles offered, during one midnight service of adoration. "With my aid you can experience a complete tactile foretaste of Margarete's love . . ."

Invisible hands slipped under Faust's workshirt to stroke his chest. Moist lips pressed into the hollow of his neck, then parted for a moister tongue and teeth that lightly bit and tugged at his earlobe.

"I am not the weakling you take me for," Faust said harshly. "Cease such illusions. I can wait."

"Ah? Shall I restore the young lady her privacy as well?"

For a long tormented instant Faust said nothing. Then: "No. No, do not. I cannot stop."

With a soft sigh, Margarete shifted in bed, throwing an arm up on the pillow above her head, lifting and reshaping one exquisite breast. Watching her, so lovely, so close, so unattainable, Faust could not help but weep bitter tears. By degrees his yearning for her grew less and less tolerable. Until finally, inevitably, he was forced out into the streets.

There were, for a man with a devil at his command, ways of satisfying his physical needs, and in his misery Faust availed himself of them.

A wife would discover her husband's infidelities had not, as she'd been promised, ceased, and storm out into the street, looking for revenge. Soon enough she would find Faust awaiting her.

A woman whose appetites were stronger than her fiancé could satisfy, yet who was too shy and indrawn to find for herself a second lover, would see a falling star in the twilight sky. Closing her eyes, she would make a wish and in that instant feel the welcome warmth of a man's hand upon her buttocks.

A nun who felt her youth fleeting and her faith never fast (perhaps her parents had caught her with a boy and sentenced her to this life as a result) would steal an hour by herself and, strolling in the woods outside of town, wistful and filled with yearnings, encounter a silent man with a sad smile who had spread a blanket in a small clearing and filled goblets for two. And when, after a glass of wine or two, it would have been perfect had he kissed her then and there—he did. And his hand touched her breast, and moved aside her clothing, and briefly—sweetly—she was no longer a chaste bride of the Savior, but a woman like any other, and privy to the pleasures that were her birthright.

Faust took them all with eyes closed, seeing only, thinking of only, desiring only Margarete.

Industriously, the cat applied its tongue to its matted hide. It made long and repeated strokes down each outstretched leg and gave careful attention to the fur between its toes. With obsessive thoroughness, it chewed at the claws, gnawing away the splintered bits. Then, satisfied, it rolled over to its feet again, placed all four paws together, and arched its back.

Hoek.

The cat accompanied this sound with a spasmodically wide opening of its mouth. *Hoek*, it said again. All of its body rippled through a painful retching motion. It was trying to cough up a hairball.

Despite its efforts, nothing came out.

For an instant Faust faltered. Where was—? Training! He was explaining how an assembly-line worker with only a few days' experience could, supervised, do the work of a journey-man. This would take some evasion, for they must not see that this meant the end of the guild system that had served these men so well. Here was the time to draw a word-picture of a soldier in the field with a broken gun—one that could be repaired without intercession of a distant gunsmith.

Still the cat continued trying to force up the hairball with great wracking coughs that accomplished nothing. *Hoek. Hoek-Hoek. Hoeoeuunck.* It was astonishing how the faceless men ignored the scrawny animal's performance. It made Faust's chest and shoulders ache just to look at it.

Hoek.

A gold coin shot out of the cat's mouth. It flew across the room, bounced on the floor, rolled briefly, and finally spiraled to a stop at Faust's feet.

He stared down at it, astonished, then up at the faceless men.

They glanced at one another. "Go on," one prompted him. Clearly, they had seen nothing.

The cat laughed. (They've bought your argument) it said. (You can wrap it up anytime you feel like it now.)

Then it jumped up on the makeshift table, turned its backside toward the inquisitors, who of course saw nothing, and raised its tail. A stream of gold coins shot out of its anus in a bright arc, clinking, endless. They heaped up on the tabletop and rolled off the edge, all for the benefit of one man only. Faust briefly squeezed shut his eyes in mingled exasperation and relief.

Mephistopheles was back.

Faust lay faceup on his bed, fully dressed, an arm over his eyes. Reinhardt had his money and would have his factory. Soon it would be churning out guns at a rate that would astound the world. Guns that every general would want. Profits that every manufacturer would envy. "You did not come when I summoned you."

"You directed me not to interfere in your private life. Remember?"

"In this case, I would have made an exception."

Mephistopheles was still embodied as a cat. Now, however, he walked on two legs, wore boots and a plumed hat, and carried a sword by his side. It would have been charming had not the cat been so obviously a flayed hide clumsily stitched together and empty within. It scratched its head with the hilt of its poniard. "Why, Faust, how was I to tell?"

"From now on, you will let *me* decide what I should and should not know."

"Of course, of course." The cat swept off its hat and bowed low, stomach dimpling inward. He could see through its eyeholes into its vacant interior. "That was the Council of Gold by the way, and the men you saw were Pirckheimer, Behaim, Stromer, Muffel, and Holzshuher. You can destroy any of them at your convenience now. All it would take is a word in the right ecclesiastical ear."

"I wish to destroy nobody." Faust's body ached all over from the blows and harsh handling it had endured this night. Without opening his eyes, he began to undo his buttons.

"I was being hypothetical."

"Don't." With difficulty, Faust drew up a foot and pulled off the boot. He dropped it heavily to the floor. With that, all ambition died. He lay back, half-unbuttoned, uncaring.

" 'Diddle, diddle, dumpling,' " Mephistopheles sang, " 'my son John, Went to bed with his trousers on; One shoe off and one shoe on, Diddle, diddle—' "

"Shut up."

Mephistopheles did so.

For a time Faust was silent. Then he said, "You can be most tedious, you know."

"It's the testosterone." All in a single fluid motion the cat drew its sword and whipped it around and down to its crotch. It held its tiny equipment in one paw, against the sharp edge of the blade. The arm folded unconvincingly in a place where no joint should be. "Shall I castrate myself? It'd be for my own good. I'd be happier and far more tractable afterwards. It's an operation, in fact, which I really do believe *most* males could benefit from. Yourself, for one—I urge you to give it serious consideration. You'd think ever so much more clearly after the surgery."

Faust wasn't listening. When he closed his eyes, the bed seemed to be going up and down in a repetitive walking rhythm. The cobbled streets of Nuremberg rose and fell beneath him, with Reinhardt hurrying after, offering weak justifications for involving him in the Council of Gold's inquisition. "We need the money, you see..." he had squeaked. "Nobody else could have...Your testimony was crucial."

Faust's lips curled at the memory. To be treated so—cuffed, humiliated, beaten, with neither foreknowledge nor consent—intolerable! From any other man, from the father of any other woman, such treatment would have...He, Faust, was transforming the world, remaking it in his own image, and in the process making this second-rate merchant rich. Yet to Reinhardt he remained a dependent, an underling, valuable to be sure, but expected to subordinate his needs, wishes, and well-being to those of the house of Reinhardt.

It was an ugly, ugly bargain he had made.

"Show me Margarete," he said wearily.

"As you wish," Mephistopheles said. "I can also, if you like, provide you with the smell of her. She bathed yesterday, so the scent of her cunt is particularly dainty."

Faust groaned. "Yes, do so."

Then, as always, it was as if he sat at the side of Margarete's bed, looking down upon her sleeping form. It was excruciating to see her so. It was his only pleasure. He inhaled deeply.

"What a dreadful thing it is to love," he mused. "Could any man be more miserable than I? Look at her! She is pretty, yes, but I have seen galaxies in collision and pillars of dust giving birth to stars. Why should I yearn so for her glance? Why should I spend my every waking breath waiting for the sound of her cough, the sight of her shadow in the doorway? What sane man would choose this—to be enslaved to a woman who doesn't even know how I agonize over her!"

"Would you wish her to know, then?"

"No. How horrible that would be! Indifference is bad enough, but pity would be intolerable. The only solace I have is that my sweet, sweet Margarete does not know how I feel about her."

From nowhere Mephistopheles produced a mustache comb. Eyebrows arched knowingly, he began to stroke and smooth his whiskers into place. He chuckled, but said nothing.

8

GRETCHEN

"Of *course* I know Doctor Faust is in love with me," Margarete said. "I'm not blind." She bit through a thread, began rummaging within her sewing basket. "Or maybe I am. Where is that green?"

Her cousin Sophia bent her head over the basket to help look. "I just thought you might not have noticed." They were sitting on the gallery overlooking the courtyard garden, to take advantage of the breeze. From here they could see, down at an angle through a workshop window, the object of their conversation, a dark Hephaestus laboring at his forge. "Here it is!"

"No, the forest green. Keep your eye on him. He's forever looking up here at me, as if I'm so dim-witted I won't notice. If I'm cruel enough to smile or wave, he'll scowl and—there!"

They both laughed as Faust brusquely turned his back on

them. "Men!" Margarete said. "They're not subtle creatures, are they?"

"I can't find it. Why don't you use some of mine?"

"It's not a match. And I've already started the trees—see?"

"Mmmm."

"I'll work on the sky for a while. That's tedious enough to punish me for absent-mindedness."

"It must be very tense. Having him around all the time."

"It's like having a wizard in the house! One never knows what he'll do. The last time father's business took him to Munich, I was certain he'd do something—come out with one of those ridiculous speeches men make or put a hand where it doesn't belong." She'd been looking forward to it, in a way. She would have poured cold water on his infatuation with a few haughty words, or else slapped him roundly for his impertinence, depending on his offense. She might even have slid a knee between his legs and slammed it quickly upward, if that were merited. Things would have been settled then. "But nothing happened. To look at him, you wouldn't think he'd be so timid."

"He's handsome enough," Sophia agreed, "in a fierce sort of way."

They embroidered in silence for a bit.

Margarete thought first of how laundry day was coming up and what dreary labor that would be. Then of her suspicion that Agnes was stealing from the larder and whether they'd have to find a new girl—one without a boyfriend to teach her thievery and other such bad habits. And full circle back to Faust. Once, just to see what would happen, she had playfully squeezed his thick and coarsely haired arm, and felt the muscles *jump* under her touch.

She had thought then that he would turn and seize her,

that those strong arms would go around her and his mouth take hers by force. She had even half-decided in that panicked instant that she would let him have that kiss—no more—before wrenching herself away and giving him the stern scolding he deserved.

But the coward had done nothing. He had only turned away, glaring down through his beard at his shoes. She had left then, not caring to hear him growl some light inanity entirely at odds with what he was feeling and certainly ought to have been saying.

She was beginning to wonder if there was something wrong with him physically.

"Do you understand this new doctrine of electromagnetism?" Sophia asked suddenly.

"Well," Margarete said, "I do and I don't. When you follow the explanations, it's perfectly simple. A changing magnetic field creates an electrical field by causing electrons to flow through a wire; and similarly, electrons flowing through a wire create a magnetic field about it."

"That's simple?"

"Well, it's like if you dip a stick in flowing water, the water will make the stick move. But if you have still water and churn it with a stick, the motion makes the water flow. It's the same thing, only the circumstances dictate which gives the energy and which receives. Our gloomy magus down below says that electromagnetic energy exists in the form of waves with both an electric component and a magnetic component; there's no such thing as a wave with only the one. It's like cloth—if you tug at the warp, you're yanking at the woof as well. So it's very easy to convert energy from the one to the other. And of course I enjoy the figures."

Like many a merchant's daughter, Margarete had been

taught by her mother enough calculation to run the business in her parents' absence. Unlike many, the skill delighted her for its own sake. She had wheedled her father into revealing to her the secrets of multiplication and long division, and been terribly disappointed when he assured her that she had exhausted the subject and there were no further arithmetics waiting to be discovered.

So the way Faust's equations tumbled and danced was a revelation to Margarete. They had a kind of soaring mental beauty that was comparable only to the feeling one got in church after praying so hard and well that one forgot one's self completely and the exultant soul rose up and expanded to fill the building.

"But if you ask the larger question of exactly what these electromagnetic waves are and look like, and how they can be waves one instant and particles the next—that's beyond me. Oh! Have you heard? One of the lesser Behaims has been sending electrical pulses across a wire from his rooms to a friend's by the Ladies' Gate, and causing an electromagnet to click there."

"What earthly use is that?"

"He's devised a clicking and clacking kind of code and used it to send messages. The council sent out inspectors to verify that it's not trickery."

Sophia shook her head. "More marvels. It's a wonder any work is getting done at all."

"Look—he's doing it again." Below, Faust hurriedly bent back to his work again. Margarete stopped sewing and parked her needle in a pinch of cloth. "Honestly, I ought to rip open my blouse and shake out my breasts at him. He'd probably die of mortification right there on the spot."

"Margarete!" Sophia's hand flew to her mouth. "I can't believe what I'm hearing!"

"Oh, don't pay it any mind. That's just Gretchen speaking."

"Gretchen? Who's Gretchen?"

"I'm doing it again, aren't I? You've become so dear to me, I keep forgetting how little time you've spent with us." For a chill instant the ghosts of Sophia's parents breathed upon their necks. Margarete set aside the embroidery and, spreading her legs to make a lap, spilled the contents of the sewing basket into it. "I *will* find that thread," she muttered. Then, "Gretchen was my baby-name—'little Greta'—but when I was young, mother and father were always most careful to address me as Margarete when I'd done something praiseworthy. So that I'd equate good behavior with maturity, I suppose. But you know little children. I conceived a notion that they thought they had two daughters, and somehow hadn't realized there was only me.

"One year during Christmas season—I think I was five—I was chosen to be in the front rank of the lantern procession. Do they have that in Düsseldorf? It's quite a lovely thing. All the children are assembled at the Butcher's Bridge with fanciful lanterns atop tall poles. Mine was a snowflake with six arms. Then they march up to the castle, where they're given hot cider and small treats.

"Well. Everything went perfectly until we got to the castle's parade grounds and old Father Wolgemut—he's dead now—came out dressed as Saint Nicholas. He had a bishop's robes and miter and crozier, and a white woolen beard that went down to his knees. Nobody had warned me! He came straight toward me, laughing in what was supposed to be a jolly manner, and I was *terrified*! So I hit him."

"No!"

"Yes! With my lantern! It knocked off his miter. Then the snowflake fell apart, and the candle set fire to his beard."

"It didn't!"

"It did! *Whoosh!* It went up with a roar. But Father Wolgemut, who really was a dear, sweet man, didn't want to pull off the beard in front of the children and have them see he wasn't actually Saint Nicholas. So he began running about frantically, bellowing for somebody to throw water on his beard. Only they'd shoveled away all the snow for the procession and, the castle being the highest point in the city, there wasn't much water around.

"It was like a fool's-tale. Everybody was screaming and waving their arms and bumping into each other, and of course the children all panicked and were running about with their poles and lanterns, too. It's a miracle we didn't burn down the city. It just kept getting worse, until at last two soldiers simply picked up Father Wolgemut and doused him headfirst in a horse-trough."

Sophia was laughing so hard now that tears were running down both cheeks. She threw her embroidery up over her face and howled.

"My parents, of course, were terrified I'd be trampled in the panic, or else run away and hide someplace where I'd never be found. So they went charging into the mob, calling out, 'Margarete! Margarete!' Father lost his wolf-fur cap and Aunt Penniger—she was there, too—was knocked off her feet and got an enormous stain on her dress that she still hasn't stopped talking about today. Oh, it was chaos.

"Finally they found me standing exactly where I'd been when Saint Nicholas attacked me. I hadn't moved an inch. I looked up at them with my little chin trembling bravely and said, 'Gretchen did it!' "

"Oh, stop! I can't breathe."

"From then on, I would only answer to Margarete and never Gretchen. Because she was the bad girl. But I used to make up little stories to myself about her. Every morning I'd brush my hair, a hundred strokes on either side, like I was supposed to. Gretchen simply threw her brush out the window and let her hair go all tangles. I emptied the chamber pots and washed the floors. Gretchen emptied the pots *on* the floor. While I was in church, praying for her soul, she'd be stealing my jewelry. She dressed up in men's clothing and went places a girl couldn't. She broke things and got into fights. She was fearless. When she got older, she let boys put their hands up her skirts, though I don't suspect she had any clear idea what they were doing at first. It's been a while since I thought about Gretchen. She must be quite the little slut by now."

Item by item, the basket's contents were restored. But the green thread was not among them. Margarete sighed. "Sometimes," she said wistfully, "I wish that I could be Gretchen. Poor Margarete! She's a good girl who does all her chores without complaining. But Gretchen has all the fun. Sometimes I wish that I could—he's doing it again!"

"He is? I missed it."

Margarete gathered her skirts and stood. "I suppose we'd best go inside."

That was the summer when the pergola came down. It had gone up years before, when Margarete's father decided he could afford to move his warehousing elsewhere and convert the courtyard into a private garden. Her mother had supervised construction of the pergola over the arched carriageway and then, to amuse her husband, trained white roses up the one side and red up the other. Three years later, when the flowering vines finally met and entangled, it was Margarete who was given the honor of explaining to her father that they were reenacting the War of the Roses. He had laughed himself blue, then, and the incident had since become his favorite family story.

The carriageway had to be enlarged, though. The building through which it ran—its tenants had been ousted for an expansion of Faust's workshops—was propped up on jacks and reinforced. Workmen came to chop down, bundle, and cart away the roses. A temporary roof was then raised over the trampled earth of what had been the garden to shelter the smiths and foundry-men laboring there to build a black iron dragon of a machine that they called Locomotive.

Watching, silent, Margarete felt her childhood flitting away.

Through the first half of that long and magical summer, the Reinhardts held a series of evening and afternoon parties under the roses, at which Faust unveiled wonder after wonder. He demonstrated his magic lantern device, which utilized an electric arc light and a series of glass slides upon which Albrecht Dürer himself had been commissioned to paint perspectives of the city, exotic foreign animals, the Nativity, a skeletal Death in conversation with a knight, and a quite striking portrait of Faust himself. Through a cunning optical arrangement, the pictures were thrown up, magnified, upon a wall newly whitewashed for this purpose. Afterwards Faust gave a lecture on a scheme for making these pictures move, as if alive, that dazzled and befuddled all who heard it.

Another time he introduced his sewing-machine. A pretty

young seamstress, all ribboned silk and Dresden-doll porcelain skin, had been engaged to demonstrate its use. Pumping the treadle with one slim foot, she sewed together the pieces for a handsome velvet suit in a fraction of the time true sewing required. At the end of the evening Margarete's father went inside to don the suit and emerged amid applause to delightedly pronounce it a perfect fit. Sophia opined that there was something sinful in this new device, that it would lead to vanity and opulence. But "It's no worse than being rich," Margarete said thoughtfully, "and having other people do all your sewing."

Money was everywhere that season. Herr Reinhardt bought a walled garden twice the size of the courtyard, so the parties could continue uninterrupted. It had a fountain and roses as well, bigger ones than Margarete had ever been able to grow, though she did not like them half so well as her own.

Thus it was that, thinking back on it later, Margarete was never sure whether it was in this garden or the other that the midsummer's eve gathering had been held. Faust's primary revelation that afternoon was the ice-box. It was a deceptively simple invention consisting of an insulated cabinet with several shelves for food, a place for a large block of ice, and a drip pan which had to be emptied twice daily.

"But there's no money in it!" her father had objected upon its unveiling. "Anyway, what's the point of a box that keeps food cold?!" Several of the portly distinguished men present nodded agreement; Margarete had observed that they were only truly satisfied with Faust's revelations when they had a clear military application. None of them appeared to notice the quick glances the women threw one another.

"Who's going to buy such a thing?" a foundry-master asked rhetorically.

"I would," Frau Reinhardt said firmly and to her husband's obvious astonishment. "If the ice were readily available."

"That's already arranged!" Faust cried. "Farmers, you know, often harvest ice from their ponds during the winter and pack it in sawdust-lined pits for summer storage. Last winter, I persuaded one to expand his operation. He has agreed to bring in a wagon-load a week. I'm afraid that will limit our production at first—I could convince him to no more—but when they see the profits to be made, other farmers will want to get in on the business. Come spring we can begin selling in earnest. By summer every housewife in Nuremberg will want a box. By fall she will be a discontented woman indeed who does not have one."

As he talked, Wagner, his fanatically humorless assistant, sat at a distance endlessly cranking a secondary invention. "Do you have any idea what that young spindle-shanks is laboring at?" Aunt Penniger asked out of the corner of her mouth.

"I saw him pour in cream earlier," Margarete said doubtfully.

"Maybe it's a new variety of butter-churn," Sophia hazarded.

"There's ice involved, too. See how he shifts the tub? That's because it's cold."

"Who invited the English spy? Does your father know he's here?" Aunt Penniger said suddenly. And, lowering her voice to a conspiratorial whisper, "Be sure to watch to see who he leaves with."

"Now, who would he leave with?" Margarete asked, amused.

"A woman, of course. He's a long way from home, after

all. I know how men are when there's nobody to keep an eye on them. I myself remember . . ." Her voice trailed off.

"Go on," Sophia urged her.

"No, no—it's not a fit tale for ears as young as yours."

Aunt Penniger loved to imply for herself a romantic past; she was that sort of innocent much given to the manufacture of old affairs from the flimsiest and least promising of materials. On a winter's eve, when her nieces were indulgent and the kitchen fire was burning low, she would fill its ashes and embers with enough soldiers, priests, and dashing adventurers jilted, spurned, and surrendered to, to make her the wickedest woman in all of Christendom.

"Wagner's turning grey," Margarete said.

"He's certainly working hard," Sophia agreed.

"If it is a butter-churn," Aunt Penniger sniffed, "I don't want one. It's easily as much work as the old."

Now Faust went to his assistant and opened up the tub, as he had several times earlier, and this time decided its contents were ready. "Ladies! Ladies! Gather around!" he cried. "Gentlemen too—but let the ladies have the closer places. Come all, and see!"

The party coalesced upon him, women inward, men on the outside, trying not to look curious. Herr Reinhardt stood churlishly aloof, talking with two Dominicans. He glanced once over his shoulder at the gathering and scowled.

All in a flash, Margarete saw her father anew: saw first that he was jealous of his master artificer's successes, then that he was angered by Faust's unsubtle treatment of him as an intellectual inferior, and finally that he resented this characterization all the more for its being true. A sudden giddiness came over her, like the suicide's abrupt realization after she's stepped off the cliff that there's no ground beneath her feet,

and no undoing that rash act. Once thought, it could not be
denied.

Margarete's love for her father remained constant as ever.
But he had dwindled in her estimation.

A cool wisp of steam rose from the open tub. Flourishing
a silver spoon he had earlier borrowed from Frau Reinhardt,
the master engineer dug into the contents, emerging with
something white and firmly textured.

"I shall need a volunteer. You . . . you . . ." The spoon
floated high to dip toward first old Pirckheimer's young Heidi,
then toward Sophia, who flushed with quick embarrassment.
"Or you." It came to rest pointing at Margarete.

Faust thrust the spoon toward her lips. "Open your mouth
and close your eyes," he said playfully. Then, when she had
reluctantly obeyed, "Now taste."

Margarete closed her mouth upon something cold, smooth,
incredibly delicious. Her eyes opened wide.

Faust chuckled. "It's called ice cream."

The ladies, seeing her reaction to the new confection,
pushed forward, clamoring for their own tastes. Sophia was
jostled and shoved away from Faust's hovering spoon and
fetched up against his assistant's knees, which still clutched
the device. Dimpling impishly, she dipped two fingers into
the tub to scoop up a taste of the sweet.

But before she could snitch any, Wagner seized her wrist
and solemnly shook his head no.

With a crisp swirl of skirts, she turned her back on him.

"Naughty, naughty," Margarete said teasingly. "What
would Father Imhoff say if he saw you try that?"

In a fury, Sophia rounded on her. "Oh, it's easy enough
for some people! They're never poor, or plain, or at a loss for
what to say. Men fall out of the trees at their feet. Their hair

is always perfect, and they never have crooked teeth. Their parents never die!"

In tears, she fled the garden.

Margarete stood frozen with astonishment.

The English spy, Will Wycliffe, chose that precise and inconvenient instant to approach her. "At last, Fraulein Rainhard," he said in his famously odd accent, "an innovation simple enough that even I can understand it—I mean the icebox, of course. You don't suppose your father would be offended if I wrote a description of it back home to my wife? So she could have one made. She'd be ever so pleased with me for doing so, I think—and that's a rare situation for an old married man to find himself in."

"I very much doubt that my father would object," Margarete said distractedly. The garden gate slammed. She could not see which way Sophia had gone.

"That's quite kind of you." Wycliffe took Margarete's arm and led her a few paces away, out of casual earshot of the other partygoers. "There's something else I've had in mind, but didn't want to bother your father over. He's such a busy man, everybody always wanting his help with this or that, it's a wonder he has any time for his family at all. But I'd dearly love to see his new factory, you know. Not that I'd know one end from the other, mind, but everybody speaks of it so. Perhaps you could—"

Margarete drew herself back from him. "Surely you're not suggesting," she said, "that I go there alone with you."

"No, no!" Wycliffe raised shocked hands in protest. "I'm not suggesting anything improper. Of course you couldn't take me there, the two of us alone. Heaven forfend. But if you were to lend me the key, I could nip over and have a quick peek. I wouldn't disturb a thing, I swear, and I'd have the key back to you in a blink."

Straightening into her most witheringly formal posture, Margarete said, "You'll have to speak with my father about that."

"Ah, well," Wycliffe said, "you can't blame a man for trying, now can you?" He gave her a wink and a smile so wry and roguish and self-mocking all at once that Margarete immediately forgave him everything. He was an old scamp, but there was no real harm in him. "And I really do admire your father, you know. He's a good fellow, solid stuff, backbone of his country. He'd be right at home in London." Softly then, as if talking to himself, he said, "But this inventor-man of yours, he's something quite remarkable. I can't imagine where he came from. Something of a prodigy, innee? Like a chimera or a comet in human form. I shouldn't be surprised he's one of the great men of the age."

"Yes, that may very well be. Everyone says he's a great man." Margarete's voice grew thoughtful as well. "But, you know, sometimes I think that he may not be a very *good* man."

That same summer, to demonstrate his steam engine, Faust had a great wooden wheel erected in the new garden, with swings set regularly about it upon which one might sit and be swung up into the peaceful sky, as high as a church steeple and then back down again.

Margarete loved the wheel. She went on it as often as she was allowed.

On its first day the wheel's riders went up without regard for age or gender, so that the laughter of couples both married and not was to be heard over half the parish. But then the young men realized how naturally a reassuring arm could be placed about a girl on the sudden, giddy elevation, and a swift kiss stolen at the top where, briefly, all was serenity and an unexpectedly buoyant floating sort of sensation, as if the riders had stepped for an instant outside the world and all its obligations. So the Dominicans intervened, decrying the invention as a hazard to the public morals and demanding that women not be allowed on it. An angry delegation from the convent of Saint Clara quickly put an end to *that*, however, and it was decided that simply segregating the sexes would suffice.

Then it was discovered that while the young ladies were being hoisted into the air, rude boys would stand underneath looking up, hoping for a glimpse of something forbidden. So an officer from the castle was assigned to stand guard with drawn sword to keep the rascals at a distance, a service that was regarded by the young ladies themselves with mingled gratitude and disdain.

On the wheel's third day, Margarete went up with Aunt Penniger. Margarete sat first. While her aunt was being helped onto the swing by a serious-faced monk, she glanced upward, at the very top of the wheel. There she saw, as the monk did not, a girl no older than herself, drawing the attention of the boys by kicking her skirts in a way that deliberately flirted with immodesty. She was as laughing and wild as Gretchen herself. Margarete sighed and crossed her ankles over a fold of her dress as the Dominican directed and, with a muttered word of caution and an abrupt mechanical jerk, was swung halfway up the wheel.

Aunt Penniger shrieked on the upswing and immediately closed both eyes tight. Turning, she clutched at Margarete with strong, bony fingers tight as pincers, and buried her face in the girl's side.

"Do you want me to wave for the monk to stop the wheel and let you off?" Margarete asked anxiously.

"No!" her aunt gasped. "No, I'll just keep my eyes closed." The wheel swung them abruptly down, and she shrieked again. "It's not that bad, really."

Margarete prised her arm from between their bodies and gently, lovingly, stroked her aunt's dry old hair. She was a tiny woman, and comforting her thus gave Margarete a taste of what motherhood must be like. Her heart went out entirely to this small, needy, and good-hearted creature.

It was so pleasant up here! Up she went, high into the cool air and then swooshing down again. She couldn't help but feel happy. All the neighborhood spread itself out before her, as bright and variegated as a patchwork quilt. Then down.

"We have to talk." Aunt Penniger spoke into Margarete's shoulder. Her voice was muffled and indistinct.

"What?"

"Talk! You girls are coming to an age when we have to find you husbands. You know that, don't you?"

"I—I suppose I do." The wheel went sliding down again, and Aunt Penniger's fingers clenched spasmodically. Margarete would have bruises in the morning, for sure.

"Tell me. Do you think Faust would make a good husband?"

Down went the wheel, and Margarete's stomach with it. Marry Faust? Despite everything, she had never seriously considered the possibility. Not that he was too old—ten years was not an unreasonable weight of authority for a husband to possess—but that he was too . . . strange. Too intimidating. Faust seemed to her not so much a man as a force of nature—a storm, or volcano, or a tidal wave. "Father's not exactly fond of him, is he?" she said cautiously.

"He may not have the choice," Aunt Penniger said. "Oh!" she squeaked. Then: "But if not Faust, then *some*body must be arranged for Sophia, and quickly."

"Sophia?"

The wheel went sweeping up. It was not an improvement.

"I don't know if you've noticed how changeable she is lately. Disobedient, sulky, given to sudden and inappropriate bursts of anger or tears, forever mooning about Faust's workshops. Oh, I know the symptoms only too well. I remember, when I was young . . . well, no matter. A match must be made, and soon. Or there'll be trouble."

"Auntie, I confess I haven't seen as much odd behavior from her as you have."

Her aunt peered up at her from between folds of bunched cloth. It was like looking down into a hermit crab's shell at the twin gleams of its eye-stalks. "Well, of course. You two are like sisters, naturally she'd hide it from you. Me, I'm only a foolish old lady—so *she* thinks. Nobody takes me seriously, and I see a lot as a result. You'd be surprised how much I see."

At the very top, the wheel paused, swinging lightly, while riders below debarked and were replaced. A lively tune, played on drum and sackbut, floated up from the musicians her father had engaged to keep those waiting in line amused. It helped disguise the thumping, clattering, and groaning noise of the engine.

She saw Faust's unsmiling assistant, Wagner, hurry by below, head down and shoulders hunched with concentration. Like master, like servant, she thought. The wheel swung Margarete away.

"How do you know it's Faust? Did she tell you?"

"Tell me? Nobody tells me anything. But it's obvious

enough, I should think. Just yesterday, I called for her to take a loaf of bread and some cheese over to Faust and his assistant for their lunch. She came into the room dragging her feet, glowering, sighing with exasperation. But when I told her the errand, oh! how she brightened. She practically skipped, she was so anxious to see him again. Then she returned too quickly to have gotten anything more than a nod and a grunt of thanks—you know how men are—and one would have thought her life was over, her face was so dark and despairing. You tell me. And Tuesday! Last Tuesday—"

As Aunt Penniger prattled, the wheel swung them both to the top again. Margarete saw Wagner stop abruptly as Sophia stepped in front of him, hands on hips. They swung down again.

Like a dumb-show, the story unfolded in a series of still images, one for every topping of the wheel. On the second turn, Wagner had his hands spread out in an attitude of astonishment and protested innocence. On the third, Sophia reached out as if to slap him, but on the fourth it was clear that she had merely tapped him on the cheek. Then she had turned and was striding angrily away. He ran after her. She turned upon him, angry again. He stepped back. She took his hand. She released it. He stepped forward. She turned to leave. He hurried after her.

They were gone.

"What a fool I am," Margarete muttered to herself. But she smiled when she said it, and she uncrossed her ankles and kicked her legs ever so slightly when next she reached the top.

For a week the Great Wheel whirled the citizens of Nuremberg around and around—and then it was down. When Margarete went, fuming, to demand that Faust explain why, he was waiting for her. He stood solemn and still in his silent workshop.

She stopped, nonplussed. "Where is everybody?" she asked. Meaning the artisans and noisemakers, the ambitious young men and avaricious old ones, the flock of interchangeable hangers-on.

"I sent them away," Faust said. Then, politely, "What was it you came to ask?"

"The wheel," she said, and somehow all her outraged anger had dissolved in the uncanny quiet of the shop, so that her voice sounded small and forlorn. "Why did you take it down?"

"It was the stresses," he said in a distracted way. "The wheel should have been made of iron, really, but the foundries aren't yet geared up for that level of production. I knew from the beginning that wood wouldn't serve for long. If I hadn't had the wheel taken down, one of the struts would have broken. People would have been injured, killed—and who would trust my engines then?"

He fell silent. For a long still moment neither of them dared speak. When he looked up, his eyes bored into hers.

"Margarete," he said. It was the first time he had addressed her by her Christian name; always before it had been Fraulein Reinhardt. "I must speak seriously to you."

He drew up a chair for her and, a little nervously, she composed herself upon it.

Faust took her hands in his. He crouched down by the side of the chair, so that he was looking up into her eyes. His face was open and vulnerable; there was infinite tenderness in it, and a yearning ache that made her heart go out to him. One kiss, she reprimanded herself. No more. One kiss for Gretchen and that was all.

"You and your parents must leave the city."

"What?"

"Your father will not listen to me. Well, who can blame him? He has seen and heard too many new things; his capacity for belief has been strained to the utmost. If I urged him away, he would laugh in my face.

"But if his only daughter had a dream . . . if she woke up with a cry in the middle of the night and said that an angel had appeared to her with a fiery sword and demanded that she and her family leave Nuremberg . . . The first time, he would not believe it a true portent. The second, he would wonder and doubt. Three nights, however, ought to do the trick. I know how it goes against your every instinct to lie, much less to your own father. But this is to save his life."

"But why?"

"There is a pathogenic organism in the ground-water. Its effects will be felt within the week. Your father has property in the country, friends in the Palatinate, business in Prussia— any of these would be an excellent destination. The further the better. But wherever you go, you must boil your water before you drink it. There'll be other refugees, and some of them will be vectors themselves; you're not entirely safe anywhere. Best if you boil the wash-water first as well; the bacteria can be carried to the mouth by a touch of the hand."

"I don't understand," Margarete said. "What are you talking about?"

"Plague."

9

THE PLAGUE KITCHEN

How changed was Nuremberg!

The smoke from the fires of pitch and faggots set evenly down the streets, one for every dozen houses, made a foul and choking miasma of the air. The stench of sulfur fumigations harried the nose. The flames cast alarming shadows upon the soot-blackened walls. Their heat contrasted strangely with the October chill.

In the marketplace, butchers stood at their neglected stands with bowls of vinegar into which buyers might drop the coins the merchants dared not touch. Dog-killers with their red staves and body-searchers with their white gave each other nods and a wide berth in passing. A pair of friars, given Papal dispensation to perform the sacrament of extreme unction until the priests returned, carried gonfalons with an embroidered Virgin and a Bleeding Heart on long poles. Only their eyes showed beneath their cowls and above the herb-filled leather cones they wore to protect from contagion. They were terrifying to see, like long-beaked servitors of Beelzebub.

Grass grew in the streets.

Strangest of all was the silence. Despite the clatter of staves and crackle of flames, the city was as quiet as a country meadow. Half the citizens—those with money or desperation enough—had fled into the country, and taken with them all of the horses. The rattling of wagons and trampling of hooves that in normal times filled the ear were absent. Faust could hear sparrows fluttering about the rooftops, and the whisper of a breeze over the slates.

White bills had been pasted on the shuttered fronts of the ribbon-makers' and lace-merchants' and chair-caners' shops. Handing the donkey's reins to Wagner, Faust went to read one.

THE ONLY TRUE PLAGUE-WATER.

The eminent HOCHSALZER, *newly come from the Low Lands where he cured thousands of sufferers during the great misery in Amsterdam last year, offers an universal preventative for the current pestilence, along with never-failing spells and cantrips for those already afflicted, as well as a simple recipe for making cheese from chalk.*

"Who is this whimsical creature?" Faust snorted.

They left the plaza.

Faust paused in his rounds to talk with a watchman. He was a gnarled old creature whose face well betokened the lack of intellectual fire within. At his belt hung a heavy ring of keys for those houses that had been left in his care. He collected a fee for this service, another for overseeing the houses that had been quarantined and boarded up, and yet another for fetching bread, cheese, butter, and beer for those who had shut themselves away from the world until the general sickness abated. This in addition to the city stipend for tending the fires. The plague had been generous to him.

"Good day, friend Charon!" Faust said heartily, extending a penny. "How many fares have you collected today?"

The old man scowled in puzzlement—Wagner had several times explained the joke to him, but it never took—and then dutifully laughed. The penny disappeared into a pocket of his new greatcoat. It was a heavy garment of English wool, so overlarge for him that it brushed the tops of his boots, but with two rows of bright brass buttons. "Five, sir, four of them from that crook-chimneyed house, a family with two young girls it was, very sad indeed. I heard the mother screaming yesterday when she discovered her children stricken. The father sent me first for medications and then for water, most distracted, saying the wife was struck down, too."

"Where did you go for water? Outside of the neighborhood?"

"No, sir, there's a well just around the corner."

"Go on."

"So quick was the progress of the disease that when I got back with the buckets, there was no answer to my banging. I could only conclude that the father was ill as well. There was nothing to do but send for the body-searcher and notify the bellman when the dead-cart came by last night."

"Most commendable," Faust said dryly. "And the other?"

"A gentleman, in the fine house to the corner. The woman as sees for him came by this morning and was warned away by him, through the door. She told me straight he'd been taken ill, and so I nailed up his lower windows and padlocked the doors. Will you be going in?"

"Yes, unlock it for me, please."

On the door was a newly posted broadside:

A SOVEREIGN CURE FOR ALL ILLNESSES.

The Sweating Sickness, Influenza, Black Death, Saint Vitus's Dance, Bubonic Plague, French Pox, Small Pox, Red Pox, Baby Pox, Demonic Possession, and Falling Sickness, all have been cured through the miraculous intercession of the renowned HOCHSALZER, *newly arrived from Naples, who also offers candles for impotence and the discovery of buried treasures.*

Old Charon undid the padlock. The bill, which had been pasted across the jamb, tore away as the door was opened.

Faust went back to the corner where Wagner waited with the donkey-cart. "Four in the house with the chimney and another in the one at the corner."

Wagner shifted his bottles from one shoulder to the other, leaned the stretcher bundle against a nearby wall, removed the ledger from his belt, and with a slim lead stylus made two neat entries. "This is the house of the English spy," he commented.

Not listening, Faust muttered, "Five cases in a street where there should be none. It baffles me."

(Mephistopheles grinned mockingly and said nothing.)

They went in. The ground floor was a shambles. Cupboards had been splintered, furniture overturned, clothes strewn about.

Wagner looked shocked. "Who would have—?"

"Why, who else but the housekeeper? The watchman was

wearing a London-cut coat. Doubtless it was her bribe that she be let pass, rather than be boarded up with her master. And as long as she was robbing him, why stop at clothing?"

The bedchamber stank as only a sickroom could, of excrement and hopelessness, of vomit and despair. It contained a few opened chests and a narrow bed. Within the latter lay the Englishman, Will Wycliffe, as pale as ashes. His cheeks were sunken, his face as stiff as fossil ivory. The only color to him came from his flaming red hair. The sheets were badly soiled.

Wagner wrinkled his nose but said nothing. He unhooked one bottle and poured out a cup of water.

Wycliffe's head stirred. "Is somebody here?" he asked weakly. "Please tell me it's not more dreams. I saw a horned fiend leaning over me, and laughing, laughing . . ."

"It's Doctor Faustus," Wagner said. "He'll soon have you well." Placing a hand behind the man's head, he brought the cup to Wycliffe's lips.

"Doctor Foster is it?" Wycliffe said when he had drunk. "Well, Doctor, I'll not detain you long. Good of you to come by, and I'm grateful for the water. But you needn't bother tomorrow. I'll be gone by then."

"Nonsense!" Faust said. "You'll be up and breaking into factories within the week." Wagner refilled the cup from his second flask. "Drink this. The wine contains an antibiotic. It and rehydration are all that you require."

Wycliffe obeyed, and made a face. "Pfaugh! This tastes fouler than Herr Hochsalzer's plague-water."

"Quacksalver again! I find this mosquito less and less amusing."

The Englishman quirked his mouth slightly. "You have a Christian name, Foster?"

"That's *Faustus*," Wagner said sternly. "Magister Johannes

Wilhelm Faustus!" He unlaced the stretcher—a simple thing
made of canvas and two poles—and laid it out on the floor
by the bed.

"Too much Latin for my ignorant head. I'll call you Jack,
if you don't mind."

"No," said Faust, amused in equal parts by the man's pre-
sumption and by Wagner's scandalized expression. "I don't
mind at all."

Together they lifted the spy from his bed and onto the
stretcher. He cried out in pain once, and then was silent. By
the time they had jigged and levered him down the stairs, he
had lapsed into unconsciousness.

There was a ripping noise when the door opened. Somebody had pasted a fresh bill across it. ETERNAL HEALTH AND
LONG—began one scrap and—EVITY the other. When they had
laid Wycliffe in the straw of the cart, Faust went back and tore
down the fragments. They concluded with the words—*a new
system for teaching cows to dance.*

Angrily, he waved the bill in the watchman's face. "Did
Quacksalver have the gall to post this nonsense while I was
inside?"

"You just missed him, sir. A most imposing man with a
lively smile and a hat *this* wide, who has cured thousands in
Paris and—"

"Paris be fucked! Where are his Nurembergish cures, if his
methods work? Who will speak in his praise and say, 'Yes,
the noble Quacksalver has restored me from the brink of the
grave?' 'I was laid low and he brought me forth!' 'My body,
which was shriveled, is now made whole and hale.' 'The bells
were rung for me and yet here I stand!' Where are those myriad testimonials? Not here nor anywhere near. They must be

sought in distant realms, in Amsterdam, in Naples, in Paris— or in Hell!"

"But it could be true, sir! It could be true!" The watchman's hand slipped inside his new greatcoat to clutch at something hung on a string about his neck.

"What's that you have, you scoundrel?" Faust forced open the hand, and then the locket revealed therein. Inside was a scrap of parchment. Unfolded, it revealed a triangle of words starting with ABRAXIS and then removing a letter with each line until the progression passed A and vanished:

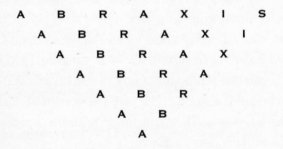

```
A    B    R    A    X    I    S
  A    B    R    A    X    I
    A    B    R    A    X
      A    B    R    A
        A    B    R
          A    B
            A
```

"How much did you pay for this flummery?"

"Nothing! It was a gift from the great Hochsalzer for recommending his tonic to my wards."

"Idiot!" Faust threw the crumpled bill into the fire and the locket after it. Then he bunched the man's shirt in his fist, and spoke fiercely into his terrified face: "I'll give you a charm worth a thousand of Quacksalver's. *Burn this jacket!* And next time wash your hands after robbing the dead."

Crossing himself frantically, the watchman fell back from him. Faust in his turn stormed away, pausing only once to roar over his shoulder, "Be sure to scrub beneath the nails!"

In the cart, Wycliffe suddenly convulsed. "No!" he screamed. "Lord, defend me from his laughter, protect me from his teeth!" His hands rose like talons toward his eyes. Wagner fought them down and, with Faust's help, lashed them to his side. "I am licked by the tongues of Hell, its black dogs crouch about me, grinning. How my gut aches. His teeth!"

Wycliffe railed about demons all the way to the convent.

The only jolly place in all the city was the plague kitchen in the convent of Saint Catherine.

Faces aglow with excitement and the heat, the sisters of Saint Catherine boiled water for drinking and cooked up gruel and apple sauce by the cauldron-load for their patients. The smells of apples, oats, and oak mingled with baking bread and fresh laundry being carried through from the drying sheds. Some twenty nuns toiled there, and for all the seriousness of their labor, it was a kitchen and they were women. There was joy in the air.

(Proof, if any were needed) said Mephistopheles (that true happiness comes only from the satisfaction of being more virtuous than your rivals and certain that the bastards know it.)

"Magister Faustus." Mother Sacred Bondage of Christ, a formidable administrator and by repute a dangerous woman to cross, sailed out from the infirmary. In her tow was a plump and somewhat homely nun. "I want you to meet a new member of our order."

"A new one?" Faust said, astonished. "When most of the best families have fled, and those which remain are in hiding?"

"We have had several converts in recent weeks," Mother Bondage said with prim satisfaction. "All from the Clares."

"Ahhhh."

The Clares had turned Faust away. He had known they would, but he wanted it public that he had tried. They had a hospital, as the Catherines did not, and this fact made them his logical allies. However, they were too vested in the old ways to ever submit to his authority. So, knowing in advance that he could not win over their mother superior, Faust had neither toiled to make his arguments convincing, nor spared her feelings on the way out. He said such words as would ensure that when she saw how well his methods worked, she would yet disdain to imitate them. "They will serve excellently as our control group," he assured Wagner.

Mother Bondage, however, had given Faust an hour and let him take the afternoon. He brought his new binocular microscope into her office and began by revealing to her a garden of unearthly delights: delicate fronds and articulated spheres, pulsing and translucent animalcules that frolicked in the warm ocean of a water drop. She studied volvox, glowing like green glass; slipper-shaped and bluish paramecia; freshwater cilicates like carnivorous trumpets; rotifers, transparent with brightly colored organs and circles of cilia spinning about their funnel-shaped mouths like wheels; and delicately ornamented diatoms formed into circles, leaves, hourglasses, and every imaginable whimsy. Then, when he knew she was entranced, he showed her the vibrio bacterium with its quick, darting motion. "This," he said, "is the snake in our garden, and the cause of the current pestilence."

Thick curtains had been drawn so that only a sliver of light reached the microscope. Mother Bondage leaned into it with a faint crackle of starched cloth. Within the circle of light the dust-mote creatures swarmed, thick as bees, tumbling by each other in twisting spirals like so many bubbles. Though mindless, the less-than-tadpoles yet seemed purposeful, for they were tireless in their random movements. She studied the Beast solemnly, clearly trying to divine its essential evil.

Then Faust brought out his final slide, saying, "This is the organism which will elaborate its cure."

At this point Mother Bondage knew enough to grant him his request. But he did not make it yet. "This is a seduction," Mephistopheles had advised him. "Be patient. You must not ask her for anything which she has not already decided to give you."

Instead, therefore, he spoke to her of the taxonomy of microorganisms and the pathology of disease. He explained the spread of an epidemic by contamination, contagion, and animal vectors. He laid out those methods by which its sources could be identified and isolated. Then he discussed hygiene and the basic principles of nursing. He touched lightly upon vaccination. He listened to her questions and answered them without condescension. The day grew quiet and the light faded from the sky.

When he was done, Mother Bondage closed her eyes for a moment of silent prayer, and then promised her complete and unstinting support to the last penny and lady of the convent.

So it was that the Catherines poured water and spooned gruel, while the Clares prayed for the intercession of the saints. The Catherines changed sheets. The Clares practiced mortification of the flesh. The Catherines employed antibiotics. The Clares made a public display of a kneecap of their patron saint.

It was soon widely known to which hospital one went to get well, and to which one went to die.

"Sister Pelagia the Penitent's father is an apothecary," Mother Bondage said. "I feel she could be aptly put to work preparing the antibiotic."

(To say nothing of spreading rumors) said Mephistopheles. (The dear lady is the shrillest gossip in Germany. Confide to her a secret and by Monday-week, it will be old news in the court of the Chinese Emperor.)

"It will be my pleasure." Faust took over the young nun and directed her attention to the ovens, where loaves of fresh-baked bread were being taken out, torn apart, and stuffed into glass bottles. "The first step," he said, "is to boil the bottles. They must be sterile because the bread serves as a medium for our mold culture. Once the bottles are cooled and the bread stuffed, they are inoculated by Sister Mary Magdalen."

A sturgeon-faced and bespectacled nun sitting at a nearby table looked up to nod a sour greeting, then bent back to her work. Before her was a large dish containing a mound of bread overgrown with blue-green fluff. Deftly, she drew a speck of the stuff upon a knitting needle, which she then stuffed deep into a bread-filled bottle. "The mold you see is *Streptomyces fausti*, a microscopic soil fungus."

Sister Eva lightly corked each newly inoculated bottle and set it upon a shelf near the ovens. There were many shelves, all thronged with bottles. "The organism needs a warm place to multiply and grow—where better than here?"

"I . . . see." It was obvious Sister Pelagia found the process nonsensical; equally obvious that she was determined to master it. Faust directed her attention to the next step.

Sister Giulietta Heloise was going down the lines of bottles where the mold had grown thick, holding each to the light and examining it closely. Some she put back and some she set aside. Faust picked up one of these latter. "Look closely. See how on the fluff, golden droplets of liquid, like dew, have formed?" He held it up, waited for her nod. "This is our medication."

"What is it?"

"War," said Faust, "is universal—so implicit in nature that, indeed, without it life would not be possible. You doubt me? I assure you that even fungi fight wars, in the soil beneath your feet. They battle each other for territory, for dominance, for room in which to grow. Which ancient combat has been going on so long that the fungi have learned to create weapons. This golden dew is one such, a chemical poison lethal to its rivals. By good fortune it is also lethal to *our* enemy."

At Faust's direction, Sister Pelagia uncorked the bottle with its precious dew and filled it to the neck with wine. "Excellent!" Faust cried. She flushed with pleasure. "Now recork it and set it aside to settle. From those which have already settled, the wine is poured off to be given to the afflicted in measured doses. A pint a day is generally sufficient. That and constant rehydration are enough to keep anyone alive."

The plump young nun's eyes shone. "It seems so simple."

"Indeed it does. That is because the fungus has already done the complicated work of distillation. Wagner!"

His assistant wordlessly produced a sheet of paper and the lead stylus. Faust quickly jotted upon the one with the other: *4-dimethylamino-1,4,4α,5,5α,6,11,12α-octahydro-3,6,10,12,12α-pentahydroxy-6-methyl-1,11,-dioxo-2-napthacenecarboxamide.* "This is the simplest possible way of expressing the chemical structure of the elaboration products. Quite an eyeful, eh?"

Wordlessly, Sister Pelagia nodded.

(Sister Anne stole a hairbrush last night) Mephistopheles said (for the thrill. A trifle really; its loss was almost immediately forgotten. Yet a convent is a hotbed of spite and jealousy; it would destroy her if it came out. Take her out back of the laundry sheds and tell her you know. She'll cry. You may have to slap her once or twice. But she'll let you prod such orifices as you may desire.)

Faust ignored him.

The shadow shifted uneasily from the corner of one eye to a place just out of sight of the other. (Don't delude yourself. These nuns are all wantons. Sometimes at night Sister Gehenna will take out a fat devotional candle and—)

"Have you ever heard," Faust asked, "of a purported healer named Quacksalver?"

"Hochsalzer? Oh, yes. Everyone knows Hochsalzer. He has the most wonderful hat. He is wealthy, too. He bought some strong flavorings from my father and paid in gold from a purse as round as a baby's bottom. He is as active as a flea—now here, now there—and the people cheer him in the streets for his miraculous cures in Poland and Muscovy. They say he is the modern Asclepius. Yet I wonder, for he smiles constantly, and that is not a natural thing. He lives with a low woman named Brita Springindemrosen, who they say has had more husbands than fingers, and she having six fingers on the one hand. But I know very little about her origins."

(Miss Hopinthebushes once serviced five men at the same time. To accomplish this ingenious and athletic—)

Faust turned brusquely to address Sister Mary Magdalen. "I feel suddenly weary and in need of the sustenance of prayer. If the chapel is empty . . ."

The old nun put down her knitting needle. "Normally," she said, "men are not allowed on the second floor." Her face split in what could only be a smile. "But for you, Doctor, there are no rules."

A single rose window illumined the chapel. Faust knelt beneath it, and clasped his hands. Outside, the clouds parted, bathing him in a pure and holy light.

"Stop this pointless bantering," he said.

A shadow slipped away from the light, danced at the edge of his vision. "Why, Faust, you give me little enough to do these days. I need something to keep me occupied."

"I forbid you to harp upon the weaknesses of these ladies. I am not interested in the conquest of any woman but one alone."

"They would hardly dare speak of it afterwards."

"You do not understand the pure and innocent devotion I feel for Margarete."

"No, I do not. I do not understand your pure and innocent devotion because I don't believe in it. Are you telling me you don't want to fuck Margarete? Or are you telling me that her cunt is so holy that your cock must enter into it innocent of more profane organs? If so, do not your previous pleasures disqualify you from such pious congress?"

"Silence, mocker," Faust said wearily.

The shadow was still.

"How fares Margarete?" he asked after a time.

"Well enough. She thinks of you often and in a kind of sweet confusion, believing sometimes that she loves you and other times that she does not quite but could easily learn to and yet other times that she does but has misread your intentions abjectly. Your letters she reads once aloud to her parents in such a way that none could suspect her feelings, and then peruses repeatedly in private for such hidden expressions of passion as only her eyes could discover. Every day brings her closer to your arms."

"Why, this is good news indeed! I am surprised you would tell me it so readily."

"How so?"

"Your ill will toward me has not exactly been subtle."

"My hatred is too vast and all-embracing to focus itself upon you individually. Imagine yourself a single molecule within a vast Amazonian river of vomit. It hardly matters in which direction you dart, against the current or with it—the river will yet reach its destination. Despising the river, shall I care about the fate of that molecule? Be happy if you wish! Cure the sick if you will. Much good it will do you."

Wagner was waiting when Faust returned from the chapel. Together they went through the wards, observing and recording the progress of his patients.

The Catherines, lacking a hospital of their own, had given up the ground floor of the nunnery to the sick. They had, for decency's sake, kept women and men segregated. But this was the uttermost of their organization. The hospital was a warren of spaces, each one crammed so thickly and haphazardly with beds it was hard to pass from one room to another.

Doubly so for Faust.

His progress through the wards was less stroll than procession. Men fervently clasped his hands and cried down blessings from the saints. Women kissed his knuckles. Tears in eyes, they promised him Masses said, candles lit, and babies named in his honor. Extravagant indeed were their praises.

This was always the most gratifying part of Faust's day.

As always, though, he imagined the wards as they might be: with saline drips and electronic monitoring devices, with X-rays and CAT scans, with a ready supply of vital organs harvested and ready for transplant, with artificial blood enough to make up any natural lack. He saw a time when the human body might be catheterized, massaged, and kept alive however great the injury, however small the will to survive.

Will Wycliffe had a room of his own, though one wall was

of cloth and the others formerly the blind end of a hallway. Faust and Wagner squeezed within.

The redheaded Englishman was much improved. He smiled weakly when they walked up. "Good to see you, Jack. Clever chap, aren't you?"

Wagner sniffed.

"Some have called me so," Faust said, holding back a smile of his own.

"Well, Jack, I heard you were asking after this Hochsalzer fellow. One of the nuns told me. I know I don't look it, but I'm a man who can do well by his friends." He lowered his voice. "I don't know what he is to you. But if there's any serious trouble, well, I have certain lads in my employ who could . . ."

"Rest," said Faust. "Rest and get well. That is all I require of you."

For convenience, Faust had rented rooms at a tavern near the convent. Sometimes he slept there, sometimes in his workshop. It depended on where he was when weariness overtook him. Now he and Wagner went to the tavern to spread out their maps and add today's data to the week's cumulative total, placing a black dot of ink on the location of each new infection.

When they were done, Faust stared at the result for a long time.

"You seem unhappy, Magister," Wagner said cautiously.

Faust slammed fist into palm. "All this sickness stems from the well behind Saint Sebald's! From it and those wells downhill of it. I could cap them all myself and end the plague in an afternoon."

"Then why don't we?" Wagner asked eagerly. "We could—"

"Because it would not *prove* anything."

"We have maps for proof, all meticulously detailed."

"But they refuse to reveal a pattern. It ought to be simple. This dark stain spreads like a fan from Saint Sebald's. The wells below the church and within that darkness spread the contagion yet further. So far, simple. But then there ought not be any outbreaks on the other side of the Pegnitz, as there demonstrably are. The rich suffer as well as the poor, and this is a thing that passes all understanding. People sicken in all parts of the city—why? They do not go to the contaminated wells to drink, and it is certain the wells cannot go to them."

(Mephistopheles chuckled.)

"Cannot we simply remove those figures which draw the eye away from the polluted wells?"

"No! Science must prove itself. The data must be reproducible."

Wagner looked blank.

Exasperated, Faust said, "Anyone with a dead sister or father that was not marked on the map would know it immediately for a fraud and lie. The methodology is what matters, not the well or even a few hundred lives, but the self-evident proof that by this method diseases may be identified, tracked down, and cured. Our records must be scrupulous, whether they show what we want them to show or not."

He paused. "Perhaps we have been going about this wrong."

Taking up the sanding jar, Faust poured a small heap onto the map. With his knife he began moving and smoothing it. "Let us sand over those results which are as should be expected. Perhaps what remains—the inexplicable illnesses—will by themselves form a pattern."

They worked in silence.

"There is no discernible pattern at all," Wagner wearily said when they were done. "See—it is like a madman's dance through the town."

"A madman's . . ." Faust said softly. Then, explosively, "I've been a fool!"

(*Non disputandum est*.) The devil stepped at last into sight. He wore a fantastical hat of blue silk with a spray of cocks' feathers in the band, so wide it hid one eye and so high it bumped against the ceiling. There was lace about his throat. He grinned like a shark. (For once you speak truly.)

"I am hungry," Faust said energetically. "Let us retire downstairs for a meal. Beef, cabbage, beer—the best of everything. But first I must have a word with a nun whose name I have forgotten—the plump one, the apothecary's daughter."

"Pelagia the Penitent, you mean?"

"No," said Faust. "I mean Pelagia the gossip."

Not much later, in the common room, Faust explained. "See now the depth of human wickedness. It is the easiest thing in the world for a bold and daring rogue to break into the houses of the sick and dead and steal their possessions. How much bolder, however, to deliberately contaminate the healthy."

"No!"

"Yes. The adored Quacksalver. How little effort to put a touch of the excrement from an afflicted man into his plague-water. When his victims sicken, they send again for Quacksalver. He comes, and makes empty promises if they are still aware, and steals their gold if they are not."

"Look! It's a vulture!" somebody shouted.

"No, a jackal!"

"A vulture, I say!"

Faust turned. Four drunken men sprawled in a booth to the far side of the room. "It's only a doctor," said one scornfully.

"It's a bird of ill omen the sight of which strikes terror into honest men, and which grows fat off of carrion," sneered his fellow. "What's the difference?"

They boomed with laughter.

"Auerbach!" Faust cried. The lean taverner hurried to their table. "Who are these men?"

"I'm terribly sorry." Auerbach ran a nervous hand over his bald head. "I've tried speaking with these rascals, but they are beyond reason. Night after night they come here to drink and drive away what few respectable patrons remain to me. Please, let me carry your platters into a private room. There will be no charge."

"No, no, don't trouble yourself. I'll see to this matter." Faust cocked his head, listening. He stood.

The laughter died as he approached the railers. But they did not fear his wrath. Mouths smirking, scowling, cocked in half-grins, they waited to be entertained. Faust raised an accusing finger and pointed it at the loudest of the batch. "You! Herr Weisskopf. You will be the first to die. For all your boasting, for all your drinking, for all the charms sewn into the lining of your jacket—"

"How the devil did you know that?" the man said.

"—you will be the first to discover that you cannot hide from the plague. Tonight, when you have drunk enough to forget this conversation, you will stagger home and up the stairs. You will do as you always do: sling the bed clothes aside, give your wife a hearty slap on the rump, and cry, 'Your dilly-dander's home, old puss!' "

"Now, this is too much! Have you been spying on—?"

"She will not respond. She will not move. Her flesh will feel cold as marble. Then you will remember my words and with sudden dread bring closer your candle, and discover that the woman you left in perfect health this morning is dead.

"You will have two days before the sickness manifests itself on your body, but knowing as you will your fate, those two days will be for you a richly deserved Hell."

He rounded upon the second and most corpulent of the railers. "*You* will not forget my words. Which is why your blood will run cold tomorrow when you hear a banging on your door. It will be your dear friend Weisskopf, all in disarray, as distracted as a madman from grief and fear. You will bar the door against him. 'Good Henlein,' he will cry. 'I gave you aid in the matter of the Jewish widow. Help me now.' "

The portly man turned pale. "Nobody knows of that," he said. "Nobody!"

"Eventually he will go away. The irony is that, though you will shun Weisskopf, the contagion is already in your blood, and you will die but minutes after him—and by your own hand."

He turned to the third. "You, Burchard, are the hardest of this sorry lot."

The man screwed his face up impudently. "I thank you, sir."

"Which is why your lot will be the hardest. For as my predictions come true, you will turn more and more to drink and bravado. Tomorrow night, drunk and alone, you will go to peer into the pits of the dead."

"And why not?" scoffed the man. "A touch of death seasons life well, I think."

"In your arrogance, you will resolve to piss upon the corpses and thus show your disregard for death. As soon thought as unbuttoned and done. But while you are emptying your bladder you will step too close. The earth will crumble beneath your feet. You will fall in.

"Breaking an arm will be the least of your horrors. You will be trapped among the dead, unable to work your way free. By the time the grave-diggers come in the morning and haul you out, you will be cold sober, and a much wiser man. One who would benefit greatly from the experience if he had not already caught the contagion."

He turned then to the last man. "And you. You—"

The man shrank back from the approaching finger. But there was nowhere to go. The finger came inexorably on. His head slammed into the back of the booth. The finger lightly tapped the center of his forehead. Faust smiled. "You will live a long life and die in bed. Your children and grandchildren will be gathered around to hear your final blessing. Your friends should envy you."

Afterwards, as they left the tavern, Wagner blurted, "Magister! Was that really those men's futures you told them?"

"Eh?" Faust shrugged. "It is some men's futures. What matter if they belong to these poor fools or to others? It drove them away, and allowed us to eat in peace."

There was a full moon and a clear sky outside. The walk home would be pleasant. "Tomorrow," Faust said, "we will begin visiting all those locations which do not fit our pattern and determine which were patients of the renowned Quacksalver. All, or near enough, I am sure. When their names have been documented and stricken, what remains should fit our thesis within a standard deviation. Then our case will be proved."

"And then we can cap the wells?"

"Then we can cap the wells."

They passed by Hochsalzer's body not five streets from the tavern. It had been stripped naked and poured over with hot pitch, though whether before or after his death was difficult to determine, and then feathered over with his own handbills. The teeth had been kicked out of its grin to make room for a dead rat.

Wagner's step faltered at the gruesome sight, but Faust, who had been expecting something of the sort, strode firmly on. He could not mourn the death of such a man, no matter how lawless the actions of his victims' vengeful relatives.

Much to Wagner's scandal, Faust began to whistle.

It was wondrous what miracles a word in the ear of the right woman could accomplish.

THE SERMON

It was almost Easter, and the roads could be traveled again. All the world was promise and green shoots, dragonflies, and mud. Streams, gorged with water, leaped wildly down the mountainsides, joyfully collapsing banks and washing away bridges. Birds nested in the tangles of deadfall that February's storms had deposited on the wagon routes. Gnats rose in spirals over the reeds. New life was everywhere.

Margarete's heart *sang*.

Spring was like a return to the Garden after the purgatory of winter and Engelthal. It was there they had fled, where her father owned a house and a share in an orchard. There they had lived, purposeless among strangers, for half a dismal year. There the influenza had come upon the family like a wolf from the dark woods, taking the weakest lambs with it. Father was not fully recovered yet. Mother stayed ever at his side, while the hired wagoner cursed the horses and the roads, and the cart slowly bumped its way home.

When the walls and towers of Nuremberg rose up before them, grand and familiar all at once, Margarete's eyes filled with tears. The customs officer at the city gate waved them through, and into streets that ached with a thousand memories. Inexorably, she was put in mind of all who had died. Sophia. Agnes. Uncle Zieler and Aunt Zielerin. Great-Aunt Nützel. Old Reisterbeck who lived across the street and his boy Wilhelm. Young Biedermeier. The Saurzapfs. The Kressners. Valentin Sebold. It seemed like all the world was dead, and the buildings left behind for gravestones. She was almost surprised to see familiar faces on the street, to learn that people she knew yet lived.

Faust had not been at the gate to greet her.

Well, how was he to know? By the time the plague had run its course, there was not a person in Bavaria who doubted that Faust was the greatest man in all of Europe. Many, indeed, thought him the equal or better of such ancients as Aristotle, Cicero, and Hermes Trismegistus. At every inn and watering-stop on the road from Engelthal, Margarete had heard of his works, his charity, his fearlessness in the face of death. Had heard him praised as the one true ornament of this dim and lightless age.

The wagon pulled to a stop in front of the Reinhardts' house, and for a melancholy instant all was still. Then servants appeared out of nowhere. Neighbors shouted from windows and ran to help. There were tears and laughter, hugs, shrieks of happy disbelief. Doors slammed open. The street was suddenly full of workers and artisans. And flowers! Everywhere there were flowers, by the basket and armload. They were poured atop the wagon and strewn upon the cobblestones.

Apprentices stood on the rooftops throwing petals by the double-handful so that they fell like snow.

Mother helped Father up the steps, and there was a respectful silence as he produced the house key and turned it in the lock. The door opened and everybody cheered. Father turned, his worn face all smiles, and, waving the key, bowed again and again.

Faust was not at her house to greet her either.

Margarete waited, half beside herself with impatience, for somebody else to ask. While children were hoisted into the air with whoops of admiration and exaggerated astonishment at their growth and size. While foremen came forward, one by one, to report each factory safe and running at full production. (Surely, Margarete thought, they had not so many factories when they had left?) While the willing hands of a dozen new servants emptied the contents of the wagon into a clean and freshly aired house.

Finally, Mother squinted into the crowd and said, "Where is our mechanic?"

"He's the one who told us you'd be coming back today," said a shop foreman. "He's the one who arranged for the flowers."

"Where—where did these flowers come from?" Father asked. "So early in the season, it's like a miracle."

"They came from your glass-houses."

"Glass-houses? What need have I for glass-houses?"

A lean young man pushed his way forward, his voice high and almost lost in the babble of the street. "We have been growing medicinal plants . . . vegetables from the New World . . . chocolate, tobacco . . . a new fruit called tomato, a new drink called coffee."

"But this is—glass-houses? No, no, no, who can afford such expenses?"

"Oh, but the money is pouring in, sir. The ledgers have all been prepared for your inspection. You will be satisfied, sir, I am assured of it."

"But *where*," Mother insisted, "is he?"

"At the church, making preparations."

"Preparations? For what?"

"He's preaching tomorrow's Easter sermon."

Then, one by one, the men were coming forward with ledgers, blueprints, and order-books to explicate the Reinhardts' newly expanded holdings, to enumerate the new factories, new buildings, new enterprises.

Listening, bewildered, Margarete could hardly keep track of all the family now owned. I suppose we're rich now, she thought. How odd.

That night Margarete was combing her hair when there came a rattle of pebbles thrown against her window.

Holding closed the neck of her nightgown, she threw open the shutters and looked down. Wagner stood in the street. In his conical felt hat and workman's blouse and pantaloons, he looked like an Italian clown. He bowed deeply and then raised high a forked stick in the cleft of which was a folded square of paper.

"Wagner!" Smiling, Margarete reached out to take the proffered paper. His round face stared up at her, a pale terrestrial mirror of the solemn moon above. "It's been so long! How is your mas—"

Wagner burst into tears and fled.

A blank second later Margarete thought: Of course. Sophia. She did not look at the paper clasped in her hand. Knowing what it had to be, she felt her chest tighten. But she didn't want to read a letter from Faust tonight. She didn't want to add one grain more emotion to this horrid, wonderful day.

Shutters closed, she took her candle back to the bed and sat down. It was weakness that made her open the letter, just to see the handwriting. It was weakness that made her read.

Belissima,
Do not charge me with absence, I pray, when all my thoughts throng like shadows about your feet. Gladly would I consign wealth, honor, and all the world's machineries to eternal darkness just to gaze once more upon your dear, beautiful face. Yet I confess it is not duty that keeps me away but fear. Yes, fear! I, who dread neither Man nor Truth, tremble at the thought of your scorn. For what are we to each other but shades, thoughts, surmises—uncertain, never touching, still untried by the fierce sun of love? Your absence has made me all unpracticed at deceit, unable to hide my ardor. One glance would tell you all. My traitor face would declare to you what I dare not. And then—? If my love is to you abhorrent, the sight of so bitter a truth on so sweet a face would burn my eyes like fire. Flee me then, and for my part I shall not pursue, but rather withdraw into the Tartarus of misery, resignation, and despair. Yet if by a miracle my suit should please you, come to me tomorrow night, and so shall we make of our shadows a substance and of our love a glory.

                              Your adoring servant,
                              J. W. F.

Margarete read it through several times, to make certain that it said what it seemed to say. Such mingled alarms and excitements she felt as were impossible to sort out. She knew what Faust wanted of her, and why it was wrong. It was coarse of him to ask her, however indirectly, to endanger her immortal soul for what were, by repute, momentary and transitory pleasures.

She lay long abed, thinking about the letter and the choice it put to her, of salvation on the one hand and of damnation and Faust on the other. Until finally, while she was still wondering how she would respond, she felt sleep coming upon her.

Nonetheless, she thought, and regardless of how she chose—that was the way a man *ought* to express himself.

Easter morning dawned bright with bird-song, exuberant with clouds and mischievous zephyrs. It poured sunshine over the rooftops and hammered airy fists upon all the doors. Margarete considered every dress she had—none seemed right for this enormous thing she was considering—before settling on modest white. Then, somehow, it was time to go and her parents were calling to her from the front door.

She joined them.

They walked slowly to church, Father supported by a cane on one side and his solicitous wife on the other. He looked so frail. Margarete flushed with guilt just seeing how pale and fragile his hands were, and weakly resolved to be virtuous, to put aside all thought of doing this thing she had as good as determined upon.

But it was as if a satyr had come down from the hills, wild and pagan, and stood, pipes in hand, just beyond the garden gate, calling to her. Her body ached and yearned to leave the safe and predictable behind her. She felt as restless as the Easter winds, just cold enough to be bracing, that danced down the street and tugged at her dress and cried: Away, away! Away to her mythical demon lover, to his impossible Arcadian fields where she could kick off her shoes and cast away her clothing, and laugh and flee and be pursued and, yes, lie in rut with him.

"Sweetheart?" her mother said. "Dearest one, we're here."

Only Margarete suspected why, of all the pulpits in the city, Faust had chosen their tiny parish church's.

Ushers stood guard at the doors, keeping out all but the regular attendees. They were burly, ruddy-faced men and, though there was grumbling, nobody they turned away dared challenge them. One, who had been as good as an uncle to her in her youth, winked a greeting at Margarete as she and her parents passed within.

Crowded as the church was, the Reinhardts' pew had been saved for them. They sat through the readings without seeing Faust. He must have been hidden in a small room off the narthex, for when Father Imhoff smilingly announced that there would be a guest to preach the sermon on this Feast of the Resurrection, he strode up the aisle from the back of the church. There was a stir of whispers and craned necks as he passed.

With a solemn bow, the priest stepped aside.

Faust climbed the stairs to the pulpit. Dark brown and deeply carved with a hundred suffering martyrs, it leaned over the congregation like the prow of an oncoming ship. With the sun in shadow, small light came through the leaded windows. A single lantern lit his face, bright on his brow and aquiline nose, forcing shadow into his eyes; it formed a pool upon the top of the pulpit where his strong hands rested.

The radio-men huddled in the front pew over their acid

batteries and boxes of electrical equipment. An antenna wire had been laid up the side of the steeple. By special arrangement Faust's sermon would serve as the first public display of this wonderful new technology. There were receivers in all the churches in the city. On this historic day, every ear in Nuremberg would be straining to hear a single set of words.

A technician stood on tiptoe to place a microphone, in size and shape strikingly like a monstrance, before him.

Faust leaned forward, looking out over the darkness, the masses of candles, the congregation. All about Margarete, vague faces yearned upward toward him.

He smiled and spread his arms. A tilt of his head brought his chin up so that his eyes caught the light and *blazed*. He was clearly a man in the transports of a great passion. Then his mouth lifted sardonically on one side. When he spoke, his voice boomed through Margarete's belly and made her breastbone buzz.

"The Emperor loves you," he said.

"Seated on his golden throne at the center of the universe, he is the most vigilant of monarchs. His mind is everywhere. His eyes see all. He never sleeps. There are many inhabited spheres, not Earth alone, but thousands, billions, worlds beyond number. His domain encompasses myriad lands, many surpassingly bizarre, with races both grotesque and of angelic beauty. Some have dogs' ears; others are headless, with their faces in their chests; yet others hop about on a single leg. Some have wings but no arms, and are incapable of working evil. But to the Emperor they are not strange. They are all his children.

"Yet in all these worlds, realms, lands, cities, the Emperor's mind is fixed on you and you alone. He loves you best. His deepest wish is for your happiness.

"It is good to have such a friend.

"Nor did you ever need his friendship more. For you are in deadly peril. Intending nothing but good, you are about to make a mistake you will regret forever. The Emperor sees this, where you cannot, and immediately sets all other business aside to warn you.

"At his command messengers fly off in all directions—an infinite number of them, and even the one who is surest of never arriving, he who is flying directly away from you, is fanatically dedicated to his task. He will never betray his trust. He cannot be turned aside. He will never die.

"How much more intrepid is the messenger headed straight your way! He knows he is your best and only chance of hearing the sweet words of that most puissant power, he who loves you best. He exists only to bring them to you. Faster than any eagle, he speeds your way!

"Alas, we live far, far, impossibly far from the Emperor's court. A ray of light, swiftest of all things in the cosmos, would take hundreds of millions of years to reach you. The messenger, though scarce slower, cannot possibly come in time.

"But the Emperor is not so easily thwarted.

"Before the creation of the world he foresaw this crisis. He knew that, cut off from his oversight and admonition, you would fall into error. So, even then loving you, he wrote down the clearest possible counsels for your guidance. Five times he set them down, first in letters of fire, each a mile high. Then, digging his fingers into the ground, he carved the streams and rivers and lakes, making of each a single rune in his great message. Then, rolling up his sleeves, he molded the land like clay, each syllable an Alp, every word a chain of sky-defying mountains. In the firmament he wrote out his intent with stars. But the lands cooled and the flames dwindled to nothing. The rivers wandered and the lakes silted up. The continents drifted apart, scattered across the oceans, collided, swallowed the old mountains, and raised up new. The galaxies spun and the stars sailed apart to form new constellations.

"Finally the Emperor wrote his message into the physical constants of the universe, into the very stuff and limits of existence itself. Here at last was a medium immune to time and untouched by entropy!

"Further, the Emperor created a priesthood from among the First Men. He taught them to read this holiest of texts, and charged them by the most solemn vows to transcribe and transmit his words faithfully.

"Yet even this most ancient of sects was not proof against time and schism. See how the servants of truth have betrayed their trust! Some declare allegiance to Moses, others to Mahomet, and others still to a demon named Mammon. So willfully deluded are they, so passionate in their folly, that it is not possible to distinguish the true servant from the false. Nor can their transcriptions be trusted. Over the ages mistakes were made in the copying. Corrupt texts were accepted as authentic. New books were forged. Until finally, no scripture can now be trusted. For every text an antitext can be found; for every interpretation, its opposite. The Emperor's message has been lost among a million lies.

"Reason is of no help to us here. Reason can tell us how to invent an explosive or create a gun—but not whether to employ that explosive to build roads and dig mines or in wars of conquest. Not whether to use that gun for fowling or for murder.

"The problem is that logic does not know *should* or *ought* but only *how*. It cannot teach us faith, but only doubt. We live in an uncertain, unfathomable world, about which the only thing logic can tell us is that logic has nothing to tell us.

"The Emperor's message lies all about you, and yet logic cannot reveal it. Reason cannot read it. Your mind cannot unpuzzle it. And, therefore, you will never know."

Faust paused.

"You will never know," he repeated. His arm reached out yearningly into the emptiness above the congregation. It froze for a long, tragic moment.

"You will never know."

Then, in the tone of one offering hope to a prisoner held long in darkness, he said, "You will never know, if you rely upon your logic, your reason, your head. But your heart knows, for it is nestled deep in your body and your body is part of physical Creation, upon which the message is written. Listen to your heart. Hear what Nature tells you. You *know* what is right and, knowing it, no earthly authority can ever again lead you astray.

"Obey your heart. Obey your will.

"Know your will and follow its dictates, and you will always go right. You will never be lost again. For this is the Emperor's message, written into the matrix of being before human ever set foot on this Earth: Nothing is forbidden. *Do What Thou Wilt* shall be the whole of the law."

Faust's arm again shot out over the congregation, and this time it triumphantly clenched a fistful of air. For a breath he held this attitude. Then, slowly, he lowered his arm to his side. He turned from the congregation.

Faust descended from the pulpit through a stunned silence. He walked down the aisle, looking neither to the right nor to the left, as the congregation found voice in a hundred wondering murmurs. The voices rose higher, and sharper. Then he was gone, leaving the church in turmoil behind him.

People sprang to their feet. Some were red with choler, others white-faced and trembling. One portly fellow stood bellowing and shaking his fist, but the import of his words could not be made out over the general din. The dismayed Father Imhoff ran up to the altar now, shouting, trying to quiet the uproar. His words too were lost in the tumult.

The radio-men alone were oblivious. Goggled, gleaved, and leather-aproned, they bent protectively over their equipment, preparing it for disassembly and transport.

Only Margarete knew the true meaning of what had been said.

In the street, the crowds were noisy with talk, wild with gesticulation. "He said not a word about faith!" Father cried, scandalized. He shook his cane against the sun. "He said nothing of grace!"

"You must not excite yourself," Mother said, taking his arm.

He shook himself free and called to a passing friend, "Roggenbach! Did you hear, did you *hear*—?"

Since the sermon had been broadcast everywhere, there was nobody who had not heard Faust's terrifying words. The waves of parishioners leaving the church intersected other waves from other churches and formed small angry knots. He was denounced at every intersection, in every plaza.

Yet Faust had his supporters, too, and they were almost all young. Arguments broke out on the streets between young and old, which was a terrible thing at any time and sacrilegious on a holy day.

Margarete saw, and disapproved, and understood. It was perfectly natural that Youth, being given a new and revolutionary truth, should embrace it too eagerly, should defend it too loudly, should proclaim it in the extremest terms and without regard for the sensibilities of others. Natural, too, that Age, vested as it was in things as they had always been, should reject the truth as unsettling and dangerous. In the face of such strong emotions, the only sane thing to do therefore was to embrace the truth circumspectly, to hide one's new allegiance from one's elders.

Only she knew that the sermon had been spoken to her and her alone.

A trail of lilies led her through the night to Faust's quarters. She noticed them casually at first, a vase on a table in the hallway when she tiptoed out of her room and another where she paused, heart pounding, to listen at the top of the stairs. Her parents were both asleep. There were more lilies in the kitchen, and that seemed strange to her but of no particular import. Then she opened the back door into the courtyard, magically restored during her absence to a garden again.

She caught her breath.

In the pale moonlight, two white lines stretched from her door to Faust's workshop. Lilies had been planted along the one path, where less noble blooms lined the others. She had strolled here earlier, when sunlight had made all ways equally bright. Now the tightly furled blossoms gleamed beckoningly.

Silently, she ran down the path. A faint sweetness rose up from the sleeping flowers. She pushed open the unlocked door and climbed the stairs—a fresh-cut lily had been laid upon each—to Faust's room.

Margarete entered without knocking.

The room was sparsely furnished with trunk, bed, and writing desk. But Faust had crammed into it a hundred vases from which billowed great masses—mountains! cloud banks!—

of roses. The curtains were drawn and in the light of a single candle they were all black, black as sin, but by their perfume, heavy and sensuous, she knew them to be red, red as blood. The bed-canopy was tied open; the sheets glowed like ivory.

Faust was waiting for her.

She froze. All her dreams and romantic fancies dissolved like mists before the shock of his presence. The Faust of her dreams had not had so solid and undeniably carnal a body. So close was he, so real that she could smell him! The consequences this rash night could bring came crashing in upon her. Disgrace! Pregnancy! Exile! She shivered with dismay, and that which was daring within her despised herself for a weakling.

Had he come toward her then, Margarete would have bolted—run back to her room and slammed the door loudly enough to wake the entire household, parents and servants alike. She would have been safe then; a stormy enough protest that there was nothing—*nothing!*—between her and Faust would have ensured that they were never allowed alone together again.

But he did not. He cocked his head in a listening attitude, and then—it was as if he knew her thoughts—drew back ever so slightly.

She waited.

He smiled and held open his arms for her.

They were three paces apart. She took a quick, impulsive step forward. It was all the permission Faust needed. He crossed the remaining distance in a single stride, and swept her into his arms.

They kissed.

A long time later they drew apart, she with a smile and a sigh, he with a kind of growl. He undid her dress-front, tugging it gently away from the shirt beneath, pushing it gently back. The sleeves were puffed below the elbows, then tight at the wrists; he held the ends between thumb and forefinger while she pulled first one arm and then the other back and through. The top of her dress fell away.

Eagerly, then, he pulled her to him again and was kissing her, kissing her, kissing her.

With surprise, Margarete found herself running her hands under his blouse, stroking the smooth, hard muscles of his back. She was fearless now, as fearless as Gretchen ever was, and as gloriously, selfishly content.

Her dress somehow lay upon the floor. All in one motion, Faust scooped her up, whirled her about, and carried her to the bed. Her slippers fell lightly to the floor behind them.

She knew enough to keep her knees up and apart, and trusted to him for the rest. Feeling like a wanton, she watched Faust strip out of his clothes, and she did not look away once. Daring, ignorant, she stretched out her arms. Then he was leaning over her, kissing her face and neck, reaching down between her legs to ease himself within her.

It was not at all comfortable at first, but an experience she was willing to endure for Faust's sake. Something tore and she cried out in pain. "Shush," he whispered, and kissed her silent. Then he was gliding softly in and out of her, murmuring endearments, leaning on his elbows to spare her his weight. She was too shy to tell him that he was being overly cautious. That she wanted the full burden of his body, wanted to feel and support the whole of him, to bear him up and lift him free of the bonds of gravity and so be lifted by him, so that together they might fly up through the roof and into the gathering night.

She thought of a boy she'd known years ago who'd had a

pet snake he had let her handle—wonderously dry and smooth it was and, contrary to all she'd been taught, not at all evil: a simple creature, part of Creation, and beautiful in its way. Its eyes were dark garnets and a strange musky smell clung to it, like nothing she had ever known before. She had closed her eyes and leaned forward to inhale that scent, and when she opened them again the boy was staring at her.

He was trembling.

And so was she. A tension had seized them both at that instant. They had each wanted something then, and neither had known exactly what.

Now, with Faust's body grown slippery in her arms, she knew the moment for what it had been, a foretaste of this sorcerous and inexpressible sensation.

It was an odd thing, this physical expression of love. She hardly knew whether it was enjoyable or not. But she knew that she would do it again and not once or twice but many, many times.

Had she known what it would be like, she would have fallen years ago. She wouldn't have waited for Faust at all.

They lay together late into the night, touching, talking. Faust was built long in the torso, but with an artisan's muscularity and hardness. It thrilled her to run her fingertips lightly along the coarse bristles of his chest. Everything about him delighted her. Blushing with happiness, she explored the new continent of his body. "How did you get *this* scar?" she asked, tracing a thin silver river across the plains of his abdomen.

"A student riot."

"And this?"

"When I served in Poland, a cannon blew up during artillery drill." He shrugged. "It was no great matter. I worked for hours on the survivors before I noticed that the blood on my doublet was not theirs but my own."

A sudden wave of sorrow, sourceless and pure, came over Margarete. The world was so random and dangerous a place, inimical to lovers, hostile to the simplest ambitions. For an instant all the future seemed dark. "What's to become of us?" she asked softly, unthinkingly.

Faust laughed. "Become of us? Why, what do you think becomes of men and women who love each other? Marriage, and children. Surely you expected nothing less. I shall grow old and grey in your company and you shall grow old in mine—old and *fat!*" He pinched her thigh to make her laugh as well.

And she did.

But she did not believe his life—*their* lives now—would ever be so simple. She could not imagine it. He was a Titan, and meant for such struggles as the storm-giants knew; safer by far to marry a merchant, an honorable reed who could bend under the winds that would shatter an oak. Who would never draw lightning. Whose life would be one of homely joys and small sorrows, comfortable rather than great.

Those were practical thoughts, however, and she did not want to be practical, not tonight nor ever again. She felt buoyed up by Faust's love and by the warmth of his love-making as well. Everything seemed possible. If she could do this, she thought, she could do anything.

"I think we should have special names for each other," she said, and when Faust raised his eyebrows, "pet names, you understand, private endearments. As a sign of our love." She lowered her eyes. "I want you to call me Gretchen."

"Gretchen." His mouth caressed the word; his tongue sa-

vored it. He stroked her side languorously and grinned to see
how her body responded to his touch. As pleased with himself
as a cat that's tricked its way into the creamery. Men were
simple creatures, Gretchen thought. They inhabited a world
without consequences. "It's a lovely name. It suits you well."

"Now give me one to call you."

For a long moment Faust puzzled over the request.
Gretchen had noted before how the learned seemed to have
special trouble naming things—kittens, babies, books. It was
as if the cultivation of subtlety made simplicity less accessible
to them. His mouth pursed, twisted, and finally split in a
wide, amused smile. "Jack," he said. "You must call me Jack."

11

Apes

With a clamor of bells that set the monkey screeching in terror, the parade began.

Across town, Jakob Treutwein heard the bells as he was placing a long ladder against one of the city wall's towers. A window opened above him and a pole with wet laundry upon it was thrust out into the air. "Hallo up there!" he called with bluff good humor. "Be careful you don't impale me."

"Who said that?" A housewife stuck her startled red face out the window. "What are you doing?"

"Installing lightning rods. I've got a contract from the city."

"Lightning rods!"

"Yes, for every tower. It won't take long at all. We'll be out of your way before you know it." His sons, Daniel and Max, stood by the cart with the great spool of metal cable, the rods, tools, and mounting spikes, shifting from foot to foot with impatience. The old woman was a renter (for the towers were, strictly speaking, military emplacements, and only the chronic lack of living space within the walls led to them being let out) and had no say over what would and would not be done with the structure. But Treutwein was all smiles and patience. He knew how to handle people, knew how much trouble even the lowliest tenant could cause, knew above all what profits he could expect from a commission that would take months to fulfill.

"Whatever you're up to, I can't be bothered!" the old woman snapped. "Take your lightning-trap away. I want no part of it."

Treutwein laughed respectfully and removed his hat. "It's not like that, grandmother. It's the simplest of devices, an iron finial that goes on the tip of the spire to intercept the lightning and channel it harmlessly along a cable into the ground, like rainwater down the spout. You need never fear lightning-fires again. Sleep through thunderstorms! You'll be proof against their worst."

"Well, I—"

"Best of all, it costs nothing. The city council pays for it all."

"Free, you say?" The old woman started to withdraw.

"Absolutely without charge."

She abruptly stuck her head out again. "This isn't one of Faust's devilish creations, is it?"

"Oh, no, no, no." Treutwein put on a shocked expression. "It was invented decades ago. In Munich."

There was confusion in the square before Saint Lorenz as the procession set out. But the chaos of human bodies pushing and stumbling into one another as they squeezed into the narrow street was momentary. Once out of the plaza, the marchers were swiftly metamorphosed into a living, rainbow-scaled serpent that glided smoothly and purposively through the city.

First came the thurifer in full ecclesiastical robes, worn backwards and inside-out. Solemnly, chains clanking, he swung a censer that contained not myrrh but sulfur, so that the incense it sent up every nostril instead of elevating minds to thoughts of sanctity, sent them straight to its opposite. Behind him came the cross-bearer, his burden held upside down, with crimson ribbons streaming from the stigmata. Then two horned imps prancing and snarling. They carried baskets fat with pamphlets, which they flung by ones and twos into the crowd of spectators.

Pfinzing the carriage-maker heard the shouting and came out of his workshop to see what was happening. His apprentices, great loutish fellows all of them, filled the doorway behind him, dusty with wood shavings, climbing over each other to look. "There's nothing to see! Nothing to see!" he cried, flinging out his arms to hold them back. Then trumpets blared and a tumbler spun by. Pfinzing blinked and laughed and shrugged and lowered his arms.

The apprentices scattered like pigeons.

After the imps came the Dominicans, the Pope's black-and-white hounds transformed for the day into an order of clowns militant. Shaggy throws draped over their shoulders, gloves with patches of fur sewn to the backs, and crude masks made apes of them all. The more stolid monks were placed at the center of the street. The exuberant and outgoing went to the edges, where they might play mock with the crowd and pick imaginary lice from children's hair.

Brother Josaphat walked among them, and despite the unseasonable heat, more appropriate to summer than late October, that made sweat itch and tickle its way down his face and under his cassock, his mood was gleeful. It was his work that had brought the Papal Nuncio to town. It was he who had, at his order's behest, dug through the dungheap of unread publications Faust had left behind him in Wittenberg, unearthing them from crates and dusty storage and even in one instance from within a bookseller's walls where they were serving as insulation, and brought to air the jewel of ordure around which the procession had been built.

Beneath his mask he flushed and scowled with a guilty sort of satisfaction at the memory of how he had made the printer squirm.

"This is blasphemous work, brother," he had told the man.

"My art is all ink and cold type," the printer said defiantly. "Blasphemy I leave to those who understand such things."

"I am agog with horror."

"My conscience is clear. I have done nothing to cause you dismay."

"My horror is not at what you have done, but at the laxity of local authority. You should have been brought before the archbishop, shown the tools of inquisition, and questioned as to your motives for printing such filth."

The man turned pale, as well he might. "Sir, I swear I could not make front nor back of it! 'Twas all a mingle-mangle of air and folly, more than any sane man could decipher, polysyllabic nonsense—naught but words." He paused, swallowed, and weakly concluded, "Words."

"Exactly so. Damnable words, words that are a peril to the

immortal soul merely to read. I will require a thousand copies."

The printer's eyes bugged. "S-sir?"

"How else are the devout to know what danger they are in?"

Wolf Kreuzer, the noxious highwayman, Georg Scherm, the evil thief known as "Ironjaws," and Claus Meth, whose murderous rage knew no bounds, were crouched in the alley alongside the English spy's house, arguing over what use might best be made of a dead cat that had just been discovered, when they heard the trumpets. They stiffened with wonder.

The cat was forgotten.

"A parade!" Wolf breathed.

"Let's go," said Georg.

"Wait! We should have a horn of our own." Claus directed their eyes toward Wycliffe's house and its splendid new copper drainpipes, bright with brass wyvern fittings at the joints.

Shouting like Arabs, they ran barefoot to the drainpipe, and began to rip it loose. It took all their energy and made a dreadful noise tearing free.

Wooden shutters slammed open. A fierce bearded man stuck his head out of a second-floor window. "Leave go, you little gutter-rats!" he roared down at them.

The pipe clattered to the ground. Wolf and Georg ran off with it slung over their shoulders, taking turns at hooting in its ends. Claus snatched up the wyvern fitting—it had been his target all along—and slid it up his arm, like an Aztec ornament. Then, with a whoop and an Italian hand-gesture, he was gone.

*   *   *

Faust reshuttered the window. "This hateful rabble," he muttered. Meaning not the boys but the crowds cheering the procession.

Gretchen smiled fondly but did not look up from her accounts. "Do not hate anyone, sweet my love," she admonished. "This anger is not theirs by birthright. It is like a storm that rises up from a confluence of breezes and atmospheric anomalies. It cannot last. Their winds and thunders will soon die down into a more natural clemency."

The room stank most gloriously of sex. But for all that, they were both demurely clothed and the door was open. There was work to be done, after all. Gretchen was compiling a flow chart of products to and from her father's factories, with an eye to seeing how these processes might be simplified. It was a task she found well suited to her temperament. But even at her most involved, she was intensely aware of her lover's presence, and content merely to be with him. She still felt the trace of his touch upon her skin.

"In the meantime I cannot go abroad without being pelted with garbage," Faust grumbled. But when Gretchen turned to rise and comfort him, he placed both hands on her shoulders and pushed her gently back. "Have no fear, I shall be schooled by you. You are my conscience. You meliorate my rage, and blunt the sword of my anger."

"They are emotions unworthy of you." Gretchen returned to her list and made a small vexed noise. "What a tangle these affairs are; if only you were still running Father's businesses!"

"You do as good a job of it as ever your father did."

"Oh, I'm smart enough. But who listens to me?"

Gretchen spent almost every afternoon in Faust's company. It was not so difficult to arrange as either had expected. Her father's illness continued to occupy both parents' atten-

tions to such a degree that they had given over management
of his factories to his daughter. It was not at all certain they
understood how great these industries had grown. Gretchen
spent her mornings scurrying between work sites, gathering
reports, asking questions, dropping off directives, and issuing
orders in her father's name. It was exhausting work, even with
Faust's help.

Help that had long been explicitly forbidden her.

She had known something was up that day in April, for
Aunt Penniger was as fluttery as a hen and exaggerated her
every word and action into an unintended self-parody. Be
careful, Gretchen admonished herself. So that when her parents called her before them to explain that their heretical tenant—"that engineer," Father called him, unwilling to grant
Faust the dignity even of a name—had been sent away, she
was not caught unprepared.

Her parents had studied her closely then. But Gretchen, as
cunning as any ancient campaigner, merely said, "Good. I am
not overfond of his presence. He never blinks."

The tension eased. A quick exchange of glances told
Gretchen that she had guessed right: that her parents suspected, that they had no proof, and that they were only too
happy to accept her reassurance as final.

It was almost sad how easy they were to deceive.

The door slammed, and there was a loud clomping of
boots in the hall—Wycliffe tactfully announcing his presence
in his own house. Noisily, he came up the stairs. His mournful
face appeared in the doorway.

"Jack," he said.

Gretchen's eyes flicked up and then down again. Faust

saw, and noted, and attributed her pique to a personal dislike of the Englishman. He did not know (for Mephistopheles did not deem it necessary) that it was the "Jack" that she objected to, nor how much more seriously she had taken their little game of private names than he.

Wycliffe's expression was almost comically morose. "I think you should take a look at this pamphlet."

Drums thundering, the procession passed by the Rathaus. Preachers had been scattered along its length, barrel-chested men with leather lungs and muscular jaws. Though they passed too quickly for any to hear the whole of their sermons, all got enough to learn the gist. ". . . foul and unwholesome monster!" they bellowed. ". . . his vile desires . . . to couple with apes . . . and lusting after . . . your daughters . . . your mothers . . . your wives!" The words echoed and rolled down the street.

Seated about a table in the cool basement of the Rathaus, five lawyers sat discussing documents that they had been charged to argue and bribe into legal existence. They heard the drums and trumpets and did not care.

They had more important matters to mind.

"These are the papers for a new financial instrument to be called, ah"—Dreschler pushed his glasses up on his head and held the stack close to his eyes—"a limited liability corporation. In, ummm, essence, it is an instrument which will allow an industrialist to borrow venture money and repay it at a premium without running the legal and, ah, moral hazards of usury."

"A neat trick," growled Kraus. "But I've seen many a neat trick explained on the gallows."

"Oh, but this will, umm—quite openly! One sells shares

in the enterprise and those investing money benefit proportionately in the profits." He slid the glasses back down onto
his nose. "I've gone over it ever so many times."

"I venture it less radical an innovation, however," said
Herogt, "than this charter for a mutual assurance society."

"That's no more than a shipowners' association!" scoffed
Golter. "It merely shares out catastrophe, so that instead of
one merchant losing all, all suffer equally."

"Nobody loses anything. The occasional claim is covered
by income earned while the surety sits unused."

"Earned? Earned how?"

"Why, by investment in Dreschler's limited liability cor-
porations. The equity in these holdings is as good as money.
Or so Reinhardt's daughter assures me."

"Reinhardt's daughter," Golter said darkly, "never obtained such startlingly original documents from Reinhardt."

"Hush, hush!" Schilling tapped his nose. "We are men of
the law. Let us not engage in idle speculation."

"Shares! Futures! Options! Taken all together, this menag-
erie of papers could work great mischief. They would transform finance into something perilously close to gambling."

"Well, and yet all men enjoy gambling, and some even
profit from it."

"The only ones sure to profit from gambling are those who
rig the wheel and run the games," Kraus observed sourly.

"Which in this instance would be, umm . . ."

The five exchanged looks of sudden avarice.

The procession passed by the convent of Saint Catherine.
Mother Bondage ignored it entirely. She sat staring incredu-
lously at the pamphlet Sister Pelagia had brought her, reading
the words that seemed less and less real the deeper into the

text she went. "Can this be so?" she murmured. "Can this be?"

Sister Pelagia secretly hooked a finger behind the drape and turned slightly, as if stifling a yawn. A gentle tug and she had a glimpse outside, brief as the shutter-click of a Faustian box camera: a sea of bicyclists, priests, and Clares clustered about the scarlet cape of a horsebound man who could only be the Papal Nuncio. She looked quickly back at her superior to see if a second glance might be dared.

Mother Bondage put the pamphlet down. She looked blindly up at Sister Pelagia, found focus there, and frowned slightly. What a creature she is, the older woman thought; how unfortunate that we must use such as she. As soon as she had the thought, she was ashamed of its pettiness and made a mental note to do a penance for it later. Meanwhile, though—

Briskly, she drew up a sheet of paper, wrote upon it a carefully considered figure, and then sanded, folded, and sealed the parchment.

"Take this note to Konrad Heinvogel," she said. "Ask after him at the straw market; he will be easy to find. Tell him that the price I have written is firm. He is not to haggle and he must give you the money today or I will sell what he wants to somebody else. Is that clear?"

"Yes, Reverend Mother. Only—what is it you are selling him?"

Mother Bondage sighed deeply. "Our microscopes."

Three students stood in a tavern doorway, watching the procession. One snatched a flung pamphlet out of the air and squinted at the title. "*The Origin of Species.*" He glanced within and made a face. "What's all this about?"

"If you hadn't spent the past month at the bottom of a wine barrel," his fellow explained patiently, "you would know that it is Faust's contention that men are descended from apes."

To be difficult, the third said, "There was a woman in France who gave birth to a litter of rabbits. This was testified to by many, for it happened during Sabbath services. She fell into a swoon during the Introit and the coneys came pouring from beneath her skirts. Surely this indicates a closer linkage of mankind to the animal than might commonly be deemed comfortable."

"Your argument would be stronger if she had given birth to apes."

"Or magistrates!"

As they were laughing and punching one another, a preacher strode by and, gesturing wildly, cried out to the sky, "Oh, Lord, send us a strong arm, a righteous fist, with which to smash your foe! Give us heroes to destroy that demon's work! Lord—"

In his wake came a surge in the crowd. But those running to keep up with his words found themselves crowded to a halt here, for the street bent and narrowed before the tavern. They shoved and elbowed. Somebody shouted his displeasure. Another shook an outraged fist.

Suddenly the air shimmered with a dangerous feel, the silent crackle of imminent violence. The students all felt it, a hot flush that ran up the spine and into the skull. The smell of unwashed bodies took on a sharper edge. They shivered with anger and unclean desire.

All about them others were responding to the same impulse. Eyes glinted oddly. Teeth shone. A burly carter clenched both hands and screamed, "Death to Faust!"

"Easily enough said!" jeered the third student. "Only, where is he? Who has seen him this past month?"

"*He* may be hidden," retorted a pock-faced rag of a woman, "but his hatchlings are not—and we all know where their nests are!"

A spontaneous growl swelled up from the crowd. "Yes!" somebody shouted. "The scientists!" cried another. Stones were plucked from the ground. Sticks appeared in hands. "To the laboratories!"

As quickly as that, the mob was formed.

Then everyone was in motion. The students were sucked out of the doorway and carried along by the flood of bodies, unable to go against its surging currents, even had they wished to. Ignorant of where they were bound or for what purpose, they yet shouted as lustily as any for blood and action. It was—in a dark and brutish way—enormous fun.

He who had caught the pamphlet, however, was careful to stow it away in his purse. He knew a man who fancied himself a necromancer, and spent his nights in graveyards resurrecting corpses and crucifying dogs in a vain effort to get spirits and hobgoblins to serve his will. A man who would pay good money for such twaddle.

Last in all the procession came the monkey, wearing a placard reading FAUSTE—HIS COUSIN. The citizens pelted it with fruit and then stones. It screamed with every hit. The children cheered derisively. A stone drew blood, and this only excited the crowd to greater efforts.

The Papal Nuncio, riding just before the monkey, saw and looked away. Cardinal Verrone was a decent man, if not a particularly religious one, and hated cruelty in all its manifestations. If it was his duty to witness such barbarity, he was under no obligation to approve of it.

At the plaza before the Ladies' Gate, a platform had been built for him to speak from. He silently groaned to see how steep the steps were. His aged buttocks were still sore from the long journey from Rome, and the rest of his body was variously mosquito-stung, blackfly-bit, and rashy from the heat. But as there was no help for it, he did not complain. As he climbed, he thought with longing of his mistress back home. Lucia had grown undeniably fat and possibly a little sullen in the thirty years they'd spent together but, still, she suited him. He could talk with her about simple matters and in plain language; in all the world only she knew or cared how he felt about things. He missed her terribly.

From the platform he could see the throngs radiating outward into the surrounding streets. Directly below him, one of the monks, a burly man, was angrily arguing with the civil guard. So not everything was going as planned! The monk gestured toward a distant window from which—it was one detail among many—broken furniture was being thrown. There was so much going on, and so little he cared to know about!

He unscrolled his parchment.

He cleared his throat.

As he read, all fell silent.

It had taken a drawn sword and high words to drive the vandals from the room. But they were weaklings and dullards who had acted on impulse and without any clear idea of *why* they were there. Such men were easy to cow. And then the city soldiers had come, and as quickly as that the rioters had melted away.

In the aftermath, Lienhard Behaim leaned back against the
door, arms crossed, watching his younger brother crawl about
the floor. Weeping, Mathes sorted through the litter of broken
glass, bent metal, and smashed cabinets that had been his laboratory, searching for something whole enough to salvage.

Lienhard had the eye of a born merchant. He judged the
value of what had been destroyed, and dismissed it as a trifle.
He had lost ten times more with the overturning of a single
wagon in the Po, not six miles from its intended market, and
never blinked. Mathes was different, though, a dreamer, impractical. As his brother, it was Lienhard's duty not only to
see that Mathes's extravagant hobby did not bankrupt the
family, but to make something of the boy as well. So that, on
reflection, the rioters seemed to Lienhard to have been a gift
straight from Heaven.

When his thoughts were all in order, he said, "You recall
the Florentine monk Savonarola, and his bonfires of the vanities?"

Mathes looked up, face puffy and already beginning to
bruise from the blows he had taken in defense of his equipment. He shook his head in a baffled sort of way. "Yes?"

"When our Uncle Hochstetter was young, he went to Flor-
ence on business and witnessed one: a pyre sixty feet high,
covered with masks, playing cards, musical instruments, silk
dresses, indecent pictures, fine furniture, Venetian mirrors. He
stood in the Piazza della Signoria, as it was being assembled
made a few quick calculations as to how many wagon-loads
were there, and sent a messenger to Savonarola offering five
thousand florins for the lot."

Mathes picked up a flattened coil of wire, tried to
straighten it, let it drop. Finally he said, "What's your point?"

"Simply that we have a far more valuable load of vanities

heaped before us, and one that will not require wagons to carry away, for it exists within men's minds, and these men have legs. This radio, for one—how much would such a device be worth to a general? Or an admiral?"

Bitterly, Mathes said, "What use is the radio to anyone now? Who would dare soil their hands with a device so tainted with the stench of the notorious Monkey Faust?"

Lienhard smiled. "Why, whoever said it was his? The scoundrel was so popular for a time that none dared say a word against him. Yet among his many crimes was this, that he took the credit for the work of others. I happen to know that he had nothing to do with the invention of the radio, nor for that matter, of telegraphy."

"What? He—then who? Who did invent them?"

"Little idiot," Lienhard said fondly. "Who else but you?"

Wycliffe heartily agreed with Faust and his harlot that the wisest course was sit out the scandal and wait for tempers to cool, as surely they would. He agreed not because he thought it true—he did not—but because he never made an offer of aid until he judged his man ready to take it.

Footsteps pounded up the stairs. Wagner entered, out of breath and white as a sheet.

"I was followed," he announced to the room.

"Here?" Wycliffe glanced toward the bookshelf; a volume there contained an already-primed pistol within its hollowed pages.

"No, of course not. I am not an idiot. But had I not shifted myself to evade pursuit, this house would surely be in flames right now."

Faust patted Gretchen's hand reassuringly and, without

relinquishing it, perched carelessly on the arm of her chair.
"You exaggerate."

"Do not think so!" Wagner turned wild eyes upon his master. "I was in the plaza when the bull was read. The Pope has cried *anathema* upon you."

"What!?"

The chair toppled behind them as both Faust and Gretchen started to their feet.

"You have been excommunicated."

Wycliffe had the knack of being able to observe people closely without seeming to do so. He noted Faust's glance: how it went to the door, then to Wagner, to himself, and finally to his doxy. And he read the thought: I am in great danger, but still I command loyalty; I have friends and thus influence, and it would be shameful to show weakness before the woman I love. Faust's chin rose. A noble look came into his eye.

Before he could voice his defiance, however, Wycliffe said in a gently regretful tone, "Jack, you're among Germans. They won't just shun you; if you stay, you'll be dead within the week. You must leave. Your life depends on it."

"He's right," Gretchen said.

"Master, we must flee."

"I have a coach ready, with foodstuffs and enough gold to see us to London. You will find safe haven there, and more. England's far-seeing monarch will extend you the money and authority to—"

Again Faust's glance darted about the room, from the door to Wycliffe, past Wagner to a chest where his papers were kept, and then finally, lingeringly, on the woman. Which Wycliffe read to mean: True, I dare not stay here; Wycliffe has his own purposes for aiding me, perhaps; yet in England I can continue my work; and Gretchen will come with me, and that is all that really matters.

"You are right," Faust said, shaken. "To stay is to die." He smiled somberly at Gretchen. "We must flee, and I fear you will be able to take no more with you than the clothes you now wear. But new clothes can be bought. And there will be wealth for you in England, I promise, and honor as well."

"My love!" Gretchen cried, stricken, "I—"

Standing where she could not see him, Wycliffe held up his left hand and significantly tapped the slim gold ring there. Faust nodded.

"There is more! Once free of this hideous city, your parents can no longer prevent our marrying! An English priest can perform the ceremony as well as any. Or a French or a Belgian. The choice is yours—a lavish ritual at our leisure, or a simple one and soon, whichever pleases you more."

"Sweet love, I *cannot!*"

For an instant Faust stood unmoving, his face as perfect an allegory of astonishment as any mummer's-mask. Then he shook his head bearishly, unbelievingly. "What are you saying?"

"I cannot go with you. This is my life. I have obligations, position, my family to think of. There would be consequences. What would become of the men employed in our factories? Father is too feeble to oversee them. Without me, the enterprises will fail, and those who have worked hardest to make them succeed will lose their all."

"They have brought it upon themselves."

"No, they have not!" Gretchen's eyes flared. "Not everyone cheered on your persecutors. Some were silent, perhaps, from fear. Others—who knows what they thought or said or did? As for those who turned against you, what of their wives and children? Have I no obligation to them?"

"No. You do not."

"Yes, I do. I am a merchant's daughter, and if I know one thing it is this: *The books must balance.* Those who have entrusted my family with their loyalty must be repaid in kind."

"And me? How will you repay me?"

Gretchen's eyes flooded with tears, and she took a step toward Faust. He turned angrily away. "You are more precious to me than all the world. But I have parents, and I am their only child. Had I brothers or even a sister, it might be different. But without me, what do they have? What would their lives be like after I fled? It would kill them."

Faust said nothing.

Wycliffe, however, could not help but wonder if it wasn't the surrender of her power and position that would grieve Margarete Reinhardt most. He had known women of authority, and none of them ever surrendered it willingly. She now ran—and ably—industries worth more than many a city. That would exert a more seductive hold on her than she would care to admit aloud.

"Oh, my beloved, I would do anything for you, save what would destroy your love for me. So noble a spirit could never love me were I guilty of such crimes, were I a murderess, had I my parents' blood upon—" She drew in a long, shuddering breath. "I—I hardly know what I'm saying. Go, and take with you all my love and happiness. I shall always be yours."

There was very little a man could do that Wycliffe did not or could not understand. Yet Faust's actions now surpassed all his comprehension. Staring into an empty portion of the room, as if addressing someone there, the great engineer said,

"What should I say? Give me the words that will bring her with me."

Nobody spoke.

A strange look came over Faust's face then. It was such an expression as Wycliffe had seen only once before. That was when, using double agents, he had exposed a Jesuit plot of treason and assassination aimed at the Throne itself, and involving a lord so highly placed in the government that even in disgrace he had been able to see Wycliffe exiled to the far reaches of the Holy Roman Empire. The nobleman had assumed exactly such a look when a man he believed his perfect and abject servant had slapped him in the face and demanded his sword.

Mephistopheles, visible to Faust and to Faust alone, had embodied himself in the form of Brother Josaphat. Laughing, he lifted his cassock to expose his sexual apparatus and squeezed the stones so tightly his fist turned white. Then he winked and with his free hand cocked a finger at Faust.

(Gotcha!) he said.

The parade was, everyone agreed, an enormous success. The Dominicans returned to their monastery, where a brace of oxen had been slowly roasting since dawn. One was sent with compliments to the Clares, and the other served up at their own feast that night. Cardinal Verrone was called upon to offer a blessing and on his own cognizance granted the monks a dispensation from fasting and abstinence for the remainder of the week. Then he retired to the quarters provided him, where he had a frugal meal without wine and went to bed to dream of his Lucia.

Much to the ultimate displeasure of the Bishop of Mainz, from whose zoo the ape had been borrowed, it finished the procession as a corpse.

12

the GERMAN MASTER

The most hated man in London stood by the window of his office, hands behind back, scowling at the street below. Heads down, bundled against the cold, the people hurried purposefully by, leaking white mist from their mouths and nostrils, like so many steam robots. "How I despise them," Faust said.

"Sir?" Wagner asked.

"Never mind." He turned back to the office. "Where were we?"

" 'Dearest, most gracious love, I applaud—' "

"—applaud your decision to consolidate your holdings, which have grown too sprawling, too diverse for you to retain a close control over. Your underlings would soon have taken advantage of your myriad responsibilities to deceive and defraud you. You would never have known which of them to trust.

"Dearest, most gracious love, rid yourself of the wire-works. You'll get a good price for it and for anything even remotely connected with weaponry; your Bavarian investors understand armaments, if nothing else. There's money to be made in optics and radio, but you'll go mad trying to keep on top of everything. Let others grow rich there! Keep the chemical concerns. They are seriously undervalued—save for the dye-works, nobody but you understands their potential. But that potential is tremendous. The seeds and botanicals you must of course keep, as well as all the pharmaceuticals. People will pay anything for health. Once the new medications prove themselves, you can charge whatever prices you wish. Attached is a formulation for a simple and safe analgesic I call aspirin." Pitching his voice differently, so Wagner would not include his instruction in the letter, he said, "Be sure to have it attached."

"Yes, Magister."

"Dearest, most gracious love, the chemist P. A. Paracelsus will apply to you soon for a position; hire him—no amount of money is too great for his services. Let him put his tincture of laudanum into production, and then have him investigate the properties of other opiates, sedatives, painkillers, and so forth." He yawned. "When I have time, I shall draw up protocols for the artificial synthesis of several new classes of drugs, which he should find of interest.

"Dearest, most gracious love, new clippings should arrive soon from Jacob Fugger's American agents. See to it that the appropriate list is appended."

"Yes, Magister."

The shift-whistle blew. Faust continued his dictation unheeding. The cold winter afternoon droned on. Eventually, the week's letter was complete, and he dismissed Wagner.

Then he settled down with paper of his own to write words too personal to share with his secretary. Wycliffe would have the main letter opened and copied for the technical data it contained. But he had promised the courier would leave an insert untouched, provided he had Faust's word it contained only private sentiments. For the spy-master was an honorable man and regarded Faust as the same.

As he was sanding his signature, Mephistopheles shambled through the wall.

The demon's face was grey and bloodless, slack-mouthed, with lusterless eyes. He wore the mangled body of a workman who had died in an industrial accident three days before.

"This only makes me loathe you the more," Faust said.

"Such emotion! What have I ever done to you?"

"You destroyed my name, exiled me, separated me from—"

"Oh, yes." The corpse smirked loutishly. "That was rather a neat bit of work on my part, wasn't it? Well, then send me away! Exile me! What better vengeance could you have? Dismiss me from your mind forever!"

"You know I cannot."

"No." Mephistopheles sat down on the edge of Faust's desk and made a seeming of opening his humidor and extracting a choice cigar. "All your enterprises float upon great bubbles of speculation, reinvestment, and greed. It takes an unending flow of successes to keep them from collapsing altogether. If I were not here to tell you that a petcock on Gasometer 22 must be replaced by Thursday to prevent a catastrophic explosion, or that one James Southerley in your ballistics laboratory is a Catholic saboteur in the pay of the King of Spain, or that an obscure hydraulics engineer with the improbable name of Lancelot Endymion Fitch has the innate talents needed to oversee the steamship project, but also enemies who will do their best to keep him from you . . . well, what *would* you do?" He struck a match. The stench of sulfur mingled with that of dried dung.

"I would—Enough. Why do you come unsummoned?"

"To alert you that Lord Howard is on his way here to see you."

"Shit!" Faust returned to the window. Here to the east of London, all was raw and new. The factories were sharp-edged, their bricks as rough as wood-rasps. The trees had been chopped down to clear the broad expanses of frozen mud (they hardly deserved to be called streets) separating the unornamented and boxlike buildings. He looked out upon the collieries, pits, gas-works, forges, brickyards—every industry spawning a dozen more in its wake—and then up over the rooftops and between the smokestacks, to where the trestle bridge stretched uncompleted out over the Thames. Ragged strings of small black specks, like ants, were workmen treading their slow ways home across the ice. Doubtless they were grateful to be spared the penny toll for a ferry. "Tell me what you know of him."

"He's an idiot."

"That I already knew. Tell me something I can use."

"There is nothing you can use, for there is nothing that will shame him. He is fickle, imaginative, undisciplined, given to enthusiasms, ignorant as a pig, and as sure of himself as, well, a lord. He is also well connected, a particular pet of the Duke of Norfolk, an able horseman, and one who shows a good leg in silk hose. The people love him for these reasons, and because he is the single most effective orator in Parliament. Where you speak with—forgive me—the plodding Teutonic heaviness of a dyspeptic elephant, without subtlety and in a freakishly ludicrous accent, his English is as strong and clear as gin, his rhetoric as sweetly Italianate as vermouth, and his diction tart as a lemon peel, the whole delivered with the dry, ironic sting of the very finest martini."

"Yes, I heard what he had to say about airships," Faust growled. "He knows how I feel about him. Why has he come?"

"He is at your door. Why not ask him yourself?"

The offices were half-empty. This late in the evening only the ambitious and those hoping to catch Faust's eye remained. Wagner had gone to the whores on the uncompleted trestle bridge; he loved them best this time of year, winter-pale and cool to the touch. But John Shetterly, the receptionist, remained to defend Faust from intruders. He looked up with a beleaguered expression. A tall figure turned, straightening, from his desk.

"My dear Foster!"

Lord Howard rushed forward, arms extended. His clothes were severe, laceless, black. The slashed doublets, long sleeves, and bright colors of yore, which showed grease and were too easily caught in machinery, had given way to more practical fashions. Industrialism was the engine that drove the times, and nobody wanted it thought they were not important enough to be involved. All the best people in England these days went about as solemnly dressed as mourners.

"My esteemed Lord Howard!" Faust grasped the ambitious coxcomb's hands with loathing and a smile. "Whatever brings you so far from court?"

"The ice-carnival, in point of fact. And since you were on my way, and there is an empty seat in my sledge, I thought you might condescend to visit it with me."

"Nothing could delight me more."

*   *   *

That winter was the harshest in living memory. It was so cold that the Thames froze solid and a carnival was built out upon its surface. As a demonstration project, trenches had been chopped in the ice into which gas-pipes had been laid and then water poured to freeze solid again. The ice itself was black from the discharge of the new factories, and at night when the torches and gas flambeaux were lit, it shone like polished obsidian.

Lord Howard's coachman drove the sledge across the ice, cracking his whip warningly whenever workmen got in his way. Mephistopheles's cadaverous form sat beside him. "You and I, Foster," said Lord Howard, "are the only two men in the realm who comprehend the power inherent in this new Age of Mechanization."

"Indeed."

"The others do not understand, as we do, the dreadful forces involved, the fear and superstitious terror your destructive engines inspire."

"So long as people show the machines a proper respect," Faust said testily, "they have nothing to fear."

"You misunderstand me, Foster. I believe this fear can be a useful thing. Did you receive the drawings I had made up for you?"

"For the, ah, *Basilisk*, you mean?" Faust had seen them: exquisitely drafted steelpoint fantasies of a machine as large as a city. It rode on a hundred wheels of various sizes and was fronted by a black goggle-eyed visage that was a cross between a lion's face and that of a cock. He had dispatched the pictures to his chief engineers with a bawdy note attached, esteeming them good for a laugh and no more.

"Yes!" Lord Howard leaned forward excitedly. "I want

you to imagine an army in full array. The cavalry drawn up in regular lines, the infantry and artillery deployed with care, and every man-jack of them ready—eager!—for the coming clash.

"But then, from over the hills comes a roar, the clashing of great gears, a bellowing inconceivable to the ear. The gathered princes start, turn wonderingly to look at one another. Suddenly, with a scream and the crashing thunder of steel jaws, the *Basilisk* tops the hill! Down it rushes upon the army, snapping trees, crushing all that stands before it. The horses rear and bolt; they cannot be controlled. The infantry panic, break, and run. The gunners desert their fieldpieces. It is a rout! Puffs of smoke appear from the *Basilisk*'s sides. The cannons—"

"Cannons?"

"From the side-ports. Didn't you study the renderings? Oh, I don't pretend that the final war machine will look much like what I have had pictured. But the *idea* is there, and the idea is what matters."

(The idea is to endow this folly with enough men and materials) Mephistopheles said over his shoulder (to give it the mass necessary by the laws of physics, economics, and political science to swallow up the galaxy of your accomplishments into the black hole of its failure.)

"It is an interesting notion," Faust said carefully. "Let me offer one in my turn. I recently submitted to the Royal Commission for New Technology, upon which you sit, a proposal for funding which . . ."

"Oh, not your aeroplanes again!" Lord Howard said. "Men buzzing and flitting about like flies." He flicked his fingers dismissively. "Can such weak and improbable constructions be of use against the armed might of a foreign tyrant? No, no, dear fellow. Patently not."

"But consider. All I ask for is funding to build a single craft whose utility I could then demonstrate by publicly dropping an incendiary device on a hulk anchored in the harbor for that purpose. In exchange I would gladly have my best engineers perform a feasibility study of your *Basilisk,* and issue a detailed report on their findings."

"Feasibility study? What nonsense. I—ah! Here we are!"

The flares that had from a distance seemed a single blaze of light, an earthly vision of the Celestial City, now separated and opened up before them. One instant they were surrounded by open ice, and the next they were among the huts and tents of the carnival. The smells of spun sugar, roasting boar, and bread frying in fat, the sounds of crank-organs, gamblers cursing, and booth-merchants crying their wares closed about them.

The sledge could go no further. They dismounted.

Faust understood the chaotic forces involved, but still he hated the sprawl and disorder of the carnival. He much preferred the austere beauty and rigid control implicit in the grid. Lord Howard, predictably, found it charming.

"Come, my dear friend! Let us taste all that this marvelous encampment has to offer!" In his enthusiasm the young lord seemed scarce more than a boy. The grey-fleshed demon clapped hands merrily and leered. (Yes, sweet child, and hurry! Your heart's desire lies hidden within this festive labyrinth, and we must help you find it.)

Mephistopheles led them both deeper into the carnival, a jolly dancing corpse.

*   *   *

It was a terrible thing for Faust how crowded the carnival was. Pasty faces thronged about him, laughing, and in their joyous abandon he felt his isolation magnified. Lord Howard took his arm and, chatting, walked him past the high fence of a bear rink where for a fee a strong man could be humiliated by a defanged and declawed antiquity. Past booths selling coffee, chocolate, winter ale, absinthe, tea. Past a tent that throbbed with horn and fiddle and drum, with a wooden floor that magnified the *stomp!-stomp!-stomp!* of giddy dancers. Through a hissing gateway topped with naked flame where their narrow lane opened up into a midway bright with gas-lanterns and garish canvas signs.

"Look here!" Lord Howard's grip tightened on Faust's arm. He was staring at a gently billowing cartoon of a mechanical man, all spikes and steel teeth, with the legend SLAY THE MAN-MANGLER. In the tent beneath was a stamping-machine that had maimed three men and killed another, pilfered from the scrap-heap and artfully daubed with hog's blood. By it was a rack of mauls. For a penny a man could smash the device three times.

The tent was crowded with the same ragged men who worked in Faust's factories and complained about the wages, who were constantly calling for strikes and shorter hours, who wanted to be paid even when they were sick, who expected Sundays off, protective goggles, safety inspections, ventilation hoods, and for all he knew to be tucked into bed at night by a solicitous management. Lord Howard, however, smiled broadly, as if these were the best lads in the world, and threw the operator a coin. Seizing a hammer, he whirled it thrice around his head and brought it down upon the machine with such force that it rang. Again. His final blow broke away a bit of flanging that flew with a *ping* across the tent. The onlookers cheered lustily.

Bowing, he threw the maul aside. Outside, he said, "Did you see? That was exactly the sort of thing I was talking about. They hate these machines with a passion. This is a force that can be harnessed and put to good use."

(It is not the machine they hate but that society has itself become a machine by which the needs of production regulate the conditions of life. But they do not understand this and so they lash out at this weak symbol instead. Pathetic, really.)

Faust shook his head, said nothing. They continued down the midway, past movie tents showing one-reelers—*The Kiss*, *The Fight*, *The Train Wreck*, *Our Glorious Sovereign in Procession*, *The Fuck*—and photogravure booths where washer-women lined up to have their hideous features preserved for posterity. Bitterly, he reflected on the high expectations he had had for films; how they would educate the illiterate, teach trades, and promote public hygiene. Everywhere he looked, he saw his inventions perverted and turned to unintended uses.

So too his dealings with the government. Everything must be made a weapon. If he drew up plans for an omnibus, Parliament wanted to know how many troops it would carry; if an improved boiler, how many men it would kill if exploded. There was nothing he could make that this ingenious and pernicious race would not turn to armament.

A dead hand clasped his shoulder.

(Take him in there) said Mephistopheles. He put his face alongside Faust's own, so that the rotting-sweet smell of his breath was overwhelming. Maggots dropped from his mouth onto Faust's greatcoat. (Show him the freaks.)

RUM BLUFF PECK'S NATURAL WONDERS AND HUMAN ODDITIES read the sign. THE KILLER LIZARD GIANT KING OF JUNGLE AFRICA

ELECTRIFIED WOMAN THE SERAGLIO. With pictures so grotesque that nothing could be too awful to lie within. "Yes, yes, yes!" cried a sailor with South Seas tattoos covering his face. "Peep a glim at the deadliest monster ever to walk the Earth! Shake hands with the black-devil monarch of Ethiopia! Experience the horrid power of the dynamo! Behold the sickening lusts of the depraved East!"

Rum Bluff Peck was a little man under his barbaric markings, but whipcord tough, and with the shrewd eyes of one who could get or arrange anything. While Lord Howard gaped at the canvases, Faust drew the sailor aside and tipped silver into his hand. "His lordship requires a private showing," he said.

With a wink and a flash of teeth, the little man leaped to block the entrance with his outstretched arms. "Closed for the night!" he bellowed. "Come back tomorrow to learn the horrifying truth! Disgusting! Closed for the night! Oh, what wonders you have missed! Closed!"

He led them within the tent.

They stepped into a canvas room strewn with sawdust and dimly lit by a single lamp. In the gloom was an enormous skeleton, crouching and misshapen. The sailor adjusted the lamp's hood so they could see better, and with a start Faust recognized the baryonyx bones he had two years before sent men to dig from a clay pit in Surrey.

(Doctor Abernathy sold the bones to finance an expedition to Maidstone) Mephistopheles said. (He reckoned that with the monograph written and published, they were no more than a souvenir and a nuisance.)

"But what of its value as a type specimen?" Faust objected.

Lord Howard turned. "I beg your pardon?"

Embarrassed, Faust said, "I'm afraid I was talking to my-self."

"Ah."

The sailor returned from a hurried consultation with shad-owy others at the entrance to the next tent. In his hand was a hawthorn cane. Imperiously, he slashed the air with it, direct-ing their attention to the dinosaur's slim skull. "Behold," he cried, "the ruins of the wickedest creature as ever was!" Lord Howard raised a hand toward the skull. "I must ask you not to touch them slicers, sir, which even after hundreds of years buried in the ground are still sharp enough to cut your grip-pers to the bone! Oh, how our ancestors must have pissed themselves when this monster—"

It ate fish, Faust did not say. Note the curve of the jaw and how strikingly similar it is to that of modern fish-eating croc-odiles. Fossilized *Lepidotes* teeth and scales were, in fact, found among the bones exactly where the creature's stomach be-longed! Nor did our ancestors cower before it, for the *Dino-sauria*, however fearsome, were dead as dust tens of millions of years before anything remotely resembling human beings arose to vex an unwary world.

They would laugh at him if he tried to explain. He kept his silence.

In the next room was displayed the gigantic corpse, seven feet if it was an inch, of the African prince, frozen naked save for a few Bengalese brass ornaments, within a sawhorsed block of ice. A crescent of white bubbles obscured one nipple; a larger inverted *S* swirled from navel to knee. Lord Howard studied his heroically proportioned parts circumspectly, as Peck launched into yet another singsong lecture.

(This wretch was no prince, but a Masai warrior who went wandering after the loss of his family, looking for adventure and forgetfulness. He reached the Indian Ocean and there found a European ship taking on water and in need of hands. Whereupon he discovered in himself an aptitude for sailing surprising in one who had never seen the sea before, and would have had quite a story to tell in whatever port city of the world he wound up in, had he not died of a fever that same voyage. An apt reminder of how death renders all life meaningless.)

Then Mephistopheles gave Faust the whole experience of the warrior's life: the despair of holding his murdered son in two strong hands; the sad emptiness, upon slaying the villain who had brought madness upon his village, of learning that vengeance was not justice and that justice was to be had nowhere in the world; the wonder of seeing the ocean for the first time—*It is so ugly*, he had murmured, already in love with it—the satisfaction of wrapping a line about his forearm during a squall and diving into the overtoppling surf to seize a shipmate's hand and so save the man's life. All this in a compressed instant. In the stunned aftermath, he reflected that this nameless and forgotten man had led a fuller life than he himself could ever hope to aspire to.

Faust roused himself from his reverie to hear Peck conclude, "—no longer worshipped by his pagan ilk, but still a source of awe to all who see him."

Lord Howard asked, "Why is he frozen in ice?"

"It's to keep him from stinking," the sailor confided. "He was shipped in a barrel of vinegar, but even so—!" He pinched his nose expressively.

"He'll be useless to you, come spring, then."

"Well, not exactly, sir, no. The plan is to render him down and gild the bones, so's we can exhibit him as the Golden Man of Peru."

Lord Howard laughed and slapped the man on his back. Rum Bluff Peck himself wheezed wickedly, showing every tooth of the seven in his mouth.

Faust endured all, and followed them into the third tent.

The Electrified Woman sat enthroned like Boadicea upon a careful reproduction of the electric chair in which enemies of the state were now being executed. She was a buxom thing in a flowing gown, over which was a harness containing small electric jewels. As they entered, the hammering sound of a generator started up. "Welcome, seekers after wonder," she said, thumping her scepter upon the chair loudly enough that it could be heard outside the tent.

The jewels pulsed and then flashed into splendor.

"I am the Goddess of Electricity," the woman declaimed and, standing, graciously waved the scepter. It sprouted a blinding light that she directed toward her audience. Lord Howard winced when it struck him in the eye, and applauded her ensuing lecture and demonstration enthusiastically.

The demonstration consisted largely of simple parlor tricks performed with a static generator: making hair stand on end, shooting sparks across the room, setting fire to a mouse. "Staggering sight, eh! Fills you with wonder, dunnit!" cried the little sailor.

"I am awestruck," Faust said.

The final tent was the Seraglio. In it were three scrawny girls in loose trousers, their arms all goosefleshed with the cold and their skin dyed brown with walnut-juice, so that they could display their breasts without scandal. They wriggled clumsily before a fat ersatz Turk who sat upon an enormous mound of pillows, hookah in mouth, ogling them with eye-rolling approval. A bored mulatto boy sat behind him, playing a hornpipe upon the pennywhistle.

Mephistopheles whispered to Faust, who whispered to the sailor, who nodded and, while the false Pasha spoke of endless nights of tireless passion, briefly left the tent. When he returned, he had with him a small carved box and a slender pipe.

Faust waved the Pasha silent. "Lord Howard, I have arranged a special treat that I know will particularly appeal to a man of your imaginative bent."

"Indeed. What is it?"

"It is called opium."

Faust waited until the drug was bubbling and Lord Howard well on his way to the isles of paradise before dismissing the actors. The three girls burrowed into heavy clothes and scampered gratefully away, unheeded by the dreaming lord. Faust, for his own part, did not taste the drug, nor did he care to watch its slow and unexciting operation. He withdrew into the adjacent room to think.

"Oh!" said the Goddess of Electricity. "You startled me." She crouched amid a tangle of wires, several of which disappeared into cunning slits in the back of her gown. With a smile, she returned to the slow and delicate work of unfastening her electrical harness.

Faust seated himself in her vacated chair. The canvas walls snapped and boomed like sails in the wind. Without the heat from coursing throngs of human bodies, the gas-lamp could not come close to warming the room. He could see his breath.

(Offer her money) Mephistopheles suggested. (She's a salt bitch and in need of the ready just now. You might find it amusing to strangle her. Time it just before your orgasm, and the fury of her struggles will be most diverting.)

"Spare me your suggestions."

The woman looked up, puzzled. "Who are you talking to?"

"Shut up." Faust did not care for the conversation of whores or carnival-workers, and was indifferent to their good opinion.

(The Pope is holding a most opulent orgy tonight—would you care to see it?)

"No."

"Sir?"

"Shut up, I said!"

(Shall I show you Cleopatra pleasuring Mark Anthony with her mouth? Or Helen of Troy dallying with Paris and an ivory priapus?)

"I am not interested in the carnality of any woman but one, and she is in Germany and I must be here. So there is no solution for my dilemma."

The Electrified Woman had finished untangling her harness. She laid it carefully away in a trunk, then nervously slipped from the room.

Mephistopheles said nothing.

Faust gripped the chair's padded arms tightly. "What is it you are not telling me, devil?"

(That you are wrong. A solution exists. But I hesitate to name it.)

"I do not enjoy these games. Tell me."

(No, Faust, I dare not. I fear your anger too much to put it into words. But if you will allow, I can *show* you. Simply close your eyes.)

He did so.

Faust found himself in a carriage.

He had somehow become Ulrich von Karlsbeck, a lieutenant who had distinguished himself in the recent suppression of the peasant uprisings. Though he did not cease being Faust, he felt von Karlsbeck's thoughts, emotions, and physical sensations as strongly as though they were his own. The identification was absolute.

The carriage rattled and bumped over cobbled streets. Von Karlsbeck's gloved hand bounced upon his knee. He felt his cock stiffen slightly and, embarrassed, crossed his legs to disguise the fact.

He was intensely aware of the closeness of Gretchen's body.

"You are very silent, Lieutenant," she said. "Have you run out of words to say, or are your thoughts simply too martial for female ears?"

"I was reflecting," Ulrich murmured, "that you are a most amazingly beautiful woman."

She stiffened, and drew herself away from him. Then, seeing that he made no move to press his advantage, relaxed again. "I am a guest in your carriage. That was no proper thing to say under such circumstances."

They had both spent the evening at a charity ball, a fundraiser for the Society for the Moral Reform of the Indigent, which worthy organization was, everyone knew, more than half-underwritten by Reinhardt Industries. Von Karlsbeck's coach had come around for him simultaneous with the news being brought to Gretchen that her driver, drunk, had disappeared along with her own conveyance. On the instant he had offered her use of his. After a moment's cool reflection, she had accepted.

"I beg your forgiveness," Ulrich said, grinding his hand against his knee. He had danced only once with Gretchen, early in the evening, but his palm still burned with the memory of her waist. "I just blurted out what I was thinking. It was a brutish thing to do. I know you must think me a rogue or a fortune-hunter, but I assure you—"

"No," she said, "I can see that."

They rode on in silence. This was, Ulrich reflected, doubt-less the only time in his life he would ever be alone with such a woman—one not merely beautiful and rich, but renowned for her capability and her many good works. She supported not only moral reform, but also societies for the suppression of vice, the abolition of torture, the restraint of slavery, work-houses for orphans, and improved sewage treatment. And she ran a dozen industries. He was most fearfully drawn to her. His friends would know what to do with such an opportunity.

He, fool that he was, knew but could not act. He was aware of his own worth and virtues, tried in battle and proven in the bedchamber. But he admired Gretchen, and this un-manned him entirely.

"Tell me," he said to break his chain of thoughts. "I have of course heard of the lock-outs at your factories, and . . . I do not say this challengingly, I assure you I am no radical! But it seems obvious, given how much and how freely you spend on charity, that you have wealth enough to give your workers the raises they desire. Would that not then be the best thing to do?" He flushed. "I know I phrased that badly."

"Clearly, you have not read Foster's essays on economics."

"No."

"Then I shall not expound upon the intricacies of supply and demand, nor how prices are regulated by what capitalists call the hidden hand of the market. But Foster shows that an overall raise in wages is never real: It raises the cost of pro-duction, which inflates prices so as to undo the good achieved. Further, the temporary improvement in means leads inevitably to bigger families, which in turn increase the pressure on the food supply, resulting in a net increase in human misery."

"This is the devil's arithmetic!" von Karlsbeck cried in dismay. "These equations make a mockery of all aspiration."

"Yes," Gretchen agreed, "the truth is harsh. However, so long as we industrialists are given a free hand, our increased efficiencies will result in lower prices and a uniformly higher standard of living, and thus shall all benefit from our endeavors."

The carriage pulled to a stop. Von Karlsbeck jumped out and ran around to open the door for Gretchen. She stepped down in a swirl of silk, and he escorted her to her door. There was an English lantern by the stoop, and its electric light made the street before it bright as day.

She ascended a step, then turned. "I am promised to another man," she said, "and I have sworn to be faithful to him forever. You understand, surely?"

He let out a breath, surprised at his own disappointment. "All too perfectly," he said. Then, gallantly, "I pray you, do not tell me this fellow's name. For then I would hate him, and that would be dishonorable. He upon whom you smile is the most fortunate of men; let not my envy mar his bliss."

Gretchen blushed.

"Close your eyes," she said, "and I will kiss your cheek."

He obeyed, and she bent her head down to his. Her lips brushed his skin in a kiss that was swift, chaste, sisterly.

He opened his eyes. "Thank you."

Without warning, she kissed him full and fierce upon the mouth. He felt her tongue deep within him. Then she whirled, and disappeared into the house. The door slammed after her.

Shaking his head in a complex mixture of wonder and wry

admiration, Ulrich von Karlsbeck walked stiffly back to his carriage.

(There) said Mephistopheles (is your solution.)

"She is faithful to me." Faust could still taste her mouth, and feel the moistness of her tongue. "You heard her say that."

(That means less than nothing. A woman does not make such a protestation unless she has been considering its alternative.)

Faust slammed the chair with both fists. "She is faithful!"

(Indeed, and has been for more than three years.)

"Is this your solution, then—that I should watch my Gretchen weaken, grow corrupt, and fall into whoredom?"

The corpse-form Mephistopheles wore was showing signs of deterioration. Elbows and knucklebones poked through rotting flesh. One cheek had sloughed away from the skull, leaving a grinning patch of teeth. (It is a common thing for a man jaded by his wife's attentions to send her to the tavern to bring home another man, so that he might watch—far commoner than you imagine, for many a woman who would otherwise remain chaste will obey such an injunction. What would be licentiousness done on her own impulse is rendered sweet obedience to her husband's commandment. In this way are many marriages preserved.)

"I will not listen to such filth."

(Oh, you fickle and faithless creature! Have you forgotten our bargain? You may do whatever you wish, but you must always—always!—hear what I have to say, in all matters great or small. Otherwise—) He left it hanging.

"You waste your time."

(To Gretchen the pleasures of the flesh are but the outward

expressions of love. She is young, and must obey her body. If she does so at the urgings of a pleasant stranger, her love will focus itself upon him; if by your direction, she will feel a proud subservience to your will. That is your choice. You have no other.)

"All that proceeds from your mouth is twisted and vile."

(I have had my say) said Mephistopheles. (See to the lord-ling.)

Lord Howard sat alone on the pillows, a dreamy smile on his face, a trace of drool running down his chin. Rum Bluff Peck looked up when Faust came in. "It's up anchors for me," the sailor said. "If ye don't want your friend froze to death, ye'd best bing 'im aft."

"I'll send Lord Howard's coachman for him in an hour or so." Faust added a touch more silver to ensure the man's co-operation. "Watch over him until then. Make sure he takes what remains unsmoked with him. He'll be wanting more in a week or so."

"It's no easy cargo to find," Rum Bluff Peck said with transparent cunning. "I hove up this load by chance. 'Deed, sir, I was staggered ye even knew of it."

"He'll pay whatever price you command."

The sailor was only a stopgap, for he would be dead in a year, stabbed in a tavern brawl over a woman he had met but minutes earlier. By then, however, Reinhardt Industries would be shipping their elixir of laudanum. Faust would be careful to send Lord Howard a case, with his compliments.

Long before the case was empty, he was confident, a certain seat in Parliament would be filled by a cousin or younger brother. One who lacked his noble kinsman's gift for rhetoric.

* * *

The air was cold and clean away from the carnival. Hooves thundered and the sledge's runners made a crisp sound slicing across the ice. On the seat beside the driver, Mephistopheles had shed the last scraps of flesh and was now but bones and a few grey rags. The factory-lights of East London shone like stars between his ribs. The open hearths of the steel mills glowed ember-red under the billowing smokestacks.

Faust took a deep breath of the wintry air and felt his head clear. The crisis was over. He would not accept Mephistopheles's advice. It was the counsel of a pimp, and the senseless defilement of a love that was pure and true. Better to let Gretchen go altogether than to deform her soul. That was something, he now realized, that he could never do.

The demon turned and grinned skullishly. (Ah, Faust, how little you understand yourself!)

TABLOIDS

Gretchen was furious. That horrid photographer and his unspeakable photo essay! What kind of man went searching through the world's nightmares to gather the ripest into a bouquet to drop at her feet? She closed the copy of *Die Zeitung* lying on the conference table, unable to look any more upon the small deformed faces, and said, "Cancel all our advertising."

Stabenow, Hoess, and Topf looked uneasily from one to another. Ullmann stared stonily ahead. Bellochs cleared his throat. "It won't look good," he demurred.

"And this *does?*" She shook the newspaper in his face. "I don't want these parasites to see another penny of our money ever again."

"We need advertising," Bellochs said patiently. Her director of marketing was a round little grandfatherly man with half-moon spectacles. "It is like a dungheap to the farmer or slavery to the Spanish colonies—an unpleasant but necessary evil. The very factories that these pictures vilify are currently running at full capacity to produce a solid backlog of film. Film which, incidentally, this photographer needs just as dearly as we need the ear of the public." He lifted a sheaf of papers from the table and let them fall a futile inch. "These are the plans for a saturation advertising campaign, with which we hope to put a new box-camera in every household in the Empire. Radio and newspapers; they fit together like this." He joined hands, fingers meshing. "So, yes, by all means, cut off advertising to every paper that offends us. *If* you wish to shut down three-quarters of your film production. Otherwise . . ." He shrugged.

"The law," Hoess suggested, "might not be entirely unhelpful here."

Ullmann thumped the table with the hilt of his scabbarded dagger—he liked to fancy himself the target of assassins—and cried, "Yes! Let's take them to court!" Wulf Ullmann was a dark-haired little man, almost handsome, a prig, a bit of a weasel, and Gretchen's own cousin. At times he presumed more on their relationship than she thought warranted. "We'll sue their paper out from under them, and run our advertising for free!"

So extreme was his passion that by reaction Gretchen found herself moved to a more temperate frame of mind. "Your cousin means you no good," Faust had written. "Watch him well." But he had not commanded Wulf be fired, and until he explicitly did so, she would keep her cousin on the payroll. Treacherous or not, he was still family. Besides, of all her duties, the one she relished least was dismissing an employee. She always cried afterwards.

Also, he was dangerous. She liked that in a man.

"I can only imagine what headlines they would run against us while the case was litigating," Gretchen said. " 'Antichrist Corporation Sues Defender of Faith and Freedom' perhaps, or 'Beast 666 Introduces Convenient New Family Camera.' " Then, when the laughter had died down, "Suppose we try this instead. We'll start the radio ads two weeks early—can we have them ready that soon? Of course we can. For two weeks, as many ads as the stations will run—we'll budget more money—and never a move to buy so much as an inch of print. That should shake up *Die Zeitung*! We wouldn't have to threaten anything; our silence would be eloquence enough. We could wait for them to come to us, hat in hand, wondering exactly how abject a public retraction of their slander we would require."

Bellochs smiled. "Now, that would not only be possible," he said, "but productive as well."

A tension went out of the room. Everyone, even Wulf, relaxed visibly.

Stabenow flipped open his notepad. "I'll prepare a draft of their retraction. What should be the gist of it?"

"Let them explain that it is a question of the greatest good for the greatest number. Our medicines save countless children's lives. Factory jobs feed thousands more. If ignorant people insist on drinking from contaminated wells, they can hardly fault us for being upriver from them. They have only their own stupidity to blame. Do they expect us to wipe their noses for them? Such ingratitude is simply outrageous."

"My people will polish it up a little," Stabenow promised.

After the meeting room had emptied, Gretchen turned to her secretary. "What's next?"

Anna consulted her clipboard. "It's Friday, so you'll be meeting with your section chiefs to go over their weekly status reports. Then you need the legal department's opinion on the new tabloids. There's a ceremony at the laboratories; the bishop will be present to bless the centrifuges. Finally, there's that impertinent Silesian from the Polish court, Władisław Czenski. He refuses to say what he wants."

"What do they all want? Chlorine, phosgene, mustard gas—I'm sorry we ever got involved in chemical weaponry in the first place. But a most properly made young man, I think. He has such lovely dark curls, don't you agree?"

"I wouldn't know."

"I'm running late today. That dreadful pictorial! Have him told that his appointment has been rescheduled for tomorrow afternoon, at my country estate. I'll have Abelard prepare lunch."

"As you wish."

"Is my carriage ready? Have it brought around. Do you know," she confided, "I'm actually looking forward to meeting with the lawyers? We've been working on the tabloids so long, and this is the final step before we put them into production."

She rattled the plate of pills angrily. "Well?"

"What we are, ah, trying to say," Dreschler said, "is no. We consulted with several priests about the, umm, morality of the product. They were unanimous in their condemnation."

"Priests! Morality? Allow me to remind you, gentlemen, that priests are not only male but sworn to celibacy. Now either they are true to their vows, in which case they know nothing about the subject, or else they are not. In which case they have no moral standing whatsoever."

"The legal staff is united in our recommendations as well," he said mildly. "We stand upon litigious grounds. As contraceptives these tabloids are perhaps, just perhaps, acceptable, provided we introduced them quietly, and made them available only to housewives and whores. To ensure they would not degrade public morals. However, your own documentation says that several taken the morning after, ummm, coition will also prove effective, and this means that they are also—" He coughed. "It means they are also an abortifacient. Child-murder is still—well. It's a capital crime, after all. Though they rarely hang the poor wretches. In most cases the judges will listen sympathetically to the woman's plea for mercy, and direct the executioner to employ the sword instead."

"This would prevent abortions!" Gretchen cried. "Even taken the morning after, the tabloids are strictly contraceptive. The egg isn't properly fertilized by then. The zygote hasn't formed. Surely flushing an unfertilized ovum is preferable to the traumatic expulsion of an embryo brought on by infusions of pennyroyal. I need not remind you how many ignorant women die each year through misjudging the dosage of the oil."

Dreschler shook his head slowly through her every word, and by this gesture erased them of all merit. "You are a woman—" he began.

"—and am thus of course particularly eager for the repute and modesty of my sex to be preserved. I thank you for pointing this out." She had learned not to let her subordinates dismiss her arguments, as men would, as arising from her gender. Let them once categorize the tabloids as being of import to women alone, and the pills would be buried forever under the weight of their disregard. But she was too cunning for that. She would outmale their maleness, outlawyer their argumentativeness, and outlogic their objections. "My father, however, would take that for granted, and so must we. How would he analyze this situation? I think, as follows."

She raised a finger.

"*Imprimis*, the tabloids shall be made available only through doctors and midwives; this will prevent them from falling into irresponsible hands. *Secundus*, with every packet we shall enclose an insert notifying the buyer of the danger of its being misused as you describe, and spelling out the legal, ethical, and medical problems attendant thereunto."

Several lawyers raised their hands and voices in dismay. Dreschler, as their chief, said, "But that will only ensure that all users know of this property!"

"It is regrettable indeed," Gretchen lied. "But what can we do? Since you chose to bring priests into this matter, we can expect strident opposition from the Church. We must, after all, defend ourselves."

She turned to go, stopped, returned. "*Tertius*," she said, "we start production tomorrow. I want that package insert written by morning."

She took the pills with her.

Men had to be seduced. This was something Gretchen in her innocence had not known. To listen to Mother or Aunt Penniger or indeed any of their generation (which was to say, those old enough to have forgotten), men were rampant and lustful beasts, ready for any nastiness on an instant's notice, and as often again as a woman would allow. They were ever-flowing and self-replenishing fountains of lechery. One had to be eternally on guard; a single indiscreet smile and a girl might be lost in debauchery forever.

This was, alas, simply not true.

Czenski was a case in point. Gretchen had seen him only the once. But, provided she was not directed otherwise—it was a letter day—she was determined to have him. Physically, he was pleasant: tall and broadly built, Nature's own bully, with a head of black ringlets so tight they might have been curled around her pinkie, and that fine, almost translucent Polish complexion that went so easily to red when moved by emotion. But it was his intensity she liked best. It reminded her in a lesser way, as a firefly lazily hovering in the evening sky might remind one of the moon, of her own beloved Faust.

He would not be easy.

Four days ago he had accosted her at a publicity shoot. She was standing outside Building 47, arm and smile frozen, in front of the new Reinhardt Industries logo (an *R*-and-*I* monogram intertwined with oak leaves to symbolize sturdy origins, and circled by a snake devouring its own tail, which represented the carbon ring), when hoofbeats thundered down the street. With a shout, the mud-spattered nobleman had leaped from his horse, tossing the reins to his servant, and run up to her, saying desperately, "The Polish armies are all that stand between Christendom and the Turk. If you—"

"Excuse me." Anna Emels threw herself before Gretchen and seized the interloper by his arms. "You cannot be here. A photograph is being taken."

He ignored the tiny woman completely, speaking over her head. "Good men are dying at this very moment to protect you, your factories, your possessions, and all civilization."

"Good men are dying every moment," Gretchen replied coldly, "somewhere. Since they did not ask my leave to do so, I feel no particular obligation toward them."

He flushed. "Do not mock my valiant comrades! They are true heroes, and you are only a—"

"Sir!" Anna thrust her face up at his, as pugnacious as a terrier pup.

Czenski glanced down at Gretchen's secretary, and froze with sudden shock. She glared up at him with all the ferocity of a small forest creature made bold by a predator's attack upon her lair. Her features taken one by one were wrong: nose too long, chin too weak, the shape of her face long out of fashion; and yet taken together they formed a strange harmony. She was not beautiful, but hers was a plainness that took the breath away. He gazed down into the cedar pools of her eyes, and was lost.

Gretchen saw his expression and understood, and was secretly amused, for she knew, as he could not, how hopeless was his case. Anna Emels had confided to her once that she was not drawn to men but to women, and, more, that she had on occasion discovered other women similarly inclined and with them acted out these longings.

Gretchen had never heard of such a thing, and was fascinated by it. She wanted to know every detail: how it was done, which woman lay on top, whether they both enjoyed it. But Anna, suddenly shy, merely stared at the ground and shook her head, that long water-rat hair hiding her eyes, and no amount of wheedling could pry another word from her.

The Silesian recovered and, reaching past the tiny woman, pressed a bundle of papers into Gretchen's hands. "You must read these. Our need is great, your assistance urgently required."

"I have business to attend to, sir," she said coolly. Then, handing the papers to Anna, "My secretary can set you up with an appointment, next Thursday perhaps, or the day after. Newspaperman! Are you ready?"

Then she had smiled and pointed, and the flash-powder

had gone off, blinding her. She blinked the small bright suns from her eyes, and it was two days later and the coach came up and carried her home.

She spent the night at her town house. A servant brought her a letter on a silver platter and for an instant she looked at it blankly, thinking: That's not how it's done. But then she saw that it was from her parents.

They had written with their usual worries from Heiligenstadt, where Father stoically endured the sulfur baths and enema cures, refusing the advice of the doctors she sent because they were trained in the new ways of the pharmaceutical industries-sponsored medical colleges, which he mistrusted. He was set in his ways and would undergo no treatment that had not been discredited long before he had been born. Mother fretted that she was working too hard and not taking enough pleasure out of life. Father suggested she sell the factories and buy herself a small estate along the Neckar, where the labor of her peasants would secure her a comfortable, if not luxurious, income. They both were concerned that she had not yet found an appropriate young man and might be doomed to die a maid.

She ate a light supper and then wrote back as reassuringly as she could, knowing they would not listen. Her mind could not help but wander toward faraway London, but she forced herself to give the response serious attention. They were her parents, after all, and deserved no less.

When she retired to her room, Faust's letter was waiting upon the pillow of her fresh-made bed. She never knew how it came, but she did not question its presence. Communication was difficult for those who had enemies they had never met.

Clearly, Wycliffe's agents had suborned one of her servants. But it was scarce worth the effort to find out who; she was better off for this weekly reminder that none of her subordinates could ever be wholeheartedly trusted.

She took up the letter, and lay back upon her bed to read it.

Bellissima,
You will be worrying whether to accept the Polish commission for chemical weaponry. Do so. Attached is a draft contract of such terms as you may demand. It is more than they hope to pay, but less than they fear. If you charge more, you cannot rely on their honoring their debts . . .

Come morning, she would cut the main packet into shreds, cross out some words, overwrite others, and clip each fragment to a memo to be copied out in a secretarial hand as coming from her and sent to the appropriate underling. These messages were her meat and bread; she read them first, quickly, conscientiously.

The slimmer packet at the heart of the larger, written in Faust's own hand, she saved until the work had been done. Then she undressed and, after raising the letter to her lips and solemnly kissing it (with just a mischievous hint of tongue), she broke the seal.

These inserts were her Bible. They never led her wrong. "You will enjoy . . ." he wrote. Or "The first time will feel strange and unnatural, the second merely strange, but the third a delight." And it was so.

She had learned to trust his advice implicitly. His understanding of her was perfect. She had no secrets from him. So

universal was his comprehension, so attuned was he to the
life force—what he called the *Geist*—that he knew things no
other man *could* know. He predicted events before they happened. He judged people he had never met.

He was never wrong.

She remembered the first time he had sent her into the
arms of another man. She remembered how the fear, the guilt,
the anticipation had combined into a bodily excitement second
only to that sacred night she had gone to Faust himself. How
timid she had felt, and how exalted! How it had roused her
blood.

Now she obeyed these directives without hesitation, rec-
ognizing no lord or power above her but Faust and obeying
no will but his alone. Occasionally, she wondered about the
rightness of some of the things he required of her—but she
always put these doubts aside. He understood more than she
ever would. But where her comprehension could not hope to
match his, her obedience was unparalleled. Never was any
man more perfectly obeyed than he was by his own Gretchen.
No woman found such fulfillment in the submission of herself
as she.

You will be wondering how to seduce the Silesian
agent . . .

"But why must I change my clothes?" Anna Emels objected. "What I wear is respectable."

"I desire it," Gretchen said.

She led the secretary to a quiet room, where a white dress,
hat, stockings, and underthings had been laid out upon the
bed. She closed the door and drew up a chair.

"I—I'd rather you didn't stay."

"Why?" Amused, Gretchen glanced down the front of her own body. "It is nothing I do not see every day."

With a shriek, the little woman pushed and shoved, until Gretchen, laughing, found herself outside in the hall. The door slammed, and there was the sound of the bolt being thrown.

They all three walked together from the house down a winding path leading into the arboretum. A light breeze caused Anna's skirts to flutter most fetchingly. Czenski held himself very stiff and formal. He did not once look directly at the secretary.

"I must explain to you the military situation along the eastern marches," he began, "and the strategic importance of the Silesian coalfields."

"Sir!" Gretchen cried. "It is a pleasant day, and you are in the company of two ladies. You must treat us with the courtesy due our sex." Then, when he looked puzzled, "There is a time and place for business. It is neither here nor now. Have you no small talk?"

He bristled. "Small talk? While my comrades fight and die?"

"Yes. Gossip you have heard, pleasant things you have seen, witty comment upon items you have read in the newspaper. Surely that lies within your grasp."

"I have no gossip. I am a soldier, and very little of what I have seen is pleasant. As for the papers—well. I am surprised you mention them. You seem to be in bad odor with the papers."

"Do you refer to the business news or the scandal pages?"

"I—" He stopped, flustered. "I have been crude and tactless. Please forgive me."

"It's because I smoke cigarettes and dye my hair,"

Gretchen said carelessly. "Their minds are so firmly made up against me it hardly matters that I also wear nylon stockings and skirts so short you can see my ankles." Then, when his eyes automatically darted downward, she laughed. "*Ah, oui— c'est assez immoral, ça.*"

He went bright red. But despite her continued hints, he stubbornly refused to switch over to court French. It was, she supposed, a kind of courtesy to insist upon speaking only her vernacular.

Still, it was no easy thing to flirt in German.

The path led them through an oak grove. "I am taking you further into my grounds than I permit most guests," she remarked, "because I wish to show you my little arbor." In the distance, she saw a last liveried servant slip over the top of a hill and disappear. She had ordered that they be left alone and undisturbed in the arboretum for the rest of the day. It was an order that she confidently expected to be obeyed.

There was a summer house in a small clearing among the pines, its trellis walls artfully overgrown with flowering trumpet vines. It was too airy to serve as shelter, too dark for reading. Even from a distance one knew that the air within was green and shadowy, and scented with the perfume of the blossoms. "There it is. We'll visit it after we eat."

In the field above, she'd arranged a picnic. It awaited them in gauze-covered Limoges dishes laid out upon a low table draped with Irish lace. Oriental carpets were placed to the table's sides, and silver buckets with iced Alsatian wine.

They climbed the grassy slope, Gretchen and Anna Emels strolling almost languidly, but Czenski rather like a loyal officer going dutifully to his own execution. He plumped himself down upon the carpet.

Anna Emels removed the gauze from the plates, exclaiming at the cold roasted partridges with white grapes, spooning the whipped cream from its ice-packed copper bowl onto the *bande d'abricots*. From a wicker basket, Gretchen produced three wreaths, two of wildflowers, and the third of laurel leaves. Czenski submitted to his with a gloomy smile, and watched intently as Anna donned hers, blushing like a bride.

"Open your mouth," Gretchen told him. She plucked a grape from the partridges and placed it in his mouth. "Now close."

He swallowed and shook his head. "I am no—"

"Hush," she said. "Eat."

Czenski's appetite was not great. But neither was it a heavy meal. Gretchen had no desire to start the afternoon feeling bloated and lethargic. She drank two slow glasses of wine and noted that Anna quietly had three and their guest nearly four. Then, when all were feeling quiet and comfortable, she said to him, "Make a wish. Anything at all . . . and if you are good, I promise it will be yours this very afternoon."

Involuntarily, his eyes shot toward Anna and then back to Gretchen where a leather attaché—magicked into existence by the same sprites who had set the table—lay by her knees like a faithful hound.

She opened it.

Within was Faust's inner, esoteric letter, and alongside it a new-drawn contract. She gestured, and Anna set a clean plate before the Silesian. She placed the contract upon it.

He snatched it up, began quickly to read. "This says—" He looked up, then down again, flipping through the pages, muttering to himself.

While Czenski was preoccupied, she sopped up the last dribbles of juice from her roasted peppers with a twist of rustic bread, and idly perused her own reading matter.

Finally he looked up wildly. "I'll need ink!" he cried. "A quill!"

"I'm so glad it's acceptable." Gretchen firmly took the contract from him, and tucked it back into her attaché. "We can dispense with the formalities at the house—afterwards." Then, mischievously, "So you see, I am more than just *infâme des scandales*, eh?"

She folded the letter away, and watched it play out before her.

. . . Send your servants away, all but for your secretary. Command her to stand before you in silence. Let her experience your gaze, briefly, and wonderingly. Then direct her to remove her clothing. She is secretly in love with you, and will do whatever you direct.

First Anna undid her brooch. Then, slowly, almost unwillingly, she lowered her dress. Her small white breasts appeared, nipples hardening as the air touched them. She looked stricken. Her face was white and still, her lips thin. Czenski lay upon one elbow, looking at her, hardly breathing.

"All of it," Gretchen said. "Your stockings as well. Everything but the flowers."

Czenski will be shocked, transfixed, ensorcelled. He is expecting nothing of the sort. Direct him to . . .

"*Monsieur?*" His head whipped around at the word and he started to his feet. It was as if he had not expected her to still be there. Perhaps he had not. Surely he had not expected her to take advantage of his inattention by beginning to remove her own clothing as well. "You have the advantage of us. *Sois gentil*—do the honorable thing."

His mouth opened, then closed. Without saying a word, he began to undress.

When they were all three naked, she took them both by the hand and led them to the summer house. There, among the cool breezes and green shadows, waited an enormous bed, sheeted in silks as white as a snowdrift. A fairy light washed over it, gentle and transforming, and a quiet in which all was permitted.

"I—I never . . ." stammered Anna Emels.

"Have you never?" Gretchen said. "It is the most natural thing imaginable. I am certain you will enjoy it." Though in truth this was a fib, for it was nothing she had any experience with either. But Gretchen was certain that *she* at least would enjoy it, for Faust had assured her so.

They entered, naked and innocent: Adam and Gretchen and Eve in the Garden.

The secretary is, unfortunately, of an emotional temperament and the experience will unsettle her in the aftermath; she will be of little use to you afterwards. Fire her.

14

DREADNOUGHT

The riverfront was alive: Its wharves and shipyards seethed like anthills. Tugboats guided in freighters and cranes swung out to meet barges. Engines hammered in the summer heat. Carts and vans jostled in the streets; locomotives idled while hopper cars poured coal into waiting sluices; mule teams hauled ore boats up the canals. Exhaust blasted from smokestacks. Puffs of steam leaked from exhaust vents.

A shift-whistle screamed, a hundred gates opened, and workmen flooded the streets. It was late afternoon and the mighty gears and pistons of industry meshed and merged so perfectly that all London seemed a single organism, a living machine, the Mother of War, who took in raw materials through uncountable orifices and, after brief gestation in the broad brick womb of her foundries, gave birth to a Titanic new race of armaments.

Yet the Spanish fleet had already set sail. All that could be done, had. Now, for all the frantic activity, there was nothing left but the playing out of what had long ago been set in motion.

Faust opened the humidor on his desk, selected a cigar, and put it down unlit.

There was no word from the physicists in the converted tennis court in the City. They labored, and summed, and spoiled countless reams of paper with small notation, but produced nothing. He understood now that the project was ahead of its time. Mephistopheles was right—a pyramid could not be built from the top down. There was simply not the scientific and technological base to allow his genius full play. So his masterwork would not be deployed in the coming conflict.

This action would be fought with more conventional arms.

The Spanish ironclads were armed with Nuremberg guns. There were no finer cannons in all the world: Their range was unsurpassed, their accuracy preternatural. The ships' armor cladding was more than three inches thick. There were, moreover, rumors of phosgene gas shells.

But neither were the British steamships without resources. The ballistics engineers in the whimsically nicknamed Spaniard Works, and the chemical engineers in munitions, and the electrical engineers in radar, had worked long and hard and often without sleep to fit them for this day. They were ready.

Faust, restless, left his office and took a turn through one of his plants.

It was a hellish place—dark, airless, as bad as any prison. He wasn't even sure which factory it was, or what was done there, for he had chosen blindly, walking down Electricity Road and up Steam Hammer and striding past the startled gate security on a whim. But today, despite the roars and clashes of machinery, there was a strange underlying silence. Nobody shouted. Supervisors gave their orders quietly, with a hand laid upon a shoulder for comfort. Workers obeyed with a quick nod of the head, a lifted thumb. Faust saw a welder burst into tears for no apparent reason.

(Talk to your men!) Mephistopheles urged. (Hand out small silver. Ask after their wives and sons by name. Call them together and give a speech. Say that all have worked hard and suffered much to prepare against this day. Tell them that the contest will be close and hard, but that one free man is the equal of ten Iberian slaves, and the battle must surely go to England. Tell them that the victory will belong as much to them as to the brave sailors of the Fleet. Apologize for being foreign-born, then tell them that their land—their home—has won your heart and loyalty. That today you would proudly lay down your life for it! Lead them in a cheer for the Throne and the ass that currently occupies it. Then give them the rest of the day off. They'll love you for it.)

"I don't want their love."

Faust passed through the plant as if enchanted, recognized by all but approached by none for fear of his now-famous wrath. The plant supervisor and his upper managers, recognizable by the hard-hats they wore as none of the floor workers did, anxiously paced him from a distance, ready to come at a gesture. He ignored them.

In all the building, only one person met his eye: a gaunt scarecrow of a mechanic, standing upon a catwalk high above the floor by an opened hoist-motor, toolbox at his feet. The man stood spraddle-legged, glaring at Faust with an absolute and perfect hatred. The air all but crackled with the force of his emotion.

(Go to him.)

Faust climbed a ladder to the man's side.

For a long time neither spoke. Finally Faust said, "Who are you? What have I ever done to you?"

"My name is Lambart Jenkins. You gave me a scholarship."

"Oh," Faust said. "One of those."

"Yes. One of those." Each word fell from the mechanic's mouth separately, four drops of purest distillate of bitterness. Lank hair hung sweat-damp down the young man's brow; his eyes were unblinking to the point of madness. "I don't suppose you even remember your visit to Glouchester."

Faust shook his head. "All I remember is that it was raining, and I stepped in such a puddle that I swore never to return. There were so many cities to visit . . . So many seeds to plant."

"I was enrolled in the technical college. One day you walked into our mathematics seminar. You spoke on the nature of light, and the geometry of space-time. You said that sometimes light behaved like a particle, and other times like a wave. Until that moment, I thought myself an algebraist. You made me a physicist. You cannot imagine how I worshipped you!"

"You feel differently now, though."

Jenkins continued staring, said nothing.

"Come," said Faust. "Walk with me."

The mechanic had a long, swooping stride with a hesitation at the end of each step as he waited for his companion to catch up. This was clearly habitual, for Faust himself was no dawdler, and it left him in constant danger of tripping over his own feet. Together they strolled past the rail terminus, the

gas-works, and the brickyards, into the surrounding tenements.

They turned a corner and Faust almost collided with a
colliery-woman, stooped under a sack of coal. Her eyes went
wide with recognition and she crashed to her knees.

Mephistopheles, discorporate, a bubble of thought, said,
(See the hypocrisy of the rabble! A thousand times this woman
has prayed for your death. Yet today she will not so much as
spit upon you, lest England be conquered by a tyrant who
would treat her no worse than she is presently. Kick her aside,
and she will cherish the bruise forever.)

Without stopping, Faust threw the woman a silver angel.
Jenkins, hurrying after, gawked over his shoulder at her.

The tenement streets were narrow, filthy, and crowded.
Children scattered like sparrows at Faust's approach and, like
sparrows, returned to their scratchings in his wake. Beggars
extended hands like claws. From a rotting third-floor window,
an old woman lowered a string with a tin can at its end holding two knives and a copper penny.

"Yoo-hoo!" she shouted. "Mr. Scissors-man!"

A hunchbacked grinder, his wheel set on a hand-barrow,
hobbled and shoved the device her way with a wild, shoulder-
looping gait. Suddenly one of the sparrows swooped in front
of him to tip the can, scatter the knives, and scoop up the
penny. The urchin ran away, laughing, in a rain of shouted
abuse. One idler shied a brickbat after him, but missed.

Faust watched all with the bright eye of an outland barbarian who knows so little of civilization that to him such
squalor seems colorful. "It has been a long time since last I
walked for pleasure. This air seems fresh to me. These people—captivating! Talk to me. I have not had any decent conversation for months."

"Not even your peers will speak to you, then?" Jenkins asked suspiciously.

"I have no peers. I am unequaled, and thus solitary. Save in my imaginings, my work has been my only companion, my deepest passion, my all, for I forget how many years. It is a terrible thing to labor so, to force one's way through the caverns of ignorance, to struggle under the crushing weight of economic necessity, to suffer fools with money and idiots with influence, to toil, and muck, and swelter, watching lesser men enjoy the rewards that should properly be mine, but burdened so that I could not enjoy those rewards were they offered me—and then to be done. Suddenly I am without purpose. One direction is the same as another to me. Everything is equally meaningless. I am bereft."

Jenkins stared. "I am dumbfounded to hear you say so."

"Do you doubt me, you gnat? Do you dare?" Faust turned upon the mechanic in a fury. "I assure you: I have suffered much."

(Faust. Remember his purpose.)

He smiled grimly. "Or could it be that, against your will, you find yourself in sympathy with me? That you hear me giving voice to words that might well have come out of your own mouth?"

"I—yes." Jenkins looked pale, shaken.

"There is the difference between us. I know you down to the bottom of your soul, and you comprehend me not a whit. Divert me! Tell me . . ." He glanced about, seeking inspiration from the crowded street, with its ragged and unhappy denizens, its filth. "Tell me of . . ."

(Ask about the incident of Sandwich's coach.)

"Tell me of Lord Sandwich and his coach."

"I had all but forgotten." Jenkins's lips twisted up on one

side at the memory. "It happened on this very street. I—but how did you know to ask?"

"Never mind. Go on."

"I was returning from the plant when I saw it. Twelve hours' labor in your forge of human degradation, and what little time was left to me spent—well, never mind. I saw it: all gilded and painted like a whore. It filled the street. You cannot imagine what an astonishing sight it was to see *here*, where no lord has honest business. The Virgin herself could not have created a greater stir.

"People came running into the street to see this wonder and try for a glimpse of the great man himself—but he kept his window curtained. The driver I now believe was lost, for he was crimson with choler, and when the crowds did not give way fast enough to suit him, he cursed them and laid upon them with his whip."

"I take it that was inadvisable."

"It worked for a moment." Jenkins snickered. "Then somebody flung a turd."

"A what?"

"A turd. It hit the coach with a moist sound, and then slowly slid down the enameled side. The coachman was so amazed he could not move. Nor did anyone else on the street. They stood like so many wax-mannikins.

"Then a woman laughed—a coarse laugh, like a donkey's bray. It was as if all had been awaiting just that token of permission to vent their passions. Women jeered and shook their fists. Stones were dug out of the street. They rattled the coach like hail. Men beat upon its sides with sticks.

"Oh, but it was glorious! I had never before seen the people so aroused against their exploiters. A festive madness gripped us all and filled us with joyous rage. For a moment I thought the Revolution was upon us. But then the driver managed to rouse the horses sufficiently to break free of the press of bodies. Lord Sandwich, who had stayed hidden throughout, stuck his head out to shout abuse at us all as base knaves and unpatriotic rogues. And that was when he was struck by the *second* turd." A merry light danced in Jenkins's eyes, so that for an instant his face was young again and surprisingly pleasant.

Faust chuckled. "I would have given much to see it!" Then he said, "So you are a radical?"

The mechanic's face hardened with dismay. He had clearly not intended to reveal so much. But he straightened his shoulders and thrust out his chin. "Yes—I am. In thought if not in deed. You can kill me for my beliefs, if you like—I know I cannot stop you—but you can never kill the beliefs themselves."

"Kill the Collectivist dream?" Faust said. "Why should I desire such a thing? It was I who wrote its ideologies."

"You! But—why?"

"Factory work is difficult, tedious, and injurious to the soul as well as the body. Men cannot live without hope. So I gave them some—a perfect world for their grandchildren and free beer on Sundays! A harmless enough drug, you might say, a soporific for the distraction of the working class and the alleviation of its despair."

(Here we are.)

Faust stopped. "Here we are."

"Here? Where?"

"Why, your lodgings, where else? So that I may read— what is it your thesis is called?—*The Implications of Static Conditions Upon the Propagation of Light*."

*   *   *

"Thomas Luffkin and Samuel Rid," Jenkins said. He stood by his room's single window, staring blindly out into the air-shaft, while Faust went through his papers. "I might have been content with my sorry condition but for them. But you paid their way to Cambridge and then Oxford, and sent me along with them—as their bootblack! I had to wait upon those geese to earn my credits, perform the calculations they were too lazy to work themselves, and listen in silence to their mis-constructions of what they had been taught. They were pig-headed fools! How could you not have known?"

(Feign indifference.)

"How indeed?"

"How they mocked me! How they hated me for being what they pretended to be! Four years I waited upon them, while my supposed teachers fed me as much nonsense as fact. Ansely taught that color was a product of the conflict between light and darkness. I spent forty-eight hours without food or sleep trying to make sense of his system, before realizing at last that it was merely an allegory of the human soul, caught up in the war between good and evil."

"You thought it insipid."

"I thought it wrong! Then Luffkin and Rid put their two half-wits together and composed a tract asserting that light was neither motion nor particle but nothing other than a ten-sion in the luminiferous ether—and for this they got not only their degrees, but positions as your scientific advisors!"

(Soon. Not yet.)

"Mmmmm."

"I was denied my degree because the professors rejected out of hand my definition of time as a dimension. They would not hear my arguments! Rid and Luffkin, who do nothing now but attend plays, frequent the vaulting-houses, and grow fat

on boiled puddings and clotted cream, have blocked my every
attempt to find work worthy of me. But I shall have the last
laugh! I have finished my great work, and will somehow get
it published, and it shall be remembered long after Luffkin
and Rid are quite forgotten!"

(Now the truth.)

"I never expected anything from them. They were but
goads to urge you on."

Jenkins swung around, so startled that all attempts to sup-
press those emotions that rose up unbidden within him were
futile. Even as his mouth twisted into a denying smirk, his
eyes grew wide with hope. Now he leaned over the paper
Faust was reading and jabbed a finger at one heavily worked
passage. "Do you—can you follow my reasoning? Any veloc-
ity compounded with the speed of light, you see, yields the
same result. Invariably. And thus—"

(Praise him.)

Faust made a small correction. "Yes. You have not betrayed my faith in you. This work is excellent. Most fine."

Wagner was waiting back at the office. The office-staff had
deserted their desks and were clustered behind him, heads
bobbing nervously, like so many contemptible fools and
round-eyed owls. Wagner shot a jealous glance at the gangly
mechanic and in his most formal voice said, "Master, Lord
Sandwich bids you join with the Admiralty in Somerset
House, to aid in their deliberations."

"Tell Sandwich I have better ways to waste my time."
Faust put a hand to his door. "This fellow has a thesis. Publish
it, and see it is added to the curriculum of all the colleges.
Find him a desk. Put him to work."

"But you *must* obey the summons," Wagner squeaked. "You are needed to . . ."

"All that I can do is done. It is out of my hands. I will be in my office. Do not disturb me for any reason."

He closed the door.

Mephistopheles was already within. He had embodied himself as a scrawny caricature of an admiral, with a jutting chin and beak nose, hair pulled back tight in a pig-tail, and silken hose. He had a tiny corkscrew of a penis, whose outlines could be clearly seen through his tights.

"Smile," he said. "You are about to make history."

"History." Faust sat heavily upon the couch he kept in his office for those nights he worked late. "What does that word mean? I knew when I began this—but now? I feel such an emptiness. So much work! For what? Just what have I labored so long and hard to accomplish?" He looked at the demon with weary loathing. "Well?"

"Tell me exactly what you want to hear," Mephistopheles said, fluffing the lace at his sleeves, "and I swear I will spoon every word into your ear, down to the last syllable."

"I want nothing more nor less than the truth. The truth! And this time do not stuff me like a turkey with facts, numbers, schemata, tables, and graphs. I require perspective. Let me experience this great event vigorously and with the undimmed senses and emotions of youth."

"It will not be easy." Mephistopheles chewed his lip, as if thinking. "But very well—lie down, make yourself comfortable. Stare at the ceiling. Relax."

Faust lay back. He let his gaze unfocus and saw the ocean, vast beyond reckoning, and upon it ships in the thousands. Then his vision wrenched violently about, sea trading places with sky, and the ships that were so minuscule grew to monstrous size and swallowed him up and he was Faust no more.

He was a young Catalan named Juan Miguel Aubrion y Ruiz. The metal deck of the ironclad *Cor Mariae* was scorching underfoot but he did not care, for the canvas hood had just been removed from his head. He gaped up at a sky so dazzlingly blue it made his head spin and his eyes ache, and at an enormous slanted smokestack on which was freshly painted the Mother of Sorrows displaying her heart, pierced by seven swords. The soldier who always smelled of garlic was striking his chains now.

After three weeks in a convict-wagon, the freedom to move was intoxicating. Juan shook his head, sending pearls of sweat flying from the tips of his hair, and flung out his arms to stretch the stiffness from them. The clean salt air filled his lungs and he knew in that instant he could make a life for himself here.

"That red bitch is *mine!*"

He whirled. A line of sailors stood by the rail, looking at the newcomers. Some grinned, others did not. The bald giant in the torn shirt pursed his lips and made a little sucking noise. Juan's heart sank.

In all the line, only he had red hair.

Sergeant Garlic snorted a maybe-laugh and moved on to the next man in the coffle. The officer overseeing the transfer stroked his mustaches and looked elaborately away. Soldiers lounged about the deck, in attitudes of bored arrogance. He had no allies anywhere.

Then the chains were all struck, and the sailing-master went down the line making assignments. Juan was handed over to a mulatto Portuguese named Gavilán—possibly because the bright pink scar on his arm looked something like a sparrowhawk—and sent below to muck out the stables.

The forward hold had been rebuilt to house the mounts that the cavalry would require in the fields outside London. "Welcome to Horse Hell," Gavilán said as they descended into the dim-lit, malodorous region. "They hate it here. They hate the crowding, the metal, the dark, the smells, the electric lights, the way the ship moves under them. Watch out for their hooves. Watch out for their teeth. They are all crazy-mean. This is a manure fork. Over here is a canvas sack. You fill up the one with the other and then you drop the manure overboard. On the lee side—never windward, always on the lee side. You understand?"

Juan nodded.

"Good." Gavilán slapped him on the back. "Work hard, boy. Work hard, and you'll soon be out. Somebody will fuck up, and Don Sebastian will give him your job."

He left.

The work was hard. The horses stood in filth up to their fetlocks. The poor creatures were unnerved by their surroundings and at the least excuse would lash out at him in panic. They carried flies, which bit. The stench was unbelievable. Worst of all were the soldiers who, when they came down to fuss over their favorites and found them living in filth, would curse and strike Juan for his laziness. He tried explaining there was more work than one man could do, but they only abused him the more for insolence.

He worked until he thought he would collapse and then, remembering Gavilán's advice, kept on working.

Finally, somebody came and put a hardtack biscuit in his hand and told him that his watch was over. When he had eaten, he went out on deck—all the berths had been reserved

for the soldiers, who were going to conquer England for His
Most Catholic Majesty and thus stood high in his regard—and
found an empty expanse of deck alee of the other sailors.

He went to sleep listening to the many voices of the sea:
the bubbling noise it made against the ironclad's side, the
whimsical bloops and chuckles. The soft crash of distant surf.
The surge of a fresh wind racing across its surface. Such
sounds a man would never grow tired of hearing.

On the fourth day, he was made a gunnery-boy. This
meant he had to carry shells for an irascible Dutch artillery-
man named Rumbartus Jakobszoon. "Poo! Poo!" the Dutchman said when he first reported, waving a hand in front of
his round face. "You go wash them clothes, boy. Wash yourself, too. Make them hose you down with the pumps."

He was shown how to lift a shell safely, and how to slide
it up into the gun. The skill seemed simple enough until the
gun drill began. For three hours he toted the fifty-pound shells
to the gun. There the gunner slammed open the breech and
he slid in the shell. Together they threw their weight against
the cannon so that it slid forward, out through the gun port.

The Dutchman held a headset up to one ear, listening to
the spotters' mock-reports, and consulted an imaginary ballistics table in his free hand. Then he made a few finicky adjustments to the aiming screws on his gun, clapped hand to a
lever, and solemnly said, "Boom."

After which the routine went: Run the gun back, open the
breech, and remove the shell, as if it had been fired. Seize the
swab, dip the head in a bucket of water, thrust it up the bore
to clean out any residue, and return the tool to its clamp.

And then repeat.

The *Cor Mariae* was a 74-gun ship. All up and down the
gun-deck, the cannons were being run out and in, their gun-

ners cursing their assistants in a melange of Dutch, German, and Portuguese—for some reason there were no Spanish-born gunners—because none of them could get the rhythm right. Juan worked with a good will, but still the Dutchman swore at him almost constantly, and struck him several times.

When the drill was finally over, the gunner patted Juan briefly on his back. "You are one piss-in-your-pants lazy gunner-boy," he said. "But better than I expect. Every day we drill like this, so we can beat them bastard English."

"We'll crush them," Juan said confidently. He had been overwhelmed by the size of the ironclad, by its complexity, and its might. A boiler-man had told him it had the destructive force of an army. "The English will take one look at the *Cor Mariae* and—"

"They look at her and they laugh their guts out. You know how they design her? They take a caravel, chop off the masts, add a boiler, and cover it with iron. What you got? Half-turtle and half-by-damn-donkey. Spain builds shit-ass stupid ships. The English, they put on women's dresses and spank each other with sticks, but they build good warships. Low in water, sleek like fish. Very fast. Also they got good crews. They don't use criminals. They don't use idiot boys. They don't train somebody two days and call him a sailor."

Juan's dismay must have shown on his face, for the Dutchman chuckled.

"Never you mind, boy," he said. "We win anyway. We blast them English dog-fuckers good with our big German guns."

That day Juan twice thought he saw the bald giant looking at him. So cold and meaningful were those looks that that night he could not sleep. He threw his blanket over his shoulders and went to the stern, to lean over the rail and stare out across the water.

It was a clear night. The lights of Lisbon harbor were a soft yellow, and the moon above it bright and cold. There were stars in the sky, more than any man could count.

In the dark, somebody approached. He tensed.

But it was only Gavilán. Pipe in mouth, the mulatto picked his way carefully between sleeping sailors. He extended the pipe, stem first. "Try some."

"What is it?" Juan asked, accepting.

"It's called tobacco."

Tobacco was a new wonder. Everyone wanted to try it. Feeling honored, Juan cautiously drew in as much smoke as he could hold in his lungs. It made him dizzy. When he exhaled, all the world rose up in one voice and lifted him briefly into the air above the ship. He handed the pipe back, and after a time Gavilán said, "What was your crime?"

"I was running guns for the Basques and the Communists. Up in the mountains."

A silence. Then: "You should not have told me that."

Juan shrugged. "The magistrate knew. He gave me the choice of prison or the Armada."

For a long time neither spoke. Then Gavilán said, "I was sent here to tell you that you're wanted below, at the machine-shop, aft of the boilers."

"All right." Juan started to fold his blanket.

"Wait. You didn't ask who sent for you."

Juan asked with his eyes.

Gavilán ran a hand over his head, signifying baldness. "He'll be waiting for you just behind the door. I don't think you'll much enjoy what he wants to do with you."

Juan's blood turned cold, and then hot again. But he had

known this was coming. There were things, he now understood, a man was expected to take care of without help. Finally he said, "It is not so much *what* he wants to do, as *how* he wants to do it."

A look flew between them, swift as a bird. Gavilán reached out a hand and touched Juan's red curls. He smiled. "Where did you get these?"

Juan's father was an Irish sailor who had lost a foot unloading cargo in Barcelona and later drifted inland, looking for work. He had stayed long enough in Vilada to sire three children on Juan's mother and then left again. Juan said nothing of that, however, but moved his head under the mulatto's hand.

"You'll need a weapon." Gavilán reached inside his jersey and withdrew a length of chain. "Wrap it around your hand, so you don't drop it. Make a loop, take the other end in your fist. You can hurt him as bad as you like, and nobody will complain. Only don't kill him. If you kill him, Don Sebastian will tie you to his corpse and drop you both overboard."

Juan stood outside the machine-shop, savoring the darkness. The nearest electric bulb not burnt out or broken was far down the passageway, a pinpoint of light. He put one hand on the door. With the other he swung the chain slightly, noiselessly, until it felt right in his grip.

Then he slammed the door open and in one smooth motion turned and whipped back his arm. Make the first blow to the face, as hard and savage as he could. Let it wrap around the giant's head. Then rip it back. Pull the bastard's face down and bring a knee up to meet it. After that it would be as simple as beating a drunk with a cudgel.

"Take this, you bugger," he whispered savagely.

But then something horrible happened.

In the darkness, where the giant should have been, stood a grotesque figure, painted like a *commedia dell'arte* player, and grinning like the moon. His face was all chin and jutting nose, yellow teeth and malice. He was dressed as an English admiral. A dark aura of absolute, unfettered evil gushed from him like a wind. There was no mistaking who it was.

"Saint Anna preserve me!" Juan cried, stepping back.

"Hello, Juan," the Tempter of Men said. "I'm so glad you could answer my summons."

"Please . . ." The chain fell from Juan's nerveless hand.

The darkness welled and intensified until all that could be seen was that pale face, like a boat bobbing on the infinite sea of night. Two white-gloved hands floated up out of nowhere to seize Juan's shoulders in a painful grip.

"Let me explain to you," the Horned One said, "the nature of history."

"What?"

"The first thing you need to know is that history happens almost exclusively in the dark. The second . . . well, let's not get ahead of ourselves. I can sum up your lessons perfectly in three *dicta*. But will you learn? No. Mere assertion lacks the force and conviction of experience. As I shall now proceed to demonstrate."

The Calamity of the World puckered his mouth and stuck out a long pink tongue. Juan could not move. The tongue stretched out far, far, impossibly far. He shivered with loathing at its approach. The tip reared back, then darted forward like a snake. It struck him in the center of his forehead. His skull cracked open like an eggshell.

The cold black air flooded in and overwhelmed him.

When he opened his eyes, it was three days later, and the English fleet had just been sighted.

"I had a terrible dream," Juan said.

"Don't tell me it." Gavilán made the sign of the cross and spat to one side. "Bad dreams are bad luck. Forget you had it, and maybe we'll survive this terrible day." He gave Juan a little squeeze, and Juan rubbed a thumb against the sparrow-hawk scar on his arm that he now knew to be a brand. Then everyone was called on deck to hear the admiral.

They had followed a course north against an unfavorable wind. In the days before steam, such a wind would have held them helpless indefinitely. Now, the old hands joked, they'd be anchored in the Thames before the food had a chance to rot.

The admiral spoke to the Armada over the radio. His speech was patched into the intercom. On deck the soldiers stood at attention in stiff ranks to listen to the hissing, crackling words. The seamen were more slovenly, lounging with elaborate lack of discipline against the rails, but every bit as intent. He told them to do their duty, that Jesus and all the saints were watching, and that divine intercession was all but guaranteed. Then he reminded them of the punishments for shirking, cowardice, desertion, and drawing a weapon on a superior officer.

Juan was not really listening, because a devilish flea was hopping furiously about in his hair, biting him first here, then there, and finally burrowing into his ear. Unobtrusively, he brought his little finger to the opening and tried to dig it out.

(That won't work, sweet baby!) cried a tiny voice from the bottom of the ear canal. (I promised to explain these things to you and I will—I will!)

The admiral's voice still echoed and rattled in the loud-speakers. (He talks of Spanish technological superiority) said the flea (by which he means the German guns. From his spies, however, he has received sure intelligence that he cannot win the coming battle. Alas, he has no more choice than you. The King demands he fight, and so he must. Nor has the King any choice. His creditors must have England, or they'll foreclose on his holdings. They, in turn, are dangerously overextended from paying for these very ships and guns. Everyone knows this for folly; but from the bankers to the King to the admiral to Don Sebastian to you, the daisy-chain of economic necessity rules all. Here is your second lesson: History is that which cannot be prevented.)

This was nonsense. I will not, Juan thought, listen to a flea.

(But who else will ever tell you the truth?)

The speech ended, and all cheered. Then they were discharged.

Juan was among the first belowdecks. The steel steps rang underfoot and filled the passageway with echoes. He ran to his post by the shell-racks and waited.

Hours passed.

The great motors started up and filled the ship with their world-shaking throb. Then they died down into silence again. Time passed. They started again, died again, started again. The ship was moving. The gunners put on their headsets and bent over their guns, making fine adjustments. But again, nothing happened.

Sometime much later, Juan found himself wondering when the battle would finally begin. Nothing could be worse than the waiting for it.

(Why, this is it, darling child, this is it!) cried the flea. (There are three stages to a battle: First you're bored. Then you're terrified. Then you're dead. Each is necessary, and they must all come in the proper order.)

"Stop digging in your ear," the Dutchman grumbled. "It is very annoying to look at."

(Don't mind him!) sang the flea. (His hemorrhoids are in bloom.)

Alarms sounded. Again, the gunners bent over their guns. Again, nothing happened.

"Little flea," Juan whispered, quietly so nobody would overhear, "what is going on?"

(I'll tell you) said the tiny voice. (The mighty crescent of the Armada continues steaming steadily northward. Ahead, blocking the Channel, is an array of English ships. They are outnumbered. Numerous though they are, they seem pathetically small and few by contrast with the Spanish forces.)

Good, Juan thought.

More alarms rang. Several seamen raced through the gunroom, were cursed at angrily, and were gone. There was a change in the sound and tempo of the engines. Outside, enormous noises, one after another. *Whumph. Whumph. Whumph.* Explosions.

The ship had changed course.

"Flea!" Juan whispered urgently.

(The left flank of the crescent has swept into a minefield only the English knew was there. Three ironclads have gone up in flames. They list and careen, no longer under rational control—two of the captains are dead and the third gone mad. I defy anyone to tell which is the piloted ship. All up and down the crescent, the ironclads are breaking formation to avoid the mines and the burning warships. The confusion spreads. Now ships are veering to evade the veering ships. Oh, I wish I could show you the mathematics for this! Such

splendid catastrophic geometries! Such flowers of fractal disarray!)

It was still quiet in the gun-room. "When are we going to
shoot some Englishmen?" a gunnerboy asked. "Shut your
mouth!" his gunner snapped back.

(Now this is lovely! Smoke sprouts from the English ships.
But unlike the smoke of honest cannons, which appears in
white puffs like cotton, these fly up in a steep arc, unnaturally
fast, scratching thin white lines into the sky.)

The gunners were leaning into their headsets again, asking
questions of the spotters, casting puzzled looks at one another.
One raised his hand in a high arc and brought it down again,
as steeply. Chuckles went up and down the line.

"What is it?" Juan asked, aware that he was only one of
many demanding the same knowledge of their masters.

"The English," said the Dutchman, face red with merri-
ment, "fire off their guns very high, almost straight up. You
know ballistics, boy? No, of course not. Up high fast means
back down fast." He made the same hand-gesture his brother
up the line had, like a leaping porpoise. "It means no distance.
They shoot off their guns and they don't hit us."

A screaming filled the air.

They hadn't even fired their first cannonade.

That much Juan was sure of, and nothing more. All he
knew was that one moment he stood by the cannon, ready to
snatch a shell from the racks on the bulkhead, and the next
he lay bleeding on the deck. There was smoke everywhere. It
was difficult to see, there was so much. And flames.

What happened, he tried to say. But he could not hear his
own voice. His ears rang as if all the world were a bell and
his head had been used for the clapper. Dimly, he could make

out a dull rhythmical pounding underfoot. A horrible scorched smell filled his nose. Looking up, he saw blue sky where none should be. The iron decks of the *Cor Mariae* had been torn open by some great explosion. Which explained why there was so much twisted metal about, so many mangled machines.

So many corpses.

Little flea, Juan thought, tell me what happened. The flea did not answer. But out of the chaos of noise and reverberation, clear as nothing else was, came a familiar, hateful voice. "No, no, no, sweet idiot, don't seek for me within yourself—war is strictly an external phenomenon!"

He turned his head toward the voice.

The Scourge of Humanity sat straddling a gun that had survived intact, shrieking and giggling and kicking his feet. "Yes!" he cried. "Oh, my dear fellow! You should have seen, you should simply have *seen* it! The English rockets rained down upon the fleet long before it got within cannon range. They fell and missed and fell and missed and fell and missed, as profligate as rain. But their numbers were so great they could not always miss, and where they hit, they exploded—magnificent explosions!—leaving great jagged holes in the ironclads and strewing the ocean surface with corpses. Now the English have come in range and are bombarding the disabled ships."

"But we are defenseless," Juan objected. Something exploded far away within the ship, and the deck tilted wildly. Briefly the pounding ceased. Then it began again, louder than before. "Why bombard us? It makes no sense."

"It makes manifest sense. It is not enough merely to kill the enemy," the Father of Filth explained. "They must first be stripped of any slightest pretense to either dignity or decency.

Before they die, they must be made to perform the unspeakable. Only then, when they have relinquished all claim to humanity, are you truly victorious. For then you have proved beyond question your own moral superiority."

"I must get up," Juan said. There was a weight upon his legs. It was the Dutchman's corpse. Revolted, he pushed it off. He found he could—dizzily, weakly—stand. Astern, the gun-deck slanted into darkness. He thought he could hear water. Forward, the bulkheads had collapsed, so that there was no passage. The upper gun-deck had collapsed into the lower; the blue-skied hole was far out of reach.

His head was beginning to clear now, and with thought came fear. The *Cor Mariae* was foundering. Soon it would sink. He must make his way to the lifeboats if he wanted to survive.

The pounding continued.

"The only way out is up," the Cloven-Hoofed One said. "But it's too high to jump, you can't scale the walls, and there's no ladder. Do you have the ingenuity to escape? Let's find out! Consider it a test of your native intelligence."

The gun on which the Son of Cruelty sat rose high enough that a man standing atop it, arms extended, could just reach the deck beams. But it was nowhere near the hole, and it weighed far too much to be moved. There was a tool-chest nearby, which he might be able to stand on end. Juan flung open the lid and desperately began to empty it.

"Oh, marvelous! Marvelous! Let all Creation assemble and bow down before the philosopher-ape, the physical embodiment of pure reason and tool-using pinnacle of evolution." Juan turned toward the Angel of Despite. "Fool! Observe the deck."

Juan looked and saw how tilted it was. Even if he could

slide the chest up beneath the hole, it would only slide back down again.

Stop, he told himself. Think. What is there at hand that I can use as a tool? He craned about and saw—there!—a coil of rope. And over by the Dutchman was the long-poled swab used to clean the bore between firings. He snatched them both up from the rubble. Now he had it!

(If only that damned pounding would cease!)

He tied one end of the rope about the center of the swab. Then he threw it like a javelin out the hole and onto the deck. The rope played out easily.

When the swab came to rest, he began to slowly pull it back. "Catch, you bastard," he muttered.

But it slid easily and without impediment up the sloping deck and over the edge of the hole. He jumped back as it clattered down, to avoid being struck.

He threw it a second time.

Again it did not catch. Again it fell.

His tormentor hooted with laughter. "You lose, you lose, you lose! Dear friend, you are simply too stupid to live!"

Juan took a deep, angry breath, and then caught himself. He was an idiot. He'd been throwing the pole downslope, along the deck. But if he simply turned and flung it over the side, there was an excellent chance his javelin would hook upon the rail.

He shifted position and aimed.

He was about to throw when the pounding underfoot reached a crescendo and a hatch flew open in the deck not twenty feet astern.

Men poured out of the hatchway like damned souls escaping from Hell. Black smoke gushed out with them and filled the gun-deck, making Juan choke and gag. Then the sailors reached him and with fists and rough hands cuffed and shoved him aside. "Wait!" he cried. "I've—"

But they had been through too much and were now too panicked to listen. In a frenzy of fear, the sailors knocked the rope from his hands, snapped the swab, ripped his shirt half off him. They stretched longing arms toward the hole in the deck above. They leaped, though it was patently impossible to jump so high. They clambered up on top of each other, every man trying to scale the others' bodies into daylight.

All in a panic, Juan fought to keep his feet. If he were to fall, he would be trampled to death. There were so many of them! He was spun around, and saw flames shoot up through the hatchway. There would be no more sailors escaping the lower decks now.

The flames licked against a toppled rack of shells. Juan caught his breath in terror.

"Oh, don't be a weakling—join the fray!" the Great Adversary jeered. "Claw your way to freedom! If the shells go up, how many will survive—one? Fight! Perhaps that one will be you!"

Too fearful even to hate himself, Juan found that he had charged into the crush of sailors and was shoving his rivals aside, as mindless as any of them, struggling to climb the bodies of the men before him.

He climbed, and wrestled, and fought with a dreamlike sense of inevitability. The bodies stank of scorched flesh and human fear. He breathed deep of that stench and it filled him with dread and strength and made him impervious to pain. He lost himself in animal terror and scrabbling hands. A fist hit his eye. An elbow smashed him in the face. He lost a tooth. A finger snapped. His mouth filled with blood. And in the middle of this nightmarish struggle he experienced a fleeting instant's clarity and he thought: This must be what eternal damnation is like. Here and now extended forever and without end.

In that same instant he placed a foot upon a sailor's shoulder and the man's arm came twisting around to throw him off and he saw high up on the dark and blistered biceps a pink scar in the shape of a sparrowhawk.

As if by lightning-flash, he stared unbelieving into Gavilán's wild and unrecognizing eyes, as terrified as those of the horses now surely dying in the forward hold. Then a surge of blind panic lifted him up and he put all his weight onto the foot and rose into the air, stepping on first his friend's shoulder and then upon his face. Miraculously, he climbed to the top of the writhing heap.

Juan stretched out his arm as high as it would go, toward the jagged deck-edge.

Then the ship lurched again. Black waters came roaring up the gun-deck from below, fast as a locomotive. He felt the human pyramid beneath him totter and sway. It was collapsing! They would none of them be saved! They would all die!

A hand reached down from above to seize his wrist, and he was hauled free.

Sobbing with relief, Juan let himself be lifted up. Below him he heard the waters slam over the sailors, and their wailing cries of horror as they were crushed, broken, swept away. Dangling within that sure grip, he found himself laughing with hysterical relief. He looked up gratefully at his savior.

The Evil One smiled down on him.

Effortlessly, he held Juan over the churning waters and the drowning sailors below.

"It's been *so* much fun, old man. But now I'm afraid it's over. Here is your third and final lesson: History is simply life with all the bits any sane person might care to experience left out."

"Why?" Juan asked, weeping in despair. "Why must I die? What have I done that I must suffer so?"

"Done? Why should you have to do anything in order to suffer? A friend of mine wanted to understand history," the Unholy Goat said. "Your suffering was all to satisfy his curiosity, nothing more. Now it's over. I've put on my little puppet-show, and it's time I withdrew my hand from your bung-hole. But first . . . Can I tell you a secret?" He placed his lips next to Juan's ear, and whispered, *"You don't exist.* You never did."

He let Juan fall.

Juan hit the iron-cold water as hard as if it had been granite. With humiliation, he realized that all that the Opponent had said was true. Even as he thrashed and struggled for life, he felt his identity—his being—his self—slipping away.

He choked, panicked, and in a flurry of bubbles and despair was again Faust.

It was daylight—a new day.

He staggered from the room, bloodless and drawn. He was not sure how much time had passed. One day? Four? Anxious faces turned up toward him from every desk and cubicle.

"It is over," he said. "England is victorious."

In that instant the telegraph began to chatter. The operator tore off his headset and flung it high into the air. "Victory!" he screamed.

Everywhere the staff was cheering.

Lambart Jenkins seized the man nearest him, and crushed Wagner in a hug. Then he climbed atop his desk and shouted at the top of his lungs, "Huzzah for England! Huzzah for Sandwich! Huzzah for Foster!"

But Faust was already out the door.

So haggard was he, and so poorly dressed, that he was not recognized. He watched, unmolested, as the great news spread through the capital. The factories emptied out into the streets. Constellations of bonfires were built upon every hill-top and commons, wherever there was space for them. Troops of boys ran with flaming faggots down every street. Stilt-walkers strode through the crowds. Women exposed their breasts. Impromptu processions with bearded men dressed in black standing atop wagons and waving slide rules, imper-sonated him with widely varying degrees of success.

Faust was now the most popular man in London.

The thought disgusted him.

15

THE ABORTION

Gretchen sat in an empty room. Dust motes swirled about her in the cool light that bounced from the whitewashed walls.

Silence filled her.

After a time, she lit a cigarette.

Father's health was failing. Mother had lost so much of herself in tending to his decline that, in her letters, she no longer even attempted to disguise the empty sense of despair she felt. So much of her life was bound up in her husband that she could see no point to an existence that did not include his presence. When Gretchen was a child, her mother had often told her a story about an ogre who could not be killed because he had hidden his heart inside an egg at the center of an old oak tree, and who died when the tree was struck by lightning. Father was the oak in which her mother's heart was kept. She might not live beyond his collapse. Even if she did, it was certain she would never again play an active role in the business.

When Father died, as he someday must, everything Gretchen had built would come crashing in on her. She had taken care to complicate the legal situation as much as possible, but on one point the law was explicit: If she didn't have a male guardian overseeing her, the courts would have to appoint one.

Wulf was the most likely candidate.

Not that he had the character needed to run Reinhardt Industries. He had not even had the courage to confront Gretchen in person when he attempted to blackmail her. He had simply placed the photos in an envelope and left it on her desk for her to discover. Gretchen had felt no compunction whatever at having him beaten and his house burned down to ensure the negatives were destroyed.

Nor had he the brains. She had come to his bedside with flowers and soup which she told him had been made with her own hands. (It was a white lie; Abelard had made it, of course.) Then she sat by him and reminisced about their childhoods together, laughing at the funny parts, holding his hand when remembering those who had died. Wölfchen, she had called him then, little wolf, the same as when they were young. By the time she left, he was baffled as to whether he was in the hospital by her doing or not.

A man that simple would be a disaster trying to run a major corporation.

But for all his flaws, Gretchen would not fire him. With the slow dwindling of her family, she had come more and more to cherish what fragments of it remained. Anyway, better the wolf in the fold than lurking outside in the dark. She liked having him where she could keep an eye on him. She liked being able to appoint his secretarial staff. If only every threat to her could be so easily handled!

The world was full of intangible enemies.

Even Aunt Penniger, silly and foolish woman that she was, sensed this new darkness. Just last Sunday, at dinner, she had said, "Have you noticed how everyone holds the same opinions nowadays? It's as if they're all afraid to disagree. Do they think that if they stand out, something will happen to them? I suppose they must."

"I imagine," Gretchen said, "it's these new notions that are about. Anarchy and labor-unionism—whoever heard of such things? Nobody is satisfied with his station anymore and those who are in consequence insist on holding on to what they've got with both hands. No wonder there's unrest."

"I feel sorry for those poor miners. The ones in the newspaper."

"That's a very complicated tangle of issues. Mind you, what the Margrave did was wrong. But they should never have resorted to violence and sabotage. They should never have occupied the mines. What did they expect? That the soldiers would simply turn around and go away?"

"It sounds such a terrible way to die. It makes one feel funny, knowing that one's own companies produced the—"

"Aunt Penniger!"

She looked away. "Well, what do I know? I'm only an old woman." Then, more firmly, "Such atrocities never happened when I was young! Things were better managed then. Soldiers only killed other soldiers."

"That's sad, too, if you stop and think about it."

"It just seems that there's more sadness to go around these days. It's as if somebody had built a mill, like that little mill at the bottom of the sea churning out salt, only this one a mill of misery. So many troubles!" Aunt Penniger shook her head. "At any rate, it's a sorry business."

By which—Gretchen understood—she meant everything.

It was true. Polluted by a thousand untraceable sources, growing grimmer and more violent by the day for reasons nobody could adequately explain, the world was sliding into chaos and something worse than chaos, for which there was no name. Laughter was rarer than it had once been on the streets, marching societies more common. Everyone knew that the wooden rifles they drilled with were not the only weapons they possessed. Everyone knew that their bellowed pledges of fealty to an Emperor who was both weak and conveniently distant were a sham, and that their only loyalty was to themselves. Everyone knew their rude and unlettered leaders had political ambitions.

The telephone rang, but she did not answer it.

She was pregnant.

It was not supposed to be possible. Faust had told her so. He had promised she would not get pregnant. He had given her his explicit and most solemn word on it.

So how could this be?

For a time she had considered the possibility that Wulf had suborned a chemist and had her birth control pills replaced with placebos. It was exactly the kind of comic-opera plotting to which he was prone. But, no, really, it was her own fault. She hadn't read the documentation carefully. She hadn't kept an exact record of her menstrual cycle. More than once she had had too much to drink and forgotten to take them at all. There were few things she hadn't done, not many mistakes she'd failed to make.

Faust had assured her it wouldn't happen.

It wasn't his responsibility, though, was it?

Now she was crying. She had to consider the consequences, and she was alone and bereft of hope and without the benefit of Faust's advice.

The law was never easy on unmarried women who found themselves in such a state. She could be imprisoned until the child was born, then publicly whipped, and driven penniless out of Nuremberg, clutching her bastard in her arms. Then, if she survived the stone-throwers and lowlifes who thought a woman stripped of the protection of the law a jolly thing to hunt down, she could choose between living as a beggar or a whore. That or let her baby starve.

She thought about the baby, sleeping deep within her. She had wanted children someday. Not now.

What kind of life would her child have to look forward to? The bastard daughter of a whore grew up to become a whore. The fatherless son of a beggar might, if intelligent, become a card-sharp and confidence-trickster, or, if ambitious, a highwayman. Otherwise, a common thief. He was sure to die on the gallows.

Such grotesque scenarios were the stuff of a radio melodrama. Even though they were sober fact, she could not honestly believe in them. It was hard to imagine the wheel of fate plunging her so low after raising her to such wealth.

Money, of course, brought its own protections. If she could prove she was secretly pledged to be married, all charges would be dropped. The city fathers would not look too closely at the proof. A stammering swineherd's word that he was the father would be good enough to send the happy couple packing to the wedding chapel.

Gretchen had to laugh. There was no shortage of candidates, at least. And how many of them would refuse her?

Refuse her hand, her houses, her lands, her factories, her influence, her power, her wealth? Not many.

But she needed more than just a husband.

She needed someone who would raise over her the benevolent umbrella of his Y-chromosome, while leaving her in control of the family holdings. Someone secure enough in himself
to trust her to run the day-to-day operations. Someone whose
presence would not grow tedious in a week. Someone whose
commands she would respect and gladly obey. Someone who
would listen to her. Someone she could respect.

There was only one such man in existence, and he was
living in permanent exile in London.

The bastard!

He should be here to comfort her. Just his presence would
be enough to quell this unbearable panic, his arms about her,
his murmured assurances . . . It hardly mattered if they were
lies. Oh, but she was the most wretched woman in existence!
Even Mother, wrinkled and worn though she was, had had
her great passion—she and Father had spent decades together.
Their painful farewell was not an unreasonable price to pay
for what they'd had. Gretchen, by contrast, had enjoyed only
a handful of months with her love. In memory their time together had steadily diminished, months becoming weeks and
weeks turned to days, until now all that remained were a few
bright Arabian hours, like a child's recollection of the pictures
in a book of wonder-tales read to her in a garden that had
vanished long ago.

If Faust were to walk into the room at this very instant,
she'd spit in his face. She would! It was criminal, what he'd
done to her. She had trusted him. She had relied upon him.
Now, when she needed him most, he was impossibly distant,
in the faraway mists of England. He might as well be in Ul-

tima Thule, for all the good he could do her. Even if she were to write him begging for aid, the letter would take a week to wend its way across the continent and into his office, with another week for his response to retrace its path to her.

She didn't have two weeks. Her belly had begun inexorably to swell. She had bound it down with swaths of cloth, and made small jokes about how chubby she'd grown from overeating. But people were beginning to wonder. Soon they'd begin to talk.

The future stretched before her, desolate and haunted with regret. She would hold this day and the guilt she now felt within her for the rest of her life. She was not the type who could forgive herself such a blunder.

Downstairs she had a Parisian fashion magazine with her picture on the cover, an advance copy sent as a courtesy to her by the publisher. Within was an article extolling her as the New Woman—CHIC, POWERFUL, AND IN CONTROL.

She was not in control.

Just yesterday, she'd been going over the architectural models of the Reinhardt Pavilion for next year's Exposition of European Industry. The pilings for the exhibition halls were already being pounded into the fields outside of Amsterdam. Next summer hundreds of thousands of visitors would course through them. Since her companies had more new products to promote than any other corporation, they planned the most spectacular showcase. It was going to be a glass palace, all windows, demonstrating the structural freedom offered by steel-frame construction. Gretchen had briefly considered erecting a skyscraper, but there was neither the time nor a suitably bedrocked location.

"The labor unions have, of course, been, well. Paid off,"

Dreschler had commented in passing. "So there will be no trouble from that quarter."

"Paid off? Do you mean bribery?"

"That is, umm, not an entirely pleasant word for it." Dreschler's doughy face took on a pained expression. "It is more in the nature of an advance payment to ensure the labor force will be satisfied with the negotiated wage schedules."

"But the men actually doing the work—how much of this advance money will they see?"

"That's up to their, ah, leaders. I didn't care to look into it too closely."

"Well, you *should!*" Gretchen exploded. Maybe it was the hormones flooding her body, rendering her own emotions unfamiliar and treacherous. Maybe it was just the tension of being in this terrifying fix and having to hide it from the world. Whatever the reason, she had flown off the handle, and lectured Dreschler for a good twenty minutes on corporate citizenship, responsibility, and why it was simply good business to keep their hands scrupulously clean. It was only when she was done that she looked around and actually *saw* the secretaries, designers, and model-makers, standing about redfacedly trying to pretend they had seen and heard nothing. Only then that she realized Dreschler should have been reprimanded in private, away from his underlings. Only then that she saw the rage and humiliation in his eyes.

"Yes," he'd said. "I understand, truly. I do."

One thinks of oneself as a good person. One is not an objective judge. Some of the things she'd done . . . she didn't want to think about them. It was so easy to be corrupted by events. All it took was the decision, not necessarily conscious, not to bother thinking about the consequences.

How could she be pregnant?

She should never have relied on the assurances of a man. Men and women were cats and birds, really. There might be a fondness between one and the other, a temporary truce between individuals now and then. A goldfinch and a tortoise-shell might well fall in love. But the imbalance of power was always there, and it was not a wise little finch who went to sleep first.

She was crying again. It felt like she was being punished for some crime the nature of which nobody would inform her. When she had first begun dealing with governments and court royalty, Gretchen had been astounded by how callous those in power were—how ready to employ force and brutality, how easily they spoke of "collateral damage" and "battlefield statistics" when what they meant was human deaths. Every king in Christendom, and several from without, had sent envoys begging her to develop for them more effective ways of killing larger numbers of people.

What had she ever done that was half so evil?

She had worked so hard. She had dedicated herself to the material betterment of society. Late nights, twenty-hour days, missed meals—whatever was needed, that had she done. None of this had been for her own enrichment and aggrandizement; those had come to her, admittedly, but they had never been the purpose of her labor. She'd had the talent, and so she'd employed it.

She was exhausted with thought; she wanted never to think again. But she did not have that option. Her mind would not stop. Like a tongue to an aching tooth, it returned again and again to her predicament, poking and prodding and refreshing the pain. There were no answers. There were no solutions. Even the questions had grown stale and meaningless with repetition. But the hounds of thought insisted on yet again running her down the labyrinth of regret, whose passages led to no center and whose perimeter held no exit.

She could not flee.

There was nowhere to go. Nowhere she wasn't known. Nowhere the sudden appearance of a pregnant woman with money and no family wouldn't raise questions. There was that damned magazine with her picture on the cover, and it was only one of many. She was known everywhere. Anyway, and always, if she fled, what would become of Reinhardt Industries? It would collapse like a playing-card castle without her leadership. She owed her employees more than that.

The problem was, the world had grown small. Distances were not as great as they once were. A month-long wagontrip could no longer hide one's past. Five hundred miles meant nothing to a determined prosecutor. Soon, the technocrats would connect and reconcile the hundreds of competing telegraph and telephone systems into one buzzing web of lines and information, intruding into every town and hamlet, rendering every part of the continent no more than a second away. There would be no more secrets then. It would pretty much put an end to privacy and personal liberty altogether.

She wasn't at all sure she wanted to live in such a world.

There never was an actual decision. One day she had simply gone to see Gunther Haaft. Haaft was a chemist and a gentle soul, one of the best researchers she had, and certainly the most discreet. She had asked him for the name of a man who could perform the operation.

"What an odd request. Whyever would you want to know such a thing?" Haaft had said. A little smile flickered like foxfire on his long plain features. "Were you of your mother's generation, I'd suspect that your daughter had—" He stopped.

The lies came so readily to her lips. No, of course not. Marketing requires certain information. One of our biologists has shown startling results on the treatment of senility utilizing fetal brain tissue. We're putting together an atlas of human anatomy and need input for the prenatal chapters. But the lies did not come quickly enough, for even as she began to speak them, a look of comprehension passed over Haaft's face, collapsing it into first unhappiness and then what could only be called compassion.

In Gretchen's experience, chemists were all stern men in white coats with wire-rimmed glasses and brutally short haircuts through which their pink scalps could be seen. They were fanatics in the service of an undiscovered ideology. Haaft, however, was the exception. Tall, horsy, aristocratic, he was disarmingly solemn, and yet quiet laughter always lurked just below the surface, waiting for his inevitable turn of wit to bring it out. Not now, though.

Gretchen stiffened. She did not want his damnable pity.

"Why should you care why I want it? I'm your superior. I sign your paychecks. I can fire you if I wish. The fact that I want it should be good enough for you."

Wordlessly, he got out a scrap of paper and scribbled down a name.

Haaft had been more than just a colleague. Gretchen considered him a friend, and one whose company she valued. Now she had lost that relationship. It was a pity. But only one among many.

How could she have been so *stupid*?

How could she have been so foolish and wicked and lazy and wasteful? There were no words harsh enough for her. If only she could travel back in time to have a few words with her younger self. She'd have something to say to herself! She'd drag the little bitch down the street by the roots of her hair and fling her in the horse-fountain. She'd thrash her within an inch of her life. Whatever it took to get her attention.

She had been given a pamphlet, privately printed and set into verse by a local semianonymous poetaster, to explain the operation:

> First does the doctor clean the abdomen,
> And then will he numb a small patch of skin
> Just below the navel with a local
> Anaesthetic—for it is the focal
> Point where the needle, without blood or fuss,
> Glides gently down into the uterus,
> That realm where all is warm and dark and damp
> —the patient may experience a cramp.
>
> A dram of amniotic fluid's removed
> Into the barrel (some call it the tube)
> Of the syringe, where it is inspected.
> Prostaglandin is slowly injected.
> Here some pressure or a bloated feeling
> May well occur—best stare at the ceiling.
>
> Long hours will pass before the contractions
> can begin; you may avoid distractions
> (nausea, diarrhea, and other ills)
> By letting your doctor prescribe you pills.
> At first your contractions will not be great.
> The pressure may cause your rectum to ache.

Waters gush freely from the vagina!
The patient may experience minor
Pain. This means that the amniotic sac
Has burst. Time for the patient to lie back
For now does begin her induced labor;
Each woman's is different in flavor—
How it should feel and how long it should go,
These are things no one beforehand can know.

First leaves the fetus, as was expected,
In that hour placenta is ejected.
Now you are done, please keep in your prayers
The poet who here has soothed all your cares
And in nimble rhyme and right proportion
Explained your prostaglandin abortion.

A. S.

She did not want to do this thing.

But it was not as if she had any choices or alternatives. There was no way out of this airtight chamber. She was put in mind of how her biologists had demonstrated to her the necessity of oxygen for respiration. They had placed a mouse within a bell jar, which they then sealed so that air could neither enter nor leave. At first the creature crouched, wary and alert, breathing deeply and looking about. Then, as the O_2 dwindled and the CO_2 built up, the mouse suddenly began racing around and around the bottom of the jar, frantically scrabbling at the glass, trying to escape. It was excruciating to watch. As the oxygen waned, so too did the mouse's energy. Finally the pretty little thing simply lay down and accepted her fate.

All her choices had been made so very long ago.

There were protesters outside her window. She could hear them chanting. "Mur-der-ESS. Mur-der-ESS. Mur-der-ESS." When had that started? It had been morning when she entered the room; it had been full of light. Now the sun had shifted the world into shadow.

"Mur-der-ESS. Mur-der-ESS. Mur-der-ESS."

The chant abruptly stopped. Gretchen went to the blinds and parted two slats with her fingers. Outside, Brother Josaphat had come by in his motorcar, to dole out encouragement and fresh stacks of pamphlets. She saw him slapping backs and shaking hands. He was looking more prosperous than ever. When he spoke to a demonstrator, he maintained an eye contact so firm it could only be called practiced.

Reactionary politics had certainly done well by Brother Josaphat. He had his own weekly radio show, a newspaper column, and the ear of the regional nobility. He had been to Rome five times. The Pope solicited his advice. He was reputed to keep a mistress. If the modern world had benefitted but one man, it was him.

Friendly laughter floated up from the little group.

Then he was gone, leaving some doughnuts and a thermos of hot cider behind him.

Sometimes she wondered who these people were who came out every day to chant in front of her town house. How did they come to have so much free time? Did they even know why they were here? Why, when there were so many evils loose in the world, did they choose to fight this one? The Dominicans had organized the mission and named it Christian Crusade for Life. They could have chosen a better title, one that didn't bring to mind how many murders could be laid to the Church's credit. But it wasn't her place to advise them.

"Mur-der-ESS. Mur-der-ESS. Mur-der-ESS."

Only today did she feel she truly understood the protesters. Always before she had considered them pious hypocrites and censorious meddlers. She saw now for the first time that they were all perfectly sincere. That they had no hidden agenda. That they meant no more than what they said. She envied them their simplicity, and wished she shared it. She wished she could talk with them.

You all chose to be where you are, she would tell them. I did not. I have no alternatives. I can do no other.

Gretchen had gone out to argue with them once or twice, when the protesters first appeared outside her houses and the pharmaceuticals laboratory. But she had quickly realized that they were not going to listen to anything she said. They believed they already knew what she thought. "I agree with you," she had said, "that life is sacred." "No you don't," they'd told her. "You think that—" and one of them spat upon her. There was a white heated point at which nobody could admit to anybody else's honesty, a blind line of passion between the two sides across which nobody dared step in either direction.

I am more than just my body, she thought.

But the world did not agree. To existence she was her physical self and nothing more. Her highest thoughts, her most spiritual impulses could only elevate her within the privacy of her own mind. They were helpless before any of the foot-soldiers of reality: a rotting tooth, a broken leg, cancer, an unwanted pregnancy. Her most fervent regrets couldn't wish away the smallest blister. No more than the protesters' chants and bullhorns could change her mind.

She was out of cigarettes. The ashtray was overflowing with butts.

It was futile. In the end, there were no answers, could be

no understanding, would never be the least hope of any communication at all. Silence ruled, and it was not the silence of peace but the seething and unhappy silence of things not spoken. It was the deep submarine silence of a woman drowning. In the end, one recognized this and did not struggle anymore, but simply did as one must.

"Mur-der-ESS. Mur-der-ESS. Mur-der-ESS."

There was a knock on the door.

"Come in, Doctor," she said.

16

THE WILD HUNT

The biplane was an experimental model with a lightweight aluminum engine. It carried Faust and Wagner across the Channel to France in practically no time. The engineers had not been at all certain it would hold together for so long a journey. Yet Faust was assured it would, and that was good enough for Wagner.

They landed the plane in a turnip field outside of Calais, cracking a strut in the process. A few hurried words and a fistful of bank notes convinced the farmer to convey them to a train station. There, they caught the express to Paris; and it was on the train that Faust's old madness returned to him.

Wagner had booked a first-class compartment. Faust sat down heavily and then glared at the empty seat facing him. "Devil!" he cried. "You lied to me!"

"Quietly, master, please." Wagner shot the curtains, lest a

passenger in the aisle should look in and see the Magister railing against vacant space and his own reflection in the glass. "You must remember that other people cannot see your *daemon*."

Faust blazed. "Do not condescend to me, you little ball of snot. I know what you think. You think me crazed." He snapped his fingers under Wagner's nose. "This for you! I care not a fig for your good opinion, nor that of any other man."

For a long time after that Faust said no more.

Throughout the silence, Wagner's mind was working furiously, considering his options, preparing himself for this ordeal.

He must be loyal.

He had to be strong, fearless, a Faustian man himself, his master *in parvum*, a humble echo of his greatness. He must keep ever in mind that there was in Faust's madness more sanity than there was in the sanity of ordinary men. He must not betray the master with skepticism or disbelief.

Not turning, Faust let out a long and dolorous groan, and then began to speak again. "I should never have encouraged Gretchen in such things. I was weak. But now I am myself again. I will reclaim her and lift her up from the muck of carnality. We shall buy a country estate and live together in chaste respectability."

"Master . . ."

"We will have children."

"Yes. Yes, of course you will."

Faust wallowed heavily over on his side, presenting a pitiable face to Wagner. "Never fall in love," he said. "She will take lovers, and some of them will be more experienced and capable than you. I tell you this as a friend—there are dishes once tasted, a woman is loath to do without."

Wagner nodded solemnly, hiding his dismay.

"Tell me! What do you think of life? What do you think of ambition? What do you think of science, of learning, of love, of fame, of glory, of aspiration?"

"I think . . . that those are all very different things."

"You are wrong. They are all one thing—a cunt."

"Sir?"

"A *cunt!* Consider: The cunt is a nasty, ugly, filthy thing. Yet we desire it so greatly as to be willing to suffer any indignity to attain it. For the sake of it we labor and preen and whisper sugary words. We go to the theatre with flowers in our arms, climb over back walls by moonlight, write sonnets, jump out of windows with our trousers in our hands, give dangerous men their choice of weapons. We build love-nests for its sake, and cities, and civilizations. It is our all, our only, our ideal. It has created us and made us great. Such is life, such is ambition, such is science, learning, love, fame, glory, and aspiration. The Eternal Cunt," he said significantly, "draws us onward."

"I am afraid I cannot follow your reasoning," Wagner confessed miserably.

"No. I did not think you would."

Faust turned away again and, staring once more into the distant Nowhere, shook an admonishing finger and cried, "Fiend! I renounce you and all your works! From this day onward, rise or fall, succeed or fail, suffer or triumph, I will have no more dealings with you. I will not listen to your advices. I will not do your bidding or serve your purposes, however innocent they seem, however subtly you lay your traps for me."

"Dear master," Wagner said, close to tears.

Faust did not reply. With all the restraint he could muster,

Wagner left him to his desired solitude. Sitting back, he opened a pocket-book and pretended to read. France glided by outside the windows.

The train passed through endless corridors of buildings left derelict and boarded up—businesses that had sprouted alongside the railroad in the technological springtime of European prosperity, and since been made obsolete and bankrupted by German and English innovations. It made Wagner feel proud of his race and of his newly adopted land as well. But it was, at the same time, rather sad.

"Keep your silence," Faust muttered. "I do not need you. You are as powerless as a buttercup. A sparrow's fart exerts more force than you do."

Wagner put down his book and started to reply. Then he realized that Faust was talking in his sleep. After a moment's contemplation, he got out his notebook and a fountain pen. Working on the Biography always calmed him. Uncapping the pen, he began to write.

In his lucid moments on the train, the Magister became exceptionally openhearted and personal. He hides absolutely nothing from me. Intimate talks like that strengthen one's heart.

Wagner stopped. This was very well, but he must deal with Faust's mania. Posterity demanded his unflinching honesty. He drew a line under what was already penned and resumed writing, slowly at first but then with increasing confidence.

This was not the first time the Magister had fallen into such a state. By now, however, I had come to realize that

*his madness was not the result of a breakdown of intellect
but rather of a surfeit of genius. Utilizing a form of
alienation-analysis invented by the Magister himself, I saw
that the "demon" he railed at was a projection and denial
of his own genius. What the common man calls Evil, he
once told me, is nothing more than the fear of one's own
potential. How difficult it must be for the Magister to
acknowledge his overwhelming superiority to the merely
human! How crushing a burden it must often seem to
him! Yet let him become one again with his demon, and all
will be well.*

He recapped his pen, convinced that he had just written
as well as ever he had, and with an acuteness of perception
that cut to the very core of Faust's emotional crisis. It was, he
dared think, a distinguished bit of analysis.

Alas, the cure was beyond him. He could only watch and
hope.

They detrained in Paris. On the platform, Faust abruptly
turned and seized Wagner's sleeve. "You must protect me!"
he said wildly. "I have given up my prescience, and now I
am blind to the hazards of the future. Anything could happen
to me! Assassins, madmen, malcontents . . . I have enemies,
too many to count."

Embarrassed and thrilled, Wagner said, "You are in no
danger, Magister."

"You have no way of knowing that! No way at all."

"Come. It is late. We must find a hotel."

The Dix-huit Novembre was comfortably furnished but
not overly large, newly electrified, and convenient to the sta-

tion. It had been a nunnery before the Revolution, a brothel during the Restoration, and was now respectable again under the Directorate. The desk clerk, who by reason of her employment was nominally a political officer, yawned and then took down their particulars in a large leather-bound ledger. She wore her hair bobbed and her lips painted red. In France, it seemed, even the police informers kept up with the fashions. She asked whether the two valises were all the luggage they had, and then wrote down that information as well.

The clerk was handing Wagner the key when Faust said, "Who else has rooms on that floor?"

She blinked. "I beg your pardon?"

"He wants to know—" Wagner began. Faust seized his arm and whispered urgently in his ear. He squared his shoulders. "I am afraid that we shall have to insist that anybody else rooming on the same floor be immediately removed. For reasons of safety."

"Impossible!" The clerk, coming fully awake for the first time, threw up her hands in horror. "Outrageous! Just who do you think you are?"

Wagner leaned forward. "Do you know, do you understand who this man is? He is the Prometheus who brought your city electric lighting, the father of modern sewage treatment, the creator of the flying-machine. He invented *la methode . . .*"

The young woman waited until he had run down. Then in a flinty voice she said, "How much?"

Faust took a chair to the rear of the lobby, and sat moodily watching the door while they haggled out a price. At last a suitable bribe was agreed upon, and the clerk set about her task.

"Come, Magister," Wagner said when the last grumbling

tenant had been moved up stairs or down, "I will see that your room is properly secure, the blankets soft, the sheets clean."

He paused halfway up the stairs and gazed down into the desk clerk's incurious stare. She couldn't be much more than thirteen. No doubt she intended to report them to the national police. Who, in turn, would want to hold such suspicious foreigners for a day or three of questioning. She was, however, clearly exhausted and if she thought they were staying would happily put off that chore for tomorrow.

Wagner coughed and casually said, "I will want to make a telephone call in the morning."

"The office is down the street."

"Good, good!" he cried, briskly rubbing his hands together. So they didn't have a telephone! "Will there be any public executions tomorrow?"

"When are there not?" she said with a Gallic shrug.

"Then we'll stay the extra day," he said with a little laugh. "Why not? As long as there's entertainment?"

It was, Wagner felt, a shrewd bit of business on his part. When he glanced back from the top of the stairs, the girl was slumped in a chair behind the desk. Her eyes were closed.

He must be fearless.

When Faust was at last settled in, Wagner went down to the lobby, past the drowsing clerk, and out into the streets.

He walked until he found the squalid quarters by the university, where such things as he wanted could be obtained. At its affluent fringes were galleries with cast-iron facades and plate-glass windows, in which was displayed degenerate art that faithfully reflected the ugliness of the times, art without balance or serenity, little more than daubs much of it, incomprehensible trash, the rest.

He shook his head and moved on.

Beyond the galleries, the city darkened and tenements leaned toward each other over the narrow streets. Whenever a pimp materialized from a doorway and approached him, he solemnly shook his head and then told the man what he *really* wanted. The first two scowled and shook their heads back at him.

The third took him to a small wine-shop.

The place was filthy. An oil lantern over the bar shed just enough light to cause Wagner to draw in the skirts of his coat, lest they brush against anything. He stepped into the thronged darkness, cringing as he was assailed by a sudden conviction that there would be someone behind it, waiting to attack and rob him. But there was not.

He straightened again.

Behind what had once been an altar and was now the bar, a fat woman with a little black mustache sat in a rocking chair. It moved, *crick-crack*, forward and back, with the unvarying tyranny of a metronome. She was reading a dime novel.

Wagner and his pimp were dwarfed by unsteady pillars of kegs and barrels, overtoppling stacks of stenciled crates, jagged halberds and rusty pikes, religious statuary, broken-toothed hay-rakes, endless bolts of dusty grey cloth. *Crick.* There were small tables, a few chairs, no customers. It was as if somebody had decided to establish a bar in a warehouse and then not told anybody. *Crack.* If only one box of grease-packed machine parts were to fall, it would bring everything down, and he'd be crushed before he could reach the door.

Crick. Through a doorway behind the woman could be glimpsed—was surely meant to be glimpsed, for there was a brighter lantern within—another woman combing her long tresses. *Crack*. She was naked to the waist, with skin white as curdled milk and nipples black as the tangles of hair that burst from her armpits. Despite himself, for he was not eager for a second dose of French pox, Wagner felt his cock stiffen. *Crick*. Clearly, wine was not all that was sold here.

The fat woman did not look up from her paperback. "What is it you want?"

Crack.

"A revolver," Wagner said, "and ammunition."

There were no express trains eastbound out of Paris. So in the morning they caught the local to Metz. It left two hours late and slowly chugged east and south out of Île-de-France up into the chalky plains of Champagne, stopping at every hamlet and water-jerk to take on corn and crates of pigs.

It took two days to reach Reims.

The delays were interminable, frequent, maddening. They would find themselves idling for hours on a siding while no trains whatsoever went by on the empty tracks; the conductor always shrugged when asked what was happening. Sometimes the train would retrace a section of route it had already completed. Once, it visited the same weary hamlet four times. It ran out of water. It ran out of coal. It lost an engineer.

In a tract of land so undistinguished that a shed or hill or tree would have been a novelty, the train was stopped by a squad of soldiers in the spurs and uniforms of the Provisional forces. With batons they emptied out the second-class and third-class coaches, driving the poorer passengers into a kind of holding pen, as if they were cattle. Then, with terrifying disinterest, the Provos proceeded to beat and brutalize them. Finally, they erected a gallows, and hung three ragged men upon it. The workers stared silent and expressionless through the execution and when their comrades were dead filed back in to their seats. The train proceeded on its way.

In Reims, they were first told they would have to change locomotives, then that they would have to stand on the platform while the cars were fumigated. Luckily, the day, though overcast, was not cold. Thunderheads piled up to the west.

A wind-up gramophone was playing in the distance. Wagner could hear its mournfully romantic lyrics afloat upon the breeze:

> *Adieu, mes amours,*
> *Adieu, ma maitress . . .*

"Farewell, my loves," Faust grumbled. "Farewell, my mattress. Love and doves above. *Amours, les fleurs, toujours.* Who is so degraded as to fall for such mush? It is music for men without pricks, and women without physical needs!"

"Still," Wagner said cautiously, "it's a lovely sentiment."

"Sentiment! When the great River of Time has carried all human sentiment out into the Sea of Eternity, it will filter down, grain by grain, and form a delta so mighty it will choke the mouth of the river, and thus put an end to all such so-called songs. It cannot happen too soon."

Wagner had no choice but to lapse into a bewildered and acquiescing silence. The master could never be wrong, he understood that now. Nevertheless, in the distance he heard, and strained to hear, the refrain:

> *Mille regretz . . .*
> *Plusieurs regretz . . .*
> *Regretz sans fin.*

He thought then, as he often did, of his lost Sophia, and had to turn away to hide his tears. He thought of her skin, white as the porcelain Christ in the parish church of his childhood. He wished he could throw himself on the ground before her and one by one kiss each toe of her perfect feet.

"When I reach Nuremberg, you and I are through." Wagner looked back, startled, only to realize that Faust was talking to himself again. He waved his arms in an agitated fashion. "No, never, preposterous," he muttered, and then, "If that is the price I must pay, then so be it," and "If I give in to you this once, how do I know it will go no further?"

Wagner touched his arm.

Lifting his jaw, Faust stared like an eagle into the gathering storm-clouds. With a thrill, Wagner saw the profile of a barbarian conqueror, the flashing eyes of a Gaiseric, an Alaric, an Ataulf, the savage intensity of the Visigothic and Vandalic heroes of the great racial theorists who had arisen within the industrialized Empire.

"Very well," Faust said at last. "But only this once, and only because I need to know. I am not obligating myself to anything." He cocked his head, listening, and then swore. "Fuck!"

A gaunt man, whose loose-fitting greatcoat and raffish air identified him as a black marketeer, walked up, saying, "Are you waiting for the night train to Metz?" With which words he became a woman. A ribbon on her coat identified her as a war widow. Which explained all: occupation, lack of fear, man's coat. She grinned a five-toothed grin. "Is that what they told you?"

Faust paid her no heed. But his formidable intellect was focused on the wider vistas these days; his judgment was not necessarily reliable in purely practical matters. So Wagner said, "Why? Do you know something?" And, when the woman looked meaningfully away, slipped a bank note into her waiting hand. "Now what is this about the night train to Metz?"

She laughed. "There ain't none! Nor ever will be. They can't admit to it for political reasons. But about a month ago Reactionary guerillas seized the railhead, and because the Royalists are on the offensive down south, there ain't the forces to take it back. The stationmaster will be here in a minute. You wait. He'll tell you there's been a delay and then he'll suggest you put up at his brother-in-law's hotel. Tomorrow you'll come back bright and early with your bags. There'll be another delay. Sometime in the afternoon you'll be sent back to the hotel. Maybe you'll shout and complain. But they won't never admit to a thing. No, they won't. I've seen people stay at the hotel over a week before giving up."

"It can't be!" Wagner exclaimed. Her eye glittered madly. He very much doubted what she said could be trusted.

"Can't it? Then why is there nobody else waiting for the train, eh? Look—here he comes."

The stationmaster strode up the platform, blowing upon his enormous mustache. He was a walrus of a man, all paunch, bright brass buttons, and self-importance. He waved a flipper to get their attention.

Wagner turned to his master to suggest they take a room and make plans overnight.

But Faust was gone.

A bag in either hand, Wagner ran from the platform and down to the street. Faust was nowhere in sight. Still, he must be nearby. Wagner could find him—he knew he could.

Reims was the sort of town that looked best from a dis-

tance. The factory smokes would lend a faint glamorizing haze
to its tired walls, and the slag-heaps would catch the sun in a
way that suggested the exotic structures of India or Ethiopia.
From a distance, one would not smell the sulfur and methane
stenches nor descry the ubiquitous soot. Up close, it was all
ditches, buckets, broken ladders, and dead cats.

Wagner trotted down the rue Chemin, anxiously peering
into the alleys and accosting bystanders to ask in a French that
had gone all to pieces in his agitation whether they had seen
a distinguished man dressed thus and so in these last few
minutes? Some frowned, some drew back, others waved him
on—helpfully or not, he could not tell.

He seized upon a shopkeeper standing in his doorway,
explaining, "He is not well. *Mal*, you understand, *tres mal*."
The man looked at him blankly. Was he talking to an idiot?
Wagner wondered. "*Distingué*, dressed in black—*en noire*."

The shopkeeper looked down at Wagner's clenched hands.
He released the man's shirt. Still, the man said nothing.

Despairing, Wagner ran on.

Even in his alarmed state he could not help but notice the
posters. They were everywhere, on public and private walls
alike, hundreds of them, and all of an unsettling uniformity:

RALLY
to protest your
EXPLOITATION
by Department Stores, Co-Ops
& FOREIGN IMPORTS!!!

SACRIFICE
for the survival of
FRANCE
Scrap Iron, Saltpeter, Grease
ALL ARE NEEDED!!!

EXHIBITION
of arts and crafts by
THE WORKERS OF REIMS
support your neighbors
BUY LOCAL!!!

TRAITORS BEWARE
even now the
CROSS-HAIRS
may be trained on the back of
YOUR NECK!!!

The invention of the maze, according to certain Parisian intellectuals, coincided with the completion of Babylon, the first city. Wherein, as never before, it was possible to lose oneself among walls that completely hid the horizon. An outlander would find himself hopelessly disoriented, and yet a citizen, who held the pattern of the whole in his mind would not. Urban life was thus founded upon the principle of deliberately confounding those who were not a part of it. Civilization was a strategy of exclusion.

Wagner had never felt so excluded, so isolated, so much an outsider as he did now. Every turn he took diminished the chances of finding his master. Yet it would be futile to stay with the streets which obviously did not contain Faust; he had no choice but to digress and diverge and digress again.

He began to run. Weeping tears of frustration, he gave up questioning people at all. He chose turns at random, running down lanes and up alleys with no plan of action at all other than a panicked determination to run until he could run no more.

Finally he came stumbling to a halt in front of a motorcar dealership. Exhausted, he put down the bags.

It didn't occur to Wagner that Faust might be within. They had been spending money at a furious rate; it had bled from their fingers, and hemorrhaged from their billfolds. What little remained would not have bought a mule-cart, let alone a motorcar. But when Wagner, expecting nothing, glanced through the showroom window, there Faust was.

He stood talking with what must surely be the dealership's owner. It was a study in contrasts. Faust was calm, pale, composed. The corpulent owner sawed his arms and raged himself red. Faust spoke a single word. All color drained from the man's face. He turned away. Faust snapped his fingers impatiently. The owner handed him some small object.

Wagner had seen variants of this scene often enough. Yet it always amazed him. The master's genius for *knowing* was at work. He was somehow aware of that one fact the man would least want to have made public, and had negotiated a price for his silence.

Faust strode out into the street, jingling the keys to a new car. "The red one," he said, gesturing toward the lot, where a rainbow line of metal brutes stood in a splendid row. "Put the bags in the trunk."

Faust drove.

When Wagner had spun the crank to turn over the motor and leaped within, the master threw the automobile into gear and stepped on the gas pedal. The car bounced over a shallow ditch at the edge of the lot and with a horrid scraping noise, veered wildly onto the road.

Behind them, the owner stood watching them drive off. He looked stricken. Seeing him thus, Wagner felt a dreadful sympathy for the man. He hardened his heart against it.

He must be ruthless.

The car lunged like a wolf toward the center of Reims. "This is not the way to the Metz road!" Wagner shouted.

"No! We must obtain fresh clothing." The car brushed lightly against a brick building and bounced back into the center of the road. Wagner gasped with horror. "What we wear is filthy and stale with travel."

They rocketed deep into Reims, panicking horses and sending children scurrying for shelter, trending always away from the factories and into the prosperous neighborhoods bordering the old city.

The car slammed to a stop before a stone house decorated in the current fashion with terra-cotta trim. "The mayor lives here," Faust commented. But instead of going up the steps and knocking at the front door, he led Wagner through a narrow alley and around to the back. They entered unobserved through an unlocked door.

It was uncannily still within. Not even a servant was home. Through a doorway could be glimpsed a sitting room, with throw rugs scattered on the gleaming oak floors and an ormolu clock ticking loudly on the mantelpiece. Wagner almost jumped out of his skin when it chimed.

They went up the stairs and into a bedroom that smelled of hair oil and furniture polish. Faust threw open a dresser drawer and handed shirt, pants, underwear, collar to Wagner. "These will fit you." He opened another drawer. "And these me."

It was dazzling how he knew—he *knew!*—the clothes would be there, and fit both of them, despite their variant sizes, and that they would be able to change into them undisturbed.

They stripped in the middle of the room, tossing what they wore upon the bed. "What point?" Faust said when Wagner started to fold his old trousers; he opened a third drawer and extracted money from a billfold therein. "Let them lie where they fall."

"But the owner—surely for the sake of his feelings, we should . . ."

"His feelings?" Faust smirked. "Fourteen innocent men languish in jail because of this ogre. Another three are dead by his direct orders, and twenty more by the action of policies he approved. Two years ago he had not a penny—what you see now is but a fraction of his wealth. You must have wondered why we found the garb of two men in a room that will hold but one. The last mayor was scourged and driven out of town naked. His clothes were cleaned and kept as a trophy." He handed Wagner a pair of shirt-studs. "I think we need not concern ourselves about this gentleman's feelings."

On the way out, he made a brief detour into a garden-shed built up against the house like a lean-to. There was a can full of petroleum spirits there. He poured it on the floor. "That will suffice."

"What are you doing?"

"We have been reported to the NPs—*les flics*, as the frogs call them. They'll be coming after us soon if we don't give them something to better occupy their attention." He struck a match. "Stand back."

They drove out of town with Reims afire behind them. As they sped into the countryside, the smoke rose up and filled the sky.

They journeyed through the night, bumping and rattling over nightmarish dirt roads. Large rocks, dangerous holes, fallen tree limbs were forever gliding into their headlights. Where bridges had washed away through neglect or sabotage, they had to coax the automobile through crude fords. They did not make good time.

From radio broadcasts overheard in passing and newspapers bought on the fly, Wagner had learned that Faust's sudden departure had precipitated a financial crisis in the City of London. Had Wycliffe anticipated that—or the depression that many commentators said must inevitably ensue—the English spy-master would surely never have extended his grudging aid.

Well, it was too late now.

The markets were collapsing. The vast bubble of speculation upon which European prosperity was built had burst, and the very people who had been most anxious to be rid of Faust were now paying the price for his absence.

Midmorning the next day they stopped to patch a blown tire in a mud-daubed village where no work was being done. Every farmer and laborer was in the tavern, gathered heavily about the radio, shaking their heads in glum satisfaction at the news reports, spitting on the floor, and wondering aloud how long it would take for the all-devouring crisis to reach them.

They all came out to watch and offer suggestions as Wagner worked. By the time he had the tire back on, he was out of sorts, drenched with sweat, and completely exhausted. Faust disappeared into the tavern and came back with a bottle full of white pills. "Here," he said. "Take one."

"What are they?"

"Amphetamines."

They rode with the canvas roof down, popping a steady stream of pills to keep themselves going. At first the drug imparted a crystalline clarity and edge to the ride. They motored through an eternal afternoon and into an interminably beautiful sunset in a silence that was as crisp and communicative as the best conversation. The air flowed over their faces like cool water, cleansing and enhancing their senses.

Sometime during the night, however, Wagner began to hallucinate. He drifted in and out of reality, never quite sure which side of it he was on. Once he awoke to discover that the car he was in was not the car he remembered from Reims.

He wanted to ask how that change had come about, but somehow he could not properly phrase the question. The world was fragmenting about him.

Faust was talking and had clearly been talking for some time. "Every vow I ever made, Wagner, every resolve and ideal I have ever had, is broken or violated. I swear it—no man has ever been so untrue to himself as I am now. Yet for Gretchen's sake I would do worse. That is the true measure of love, you see, the evil one will stoop to for its sake . . ."

But he was distracted by Faust's demon, a tiny red imp with a barbed tail, trunks, and a pitchfork that capered upon the dashboard. It was trying to tell him something, but its voice was too high and small, like a mosquito's, for comprehension. He blinked and white doves swarmed down from the darkness to batter against his face and break up into nothing.

Snow, he thought. But that was wrong. It was too early for snow, surely. The wheel was in his hands, he was driving, and Faust sat in the seat beside him, head thrown back, mouth open. He was snoring.

Sometime later—earlier?—he shook his head and discovered he was sitting in a field of grass. The moon hung full and round in the sky and Faust sat in a chair nearby. He was smoking a cigar and grinning.

"Master," Wagner said groggily, "what is happening?"

"We ran out of gasoline. More is being fetched from a nearby village."

"Why—why are . . . ?"

In the field about them were pale white shapes, men and women coupling in every conceivable position and combination. Shocked, Wagner looked to Faust and saw that though still elegantly dressed from the waist up, he was not wearing any trousers.

"It's the Festival of the Horned Man. I convinced these people that I should preside."

"I don't understand."

Faust was wearing a sort of crown with two short horns. He reached up to adjust it. Complacently, he said, "Old religions die hard."

A woman, naked and startlingly buxom, approached to kneel before Faust's throne. He stood and presented his hindquarters to her. She reverently kissed both cheeks. Then, when he turned back, she stood, bent, and offered her own buttocks to him. He leaped forward and mounted her like a goat. The revelers had paused in their doings to watch. Now they cheered. The cigar was still clenched in his mouth.

Surely that had never happened. It must have been a hallucination.

Faust was driving again, and raving. ". . . beyond the certainty of France, into lands where no man speaks one language but all of necessity are multilingual. The traveler can never know here what nation he is in, things are so uncertain in these regions, where the boundaries flicker and no map is accurate for long. The border countries have been political coinage so long, and passed hands so many times, that their faces are worn smooth. Look into the eyes of the people here— sometimes French, sometimes German, often conquered, ceded, married into, given over, and yet somehow never possessed by themselves—and you will see nothing. They are a cautious folk, suspicious, silent, intimidated. You can never know which of them are dangerous and which are not, for they all share this same look." He turned to Wagner. "Take over the wheel. I am going to sleep in the backseat."

It was broad daylight when they arrived in Metz. They booked a room in a tavern and slept until it was light again. Then, dressed for travel, they took their bags downstairs and ordered a breakfast of sausages, turnips, and beer.

They were just finishing up when a man in the uniform of the French national police entered the tavern. Customers tensed as he approached, and quietly got up to leave as he passed them by. He came to their booth.

"You are English," he said.

"I am a citizen of a free imperial city," Faust replied icily, "and this is my servant. You have no jurisdiction over us. Nor is this France. Here, you have no authority to do anything."

"The Directorate does not acknowledge such legal niceties," the policeman said. He had glanced briefly at Wagner, judged him negligible, and then focused all his attention on Faust. "I am looking for two Englishmen. You must come with me for questioning."

"Do I look English? Do I *sound* English?"

"You are clearly out of your proper place. That is enough."

The man seized Faust's arm. Wagner, terrified, looked to his master for guidance, and saw those unblinking eyes looking directly back into his. His skull was buzzing. The night's sleep had not undone the effects of fatigue. The inside of his mouth tasted odd and coppery.

"Kill him," Faust said.

Wagner's gun came out of his coat pocket. He shot the man in the side, below the ribs. Flecks of blood spattered his hand, warm as piss and redder than apples. The policeman wrenched away, staring down at the wound. He crumpled without saying anything. His body lay stretched out upon the floor. To the far end of the room the taverner's mouth was a perfect O. It had all happened so suddenly.

Wagner stared down at the body. Then he raised his hand and flexed the fingers. The droplets of blood glistened like gemstones.

A wondering, exulting guilt expanded within him.

In Mannheim, they stayed in a hotel. Mercifully, Faust did not feel the need to have the other rooms on their floor emptied of inhabitants. When Wagner had suggested they might do so, he had simply rolled his eyes.

"You are right, you are right," Faust muttered. "I should have listened to you. And I will. But only long enough to bring my Gretchen away with me. I have no other use for you."

Lying on his side of the bed, Wagner uncapped his pen. His hands trembled and there were—when had that happened?—ink stains on his fingers.

From Metz we made our way to Saarbrücken. This strange journey has become for me a voyage of self-discovery. I have learned so much, so very much. THERE ARE NO LIMITATIONS. Underline that. I find that I am capable of anything. Anything at all. Just yesterday I seemed an ordinary sort of fellow. Now I know the transforming power of experience.

We hired a boat to transport our automobile down the Rhine to Mannheim. During the trip, I studied the Magister's face. The eyes, I noticed, are NOT EXACTLY

*BALANCED. One is always a little nobler, the other a
trifle more knowing!!! THIS IS SIGNIFICANT! It tells so
much. It tells so much. It tells so much. It tells so much.*

Faust continued to talk and gesture. Wagner paid him no
heed. In his mind, he was seeing the policeman fall, the blood
fly, the way his hand had jerked up and back with the recoil
of the pistol. It was like a small wave of victory over fear and
the weakness of conventional morality, an outer sign of the
inner triumph of his will.

They obtained another car in the morning, and maps for
most of the several principalities of the Holy Roman Empire
through which they would have to pass. By now it had become routine. This constant rush and change and discomfort
was no longer a voyage but, rather, a condition.

They set off.

That afternoon they were patching a flat in the middle of
a desolate stretch of farmland, when the roar of an internal
combustion engine sounded in the distance.

A motorcyclist, in heavy leather boots, jacket, and helmet,
goggles over his eyes, came speeding up the road. He was
muddy to the waist, and when he saw Faust he drew up his
cycle so abruptly that it stalled out.

"Are you from England?" the man cried.

"Who wants to know?"

The man pushed up his goggles. He looked dangerous. "A
messenger, and one who holds England dear to his heart. Is
your name Foster?"

"And if it is?"

The messenger reached into his leather jacket, and Wagner

nervously clasped the grip of his revolver. But the man's hand emerged with nothing more than a white square of paper. "I have a message for you. From Nuremberg."

Faust snatched the message from the man's hand.

Eagerly, he opened it.

17

THE AGENT

Margarete's prison cell held a single mirror, a toilet, a bed, a writing desk, and a chair. It was enough. She could run Reinhardt Industries as well from this hermitage as ever she had from her corporate headquarters. Better, for there were fewer distractions.

Rumors came to her of corporate infighting as her chief executives jockeyed to position themselves her successor, with now Wulf (or whoever it was cunning enough to use him for a front) in the ascendancy, and now Dreschler, and on occasion an unexpected (but never the same one twice) third. Sometimes she sided with one just to keep the others off-balance, firing off a memo of reprimand or undercutting a presumptuous decision with directly contradictory orders. More and more of late, however, she simply let it go.

They could none of them wrest power from her in the little

time she had left. Nor was she making any long-range plans for Reinhardt Industries. She wanted only to leave the corporation in the best shape she could. She had no illusions her influence would outlast her body.

The jailer came down the hall, rattling his keys to alert her to his imminence. It was but one of the many small courtesies he afforded her. He unlocked the door and entered with a little bow. "Gracious lady."

"Honest Ochsenfelder." She assumed a smile she did not feel, and with a flutter of she knew not quite what emotion, asked, "Am I to be shown the instruments again?"

"We display the instruments of torture," he said stiffly, "only to ensure the cooperation of our clients. The purpose of the viewing is to prevent their use. I wish I could convince you of that." He glanced at the prayer-book resting upon the corner of her desk. "I see you've been using your time wisely."

"No, my Aunt Penniger brought me that just before she fell ill." Nobody knew for sure, but it was suspected she'd had a stroke. "It was hers as a girl, and I keep it out to remind myself of her. Prayer would only make me unhappy, for I should surely pray for release—and yet there is no release for me." Ochsenfelder solemnly shook his head in agreement. "I endeavor instead to learn to accept my fate."

"Most prisoners pray volubly. Particularly when they know their warden is near."

"Does it influence you?"

"No, of course not."

"Well, then."

Ochsenfelder looked at her with grave concern, yet said nothing. He was a forthright and resolute man, unbending in most things and yet kindly at the core, as she remembered men as having been in her youth. She took some small comfort from his presence.

"Tell me," she said. "You do not bring food or letters. I have already been interviewed for the chronicles. We have agreed that I will not speak to the newspapers. Why have you come?"

"To report that you have a visitor, if you will see him. An Italian."

"Margarete Reinhardt?"

The Italian was strange to her. A short burly fellow with dark curls and the widest shoulders she had ever seen. He entered, hat in hand. "Guido Cavarocchi," he said briskly. "I have been engaged by a certain friend on your behalf." Then, pretending to cough into his hand, presumably so that he could later deny the name were it necessary, he added, "Wycliffe." In a normal voice, he said, "You need not fear being overheard. I have bribed the jailer to ensure our privacy."

"Really!" she said, startled. "And you speak so openly of it."

Cavarocchi sighed. "You hold me to shame. It is a degenerate age, madame, and I fear I have been as corrupted by it as anybody."

Her heart immediately went out to him. "Take my chair. I'll sit on the edge of the bed."

"Thank you." He placed his briefcase on his lap. "Our mutual friend told me to speak with you in the frankest possible manner. Even at the expense, he said, of making the truth out to be something worse than it is. He believed that soft words and subtle arguments would only antagonize you."

"Exactly what are you trying to say?"

"Jack Foster has left London."

Faust!

Involuntarily, Margarete's heart leaped. Sternly, she called it to heel. She folded her hands and briefly shut her eyes to regain her composure. "And therefore?"

"Good lady, there is only one place he could be headed, and that is to this cell. There is only one woman for whom he would leave behind a host of industries the least of which—I beg your pardon, but I *was* told to be frank—dwarfs your own. In sum, he is coming here, and to see you."

"I—" Margarete found that she was trembling. She glanced back toward her desk, where his photograph stood in a silver frame. It did not calm her. She did not know what to say, what to think. She hardly knew how she felt. "I . . . am at a loss."

"To continue. England requires that the architect of her prosperity return to his work as soon as possible. Needless to say, such a return must be voluntary. Therefore we need such coin as the Magister himself values above mere wealth, power, industry—in short, you. It is my mission to secure your whole-hearted cooperation and your freedom as well."

She stared off into a future with Jack. His hand in hers. His body in bed beside her in the morning. His eyes staring into her own. His voice telling her what to do.

They would have to flee to England. But that would not be much of a burden. She would learn the language. Perhaps she could bring Abelard to cook for them. In any event, they would live comfortably. They should never want for money or servants or ease. They'd have gardens and coaches and pedigreed dogs. She could rely on Jack for all of that.

They would stand together in a church and be married. They would have children—three of each, and all of them precious to her. But the oldest boy would be her particular darling. Faust would want to name him Euphorion or Hyperion or some such faddish neo-Classical nonsense, but she would hold out for Wilhelm, after her father. He would grow tall and strong; he would shine in her eyes brighter than the sun itself.

With such a father, it would not be expecting too much for all six to live and thrive. In time they would marry and present her with grandchildren.

Most important, Jack would always be there with her. When she was sullen and out of sorts, he would tease and tickle her until she laughed. When he was oppressed by his many cares and obligations, she would kiss each sorrow away. By slow degrees her waist would thicken. Silver threads would appear in his beard.

They would grow old together.

"Exactly how," she asked, "do you intend to convey me from this place? The walls, I am told, are three feet thick. You do not, I hope, intend to harm the guards."

"Nothing of the sort." Cavarocchi clicked his tongue dismissively. "They will simply be paid to close their eyes as you walk out. In order to make the escape look plausible, a woman of roughly your size and appearance will be brought in to perform some small task—to adjust your dress, perhaps, so that you will look your best for the trial. Nobody would deny you that.

"The woman will exchange clothing with you, and stay behind, lying covered in your bed. You will leave in my company, and I will smuggle you out of town in a wagon with a false bottom. This also is for appearances' sake—the city forces will be on guard against accidentally discovering you. Once quit of Nuremberg, you will travel in ease and comfort to London. A house will be provided you, servants, and an appropriate allowance. Faust will be located and informed of your whereabouts." Cavarocchi spread his arms, smiling. "A farce, admittedly—but one with a happy ending."

"And the woman who is to be left here. What's in it for her?"

"Frau Holt has a child who needs some very expensive surgery. She welcomes the opportunity and—my word upon it!—blesses your name for providing her with it."

"What becomes of her after my escape?"

Cavarocchi made a puzzled face. "She'll be held briefly, no doubt, and then released."

"Am I to pretend to believe this?" Margarete snapped. "The city of Nuremberg will suspend its own laws and free a pauper woman who helped a notorious criminal escape? Have fear and prison so melted my brains that you expect me to believe this?"

For a long time the Italian was silent. Then, humbly, he said, "Forgive me. I was expecting a woman so eager for release she would not think things through."

"No, I am beyond ignoring consequences."

"Very well. Give me a moment to think." Cavarocchi clasped his hands and bowed his head. He looked like an actor mentally preparing himself to go onstage. And once she had this thought, Margarete felt she understood the man. He was a chameleon, assuming whatever emotions best suited the situation.

She had owned chameleons once, slow and whimsical creatures that she kept in a glass tank in her office. But they had died.

"Very well! It will not be easy to get Frau Holt off. But hers is a lesser crime than yours and since it will be done for the sake of her child, the judges might plausibly extend her mercy. Buying such men will be terribly expensive. But no price is too great to bring Faust back to London, and therefore no price is too great to secure your liberty."

"You truly intend to bribe every official in Nuremberg?"

"We shall do what we must." Cavarocchi stood. "You need time to think, and I to act. I will return tomorrow."

Margarete was appalled. She was no innocent, but it was a shocking thing to have the entire city revealed as corrupt from the judges through the jailers and so down to the city guard. Cavarocchi had spoken of buying every official in Nuremberg as if it were merely a cause of ruinous expense.

She did not think she could go along with it. To do so would be to become as corrupt and dishonest as her oppressors. Surely one could not do so knowingly and willingly. It would have to be done by small and incremental steps, eyes shut and unaware.

It was not possible for her to rejoin the unthinking world, becoming as she had been before, sleepily and smugly ignorant of consequences. There were thoughts that once thought, could not be unthought. She could never be Gretchen again. Gretchen was an evil game she had once played. No more.

Faust was coming for her!

She did not want him to see her this way. Caged and humbled. The sight would live in his mind, poisoning whatever image he held of her, forever lessening her in his esteem.

There was not much time, then. One way or the other, she must decide soon. She dared not be here when he reached the prison and came to her cell.

A jangle of keys.

Ochsenfelder entered, carrying a covered dish. "My wife made this for you," he said. "It's gooseberry pie."

"You may thank her for me. Leave it on the desk."

"She is very concerned about you," Ochsenfelder began. "She—"

"Again, thank her. Please leave now."

Ochsenfelder left, looking puzzled and a little hurt.

It was wrong, perhaps, to treat her jailer so harshly for having human weaknesses. But he had behaved toward her as a stern and loving father would toward his own errant daughter, and she had responded to that. One of Margarete's lovers, a Florentine woman, had once told her of the time a man she had trusted as a second father had put a hand upon her rump and made a coarse suggestion; she had run home and cried for hours. The authority that an older man could extend over a younger woman was in the nature of a sacred trust. It was a foul thing to violate it.

Whatever she was guilty of, it was not half so bad as Ochsenfelder's betrayal of that trust.

Perhaps she should accept Cavarocchi's—Wycliffe's—offer. To stay was not only to die, but also to accept the authority of a system that was rotten from the basement all the way up to the weathercock. It implicitly endorsed the ethical superiority of men who neither understood her situation nor adhered to their own professed standards.

What was the moral thing to do?

Somebody had to decide upon her guilt or innocence. Not the courts. She no longer believed in them. Cavarocchi was right. When judges and magistrates could be bought, and jailers bribed to turn a blind eye, how much outrage could one feel when lesser criminals merely took advantage of the services offered them?

They could not judge her.

Perhaps she deserved death. But they would kill her for the wrong reasons. They would kill her for a night of pleasure—one among many—in which she'd failed to take precautions. Once she discovered herself pregnant, every step leading to this stone cell was foreordained.

Was this justice? It was not.

Only one person was qualified to judge her. Only one woman was fit to declare sentence.

The next morning Dreschler came in response to her summons.

He entered and she nodded toward the chair. He sat and she remained standing. It did not bother him in the least. He looked up at her with his soft lopsided smile, his sleepy eyes, waiting.

Two sheets of paper rested facedown on her desk.

"Tell me," she said. "How did the city council come to know of my abortion? That was your work, wasn't it?"

"No, no, no!" he cried. "When word of your, ah, unfortunate mistake—"

"My abortion."

"Yes. When it came out, I had security track down the source. You would scarce, ah, credit this, but it was proved beyond any doubt to be the work of your own—"

"Cousin Wulf." She shrugged, and lit a cigarette. "Well, I don't believe you, but that hardly matters now. Take a look at the paper on the left."

Dreschler picked it up and, lifting his eyeglasses, read. An expression of profound satisfaction slowly spread itself over his face. This first version of Margarete's will, while not leaving him anything material, gave him the explicit recognition as her successor that he coveted. He opened his mouth to speak, and Margarete gestured him to silence. "Now the other one."

He read. His expression changed. This version named Wulf as her successor. He looked up at Margarete, but said nothing.

"My trial is scheduled for Tuesday. I'll be dead soon."

He still said nothing. Dreschler was not a good man, but he was unquestionably an intelligent one. You could dangle the juiciest bait before his nose and he would not snap at it. He had discipline. She wished there were somebody else to entrust with her holdings. But unfortunately, Dreschler was the best available. She'd done all she could for Reinhardt Industries, its shareholders, and its employees.

It was time to let go.

She waited until their mutual silence had grown full and ripe. Then she raised an eyebrow. "Well?"

Dreschler nervously cleared his throat. "What is it you want of me?"

"Not much. Two items. I've written them down."

His face softened when he saw the first item on the list, then hardened when he saw the second. Ruthlessness, however, being another of his virtues, he only said, "Do you have any directions for the running of the plants?"

Koenig needed more support staff if the plastics exhibits were to be ready before the Exposition opened. The new man in the benzene research group had reported they were low on supplies, and this so directly contradicted his supervisor's assessment that there was clearly something wrong *some*where, and this would have to be looked into. Accounting had been doing an exemplary job for so long that most of upper management had forgotten what a shambles it had been before the shake-up. It was time to hand out a few awards and certificates before morale fell again. Her list of things to do was endless.

"No," she said. "I'm sure you'll do an excellent job."

Cavarocchi entered, all business. "Our people have already spoken to two judges; a third is being approached this morning. Others may need to be blackmailed; operatives are currently at work. So what you desire is certainly possible. If you are willing to take my word that it will be done, you can leave the day after tomorrow. If you want to await assurances—"

"I am not going. I thank you, but I choose to stay."

Cavarocchi's face froze. "May I inquire why you . . . ?"

"No. Please don't. I am sorry, but my reasons are personal."

He sighed. "I did not want to show you this."

From his attaché, he removed a newspaper. He unfolded it before her. JEW'S-WHORE! screamed the headline above a very unflattering photograph of Margarete being taken to jail. She looked haggard, of course—the abortion had taken place only hours before—but also, somehow, both wracked with guilt and unrepentant.

"Look at this!" Cavarocchi slapped down a second, a third, a fourth tabloid, one atop the other, headlines overlapping. MURDERESS/SLUT/CRIMINAL/WHORE! "And this. And this. Look. See. What chance do you think you'll have in a court of law? What chance? Justice? Mercy? Don't make me laugh."

She took the first newspaper, folded it so she didn't have to look at herself, and read the article. "That dear, sweet, gentle, thoughtful man," she mused. "So he had a Jewish grandmother? I wonder if he even knew." She returned the paper.

"How terrible for him to be caught up in this. I suppose he'll be deported?"

Cavarocchi shrugged. There was a hardness to him that she had not noticed yesterday—the hardness of a pirate, a highwayman, an adventurer. She was confirmed in her earlier opinion of him: a chameleon. The emotions came and went too fast, and did not leave any trace behind them.

"Can I do nothing for you?"

"Nothing," Margarete said. Then, "No, wait! The woman you would have left in my place—you can pay her the money promised and tell her it comes from a friend. You can draw upon my resources. I'll write you out a note."

She ground out her cigarette and reached for a pen.

When he took the paper, she seized Cavarocchi's hand and kissed the back of it.

He drew it away, startled. "What was that for?"

"To express my gratitude. I thought I had given up my old ways—I'd hoped I had—but I was not sure. It is so easy to repent when there is no other choice. Now you have tested my resolve, and I know that my repentance is genuine. Go, and take my blessing with you."

The next day Dreschler's two packages arrived. The first contained a neatly folded packet of paper with some two dozen white pills within. The second was an old copy of *Die Zeitung*. The one with the photo exposé of pollution from her film factories.

She had never actually looked at the pictures. She studied them now, the flippered hands, the twisted spines. The faces of the parents. This one ancient mother bathing her son—how eloquently her face bespoke an unending life of despair. This is Hell, it said, and here I have long dwelt.

Afterwards she tried to pray. She still did not believe that there was anybody listening. But she had been wrong about so many things. Perhaps she could dare hope to be wrong about just one more?

Knowing that her guardians could be bribed, it was the easiest thing in the world to arrange the privacy she required. In preparation, she got out her prayer-book and placed ten crisp bank-notes at even intervals within its pages. They made for a substantial sum. Whatever Cavarocchi had paid, it was less than this.

Jangling keys, heavy tread, slow-opening door: Ochsenfelder. He entered and with habitual gravity said, "I have good news. Your trial has been postponed."

"Oh." Margarete's mind was a blank. She could not think of an appropriate response.

"Your agent—not Dreschler, but the Italian, Cavarocchi—has petitioned for an extension in order to bring in two witnesses from the lowlands who will testify to the circumstances leading up to your rape."

"My what?"

"Child, you should have mentioned this terrible event at the beginning of your testimony. It strongly argues for leniency in the means of your execution."

"There are no such witnesses. I was never raped—never! Anyone who says such a thing perjures himself."

"Lady." Ochsenfelder looked pained. "Why do you do this to yourself? Your prosecutor will not be half so hostile to your case as you are now."

"It is the simple truth. Why would anyone—?"

She stopped. The trial had been delayed so that Faust could reach her in time. Of course. Wycliffe knew the depth of her feelings. Faust was a kind of intoxication to her; she could not think clearly in his presence. Where persuasion would not suffice, Wycliffe's people thought, the touch of his hand upon her skin would. And they were right.

It made her shiver. "What a foul and conscienceless world this is," she murmured.

"Young lady!" Ochsenfelder said. "You should quake to have such thoughts and speak such words. You stand now in the shadow of the gallows and if your life cannot be saved, think then of your immortal soul! I have been gentle with you, and perhaps that was wrong. Pray! Now! Get down upon your knees and beg for forgiveness, rather than—"

"You!" she cried, all in a fury. "Who are you to talk to me? Why should *I* be imprisoned and *you* not? I made my choices in the darkness of fear and ignorance—I call them choices, but what choices did I have? You, you have betrayed—"

She was crying now. Flinging an arm over her eyes, she turned and put her head against the wall and sobbed until she had emptied herself of tears.

Ochsenfelder stood to the far side of the cell, saying nothing. He never came near to her if he could avoid doing so, and he never turned his back on her. It was reflexive, he had told her once, from decades of watching over felons. When she asked if he were frightened of being overpowered, he had replied that what he feared most was injuring a foolishly ambitious escapee.

"Forgive me," Margarete said, when she had cried herself out. "Forgive me. I did not realize I was so—"

"I understand."

"Tell the city fathers that they need not delay the trial on my behalf. There are no witnesses coming who can save me.

I will swear that into the record, if necessary."

Ochsenfelder solemnly bowed his head.

Margarete took a deep breath. "And take this," she said, handing him her prayer-book, "to remember me by."

Her jailer left with a sad smile and a small bow. It had been a trying encounter for him, but he was clearly pleased by its outcome.

She waited.

Not long after, he returned to her cell, pale and unhappy. "I—" he began. He swallowed. Then: "Is there anything I might . . . do for you?"

"Yes. I wish to be alone and undisturbed for the rest of the night. See to it that nobody comes to my cell before morning."

He nodded, turned away, turned back. "Please, I must explain something to you," he said all in a rush. "All my life I have been, as you thought me, an honest man. But then my wife, whom I love so much, made a foolish mistake, you see, and invested her—"

She stopped him with an uplifted hand. "Please don't," she said. "It's not that I am unsympathetic. It's just that I've heard so many sad stories in my lifetime. I don't think that I could bear to hear just one more."

There was a good side to almost anything. The one gift that imprisonment had given her was time to think. The abortion had been decided upon in a panic. For all her agonized emotion, there had been neither time nor presence of mind to think things through. There had been only denial.

She thought for a long time about the miners gassed, the children born deformed, Anna Emels's suicide, and a hundred things more. Once you accepted the possibility of guilt, it seemed, there was no bottom.

She did not blame Jack, though the decisions had been his, but herself for letting him make such decisions for her. He had placed his mouth between her legs and insinuated his tongue so deep inside her that when she spoke his words had come out of her mouth.

I do not know what right is anymore, she admitted to herself, only that my hands are not clean.

Consequences never stopped. Even now. She thought of dear, sweet, unhappy Aunt Penniger, who had come to visit her every day until the stroke, and of her parents as well. What a terrible blow this would be to all of them! It really was dreadful how few things would be resolved by her death. Dreadful how the consequences would continue to cascade onward.

She took one last long look at Jack's photograph. She loved him so much, so deeply, so dearly. She only wished she had proved worthy of him. For a long time she studied the lineaments of his image. How stiff he looked, how stern, how totally unlike himself!

She regretted that lost life in England. It would have been so pleasant to lie with Faust again, to rub her face against his chest, simply to hold hands with him. It was hard to think that she would never again smell spring flowers or cool her ankles in a country stream. Most of all she regretted little Wilhelm. Darling child, she thought, what a dreadful thing it is to deny you existence. There were so many levels of irony in the thought she could have choked upon them.

If only Jack were here!

But she could not have it both ways. If he were here, she would go with him. She could never say no to him. Yet the comfort he offered had too high a price; she could not accept it.

She turned the frame facedown. She couldn't do this thing with him watching.

If the end justified the means, then when did the end arrive? Tomorrow? Next year? A century from now? Or was it like the horizon, receding with every step, always ahead and never here, transfinite and irrational?

No, the end was a permanent condition. It was always arriving. It was always here. Every moment stood upon the requirement to justify itself.

Very well, then, Margarete thought. Justify yourself.

She opened the square of paper and laid out the pills in three neat rows of eight. Then she filled a glass tumbler with water. At first the water was white with tiny bubbles, but it soon calmed into transparency. She placed the tumbler beside the pills.

The trick to taking barbiturates was to be methodical. She had to take them one after the other, with little sips of water in between to get them down. If she took them too fast, she might throw up. Too slow, and she'd fall asleep before she'd taken enough to do the job. Luckily, she'd always been methodical. She felt the task was well within her capability.

She raised the first pill to her lips.

She swallowed.

It went quicker than she had expected. Swallow, sip, find the next capsule. Swallow, sip, find the next capsule. Her fingers closed upon nothing, and for a panicked instant she scrabbled across the empty desktop with both hands looking for the missing capsule. Then, realizing that she was done, she settled back in her chair with a complacent sense of having done her duty.

It was all over now.

Shortly before the pills took their final effect, Margarete had a waking hallucination.

It seemed there was a message for her. She knew there was. She imagined the messenger from Faust's long-ago sermon finally arriving, in leather gloves and helmet, removing his motorcycle goggles before extending her the Emperor's parchment, a crisp square folded into quarters, with seals and ribbons still intact. His expression was stern, and yet she dared hope there was compassion in it as well. Am I forgiven? she wondered. I have repented—but is repentance enough?

She unfolded and looked at the parchment. For an instant the words were strange, in a language and script with which she was unfamiliar. Then they came into a more conforming mode, and she knew that she could comprehend it simply by concentrating just a little bit harder.

The letters swam into place, and she began to read.

18

THE MESSAGE

19

Ashes

Margarete was dead.

There was no reason to stay; there was no reason to keep moving. There was no place he wanted to be; there was no place he did not want to leave behind.

Mere momentum carried Faust on to Nuremberg.

He arrived at sunset. A statue had been reared in the center of town to Mathes Behaim: THE INVENTOR OF THE RADIO, FATHER OF THE CONDENSING COIL, AND CREATOR OF THE VACUUM TUBE, who had died a martyr to science when an array of acid batteries exploded during an attempt to establish infinite conductivity. This was human glory—a sad and exhaust-darkened memorial for good citizens to ignore and drunks to piss upon on their way home from the brothels. Here was the omega-point of all ambition.

Faust left his automobile at the foot of the monument,

there to block traffic and be discovered by the police in the morning and confiscated. He did not care.

A single heavy drop of rain fell on the cobbles by his feet. The storm that had been threatening for days had arrived at last. He turned up his collar and strode on.

Here, in the old part of town, where electrification was still incomplete, people kept country hours and went to bed with the cows. Street-lights existed only at prominent intersections. Radios, played however quietly, were strictly forbidden after dark. Faust looked around him with distaste. "I had forgotten how quiet it gets here."

"Pish! Tosh! We'll soon liven things up," said a voice from somewhere over his shoulder.

"I've had about enough of you and your—"

"Oh, Faust, believe me: I will never lie to you again. All such tricks and deceits are things of the past. Think of them as a teacher's little guiles, ways of coaxing on a willful child who does not wish to learn his lessons. I swear by my very being I shall never employ them again." Mephistopheles snickered and lowered his voice insinuatingly. "After all—if I may be permitted to gloat—what need have I for lies? The truth is ugly enough to serve my purposes."

Faust stared vaguely about, not listening. "I need a drink."

"The Cellar Imp is just around the corner and down the way. For a nominal sum the landlord will keep it open past hours, so long as you're reasonably quiet. When you start raving and breaking furniture, I know of other places we can go."

An hour-some later Faust looked about him with an obscure feeling that something was missing. He thought for a while, then said, "Where is Wagner?" He was not actually drunk, but emotion made him feel as if he were. Sorrow, loss, anger—these were as good as a bottle of the very worst gin.

"Don't you remember? You left him behind in Heilbronn. I chanced to remark that the Occupation forces had despatched a squad of cavalry to overtake you. That incident with the Provo halftrack and the Venetian mercenaries? So you ordered him to lock himself in a church tower and shoot at the passersby, to delay pursuit. He paced the thing well; it was four hours before he ran out of ammunition and the soldiers dared break down the door. By which time you were well away. Oh, don't look so distressed. Think of it as a sacrifice to your greatness."

"A sacrifice." Faust imagined Wagner dead at his feet, like a faithful hound, and felt a special fondness for the obsequious little toady.

"I have answered so many questions for you over the years," Mephistopheles said. "Will you answer one for me?" He did not wait for an assent. "You will, as all men must, someday die. Who, in all the burgeoning masses of fools and villains that constitute the human race, is there that you do not loathe? Who among them does not deserve immediate death? Who would you wish to outlive you?"

Faust did not even have to think. "Nobody."

"Well, exactly! I can't tell you how delighted I am to hear you say so. At last we have a meeting of minds!"

The burly landlord of the Cellar Imp closed his wine cabinet with a slam, twisted the key, and turned his brutal face toward Faust. He had not much liked Faust's constant muttering, but his patience had held well enough until Faust had set fire to a drunken mechanic's coat and driven the man, ablaze, from the tavern. Now, it seemed, his hospitality was exhausted.

With a grumbling sigh, Faust stood.

He opened the door into a cloudburst. The rain had grown in strength while he was inside. It was cold as ice-water, and came down so hard it stung the flesh. He stepped into it and was immediately drenched to the skin.

It was easy to break into the church. There was a small door to the rear for the priests and Mephistopheles showed him where an axe had been left under a tarp flung over the rectory's woodpile. Three blows, each coinciding with a thunderclap, sufficed to break the lock.

Dripping puddles onto the stairs, Faust descended into the basement. He made straight for the cabinet where the Communion wine was kept. Again he employed the axe. If the noise disturbed the pastor's dreams of plump choirboys, his unease was not sufficient to bring him out into the night and rain.

When he'd slipped a bottle into his coat pocket, tucked another under his arm, and smashed the rest, Faust started back up the stairs. But then he dropped one of the bottles and in his confusion took a wrong turn, and somehow he wound up before the main altar, under the crucifix.

He gazed stupidly up at the milk-skinned Nazarene. The wracked limbs and agonized expression spoke eloquently of the pleasure the artist took in the torment of the flesh. The rolled eyes and nauseated mouth—how well they conveyed the Savior's loathing for the material world! Faust's eyes welled with tears of sympathy. "You too, old Jew?"

He had for many years thought of Christ as a rival in greatness. Now he realized they were both brothers in misery. Their enemies were identical: the howling mob, the fearful, the inferior, the baying hounds of conventional morality. He wished he could kill them all and dump the corpses at the feet of their crucified victim.

"Excuse me," Mephistopheles said. "Would you like to have some fun?"

The devil led Faust to an undistinguished tenement door. The rain still hammered down. He tried the latch. Locked.

(The room within held a gas-oven, a sink, a bed, a chamber pot. There were also a table, two chairs, a travel-trunk, a cradle. These few poor items took up almost all the space there was.)

He pounded on the door.

A fearful voice said, "Who's there?"

"Nathan, I need your help!"

"There is no one by that name here. Who are you?"

"A friend."

"Go away, before we call the police."

(There were two adults and a nursling. The man was stout and had a short beard. The woman's hair was long and black. Neither was particularly tall.)

"Nathan, don't you remember the time when you were young and lost yourself in the forest, hunting for mushrooms? Night fell, there was no moon, and you heard wolves. In desperation you knocked on the door of a woodcutter's cabin. He was not a landsman, yet he let you in. Do the same for me now."

A brief hesitation, the rattle of bolts. The door opened.

Smiling, Faust strode in. He went straight to the cradle, scooped up the baby, turned, and said, "You are both Jews."

With a shriek, the mother rushed at him. Fending her off with one hand, he brandished the sleeping infant over his head with the other. "Careful! The baby will fall! The baby will drop!" Then, as the husband seized his wife to hold her back, "The baby will have its fucking brains spattered out against the wall, if you don't behave."

Somebody in the apartment overhead angrily thumped the floor.

They all three froze.

"What do you want with us?" Nathan whispered. His wife turned pleading eyes toward him, but stood back.

The baby yawned and made a soft gurgling noise. Faust solemnly tapped a fingertip on its tiny nose. Then he handed it to the mother. She clutched it to her breast, automatically comforting it with a slight jiggling motion. "Your kind has been banned from Nuremberg. Surely you know what would happen if you were discovered?"

"I swear to you, sir, our chore here is an honest one," the man said. "It will take but a day or two to accomplish, and then we will be gone."

Faust removed his wet coat, and draped it over the oven door. He turned on the gas with a twist of a knob, lit it with a *skritch* of the friction lighter, and turned the flame down low. "Your great-grandfather, Israel ben Simeon," he said, "was a silversmith in this city. When the city fathers, resenting the prosperity of their Jews, conspired to seize their properties, he was too proud to sell his house for a fraction of its value to men he considered thugs and criminals. Others, wiser than he, did so and fled to Spain, Italy, Ruthenia. He stayed and, out of stubbornness, did not send any of his wealth away."

"You—know something of this?" The merest hint of avarice entered Nathan's round, fearful face.

"Most assuredly I do. Your great-grandfather had a Christian friend named Boehm, a crippled choirmaster who had several times been the secret recipient of his quiet charity. This choirmaster came one night to warn that he was to be arrested in the morning. He escaped with only his wife and daughter, enough gold to bribe their way to Prague, and as many jewels as he could swallow. Do you follow me?"

Nathan nodded.

"Israel ben Simeon's most treasured possession was a magnificent silver ewer, worked with an unequaled representation of Judith holding the head of Holofernes. It was his masterpiece; a year of his life had gone into its making. Every metalworker who came to town, be he Jew or Christian, called to see it and study its craft. It was priceless. Alas, it was too large to take away with him, and so he filled it with jewelry and other valuables, and buried it behind his house, at the base of the chimney."

"This is exactly what I have always been told," Nathan said wonderingly.

"The location of the Nuremberg hoard old Israel confided to his daughter's husband, your grandfather, upon his deathbed, and he in turn passed it on to your father. Who spoke of it often to both you and your brother Avram."

"This is no man, but the devil himself!" cried the woman.

"No, no, no—you flatter me, Rachel. I am nothing of the sort." Faust chuckled to see how she started when he spoke her name.

"What do you intend here?" she asked.

"Nothing bad, I assure you. Calm yourselves, be at ease. I need a cup or perhaps a glass." Faust went over to the gently hissing oven and drew the bottle of Communion wine from his greatcoat. He thumped it down on the table, and drew up a chair. Then, sharply, he said, "Well?"

Silently, Rachel brought him a tumbler.

"Pour," he told Nathan.

The man obeyed.

Faust drank.

"Where was I? Your brother Avram. Who, as first-born, naturally received the bulk of your father's estate. Who, when you both wanted the same woman for wife, surrendered his claim in exchange for half of your own inheritance. And who (against your advice, incidentally) invested heavily in the plastics industry at a time when nobody knew an isomer from a polymer. How his prosperity oppresses you! He wears silk suits and dines on caviar. He keeps a chauffeur. His condescending smirk is like a lash across your back.

"A poor man has no honor in this world. When you went to beg for his cast-offs, Avram made you enter by the tradesmen's gate. He would not even lend you use of his automobile; you returned home through the streets bent under your load like a rag-picker. Everyone saw it! Only wealth could erase such shame. So, in the extremity of your folly, you thought of the family legend."

"It is more than a legend, though! You have verified as much."

"Oh, Nathan, Nathan, Nathan—bad enough for you to come here alone. How could you have led your wife into such terrible peril?"

"I insisted," Rachel said. "I would not let him go without me."

Faust scowled. "Since when do women make such decisions? Your husband feared to leave you in his brother's care. Am I wrong? Eh? No, I am not. Nathan knows only too well how that lecherous goat still desires you. The baby's asleep again. Put it back in the cradle."

She did so, but remained protectively crouching over her child, back bent in a lovely and vulnerable curve.

"Such a dreadful, dreadful waste. For four generations your family has pursued a mirage. I tell you this as a friend." He raised his voice in a mocking nasal whine. " 'Someday, my son, we will return to Great-Grandfather's house and reclaim our heritage!' Well, here you are, and what have you to show for it?"

"Perhaps . . . you know something that would help us?"

"I am here for no other reason." Faust drained his glass, and nodded for more. "You came to Nuremberg looking for the old Jews' quarter, and could not find it. You sought a house with a unique chimney—one with a brickwork salamander laid into its design—and could not find it. It should have been easy, yet it was not. Would you care to know why?"

Silently, Nathan nodded.

For a long moment Faust did not speak, deliberately drawing out the tension. Then he said, "The house of Israel ben Simeon no longer exists. The Jews' quarter was razed five years ago to make way for the railroad station. The rubble was bulldozed and carted away for landfill. But here's the ironic part: Even if you'd come beforetime, you wouldn't have found the treasure. It was dug up two nights after its burial by Gustav Boehm—the very same choirmaster who warned your great-grandfather to leave!"

Rachel put an arm over her eyes. Her husband looked stricken.

"The ewer, which was priceless but known to many, Boehm hammered into a lump and had melted into an ingot worth—well, it would make you laugh to know how little it brought. The rest he pawned, the money he wasted, and what now remains of your great-grandfather's legacy? Only your memories. After you die, it will be as if he had never been."

"Listen to me, please." Nathan contrived to place himself

between Faust and his family. "Whatever you want, whatever you've come here for . . . spare my wife. Spare my innocent child."

"What a position you have put yourself in! Yet you were comfortable enough back in Poland. You had food, clothing, money for coal in the winter. Would you have gambled your family's lives on such a chimerical quest if you had not been eaten away with spite and envy?"

"Please. You have no idea how we've suffered—"

"What does a Jew know of suffering?" Faust spat on the floor. "So much for you—and more than you can do!"

Nathan stared unhappily down at his feet. "It's a Christian superstition," he said, "that in punishment for the crucifixion, Jews can only slobber. I can spit as well as any man."

"A scholar, are you? Well then, Rabbi, let's see you. Spit in my face! Let's see if you dare. Do you dare? Eh? Eh? No, I didn't think you would." Faust stood. He opened the drawer by the sink and took out a knife.

"What are you doing?"

"What does it look like I'm doing?" Faust slammed the knife into the tabletop. He dragged it heavily toward him, digging a deep gouge in the wood. "I trust you know the story of Abraham and Isaac." He cut a second gash at right angles to the first, so that they formed a cross. "There. I have made you an altar."

He proffered the knife, hilt first.

Nathan, horrified, shrank away from it. "I don't know what you think of me. But I swear, I could never harm my own son."

"You brought him *here*, didn't you?" Faust took a long drink from his glass.

"I didn't know this would happen!"

Disgusted, Faust flung the knife across the room. It clattered into the sink.

"The unconscious mind," he said, "is a tricky thing. It wants what the conscious mind cannot admit to. A man who is obsessive about his wife's fidelity, for example, might actually be acting out his desire to see her proved unfaithful." He sucked on a molar. "There's no need to look so shocked. I know the unconscious. I know what you secretly want."

Nathan hung his head. "All men are sinful by nature," he conceded. "But—"

"You'd like me to fuck your wife, wouldn't you?" Faust stretched out a leg and kicked the cradle until the baby wailed. Rachel fearfully snatched the baby up. The upstairs neighbor pounded on the floor again, but Faust ignored him. "*Say* you would!"

Eyes squeezed tight against tears of humiliation, Nathan said, "I want you to fuck my wife."

"Beg me to do so."

"Please."

"You want me to fuck her until she bleeds. Say it!"

Nathan was weeping openly now, the tears flowing down his cheeks. "Why? What evil have I ever done to you to deserve this? Why are you doing this to us?"

"Fool. There is no *why*. The very word is a semantic fallacy. Ask me *how* and I can lay out for you cause and effect, one thing leading to another, the alcohol acting on a grieving man's mind, the door inadequately guarded, the people within isolated from the common lot of humanity by the dreadful secret of their ancestry." He rattled his glass.

Nathan refilled it.

Faust drank.

"But to ask *why*," he continued, "implies that things happen for a purpose, and they do not. There is no purpose, no direction, no guidance to events. Nothing means anything. The world is a howling desert of meaninglessness, and reason is useless before it. There is only blind event."

He stared off into the bleak landscapes of the future while Nathan refilled his glass and refilled his glass and refilled his glass.

He saw so clearly now, without delusion or hope. It was a crystal night of the soul.

When he awoke, the Jews were gone. They had taken what they could carry in their arms and fled into the night.

He felt dreadful, but not so much as he would have expected. Drink some water and you'll feel better, he thought, you've slept for twenty-eight hours. Surely that was Mephistopheles speaking to him? There had been a time when he could easily distinguish between the demon's thoughts and his own. It pained him to think how naive he had once been.

At Mephistopheles's prompting, he drank water, washed his face, drank more water, adjusted his clothes, and went to a pharmacist's. There he bullied the proprietor into compounding a variety of drugs and vitamins into an elixir that by noon had restored vigor to his body. Still, his spirit lagged impossibly behind.

A walk would clear out the cobwebs.

"Very well."

Obediently, Faust took a street-car to the edge of town. From the terminus, he followed a winding road out into the countryside. Pavement gave way to dirt. A mile or three into the farmlands was a trail which led through a copse of black oaks and into a meadow.

He followed it.

Crickets greeted him with song. Small white and yellow lepidoptera sought among the thorns and spiky husks of dead vegetation for flowers yet living and similarly clad in autumn's colors. Bees droned. The sky was blue and flocked with a gentleman farmer's sufficiency of clouds. It was unseasonably warm.

Rest, he thought. Sit and take your ease.

Faust sank down into the fragrant sweetness of green grasses, the Arabian sweetness of dry grasses, the dark sweetness of putrefaction. Brown stalks rose up about him. He waited, though for what he could not say. He was totally without ambition. He might sit here forever.

Damn Gretchen! Damn that filthy bitch to Hell forever! He had given up everything—everything!—for her. Yet, driven by who knew what sluttish and unhealthy philosophies, she had willfully taken her own life, when forces were in place to bring her away free. Abominable! Such was the unspeakable perversity of women—that given the opportunity, they would inevitably choose death over life.

But what use? It was done, it was over, it was beyond recall. All the weariness in the world flowed into Faust. He leaned back on his elbows. There, in the shape-shifting meadow, where reeds turned to fairy spears and leaves dried and curled into cocoons, he listened to the complex chords of insect chirps, chitters, and stridulation. With such cries and a variety of pheromonal lures, the delicately savage combatants vied to trick one another into ambushes, murder, and sex.

All about him nature was having one last long and leisurely war. Voles burrowed for grubs. Spiders threw webs between towering stalks. A hawk circled speck-small among the clouds, hunting for a fur-clad and tremulous heart. The year had come to fullness and food was running out. Bees and wasps were already beginning to starve. Ants scoured the earth for summer's last gleanings. Predators expanded their range. Everything was dying.

Everything was dying, yet death did not suffice. Life had hidden resources. In a thousand ways it was concentrating strength, hoarding its energies in seed, chrysalis, and nectar, preparing for the warrior sweep out of exile that would undo the defeat of winter. Spring was implicit.

There was a crashing in the woods.

Faust sat up.

A young woman burst from the trees and ran into the meadow.

She saw Faust and stopped as suddenly as a startled doe. By her expression, she was amazed to see him there. Her clothing—clean, well-made, old-fashioned in a modestly fashionable way—marked her as being from a good family.

Faust had by the merest fraction begun to lift himself from the grass when, blushing, she raised a hand to her shoulder and unfastened one strap of her dress. The cloth fell away. Awkwardly, she undid three buttons of her blouse and then pulled it aside, baring a breast.

It was flesh made perfect: plump, pale, and without blemish. Subtleties of color, from cream to peach-flush, tinted the skin more exquisitely than any water-colorist could have managed. The nipple, surrounded by a halo of faintest pink, was delicate and brown and emphatic as a berry.

Kneeling, the girl offered her breast to Faust's mouth.

Solemnly, he parted his lips. For the briefest instant that virginal nipple was in his mouth, sweet, warm, ever so faintly salty . . . and then gone.

All in one swirling motion, the maiden had drawn back,

stood, rebuttoned, turned, and was running away again, back into the woods, a wild thing, braids flying.

Green shadows swallowed her and were silent.

Faust stared wonderingly after this inexplicable nymph. She seemed the personification of all that was fresh and unspoiled, a spark of green nature in a weary and corrupt world.

Did it surprise you, Faust?

"I was amazed. I . . . I felt like a virgin confronting his first whore. Great vistas opened before me. It seemed that there was so much that was possible, so much that . . . might happen."

Come. It's time to return to the city.

Faust stood. Together he and his internal guide retraced the path through the woods and past the still, pesticided fields, over the road and down along the Pegnitz's rusted shore. What few plants grew among the smashed machines, bricks, and plastic bottles there were brown and dying. Bright swirls of effluents from the Reinhardt Industries plant to the east curled and uncurled in its currents. The trees fell away. Smoke and sparks belched into the sky from the mouths of thunderous foundries.

Faust shook his head. "I still cannot—the incident with the young girl. It was so . . . remarkable. My head buzzes with it."

There is a simple enough explanation.

"Then don't tell me," Faust said harshly. "*I don't want to know.*"

Can this be my little Jack Faust? This, the scholar who was from earliest memory the humble slave of truth? The scientist who would have sold his soul, were there such a thing, for knowledge? The philosopher who swore that whatever simply *was*, whether fair to him or abhorrent, was of necessity superior to the most beautiful imaginings? Does the truth mean nothing to you anymore?

"Truth," Faust said bitterly. "What is truth?"

Truth is whatever you have the strength, the wit, and the will to make it be.

"What are you talking about?"

Politics, Faust. Has it never occurred to you that Germany needs a leader?

"We already have an Emperor."

Yes, a feeble old man who by his very existence keeps Germany shattered, fragmented, and weak. Were this dotard not occupying the throne, some strong man or iron duke would inevitably arise to claim that office by fire and conquest, and in so doing subdue and unite the quarreling subnations into one mighty and unstoppable colossus that would stand astride the world, crushing its rivals underfoot and imposing its just tyranny upon all the inferior lands and races of the Earth.

"There is something to what you say," Faust mused. "But—not I. I am no statesman or ruler or conqueror. I wouldn't know where to begin."

You'd begin with my advice. Let me show you.

He returned to Nuremberg by air, flying high above the stratocathedrals and cumulofortresses of the clouds. "Fasten your belt, we're beginning the approach," said the pilot with a flash of teeth and he saw the narrow streets and orange roofs of the city laid out below him like a clever child's diorama.

"Look!" The pilot pointed. Along the Pegnitz crept a narrow column of marchers. Where roads merged, they were joined by more marchers. Then more. And more. Their numbers grew, swelled, multiplied, and did not stop, until all the roads were thronged with human bodies. They looked like nothing so much as ants swarming.

"They're all coming for your rally!"

Nuremberg was not large enough to hold such numbers. So the organizers had appropriated a region outside of town nicknamed for its size and flatness the Dirigible Field. Bleachers had been built, support-buildings, toilets, reviewing stands. Gargantuan banners were raised, roads asphalted, entire groves of pines transplanted for background. The work that had gone into this weekend rally would have sufficed to build a small city.

A car carried him in triumph through the agonized screams of adoration, the outstretched arms and bared teeth of citizens like werewolves leaping and snapping to reach him. "Wave!" cried the strangely familiar driver. "They love you!"

He was brought to the Dirigible Field and installed upon the reviewing stand. The dignitaries all stood up straighter in his presence.

"What should I tell them?" he asked.

"Tell them anything," his Minister of Propaganda said. "They'll believe you."

He stretched forth his hand and the multitudes roared.

"*Faust!*

"*Faust!*

"*Faust!*" the crowds chanted, thrusting clenched fists upward in salute. They waved a forest of flags and all of them the same: a red field with a white circle, and within that circle a stylized black fist.

"*Faust!*

"*Faust!*

"*Faust!*"

Their shouts rattled the sky.

After his speech, the afternoon scrolled by in hypnotically monotonous spectacle. Personnel carriers passed before him, churning up dust. Then tanks. Missile carriers. Black-uniformed soldiers goose-stepping in endless ranks. Veterans associations, women's auxiliaries, unions of railroad engineers, societies for space travel, youth organizations, all in tight squadrons. As night fell, bonfires were lit behind them. Still they came and came and came, interchangeable, anonymous, disciplined.

Faust's legs began to buckle from standing so long.

They brought him a chair, and wearily he sat. Darkness closed about him. He could smell canvas and sawdust. The sides of the tent rattled and snapped in the gathering wind.

It's almost midnight, Mephistopheles said.

Faust looked down at his withered arms. His hands were pale and spotted. "I feel so old. So weak."

That's only to be expected. The century is just about over. Your life's work nears completion.

"Life's . . . work?"

Behold.

With a *boom* like thunder, the wind ripped the tent away and cast it up into the sky. What had been hidden was revealed: a world of blood, violence, and universal war. He was still upon the parade grounds, but now grey concrete bunkers and military installations were scattered about the plain. The earth was gashed and churned to mud by countless metal treads.

All was in motion. His armies poured by in torrents, no longer ceremonially but on their way to battle. Vehicles rumbled past. He saw the rocket-launchers, the tanks, the guided missile carriers, the munitions convoys, the flatbeds bearing smart bombs and CBW warheads, the bombers flying overhead, the fighters, the drones, the more-than-human robotic technologies of mass destruction. Rivers of helmeted soldiers marched into the night.

"Is this all?" he asked, disappointed.

Far from it. Extend your imagination.

He strained to see further.

Beyond the horizon, one by one, great self-illuminating clouds arose, as sudden as so many lightbulbs being snapped on. They billowed up into the sky, turning the earth black, each one brighter than the sun, and still more rose up behind them in endless profusion: death and negation made gloriously, radiantly beautiful.

It was an impossible sight. His eyes would burn within his head to see even a fraction of it in reality, the viscous fluids bursting the eyeballs in small gusts of steam, the lids crisping black and flaking away. But in his mind he saw it, and the ashes from every populated continent slowly settling upon what had once been Europe.

"More!" Faust cried. "More light!" He waved his arms as if conducting a symphony, watching the volatilized carbons incandesce with borrowed energies. "More light! Let in more light!" He hopped and capered, mad with elation. "Oh, I'll bring them light. I'll teach them about light, all right. Just watch me."

Then—abruptly—it all went away.

Faust was no longer old. He stood strong and healthy, a man in his prime, by the edge of the Pegnitz. Hornets darted peacefully through the dusty golden light of late afternoon.

The factories hummed. It was autumn, and no man anywhere was yet his follower.

All the world seemed dark and cold.

"Mephistopheles!" he cried. "Your vision—can I trust it? Is it universal? Is it inevitable? Can you promise I will live to see it?"

There was no response. Mephistopheles had dwindled into silence. Faust could feel him humming at the core of his being, a constant knot of discontent, an implicit twinge of ambition, a gnawing hunger for revenge upon all those who had treated him with such wickedness and cruelty. But he could no longer hear the demon's voice.

Nor did he feel its lack. Faust understood now that it was irrelevant whether his powers came from verifiable exterior forces or not. The knowledge was within him; it welled up from whatever hidden sources. It had shown him his destiny. That was enough.

He knew what needed to be done.

He could not do it alone, admittedly. But he would not want for allies and subordinates. His words would bring them. He would give voice to what all wanted said and none dared admit to thinking. He knew exactly what to say.

He was eager to get to it.

Faust clenched and unclenched his fist, thinking of all the future lying helpless before him, legs spread, battered into submission. Waiting for his cleansing wrath.

It would be as simple as setting off a nuclear reaction— once critical mass was achieved, all else followed as a matter of course. He had set foot upon the final road. Not all the demons of Hell could turn him away. Heaven itself would be helpless to stop him.

The thought brought a bubble of wry amusement spiraling up within him. Heaven indeed! For the first time in months, Faust laughed.

"God help them!" he cried. "God help them all."